George Eliot

The Mill on the Floss

COMPACT EDITIONS

PHOENIX

A PHOENIX PAPERBACK
COMPACT EDITIONS

This paperback edition, a condensed version of the
original, first published in Great Britain in 2007
by Phoenix,
an imprint of Orion Books Ltd,
Orion House, 5 Upper St Martin's Lane,
London WC2H 9EA

1 3 5 7 9 10 8 6 4 2

A CIP catalogue record for this book
is available from the British Library.

ISBN 978-0-7538-2271-5

Typeset by Deltatype Ltd,
Birkenhead, Merseyside

Printed and bound in Great Britain by
Clays Ltd, St Ives plc

The Orion Publishing Group's policy is to use papers that
are natural, renewable and recyclable products and
made from wood grown in sustainable forests. The logging
and manufacturing processes are expected to conform to
the environmental regulations of the country of origin.

www.orionbooks.co.uk

Contents

The Mill on the Floss

BOOK FIRST Boy and Girl

BOOK SECOND School-time

BOOK SIXTH The Great Temptation

BOOK SEVENTH The Final Rescue

About the Author

George Eliot was born Mary Anne (later Marian) Evans on 22 November 1819 at South Farm, Arbury in Warwickshire, where her father was estate manager. When she was five months old, the family moved to a farmhouse at Griff, her beloved home until she was twenty-one. Because of her father's position, the young Marian had access to the library at Arbury Hall and made full use of it. She boarded at schools in Coventry and Nuneaton, where she studied a considerable range of literature and excelled at English composition and piano playing.

After her mother's death in 1836 she became her father's housekeeper. In 1841 the family moved to Coventry, where Marian was introduced to the free-thinking Charles Bray and his wife Cara. Their social circle greatly enriched her life, influencing her reading, her thinking and her early career. Her father died in 1849 when she was 30 – well past the normal marriageable age – but he left her £100 a year which gave her a certain amount of independence. She moved to London and became a distinguished editor of the *Westminster Review*, where she met the talented and many-sided author, George Henry Lewes. Lewes was still married to his wife but he had condoned her adultery, so he and Marian were unable to marry. Despite this, they lived together until his death in 1878. Marian's rejection by her friends, family and society in general over her common law marriage is reflected in the ostracizing of Maggie Tulliver in *The Mill on the Floss*.

Lewes was extremely supportive of Marian's artistic endeavours and it was he who first encouraged her to write fiction. The success of *Adam Bede*, published in 1859, confirmed her literary powers. She adopted the masculine name George Eliot partly to distance herself from 'silly' female romance writers but also to cover up the tricky subject of her marital status. The publication of *Adam Bede* led to intense speculation about the author and eventually Marian came forward. Despite her fears of being shunned, her marital situation did not affect her popularity and she was even introduced to Princess Louise, who was a fan.

Her last novel was *Daniel Deronda*, which was published in 1876. After Lewes's death she once again courted controversy by marrying John Cross, a man twenty years younger than herself. However, she died not long afterwards of kidney disease, on 22 December 1880, at the age of 61. Her other major novels apart from those mentioned above are *Silas Marner* and *Middlemarch*.

Chronology of George Eliot's Life

Year	Age	Life
1819		Born at South Farm, Arbury, Warwickshire on 22 November as Mary Anne Evans
1820	5 months	The Evans family move to Griff
1824–36	5–16	Attends boarding schools in Attleborough, Nuneaton and Coventry
1836	16	Death of mother
1837	17	Marriage of sister, Christiana. Becomes father's housekeeper
1838	18–19	Reads widely, including many religious works
1841	21	Moves, with father, to Coventry. Introduced to Charles Bray and his wife Cara, Charles Hennell's sister
1842	22	Breaks with orthodox Christianity. Meets Sara Hennell, Cara Bray's sister; friendship generates much correspondence
1844–8	25–8	Translates Strauss's *Das Leben Jesu* (1846)
1849	29	Death of father. Visits France, Italy and Switzerland with Brays; winters in Geneva alone
1850	30	Returns to England in March but finds the experience painful; decides to earn her living by writing

Chronology of her Times

Year	Literary Context	Historical Events
1819	Birth of Ruskin	Birth of Victoria
1820	Scott, *Ivanhoe* Birth of Flaubert	Death of King George III; accession of George IV
1824	Death of Byron	
1830	Tennyson, *Poems, Chiefly Lyrical*	Catholic Emancipation Death of King George IV; accession of William IV
1831		First Reform Bill introduced by Lord John Russell
1833		First Factory Act, regulating child labour
1837		Death of William IV; accession of Victoria
1838	Charles Hennell, *An Inquiry into the Origins of Christianity*	Chartists demand suffrage
1842	Wordsworth, *Poems*	Chartist Riots
1844	Disraeli, *Coningsby*	
1846	The Brontës, *Poems*; Ruskin, *Modern Painters*	Repeal of the Corn Laws
1847	Charlotte Brontë, *Jane Eyre*; Thackeray, *Vanity Fair*	
1850	Death of Wordsworth Herbert Spencer, *Social Statistics*; Dickens, *David Copperfield*	

Year	Age	Life
1851	31	Joins Chapman's household in London; secretly becomes managing editor of his *Westminster Review* for which she writes articles 'as a man'. Visits Great Exhibition twice.
1852	32	Meets and befriends Herbert Spencer, social philosopher and journalist; and George Henry Lewes. Falls in love with Spencer and is rejected.
1853	33	Occupied with Westminster Review
1854	34	Translation work. Travels to Weimar and Berlin with Lewes; reports her happiness to Charles Bray
1855	35	Returns to England; sets up house with Lewes in Richmond.
1857	37	Begins to write fiction. 'Amos Barton', 'Mr Gilfil's Love-Story' and 'Janet's Repentance' appear serially in Blackwoods'. Tells her family about relationship with Lewes, and they break off all communication with her
1858	38	Writes *Adam Bede*.
1859	39	*Adam Bede* published; has begun *The Mill on the Floss*. Dickens expresses admiration and invites her to contribute to his weekly periodical, *All the Year Round*.
1860	40	Writes 'Brother Jacob', begins *Silas Marner*
1862–3	42–3	*Romola* serialized in the *Cornhill Magazine*
1866	46	*Felix Holt* published
1867	47	Subscribes £50 'from the author of *Romola*' to the foundation of Girton College, Cambridge
1869	49	Begins *Middlemarch*
1871–2	51–2	*Middlemarch* published in independent parts
1873–6	53–6	Writes *Daniel Deronda*
1878	58	Death of George Henry Lewes
1880	60	Marries John Walter Cross on 6 May. Death in London on 22 December, one month after her 61st birthday.

Year	Literary Context	Historical Events
1851	Ruskin, *The Stones of Venice*	Great Exhibition at the Crystal Palace
1853	Dickens, *Bleak House*; Elizabeth Gaskell, *Cranford*; *Ruth*, Charlotte Brontë, *Villette*	
1854–6		Crimean War
1855	Lewes, *Life of Goethe* Elizabeth Gaskell, *North and South*	
1857	Flaubert, *Madame Bovary*; Elizabeth Gaskell, *The Life of Charlotte Brontë*; Dickens, *Little Dorrit*	Indian Mutiny
1860		Unification of Italy
1862		American Civil War
1866	Elizabeth Gaskell, *Wives and Daughters*	
1867	Turgenev, *Fathers and Sons*	Second Reform Bill brought in by Disraeli
1869	J S Mill, *The Subjection of Women*	
1870–1		Franco-Prussian War
1874	Hardy, *Far From the Madding Crowd*	Disraeli becomes Prime Minister
1880	Tennyson, *Ballads and the Other Poems*	Parnell demands Home Rule for Ireland

BOOK FIRST

Boy and Girl

1

Outside Dorlcote Mill

A wide plain, where the broadening Floss hurries on between its green banks to the sea, and the loving tide, rushing to meet it, checks its passage with an impetuous embrace. On this mighty tide the black ships – laden with the fresh-scented fir-planks, with rounded sacks of oil-bearing seed, or with the dark glitter of coal – are borne along to the town of St Ogg's, which shows its aged, fluted red roofs and the broad gables of its wharves between the low wooded hill and the river brink, tinging the water with a soft purple hue under the transient glance of this February sun. Far away on each hand stretch the rich pastures, and the patches of dark earth, made ready for the seed of broad-leaved green crops, or touched already with the tint of the tender-bladed autumn-sown corn. The distant ships seem to be lifting their masts and stretching their red-brown sails close among the branches of the spreading ash. Just by the red-roofed town the tributary Ripple flows with a lively current into the Floss. How lovely the little river is! It seems to me like a living companion while I wander along the bank and listen to its low placid voice. I remember those large dipping willows. I remember the stone bridge.

And this is Dorlcote Mill. I must stand a minute or two here on the bridge and look at it, though the clouds are threatening, and it is far on in the afternoon. Perhaps the chill damp season adds a charm to the trimly-kept, comfortable house, as old as the elms and chestnuts that shelter it from the northern blast. The stream is brimful now, and lies high in this little withy plantation, and half drowns the grassy fringe of the croft in front of the house.

The rush of the water, and the booming of the mill, bring a dreamy deafness, which seems to heighten the peacefulness of the scene. I turn my eyes towards the mill again. That little girl is watching it too; she has been standing on just the same spot at the edge of the water ever since I paused on the bridge. And that queer white cur with the brown ear seems to be leaping and barking in ineffectual remonstrance with the wheel; perhaps he is jealous, because his playfellow in the beaver bonnet is so rapt in its movement. It is time the little playfellow went in, I think; and there is a very bright fire to tempt her: the red light shines out under the deepening grey of the sky. It is time, too, for me to leave off resting my arms on the cold stone of this bridge ...

Ah, my arms are really benumbed. I have been pressing my elbows on the arms of my chair, and dreaming that I was standing on the bridge in front of Dorlcote Mill, as it looked one February afternoon many years ago. Before I dozed off, I was going to tell you what Mr and Mrs Tulliver were talking about, as they sat by the bright fire in the left-hand parlour on that very afternoon I have been dreaming of.

2

Mr Tulliver, of Dorlcote Mill, Declares His Resolution about Tom

'What I want, you know,' said Mr Tulliver – 'is to give Tom a good eddication; an eddication as'll be a bread to him. That was what I was thinking of when I gave notice for him to leave th' academy at Ladyday. I mean to put him to a downright good school at Midsummer. The two years at th' academy 'ud ha' done well enough, if I'd meant to make a miller and farmer of him; for he's had a fine sight more schoolin' nor I ever got. But I should like Tom to be a bit of a scholard, so as he might be up to the

tricks o' these fellows as talk fine and write with a flourish. It 'ud
be a help to me wi' these lawsuits, and arbitrations, and things. I
wouldn't make a downright lawyer o' the lad – I should be sorry
for him to be a raskill – but a sort o' engineer, or a surveyor,
or an auctioneer and vallyer, like Riley, or one o' them smartish
businesses as are all profits and no outlay, only for a big watch-
chain and a high stool. They're pretty nigh all one, and they're
not far off being even wi' the law, *I* believe; for Riley looks Lawyer
Wakem i' the face as hard as one cat looks another. *He's* none
frightened at him.'

Mr Tulliver was speaking to his wife, a blond comely woman
nearly forty, in a fan-shaped cap which were new at St Ogg's, and
considered sweet things.

'Well, Mr Tulliver, you know best; *I've* no objections. But
hadn't I better kill a couple o' fowl and have th' aunts and uncles
to dinner next week, so as you may hear what sister Glegg and
sister Pullet have got to say about it? There's a couple o' fowl
wants killing!'

'You may kill every fowl i' the yard, if you like, Bessy; but I
shall ask neither aunt nor uncle what I'm to do wi' my own lad,'
said Mr Tulliver, defiantly.

'Dear heart!' said Mrs Tulliver, shocked at this sanguinary
rhetoric, 'how can you talk so, Mr Tulliver? But it's your way to
speak disrespectful o' my family; and sister Glegg throws all the
blame upo' me. Howiver, if Tom's to go to a new school, I should
like him to go where I can wash him and mend him.'

'Well, well, we won't send him out o' reach o' the carrier's cart,
if other things fit in,' said Mr Tulliver. 'But you mustn't put a
spoke i' the wheel about the washin', if we can't get a school near
enough. That's the fault I have to find wi' you, Bessy: if you see
a stick in the road, you're allays thinkin' you can't step over it.
You'd want me not to hire a good waggoner, 'cause he'd got a
mole on his face.'

'Dear heart!' said Mrs Tulliver, in mild surprise, 'when did I
iver make objections to a man because he'd got a mole on his
face?'

'No, no, Bessy; I didn't mean justly the mole; I meant it to stand for summat else; but niver mind – it's puzzling work, talking is. What I'm thinking on is how to find the right sort o' school to send Tom to. It's an uncommon puzzling thing to know what school to pick.'

Mr Tulliver paused a minute or two, and dived with both hands into his breeches pockets as if he hoped to find some suggestion there. Apparently he was not disappointed, for he presently said, 'I know what I'll do – I'll talk it over wi' Riley: he's coming tomorrow, t'arbitrate about the dam. Riley's as likely a man as any to know o' some school; he's had schooling himself, an' goes about to all sorts o' places; arbitratin' and vallyin' and that. I want Tom to be such a sort o' man as Riley, you know – as can talk pretty nigh as well as if it was all wrote out for him, and knows a good lot o' words as don't mean much; and a good solid knowledge o' business too. But,' continued Mr Tulliver after a pause, 'what I'm a bit afraid on is, as Tom hasn't got the right sort o' brains for a smart fellow. I doubt he's a bit slowish. He takes after your family, Bessy.'

'Yes, that he does,' said Mrs Tulliver, accepting the last proposition entirely on its own merits; 'he's wonderful for liking a deal o' salt in his broth.'

'It seems a bit of a pity, though,' said Mr Tulliver, 'as the lad should take after the mother's side instead o' the little wench. The little un takes after my side, now: she's twice as 'cute as Tom. Too 'cute for a woman, I'm afraid,' continued Mr Tulliver. 'It's no mischief much while she's a little un, but an over-'cute woman's no better nor a long-tailed sheep – she'll fetch none the bigger price for that.'

'Yes, it *is* a mischief while she's a little un, Mr Tulliver, for it all runs to naughtiness. How to keep her in a clean pinafore two hours together passes my cunning. An' now you put me i' mind,' continued Mrs Tulliver, rising and going to the window, 'I don't know where she is now. Ah, I thought so – wanderin' up an' down by the water, like a wild thing: she'll tumble in some day.'

Mrs Tulliver rapped the window sharply, beckoned, and shook

her head more than once before she returned to her chair.

'You talk o' 'cuteness, Mr Tulliver,' she observed as she sat down, 'but I'm sure the child's half an idiot i' some things; for if I send her upstairs to fetch anything, she forgets what she's gone for, an' perhaps 'ull sit down on the floor i' the sunshine an' sing to herself all the while I'm waiting for her downstairs. That niver run i' my family, thank God, no more nor a brown skin as makes her look like a mulatter.'

'Pooh, nonsense!' said Mr Tulliver; 'she's a straight black-eyed wench as anybody need wish to see. I don't know i' what she's behind other folk's children; and she can read almost as well as the parson.'

'But her hair won't curl and I've such work as never was to make her stand and have it pinched with th' irons.'

'Cut it off – cut it off short,' said her father, rashly.

'How can you talk so, Mr Tulliver? She's too big a gell, gone nine, and tall of her age, to have her hair cut short; an' there's her cousin Lucy's got a row o' curls round her head, an' not a hair out o' place. It seems hard as my sister Deane should have that pretty child; I'm sure Lucy takes more after me nor my own child does. Maggie, Maggie,' continued the mother, in a tone of half-coaxing fretfulness, as this small mistake of nature entered the room, 'where's the use o' my telling you to keep away from the water? You'll tumble in and be drownded some day, an' then you'll be sorry you didn't do as mother told you.'

Maggie's hair, as she threw off her bonnet, painfully confirmed her mother's accusation: Mrs Tulliver, desiring her daughter to have a curled crop, 'like other folks's children,' had had it cut too short in front to be pushed behind the ears.

'Oh, dear, oh, dear, Maggie, what are you thinkin' of, to throw your bonnet down there? Take it upstairs, there's a good gell, an' let your hair be brushed, an' put your other pinafore on, an' change your shoes – do, for shame; an' come an' go on with your patchwork.'

'Oh, mother,' said Maggie, in a vehemently cross tone, 'I don't *want* to do my patchwork. It's foolish work, tearing things to pieces to sew 'em together again.'

Exit Maggie, dragging her bonnet by the string, while Mr Tulliver laughs audibly.

'I wonder at you, as you'll laugh at her, Mr Tulliver,' said the mother, with feeble fretfulness in her tone. 'You encourage her i' naughtiness. An' her aunts will have it as it's me spoils her.'

3

Mr Riley Gives His Advice
Concerning a School for Tom

The gentleman in the ample white cravat and shirt-frill, taking his brandy-and-water so pleasantly with his good friend Tulliver, is Mr Riley, a gentleman with a waxen complexion and fat hands, rather highly educated for an auctioneer and appraiser, but large-hearted enough to show a great deal of *bonhomie* towards simple country acquaintances of hospitable habits.

The conversation had come to a pause. Mr Tulliver was on the whole a man of safe traditional opinions; but on one or two points he had trusted to his unassisted intellect, and had arrived at several questionable conclusions; among the rest, that rats, weevils, and lawyers were created by Old Harry. But today it was clear that the good principle was triumphant: this affair of the water-power had been a tangled business somehow, for all it seemed – look at it one way – as plain as water's water; but, big a puzzle as it was, it hadn't got the better of Riley.

But the dam was a subject of conversation that would keep; there was another subject, as you know, on which Mr Tulliver was in pressing want of Mr Riley's advice.

'There's a thing I've got i' my head,' said Mr Tulliver at last, in rather a lower tone than usual, as he turned his head and looked steadfastly at his companion.

'Ah!' said Mr Riley, in a tone of mild interest.

'It's a very particular thing,' he went on; 'it's about my boy Tom.'

At the sound of this name, Maggie, who was seated on a low stool close by the fire, with a large book open on her lap, looked up eagerly. There were few sounds that roused Maggie when she was dreaming over her book, but Tom's name served as well as the shrillest whistle.

'You see, I want to put him to a new school at Midsummer,' said Mr Tulliver; 'he's comin' away from the 'cademy at Ladyday, an' I shall let him run loose for a quarter; but after that I want to send him to a downright good school, where they'll make a scholard of him.'

'Well,' said Mr Riley, 'there's no greater advantage you can give him than a good education. Not,' he added, with polite significance – 'not that a man can't be an excellent miller and farmer, and a shrewd sensible fellow into the bargain, without much help from the schoolmaster.'

'I believe you,' said Mr Tulliver, 'but I don't *mean* Tom to be a miller and farmer. I shall give Tom an eddication an' put him to a business, as he may make a nest for himself, an' not want to push me out o' mine. Pretty well if he gets it when I'm dead an' gone.'

This was evidently a point on which Mr Tulliver felt strongly, and the impetus which had given unusual rapidity and emphasis to his speech, showed itself still unexhausted for some minutes afterwards in a defiant motion of the head from side to side.

These angry symptoms were keenly observed by Maggie. Tom, it appeared, was supposed capable of turning his father out of doors. Maggie jumped up from her stool, forgetting all about her heavy book, which fell with a bang within the fender; and going up between her father's knees, said, in a half-crying, half-indignant voice—

'Father, Tom wouldn't be naughty to you ever; I know he wouldn't.'

Mrs Tulliver was out of the room superintending a choice supper-dish, and Mr Tulliver's heart was touched; so Maggie was not scolded about the book. Mr Riley quietly picked it up and looked at it, while the father laughed and held her hands.

'What! they mustn't say any harm o' Tom, eh?' said Mr Tulliver, looking at Maggie with a twinkling eye. Then, in a lower voice, turning to Mr Riley, as though Maggie couldn't hear, 'She understands what one's talking about so as never was. And you should hear her read – straight off, as if she knowed it all beforehand. But it's bad – it's bad,' Mr Tulliver added, sadly, checking this blamable exultation; 'a woman's no business wi' being so clever; it'll turn to trouble, I doubt. But, bless you!' – here the exultation was clearly recovering the mastery – 'she'll read the books and understand 'em better nor half the folks as are growed up.'

Mr Riley was turning over the leaves of the book, and he presently looked at her and said—

'"The History of the Devil" by Daniel Defoe; not quite the right book for a little girl. How came it among your books, Tulliver?'

Maggie looked hurt and discouraged, while her father said—

'Why, it's one o' the books I bought at Partridge's sale. They were all bound alike – sermons mostly, I think; but they've all got the same covers and I thought they were all o' one sample, as you may say. But it seems one mustn't judge by th' outside. This is a puzzlin' world.'

'Well,' said Mr Riley, in a patronising tone, as he patted Maggie on the head, 'have you no prettier books?'

'Oh, yes,' said Maggie, reviving a little in the desire to vindicate the variety of her reading, 'I've got "Aesop's Fables" and a book about Kangaroos and things, and the "Pilgrim's Progress …"'

'Ah, a beautiful book,' said Mr Riley; 'you can't read a better.'

'Well, but there's a great deal about the devil in that,' said Maggie, triumphantly, 'and I'll show you the picture of him, as he fought with Christian.'

Maggie ran in an instant to the corner of the room, jumped on a chair, and reached down from the small book-case a shabby old copy of Bunyan, which opened at once at the picture she wanted.

'Here he is,' she said, running back to Mr Riley, 'and Tom coloured him for me with his paints when he was at home last holidays – the body all black, you know, and the eyes red, like fire, because he's all fire inside, and it shines out at his eyes.'

'Go, go!' said Mr Tulliver, peremptorily, beginning to feel rather uncomfortable at these free remarks on the personal appearance of a being powerful enough to create lawyers; 'shut up the book, and let's hear no more o' such talk. It is as I thought – the child 'ull learn more mischief nor good wi' the books. Go, go and see after your mother.'

Maggie shut up the book at once, with a sense of disgrace, but not being inclined to see after her mother, she compromised by going into a dark corner behind her father's chair, and nursing her doll, towards which she had an occasional fit of fondness in Tom's absence.

'Did you ever hear the like on't?' said Mr Tulliver, as Maggie retired. 'It's a pity but what she'd been the lad – she'd ha' been a match for the lawyers, *she* would. It's the wonderful'st thing' – here he lowered his voice – 'as I picked the mother because she wasn't o'er 'cute – bein' a good-looking woman too, an' come of a rare family for managing; but I picked her from her sisters o' purpose, 'cause she was a bit weak, like; for I wasn't a-goin' to be told the rights o' things by my own fireside. But you see, when a man's got brains himself, there's no knowing where they'll run to; an' a pleasant sort o' soft woman may go on breeding you stupid lads and 'cute wenches. It's an uncommon puzzlin' thing.'

Mr Riley's gravity gave way, and he shook a little under the application of his pinch of snuff, before he said—

'But your lad's not stupid, is he?'

'Well, he isn't not to say stupid – he's got a notion o' things out o' door, an' a sort o' common-sense, as he'd lay hold o' things by the right handle. But he's slow with his tongue, you see, and he reads but poorly, and spells all wrong, they tell me, an' as shy as can be wi' strangers, an' you never hear him say 'cute things like the little wench. Now, what I want is to send him to a school where they'll make a smart chap of him. I want my son to be even wi' these fellows as have got the start o' me with having better schooling. Not but what, if the world had been left as God made it, I could ha' seen my way, and held my own wi' the best of 'em;

but things have got so twisted round and wrapped up i' unreasonable words, as arn't a bit like 'em, as I'm clean at fault, often an' often. Everything winds about so – the more straightforrard you are, the more you're puzzled.'

'You're quite in the right of it, Tulliver,' observed Mr Riley. 'Better spend an extra hundred or two on your son's education, than leave it him in your will.'

'I daresay, now, you know of a school as 'ud be just the thing for Tom?' said Mr Tulliver.

Mr Riley took a pinch of snuff, and kept Mr Tulliver in suspense by a silence that seemed deliberative, before he said—

'I know of a very fine chance for any one that's got the necessary money, and that's what you have, Tulliver. The fact is, I wouldn't recommend any friend of mine to send a boy to a regular school, if he could afford to do better. But if any one wanted his boy to get superior instruction and training, where he would be the companion of his master, and that master a first-rate fellow, I know his man. I wouldn't mention the chance to everybody, but I mention it to you, Tulliver – between ourselves.'

Mr Tulliver became quite eager.

'Ay, now, let's hear,' he said, with the complacency of a person who is thought worthy of important communications.

'He's an Oxford man,' said Mr Riley, looking at Mr Tulliver to observe the effect of this stimulating information.

'What! a parson?' said Mr Tulliver, rather doubtfully.

'Yes – and an MA. The bishop, I understand, thinks very highly of him; why, it was the bishop who got him his present curacy.'

'Ah!' said Mr Tulliver. 'But what can he want wi' Tom, then?'

'Why, the fact is, he's fond of teaching, and wishes to take one or two boys as pupils to fill up his time profitably. The boys would be quite of the family – the finest thing in the world for them; under Stelling's eye continually.'

'And what money 'ud he want?' said Mr Tulliver. Instinct told him the services of this admirable MA would bear a high price.

'Why, I know of a clergyman who asks a hundred and fifty with his youngest pupils, and he's not to be mentioned with Stelling.'

'Ah,' said Mr Tulliver; 'but a hundred and fifty's an uncommon price. I never thought o' payin' so much as that.'

'A good education, let me tell you, Tulliver – a good education is cheap at the money. But Stelling is moderate in his terms – I've no doubt he'd take your boy at a hundred. I'll write to him about it, if you like.'

Mr Tulliver rubbed his knees, and looked at the carpet in a meditative manner.

'But belike he's a bachelor,' observed Mrs Tulliver, who was now in her place again. 'It 'ud break my heart to send Tom where there's a housekeeper, an' I hope you won't think of it, Mr Tulliver.'

'You may set your mind at rest on that score, Mrs Tulliver,' said Mr Riley, 'for Stelling is married to as nice a little woman as any man need wish for a wife. There isn't a kinder little soul in the world; I know her family well. She has very much your complexion – light curly hair. She comes of a good Mudport family. Stelling's rather a particular fellow as to the people he chooses to be connected with. But I *think* he would have no objection to take your son – I *think* he would not, on my representation.'

'I don't know what he could have *against* the lad,' said Mrs Tulliver, with a slight touch of motherly indignation.

'But there's one thing I'm thinking on,' said Mr Tulliver, looking at Mr Riley, after a long perusal of the carpet. 'Wouldn't a parson be almost too high-learnt to bring up a lad to be a man o' business? I want Tom to know figures, and write like print, and see into things quick, and know what folks mean, and how to wrap things up in words as aren't actionable. It's an uncommon fine thing, that is,' concluded Mr Tulliver, 'when you can let a man know what you think of him without paying for it.'

'Oh, my dear Tulliver,' said Mr Riley, 'you're quite under a mistake about the clergy. A clergyman has the knowledge that will ground a boy, and prepare him for entering on any career with credit. Drop Stelling a hint, and that's enough. You talk of figures, now; you have only to say to Stelling, "I want my son to be a thorough arithmetician," and you may leave the rest to him.'

Mr Riley paused a moment. 'You see, my dear Tulliver,' he continued, 'when you get a thoroughly educated man, he's at no loss to take up any branch of instruction. When a workman knows the use of his tools, he can make a door as well as a window.'

'Ay, that's true,' said Mr Tulliver, almost convinced now that the clergy must be the best of schoolmasters.

'Well, I'll tell you what I'll do for you,' said Mr Riley, 'and I wouldn't do it for everybody. I'll see Stelling's father-in-law, or drop him a line when I get back to Mudport, to say that you wish to place your boy with his son-in-law, and I daresay Stelling will write to you and send you his terms.'

'But there's no hurry, is there?' said Mrs Tulliver; 'for I hope, Mr Tulliver, you won't let Tom begin at his new school before Midsummer.'

'It might be as well not to defer the arrangement too long,' said Mr Riley quietly, 'for Stelling may have propositions from other parties, and I know he would not take more than two or three boarders. If I were you, I would enter on the subject with Stelling at once: there's no necessity for sending the boy before Midsummer, but I would make sure that nobody forestalls you.'

'Ay, there's summat in that,' said Mr Tulliver.

'Father,' broke in Maggie, who had stolen unperceived to her father's elbow again, listening with parted lips – 'Father, is it a long way off where Tom is to go? Shan't we ever go to see him?'

'I don't know, my wench,' said the father, tenderly.

'About fifteen miles, that's all,' said Mr Riley. 'You can drive there and back in a day quite comfortably.'

'But it's too far off for the linen, I doubt,' said Mrs Tulliver, sadly.

The entrance of supper opportunely adjourned this difficulty, and relieved Mr Riley from the labour of suggesting some solution or compromise – a labour which he would otherwise doubtless have undertaken; for, as you perceive, he was a man of very obliging manners. And he had really given himself the trouble of recommending Mr Stelling to his friend Tulliver without any positive expectation of a solid, definite advantage resulting to himself.

4

Tom Is Expected

Maggie was not allowed to go with her father in the gig when he went to fetch Tom home from the academy; the morning was too wet, Mrs Tulliver said, for a little girl to go out in her best bonnet. Maggie took the opposite view very strongly, and it was a direct consequence of this difference of opinion that when her mother was in the act of brushing out the reluctant black crop, Maggie suddenly rushed from under her hands and dipped her head in a basin of water standing near – in the vindictive determination that there should be no chance of curls that day.

'Maggie, Maggie,' exclaimed Mrs Tulliver, 'what is to become of you if you're so naughty? Oh dear, oh dear! look at your clean pinafore, wet from top to bottom. Folks 'ull think it's a judgement on me as I've got such a child – they'll think I've done summat wicked.'

Maggie was already out of hearing, making her way towards the great attic that ran under the old high-pitched roof, shaking the water from her black locks as she ran. This attic was Maggie's favourite retreat on a wet day, when the weather was not too cold; here she fretted out all her ill-humours, and here she kept a Fetish which she punished for all her misfortunes. This was a large wooden doll, now entirely defaced by a long career of vicarious suffering. Maggie had soothed herself by alternately grinding and beating the wooden head against the rough brick of the great chimneys. That was what she did this morning, sobbing all the while with a passion that expelled even the memory of the grievance that had caused it. As, at last, the sobs were getting quieter, a sudden beam of sunshine made her throw away the Fetish and run to the window. The sun was breaking out; the sound of the mill seemed cheerful again; the granary doors were open; and there was Yap, the queer white-and-brown terrier, with one ear turned back, trotting about and sniffing vaguely, as if he were in search of a companion. It was irresistible. Maggie tossed her hair back and ran downstairs, seized her bonnet without putting it on, peeped, and then dashed along the passage lest she should encounter her mother, and was quickly out in the yard, whirling round and singing, 'Yap, Yap, Tom's coming home!' while Yap danced and barked round her, as much as to say, if there was any noise wanted he was the dog for it.

'Hegh, hegh, miss! you'll make yourself giddy, an' tumble down i' the dirt,' said Luke, the head miller, a tall, broad-shouldered man of forty, black-eyed and black-haired.

Maggie paused in her whirling and said, staggering a little, 'Oh, no, it doesn't make me giddy, Luke; may I go into the mill with you?'

Maggie loved to linger in the great spaces of the mill. The resolute din, the unresting motion of the great stones, giving her a dim delicious awe as at the presence of an uncontrollable force – the meal forever pouring, pouring – the fine white powder softening all surfaces – the sweet pure scent of the meal – all helped to make Maggie feel that the mill was a little world apart from her outside everyday life. The part of the mill she liked best was the topmost storey – the corn-hutch, where there were the great heaps of grain, which she could sit on and slide down continually. She was in the habit of taking this recreation as she conversed with Luke, to whom she was very communicative, wishing him to think well of her understanding, as her father did.

Perhaps she felt it necessary to recover her position with him on the present occasion, for, as she sat sliding on the heap of grain near which he was busying himself, she said, at the shrill pitch which was requisite in mill-society—

'I think you never read any book but the Bible – did you, Luke?'

'Nay, Miss – an' not much o' that,' said Luke, with great frankness. 'I'n got to keep count o' the flour an' corn – I can't do wi' knowin' so many things besides my work.'

'Why, you're like my brother Tom, Luke,' said Maggie, wishing to turn the conversation agreeably; 'Tom's not fond of reading. I love Tom so dearly, Luke – better than anybody else in the world. But I think Tom's clever, for all he doesn't like books; he makes beautiful whipcord and rabbit-pens.'

'Ah,' said Luke, 'but he'll be fine an' vexed, as the rabbits are all dead.'

'Dead!' screamed Maggie, jumping up from her sliding seat on the corn. 'Oh dear, Luke,' she said, in a piteous tone, while the big tears rolled down her cheek; 'Tom told me to take care of 'em, and I forgot. What *shall* I do?'

'Well, you see, Miss, they were in that far tool-house, an' it was nobody's business to see to 'em. I reckon Master Tom told Harry to feed 'em, but there's no countin' on Harry – he remembers nothing but his own inside.'

'Oh, Luke, Tom told me to be sure and remember the rabbits every day; but how could I, when they did not come into my head, you know? Oh, he will be so angry with me, I know he will, and so sorry about his rabbits – and so am I sorry. Oh, what *shall* I do?'

'Don't you fret, Miss,' said Luke soothingly, 'they're nash things, them lop-eared rabbits – they'd happen ha' died, if they'd been fed. Master Tom 'ull know better nor buy such things another time. Don't you fret, Miss. Will you come along home wi' me, and see my wife? I'm a-goin' this minute.'

The invitation offered an agreeable distraction to Maggie's grief.

5

Tom Comes Home

Tom was to arrive early in the afternoon, and there was another fluttering heart besides Maggie's when it was late enough for the sound of the gig-wheels to be expected; for if Mrs Tulliver had a strong feeling, it was fondness for her boy. At last the sound came – that quick light bowling of the gig-wheels – and in spite of the wind, which was not likely to respect Mrs Tulliver's curls and cap-strings, she came outside the door, and even held her hand on Maggie's offending head, forgetting all the griefs of the morning.

Mrs Tulliver stood with her arms open; Maggie jumped first on one leg and then on the other; while Tom descended from the gig, and said, with masculine reticence as to the tender emotions, 'Hallo! Yap – what! are you there?'

Nevertheless he submitted to be kissed willingly enough, though Maggie hung on his neck in rather a strangling fashion, while his blue-grey eyes wandered towards the croft and the lambs and the river. He was one of those lads that grow everywhere in England, and, at twelve or thirteen years of age, look as much alike as goslings: a lad with light-brown hair, cheeks of cream and roses, full lips, indeterminate nose and eyebrows – a physiognomy in which it seems impossible to discern anything but the generic character of boyhood; as different as possible from poor Maggie's phiz, which Nature seemed to have moulded and coloured with the most decided intention.

'Maggie,' said Tom confidentially, taking her into a corner, as soon as his mother was gone out to examine his box, and the warm parlour had taken off the chill he had felt from the long drive, 'you don't know what I've got in *my* pockets.' He drew something half out of his right-hand pocket.

'What is it?' said Maggie, in a whisper.

'Why, it's … a … new … guess, Maggie!'

'Oh, I *can't* guess, Tom,' said Maggie, impatiently.

'Don't be a spitfire, else I won't tell you,' said Tom.

'No, Tom,' said Maggie, imploringly, laying hold of the arm that was held stiffly in the pocket. 'I'm not cross, Tom; it was only because I can't bear guessing. *Please* be good to me.'

Tom's arm slowly relaxed, and he said, 'Well, then, it's a new fish-line – two new uns – one for you, Maggie, all to yourself. I wouldn't go halves in the toffee and gingerbread on purpose to save the money; and Gibson and Spouncer fought with me because I wouldn't. And here's hooks; see here! ... I say, *won't* we go and fish tomorrow down by the Round Pool? And you shall catch your own fish, Maggie, and put the worms on, and everything – won't it be fun?'

Maggie's answer was to throw her arms round Tom's neck and hug him, and hold her cheek against his without speaking, while he slowly unwound some of the line, saying, after a pause—

'Wasn't I a good brother, now, to buy you a line all to yourself? You know, I needn't have bought it, if I hadn't liked.'

'Yes, very, very good ... I do love you, Tom.'

Tom had put the line back in his pocket, and was looking at the hooks one by one, before he spoke again.

'And the fellows fought me, because I wouldn't give in about the toffee.'

'Oh dear! Tom. Didn't it hurt you?'

'Hurt me? no,' said Tom. Then he added—

'I gave Spouncer a black eye, I know – that's what he got by wanting to leather *me*; I wasn't going to go halves because anybody leathered me.'

'Oh, how brave you are, Tom! If there came a lion roaring at me, I think you'd fight him – wouldn't you, Tom?'

'How can a lion come roaring at you, you silly thing? There's no lions, only in the shows.'

'But I like to fancy how it would be,' said Maggie. 'Just think what you would do, Tom.'

'Oh, don't bother, Maggie! you're such a silly – I shall go and see my rabbits.'

Maggie's heart began to flutter with fear.

She dared not tell the sad truth at once, but she walked after Tom in trembling silence as he went out, thinking how she could tell him the news so as to soften at once his sorrow and his anger; for Maggie dreaded Tom's anger of all things – it was quite a different anger from her own.

'Tom,' she said timidly, when they were out of doors, 'how much money did you give for your rabbits?'

'Two half-crowns; and a sixpence,' said Tom, promptly.

'I think I've got a great deal more than that in my steel purse upstairs. I'll ask mother to give it you.'

'What for?' said Tom. 'I don't want *your* money, you silly thing.'

'Well, but, Tom – if mother would let me give you two half-crowns and a sixpence out of my purse to put into your pocket and spend, you know; and buy some more rabbits with it?'

'More rabbits? I don't want any more.'

'Oh, but, Tom, they're all dead.'

Tom stopped immediately in his walk and turned round towards Maggie. 'You forgot to feed 'em, then, and Harry forgot?' he said, his colour heightening for a moment, but soon subsiding. 'I'll pitch into Harry – I'll have him turned away. And I don't love you, Maggie. You shan't go fishing with me tomorrow. I told you to go and see the rabbits every day.' He walked on again.

'Yes, but I forgot – and I couldn't help it, indeed, Tom. I'm so very sorry,' said Maggie, while the tears rushed fast.

'You're a naughty girl,' said Tom, severely, 'and I'm sorry I bought you the fish-line. I don't love you.'

'Oh, Tom, it's very cruel,' sobbed Maggie. 'I'd forgive you, if *you* forgot anything – I wouldn't mind what you did – I'd forgive you and love you.'

'Yes, you're a silly – but I never *do* forget things – *I* don't.'

'Oh, please forgive me, Tom; my heart will break,' said Maggie, shaking with sobs, clinging to Tom's arm, and laying her wet cheek on his shoulder. 'I ... lo-lo-love you so, Tom.'

'But you're a naughty girl and you shan't go fishing with me tomorrow.'

With this terrible conclusion, Tom ran away from Maggie towards the mill, meaning to greet Luke there, and complain to him of Harry.

Maggie stood motionless, except from her sobs, for a minute or two; then she turned round and ran into the house, and up to her attic, where she sat on the floor, and laid her head against the worm-eaten shelf, with a crushing sense of misery. Tom was come home, and she had thought how happy she should be – and now he was cruel to her. What use was anything, if Tom didn't love her? Oh, he was very cruel! Hadn't she wanted to give him the money, and said how very sorry she was? She had never *meant* to be naughty to Tom.

Maggie soon thought she had been hours in the attic, and it must be tea-time, and they were all having their tea, and not thinking of her. Well, then, she would stay up there and starve herself – hide herself behind the tub, and stay there all night; and then they would all be frightened, and Tom would be sorry. This resolution lasted in great intensity for five dark minutes behind the tub; but then the need of being loved, the strongest need in poor Maggie's nature, began to wrestle with her pride, and soon threw it. She crept from behind her tub into the twilight of the long attic, but just then she heard a quick footstep on the stairs.

Tom had been too much interested in his talk with Luke, in going the round of the premises, walking in and out where he pleased, and whittling sticks without any particular reason, except that he didn't whittle sticks at school, to think of Maggie and the effect his anger had produced on her. He meant to punish her, and that business having been performed, he occupied himself with other matters, like a practical person. But when he had been called into tea, his father said, 'Why, where's the little wench?' and Mrs Tulliver, almost at the same moment, said, 'Where's your little sister?' – both of them having supposed that Maggie and Tom had been together all the afternoon.

'I don't know,' said Tom. He didn't want to 'tell' of Maggie, though he was angry with her; for Tom Tulliver was a lad of honour.

'What! hasn't she been playing with you all this while?' said the father. 'She's been thinking o' nothing but your coming home.'

'I haven't seen her this two hours,' said Tom, commencing on the plumcake.

'Goodness heart! she's got drownded!' exclaimed Mrs Tulliver, rising from her seat and running to the window.

'Nay, nay, she's none drownded!' said Mr Tulliver. 'You've been naughty to her, I doubt, Tom?'

'I'm sure I haven't, father,' said Tom, indignantly. 'I think she's in the house.'

'Perhaps up in that attic,' said Mrs Tulliver, 'a-singing and talking to herself, and forgetting all about meal-times.'

'You go and fetch her down, Tom,' said Mr Tulliver, rather sharply, his perspicacity or his fatherly fondness for Maggie making him suspect that the lad had been hard upon 'the little 'un,' else she would never have left his side. 'And be good to her, do you hear? Else I'll let you know better.'

Tom never disobeyed his father but he went out rather sullenly, carrying his piece of plumcake, and not intending to reprieve Maggie's punishment, which was no more than she deserved. Tom was only thirteen, but he was particularly clear and positive on one point – namely, that he would punish everybody who deserved it.

It was Tom's step, then, that Maggie heard on the stairs, when her need of love had triumphed over her pride, and she was going down with her swollen eyes and dishevelled hair to beg for pity. At least her father would stroke her head and say, 'Never mind, my wench.'

But she knew Tom's step, and her heart began to beat violently with the sudden shock of hope. He only stood still at the top of the stairs and said, 'Maggie, you're to come down.' But she rushed to him and clung round his neck, sobbing, 'Oh, Tom, please forgive me – I can't bear it – I will always be good – always remember things – do love me – please, dear Tom!'

Maggie and Tom were still very much like young animals, and so she could rub her cheek against his, and kiss his ear in a random, sobbing way; and there were tender fibres in the lad that had been used to answer to Maggie's fondling; so that he behaved with a weakness quite inconsistent with his resolution to punish her as much as she deserved: he actually began to kiss her in return, and say—

'Don't cry, then, Magsie – here, eat a bit o' cake.'

Maggie's sobs began to subside, and she put out her mouth for the cake and bit a piece; and then Tom bit a piece, just for company.

'Come along, Magsie, and have tea,' said Tom at last, when there was no more cake except what was downstairs.

So ended the sorrows of this day, and the next morning Maggie was trotting with her own fishing-rod in one hand and a handle of the basket in the other, stepping always, by a peculiar gift, in the muddiest places, and looking darkly radiant from under her beaver-bonnet because Tom was good to her. Maggie was rather in awe of Tom's superiority, for he was the only person who called her knowledge 'stuff,' and did not feel surprised at her cleverness. Still he was very fond of his sister, and meant always to take care of her, make her his housekeeper, and punish her when she did wrong.

They were on their way to the Round Pool. The sight of the old favourite spot always heightened Tom's good-humour, and he spoke to Maggie in the most amicable whispers, as he opened the precious basket, and prepared their tackle. He threw her line for her, and put the rod into her hand. But she had forgotten all about the fish, and was looking dreamily at the glassy water, when Tom said, in a loud whisper, 'Look, look, Maggie!' and came running to prevent her from snatching her line away.

Maggie was frightened lest she had been doing something wrong, as usual, but presently Tom drew out her line and brought a large tench bouncing on the grass.

Tom was excited.

'Oh, Magsie! you little duck! Empty the basket.'

Maggie was not conscious of unusual merit, but it was enough that Tom called her Magsie, and was pleased with her.

It was one of their happy mornings. They trotted together, with no thought that life would ever change much for them.

6

The Aunts and Uncles Are Coming

It was Easter week, and Mrs Tulliver's cheese-cakes were more exquisitely light than usual: 'a puff o' wind 'ud make 'em blow about like feathers,' Kezia the house-maid said – feeling proud to live under a mistress who could make such pastry; so that no season or circumstances could have been more propitious for a family party, even if it had not been advisable to consult sister Glegg and sister Pullet about Tom's going to school.

'I'd as lief not invite sister Deane this time,' said Mrs Tulliver, 'for she's as jealous and "having" as can be, and 's allays trying to make the worst o' my poor children to their aunts and uncles.'

'Yes, yes,' said Mr Tulliver, 'ask her to come. I never hardly get a bit o' talk with Deane now. What's it matter what she says? Your sister Deane won't get 'em to leave all to one, I reckon, and make the country cry shame on 'em when they are dead?'

'I don't know what she won't get 'em to do,' said Mrs Tulliver, 'for my children are so awk'ard wi' their aunts and uncles. Maggie's ten times naughtier when they come than she is other days, and Tom doesn't like 'em, bless him. And there's Lucy Deane's such a good child – I can't help loving the child as if she was my own; and I'm sure she's more like *my* child than sister Deane's, for she'd allays a very poor colour for one of our family, sister Deane had.'

'Well, well, if you're fond o' the child, ask her father and mother to bring her with 'em. And won't you ask their aunt and uncle Moss too? and some o' *their* children?'

'Oh dear, Mr Tulliver, why, you know as well as I do, as *my* sisters and *your* sister don't suit well together.'

'Well, well, do as you like, Bessy,' said Mr Tulliver, taking up his hat and walking out to the mill. Few wives were more submissive than Mrs Tulliver on all points unconnected with her family relations; but she had been a Miss Dodson, and the Dodsons were a very respectable family indeed – as much looked up to as any in their own parish, or the next to it. There were particular ways of doing everything in that family: particular ways of bleaching the linen, of making the cowslip wine, curing the hams, and keeping the bottled gooseberries; so that no daughter of that house could be indifferent to the privilege of having been born a Dodson. When one of the family was in trouble or sickness, all the rest went to visit the unfortunate member, usually at the same time, and did not shrink from uttering the most disagreeable truths that correct family feeling dictated: if the illness or trouble was the sufferer's own fault, it was not in the practice of the Dodson family to shrink from saying so. In short, there was in this family a peculiar tradition as to what was the right thing in household management and social demeanour. Mrs Tulliver was a thorough Dodson, though a mild one, and though she had groaned a little in her youth under the yoke of her elder sisters, and still shed occasional tears at their sisterly reproaches, it was not in Mrs Tulliver to be an innovator on the family ideas. She was thankful to have been a Dodson, and to have one child who took after her own family at least in his features and complexion, in liking salt and in eating beans, which a Tulliver never did.

In other respects the true Dodson was partly latent in Tom, and he was as far from appreciating his 'kin' on the mother's side as Maggie herself; generally absconding for the day with a large supply of the most portable food, when he received timely warning that his aunts and uncles were coming.

On Wednesday, the day before the aunts and uncles were coming, there were such various and suggestive scents, as of plumcakes in the oven. Tom and Maggie made several inroads into the kitchen, and were induced to keep aloof for a time only by being allowed to carry away a sufficient load of booty.

'Tom,' said Maggie, as they sat on the boughs of the elder-tree, eating their jam puffs, 'shall you run away tomorrow?'

'No,' said Tom, slowly, when he had finished his puff, and was eyeing the third, which was to be divided between them, 'no, I shan't.'

'Why, Tom? Because Lucy's coming?'

'No,' said Tom, opening his pocket-knife and holding it over the puff, with his head on one side in a dubitative manner. (It was a difficult problem to divide that very irregular polygon into two equal parts.) 'What do *I* care about Lucy? It's the pudden. I know what the pudden's to be – apricot roll-up – oh my buttons!' With this interjection, the knife descended on the puff and it was in two, but Tom eyed the halves doubtfully. At last he said—

'Shut your eyes, Maggie.'

Maggie obeyed.

'Now, which'll you have, Maggie – right-hand or left?'

'I'll have that with the jam run out,' said Maggie, keeping her eyes shut to please Tom.

'Why, you don't like that, you silly. You may have it if it comes to you fair, but I shan't give it you without. You choose.'

Maggie said, 'Left-hand.'

'You've got it,' said Tom, in rather a bitter tone.

'What! the bit with the jam run out?'

'No; here, take it,' said Tom firmly, handing decidedly the best piece to Maggie.

'Oh, please, Tom, have it: I don't mind – please take this.'

'No, I shan't,' said Tom, beginning on his own inferior piece.

Maggie, thinking it was no use to contend further, began too, and ate up her half puff with considerable relish as well as rapidity. But Tom had finished first, and had to look on while Maggie ate her last morsel or two, feeling in himself a capacity for more.

'Oh, you greedy thing!' said Tom, when she had swallowed the last morsel. He was conscious of having acted very fairly, and thought she ought to have considered this, and made up to him for it. He would have refused a bit of hers beforehand, but one is naturally at a different point of view before and after one's own share of puff is swallowed.

Maggie turned quite pale. 'Oh, Tom, why didn't you ask me?'

'*I* wasn't going to ask you for a bit, you greedy. You might have thought of it without, when you knew I gave you the best bit.'

'But I wanted you to have it – you know I did,' said Maggie.

'Yes, but I wasn't going to do what wasn't fair. If I go halves, I'll go 'em fair – only I wouldn't be a greedy.'

With this cutting innuendo, Tom jumped down from his bough, and threw a stone with a 'hoigh!' as a friendly attention to Yap.

But Maggie sat still on her bough, and gave herself up to the keen sense of unmerited reproach. She would have given the world not to have eaten all her puff, and to have saved some of it for Tom. She would have gone without it many times over, sooner than Tom should call her greedy and be cross with her. The tears flowed so plentifully that Maggie saw nothing around her for the next ten minutes; but by that time resentment began to give way to the desire of reconciliation, and she jumped from her bough to look for Tom. He was no longer in the paddock behind the rickyard. Maggie ran to the high bank against the great holly-tree, where she could see far away towards the Floss. There was Tom; but her heart sank; he had another companion besides Yap – Bob Jakin, whose official function of frightening the birds was just now at a standstill. When Tom had Bob for a companion, he didn't mind about Maggie, and would never let her go with him.

It must be owned that Tom was fond of Bob's company. How could it be otherwise? Bob knew, directly he saw a bird's egg, whether it was a swallow's, or a tomtit's, or a yellow-hammer's; he found out all the wasps' nests, and could set all sorts of traps; he could climb the trees like a squirrel, and had quite a magical power of detecting hedgehogs and stoats; and he had courage to do things that were rather naughty; such as making gaps in the hedgerows, throwing stones after the sheep, and killing a cat that was wandering *incognito*. Such qualities in an inferior, who could always be treated with authority in spite of his superior knowingness, had necessarily a fatal fascination for Tom; and every holiday-time Maggie was sure to have days of grief because he had gone off with Bob.

Well! there was no hope for it: he was gone now, and Maggie could think of no comfort but to sit down by the holly, or wander by the hedgerow, and fancy it was all different, refashioning her little world into just what she should like it to be.

Meanwhile Tom, forgetting all about Maggie, was hurrying along with Bob, whom he had met accidentally, to the scene of a great rat-catching in a neighbouring barn. Bob knew all about this particular affair, and spoke of the sport with an enthusiasm which no one who is not either divested of all manly feeling, or pitiably ignorant of rat-catching, can fail to imagine. There was something agreeable in Bob's snub-nosed face, with its close-curled border of red hair. But then his trousers were always rolled up at the knee, for the convenience of wading on the slightest notice.

At this moment a striking incident made the boys pause suddenly in their walk. It was the plunging of some small body in the water from among the neighbouring bulrushes: if it was not a water-rat, Bob intimated that he was ready to undergo the most unpleasant consequences. Bob chose now to walk in the shallow edge of the overflowing river by way of change.

'He's none so full now, the Floss isn't,' said Bob, as he kicked the water up before him, with an agreeable sense of being insolent to it. 'Why, last 'ear, the meadows was all one sheet o' water, they was.'

'Ay, but,' said Tom, whose mind was prone to see an opposition between statements that were really quite accordant, 'but there was a big flood once, when the Round Pool was made. I know there was, 'cause father says so. And the sheep and cows were all drowned, and the boats went all over the fields ever such a way.'

'I don't care about a flood comin',' said Bob; 'I don't mind the water, no more nor the land. I'd swim – I would.'

'Ah, but if you got nothing to eat for ever so long?' said Tom, his imagination becoming quite active under the stimulus of that dread. 'When I'm a man, I shall make a boat like Noah's ark, and keep plenty to eat in it – rabbits and things. And then if the flood came, you know, Bob, I shouldn't mind ... And I'd take you in, if I saw you swimming,' he added, in the tone of a benevolent patron.

'I aren't frightened,' said Bob, to whom hunger did not appear so appalling. 'But I'd get in an' knock the rabbits on th' head when you wanted to eat 'em.'

'Ah, and I should have halfpence, and we'd play at heads-and-tails,' said Tom, not contemplating the possibility that this recreation might have fewer charms for his mature age.

'I've got a halfpenny o' my own,' said Bob, proudly, coming out of the water and tossing his halfpenny in the air. 'Yeads or tails?'

'Tails,' said Tom, instantly fired with the desire to win.

'It's yeads,' said Bob, hastily, snatching up the halfpenny as it fell.

'It wasn't,' said Tom, loudly and peremptorily. 'You give me the halfpenny – I've won it fair.'

'I shan't,' said Bob, holding it tight in his pocket.

'Then I'll make you – see if I don't,' said Tom.

'You can't make me do nothing, you can't,' said Bob.

'Yes, I can. I'm master,' said Tom, collaring Bob and shaking him.

'You get out wi' you,' said Bob, giving Tom a kick.

Tom's blood was thoroughly up: he went at Bob with a lunge and threw him down, and Bob seized hold and kept it like a cat, and pulled Tom down after him. They struggled fiercely on the ground for a moment or two, till Tom, pinning Bob down by the shoulders, thought he had the mastery.

But at this moment, Yap saw a favourable opportunity for biting Bob's bare leg not only with impunity but with honour. The pain from Yap's teeth, instead of surprising Bob into a relaxation of his hold, gave it a fiercer tenacity, and with a new exertion of his force, he pushed Tom backward and got uppermost. But now Yap set his teeth in a new place, so that Bob let go his hold of Tom and, almost throttling Yap, flung him into the river. By this time Tom was up again, and before Bob had quite recovered his balance after the act of swinging Yap, Tom fell upon him, threw him down, and got his knees firmly on Bob's chest.

'You give me the halfpenny now,' said Tom.

'Take it,' said Bob, sulkily.

'No, I shan't take it; you give it me.'

Bob took the halfpenny out of his pocket and threw it away from him on the ground.

Tom loosed his hold, and left Bob to rise.

'There the halfpenny lies,' he said. 'I don't want your halfpenny; I wouldn't have kept it. But you wanted to cheat: I hate a cheat. I shan't go along with you any more,' he added, turning round homeward, not without casting a regret towards the rat-catching which he must relinquish along with Bob's society.

'You may let it alone, then,' Bob called out after him. 'I shall cheat if I like ... An' you're a nasty fightin' turkey-cock, you are ...'

Tom walked on without looking round, and Yap followed his example, the cold bath having moderated his passions.

'Go along wi' you, then, wi' your drownded dog; I wouldn't own such a dog – *I* wouldn't,' said Bob. But Tom was not to be provoked into turning round, and Bob's voice faltered a little as he said—

'An' I'n gi'en you everything, an' showed you everything, an' niver wanted nothin' from you ... An' there's your horn-handed knife, then, as you gi'en me ...' Here Bob flung the knife as far as he could after Tom's retreating footsteps. But it produced no effect, except the sense in Bob's mind that there was a terrible void in his lot, now that knife was gone.

He stood still till Tom had passed through the gate and disappeared behind the hedge. The knife would do no good on the ground there – it wouldn't vex Tom, and pride or resentment was a feeble passion in Bob's mind compared with the love of a pocket-knife. What is life without a pocket-knife to him who has once tasted a higher existence? So Bob shuffled back to the spot where the beloved knife lay in the dirt, and felt quite a new pleasure in clutching it again after the temporary separation, in opening one blade after the other, and feeling their edge with his well-hardened thumb. Poor Bob! he was not sensitive on the point of honour – yet for all that he was not utterly a sneak and a thief, as our friend Tom had hastily decided.

7

Enter the Aunts and Uncles

The Dodsons were certainly a handsome family, and Mrs Glegg was not the least handsome of the sisters; for a woman of fifty she had a very comely face and figure, though Tom and Maggie considered their aunt Glegg as the type of ugliness. It is true she despised the advantages of costume, for though, as she often observed, no woman had better clothes, it was not her way to wear her new things out before her old ones. So of her curled fronts: Mrs Glegg had doubtless the glossiest and crispest brown curls in her drawers, as well as curls in various degrees of fuzzy laxness; but to look out on the week-day world from under a crisp and glossy front, would be to introduce a most dreamlike and unpleasant confusion between the sacred and the secular. Occasionally, indeed, Mrs Glegg wore one of her third-best fronts on a week-day visit, but not at a sister's house; especially not at Mrs Tulliver's, who, since her marriage, had hurt her sisters' feelings greatly by wearing her own hair, though, as Mrs Glegg observed to Mrs Deane, a mother of a family, like Bessy, with a husband always going to law, might have been expected to know better. But Bessy was always weak!

So if Mrs Glegg's front today was more fuzzy and lax than usual, she had a design under it; she intended the most pointed and cutting allusion to Mrs Tulliver's bunches of blond curls, separated from each other by a due wave of smoothness on each side of the parting. Mrs Tulliver had shed tears several times at sister Glegg's unkindness on the subject of these unmatronly curls, but the consciousness of looking the handsomer for them, naturally administered support. Mrs Glegg chose to wear her bonnet in the house today – untied and tilted slightly, of course – a frequent practice of hers when she was on a visit, and happened to be in a severe humour.

Mrs Glegg held her large gold-watch in her hand and observed to Mrs Tulliver that whatever it might be by other people's clocks and watches, it was gone half-past twelve by hers.

'I don't know what ails sister Pullet,' she continued. 'It used to be the way in our family for one to be as early as another and not for one sister to sit half an hour before the others came. But if the ways o' the family are altered, it shan't be *my* fault – *I'll* never be the one to come into a house when all the rest are going away. I wonder *at* sister Deane – she used to be more like me. But if you'll take my advice, Bessy, you'll put the dinner forrard a bit, sooner than put it back, because folks are late as ought to ha' known better.'

'Oh dear, there's no fear but what they'll be all here in time, sister,' said Mrs Tulliver, in her mild-peevish tone. 'The dinner won't be ready till half-past one.'

'Well, Bessy!' said Mrs Glegg, with a bitter smile, and a scarcely perceptible toss of her head, 'I should ha' thought you might have it at one. You was never brought up in that way, Bessy.'

'Why, Jane, what can I do? Mr Tulliver doesn't like his dinner before two o'clock, but I put it half an hour earlier because o' you.'

'Yes, yes, I know how it is with husbands – they're for putting everything off – but it's a pity for you, Bessy, as you haven't got more strength o' mind. It'll be well if your children don't suffer for it. And I hope you've not gone and got a great dinner for us – going to expense, for your sisters as 'ud sooner eat a crust o' dry bread nor help to ruin you with extravagance. I wonder you don't take pattern by your sister Deane – she's far more sensible. And here you've got two children to provide for, and your husband's spent your fortin i' going to law, and 's likely to spend his own too.'

With sister Glegg in this humour, there was a cheerful prospect for the day. Mrs Tulliver never went the length of quarrelling with her. But this point of the dinner was not at all new, so that Mrs Tulliver could make the same answer she had often made before.

'Mr Tulliver says he always *will* have a good dinner for his friends while he can pay for it,' she said; 'and he's a right to do as he likes in his own house, sister.'

'Well, Bessy, *I* can't leave your children enough, out o' my savings, to keep 'em from ruin.'

The sound of wheels while Mrs Glegg was speaking was an interruption highly welcome to Mrs Tulliver.

Sister Pullet was in tears when the one-horse chaise stopped before Mrs Tulliver's door.

'Why, whativer is the matter, sister?' said Mrs Tulliver.

There was no reply but a shake of the head, as Mrs Pullet slowly rose and got down from the chaise, not without casting a glance at Mr Pullet to see that he was guarding her handsome silk dress from injury. Mr Pullet was a small man with a high nose, small twinkling eyes, and thin lips, in a fresh-looking suit of black, and a white cravat, that seemed to have been tied very tight on some higher principle than that of mere personal ease. He bore about the same relation to his tall, good-looking wife, with her balloon sleeves, abundant mantle, and large be-feathered and be-ribboned bonnet, as a small fishing-smack bears to a brig with all its sails spread.

Mrs Pullet brushed each doorpost with great nicety, about the latitude of her shoulders (at that period a woman was truly ridiculous to an instructed eye if she did not measure a yard and a half across the shoulders), and having done that, sent the muscles of her face in quest of fresh tears as she advanced into the parlour where Mrs Glegg was seated.

'Well, sister, you're late; what's the matter?' said Mrs Glegg, rather sharply, as they shook hands.

Mrs Pullet sat down – lifting up her mantle carefully behind, before she answered—

'She's gone,' unconsciously using an impressive figure of rhetoric.

'Died the day before yesterday,' continued Mrs Pullet; 'an' her legs was as thick as my body,' she added, with deep sadness, after a pause. 'They'd tapped her no end o' times, and the water – they say you might ha' swum in it, if you'd liked.'

'Well, Sophy, it's a mercy she's gone, then, whoever she may be,' said Mrs Glegg, 'but I can't think who you're talking of.'

'But *I* know,' said Mrs Pullet, sighing and shaking her head; 'it's old Mrs Sutton's o' the Twentylands.'

'Well, she's no kin o' yours, nor much acquaintance as I've ever heared of,' said Mrs Glegg, who always cried just as much as was proper when anything happened to her own 'kin,' but not on other occasions.

'She's so much acquaintance as I've seen her legs when they was like bladders … There isn't many old parish'ners like her, I doubt.'

'Sophy,' said Mrs Glegg, unable any longer to contain her spirit of rational remonstrance – 'Sophy, I wonder *at* you, fretting and injuring your health about people as don't belong to you.'

Mrs Pullet was silent, having finished her crying, and rather flattered than indignant at being upbraided for crying too much. It was not everybody who could afford to cry so much about their neighbours who had left them nothing; but Mrs Pullet had married a gentleman farmer, and had leisure and money to carry her crying and everything else to the highest pitch of respectability.

She had recovered sufficiently to take off her veil and fold it carefully. 'Sister, I may as well go and take my bonnet off now. Did you see as the cap-box was put out?' she added, turning to her husband.

Mr Pullet, by an unaccountable lapse of memory, had forgotten it, and hastened out to remedy the omission.

'They'll bring it upstairs, sister,' said Mrs Tulliver.

Mrs Tulliver was fond of going upstairs with her sister Pullet, and looking thoroughly at her cap before she put it on her head, and discussing millinery in general. This was part of Bessy's weakness that stirred Mrs Glegg's sisterly compassion: Bessy went far too well dressed, considering. Of all her sisters, Mrs

Tulliver certainly preferred her sister Pullet, not without a return of preference; but Mrs Pullet was sorry Bessy had those naughty awkward children; she would do the best she could by them, but it was a pity they weren't as good and as pretty as sister Deane's child. Maggie and Tom, on their part, thought their aunt Pullet tolerable, chiefly because she was not their aunt Glegg. Still, it was agreed by the sisters, in Mrs Tulliver's absence, that the Tulliver blood did not mix well with the Dodson blood; that, in fact, poor Bessy's children were Tullivers, and that Tom, notwithstanding he had the Dodson complexion, was likely to be as 'contrairy' as his father. As for Maggie, she was the picture of her aunt Moss, Mr Tulliver's sister – a large-boned woman, who had married as poorly as could be. But when Mrs Pullet was alone with Mrs Tulliver upstairs, the remarks were naturally to the disadvantage of Mrs Glegg, and they agreed, in confidence, that there was no knowing what sort of fright sister Jane would come out next. But their *tête-à-tête* was curtailed by the appearance of Mrs Deane with little Lucy; and Mrs Tulliver had to look on with a silent pang while Lucy's blond curls were adjusted. It was quite unaccountable that Mrs Deane, the thinnest and sallowest of all the Miss Dodsons, should have had this child, who might have been taken for Mrs Tulliver's any day. And Maggie always looked twice as dark when she was by the side of Lucy. She did today, when she and Tom came in from the garden with their father and their uncle Glegg. Maggie had thrown her bonnet off very carelessly, and, coming in with her hair rough as well as out of curl, rushed at once to Lucy, who was standing by her mother's knee. Certainly the contrast between the cousins was conspicuous. It was like the contrast between a rough, dark, overgrown puppy and a white kitten. Lucy put up the neatest little rosebud mouth to be kissed: everything about her was neat – her little round neck, with the row of coral beads; her little straight nose; her little clear eyebrows, rather darker than her curls, to match her hazel eyes, which looked up with shy pleasure at Maggie, taller by the head, though scarcely a year older. Maggie looked at Lucy with delight.

'Oh, Lucy,' she burst out, after kissing her, 'you'll stay with Tom and me, won't you? Oh, kiss her, Tom.'

Tom, too, had come up to Lucy, but he was not going to kiss her – no; he came up to her with Maggie, because it seemed easier, on the whole, than saying, 'How do you do?' to all those aunts and uncles; he stood looking at nothing in particular, with the blushing, awkward air and semi-smile which are common to shy boys.

'Heyday!' said aunt Glegg, with loud emphasis. 'Do little boys and gells come into a room without taking notice o' their uncles and aunts? That wasn't the way when *I* was a little gell.'

'Go and speak to your aunts and uncles, my dears,' said Mrs Tulliver, looking anxious and melancholy.

'Well, and how do you do? And I hope you're good children, are you?' said aunt Glegg as she took their hands, hurting them with her large rings, and kissing their cheeks much against their desire. 'Look up, Tom, look up. Boys as go to boarding-schools should hold their heads up. Look at me now.' Tom declined that pleasure apparently, for he tried to draw his hand away. 'Put your hair behind your ears, Maggie, and keep your frock on your shoulder.'

Aunt Glegg always spoke to them in this loud emphatic way, as if she considered them deaf, or perhaps rather idiotic: it was a means, she thought, of making them feel that they were accountable creatures. Bessy's children were so spoiled – they'd need have somebody to make them feel their duty.

'Well, my dears,' said aunt Pullet, in a compassionate voice. 'You grow wonderful fast,' she added, looking over their heads with a melancholy expression at their mother. 'I think the gell has too much hair. I'd have it thinned and cut shorter, sister, if I was you: it isn't good for her health. It's that as makes her skin so brown, I shouldn't wonder. Don't you think so, sister Deane?'

'I can't say, I'm sure, sister,' said Mrs Deane, shutting her lips close again, and looking at Maggie with a critical eye.

'No, no,' said Mr Tulliver, 'the child's healthy enough – there's nothing ails her. But it 'ud be as well if Bessy 'ud have the child's hair cut, so as it 'ud lie smooth.'

A dreadful resolve was gathering in Maggie's breast, but it was arrested by the desire to know from her aunt Deane whether she would leave Lucy behind: aunt Deane would hardly ever let Lucy come to see them.

'You wouldn't like to stay behind without mother, should you, Lucy?' Mrs Deane appealed to her daughter.

'Yes, please, mother,' said Lucy, timidly, blushing very pink.

'Well done, Lucy! Let her stay, Mrs Deane, let her stay,' said Mr Deane, a large but alert-looking man, with a type of physique to be seen in all ranks of English society – bald crown, red whiskers, full forehead, and general solidity without heaviness – but the keenness of his brown eyes was less common than his contour. He held a silver snuff-box very tightly in his hand, and now and then exchanged a pinch with Mr Tulliver. Mr Deane's box had been given him by the superior partners in the firm to which he belonged, at the same time that they gave him a share in the business, in acknowledgement of his valuable services as manager. No man was thought more highly of in St Ogg's than Mr Deane, and there was no knowing where a man would stop, who had got his foot into a great mill-owning, ship-owning business like that of Guest & Co., with a banking concern attached.

'Maggie,' said Mrs Tulliver, beckoning Maggie to her, and whispering in her ear, as soon as this point of Lucy's staying was settled, 'go and get your hair brushed – do, for shame. I told you not to come in without going to Martha first; you know I did.'

'Tom, come out with me,' whispered Maggie, pulling his sleeve as she passed him; and Tom followed willingly enough. 'There's something I want to do before dinner.'

Tom followed Maggie upstairs into her mother's room, and saw her go at once to a drawer, from which she took out a large pair of scissors. Maggie seized her front locks, cutting them straight across the middle of her forehead.

'Oh, my buttons, Maggie, you'll catch it!' exclaimed Tom; 'you'd better not cut any more off.'

Snip! went the great scissors again while Tom was speaking; and he couldn't help feeling it was rather good fun.

'Here, Tom, cut it behind for me,' said Maggie, excited by her own daring, and anxious to finish the deed.

'You'll catch it, you know,' said Tom, hesitating a little as he took the scissors.

'Never mind – make haste!' said Maggie. Her cheeks were quite flushed. The black locks were so thick – nothing could be more tempting to a lad who had already tasted the forbidden pleasure of cutting the pony's mane. One delicious grinding snip, and then another and another, and Maggie stood cropped in a jagged uneven manner.

'Oh, Maggie,' said Tom, jumping round her, and slapping his knees as he laughed, 'oh, my buttons, what a queer thing you look! You look like the idiot we throw our nutshells to at school.'

Maggie felt an unexpected pang. She had thought beforehand chiefly of her own deliverance from her teasing hair and teasing remarks about it, and something also of the triumph she should have over her mother and her aunts by this very decided course of action: she didn't want her hair to look pretty – that was out of the question – she only wanted people to think her a clever little girl, and not to find fault with her. But now the affair had quite a new aspect. She looked in the glass. Tom laughed and clapped his hands, and Maggie's flushed cheeks began to pale, and her lips to tremble a little.

'Don't laugh at me, Tom,' said Maggie, in a passionate tone, with an outburst of angry tears, stamping, and giving him a push.

'Now, then, spitfire!' said Tom. 'What did you cut it off for, then? I shall go down: I can smell the dinner going in.'

He hurried downstairs. Poor Maggie could see clearly enough, now the thing was done, that it was very foolish, and that she should have to hear and think more about her hair than ever; for Maggie rushed to her deeds with passionate impulse, and then saw not only their consequences, but what would have happened if they had not been done, with all the detail and exaggerated circumstance of an active imagination. Tom never did the same sort of foolish things as Maggie, having a wonderful, instinctive discernment of what would turn to his advantage or disadvantage; and so it happened, that though he was much more wilful and inflexible than Maggie, his mother hardly ever called him naughty. But if Tom did make a mistake of that sort, he espoused it, and stood by it: he wasn't going to be sorry. But Maggie, as she stood crying before the glass, felt it impossible that she should go down to dinner and endure the severe eyes and severe words of her aunts, while Tom, and Lucy, and Martha, who waited at table, and perhaps her father and her uncles, would laugh at her; and if she had only let her hair alone, she could have sat with Tom and Lucy, and had the apricot-pudding and the custard! What could she do but sob? She sat helpless and despairing among her black locks.

'Miss Maggie, you're to come down this minute,' said Kezia, entering the room hurriedly. 'Lawks! what have you been a-doing? I niver *see* such a fright!'

'Don't, Kezia,' said Maggie, angrily. 'Go away! I don't want any dinner. I shan't come.'

'Oh, well, I can't stay. I've got to wait at dinner,' said Kezia, going out again.

'Maggie, you little silly,' said Tom, peeping into the room ten minutes after, 'why don't you come and have your dinner? There's lots o' goodies, and mother says you're to come. What are you crying for, you little spooney?'

Oh, it was dreadful! Tom was so hard and unconcerned; if *he* had been crying on the floor, Maggie would have cried too. And there was the dinner, so nice; and she was *so* hungry. It was very bitter.

But Tom was not altogether hard. He went and put his head near her, and said in a lower, comforting tone—

'Won't you come, then, Magsie? There's the dessert-nuts, you know – and cowslip wine.'

Maggie's tears had ceased, and she looked reflective as Tom left her. His good-nature had taken off the keenest edge of her suffering, and nuts with cowslip wine began to assert their legitimate influence.

Slowly she rose from amongst her scattered locks, and slowly she made her way downstairs. Then she stood leaning with one shoulder against the frame of the dining-parlour door, peeping in when it was ajar. She saw Tom and Lucy with an empty chair between them, and there were the custards on a side-table – it was too much. She slipped in and went towards the empty chair. But she had no sooner sat down than she repented, and wished herself back again.

Mrs Tulliver gave a little scream as she saw her, and felt such a 'turn' that she dropped the large gravy-spoon into the dish with the most serious results to the table-cloth. For Kezia had not betrayed the reason of Maggie's refusal to come down, not liking to give her mistress a shock in the moment of carving, and Mrs Tulliver thought there was nothing worse in question than a fit of perverseness, which was inflicting its own punishment by depriving Maggie of half her dinner.

Mrs Tulliver's scream made all eyes turn towards the same point as her own, and Maggie's cheeks and ears began to burn, while uncle Glegg, a kind-looking, white-haired old gentleman, said—

'Heydey! what little gell's this – why, I don't know her. Is it some little gell you've picked up in the road, Kezia?'

'Why, she's gone and cut her hair herself,' said Mr Tulliver in an under-tone to Mr Deane, laughing with much enjoyment. 'Did you ever know such a little hussy as it is?'

'Why, little Miss, you've made yourself look very funny,' said uncle Pullet, and perhaps he never in his life made an observation which was felt to be so lacerating.

'Fie, for shame!' said aunt Glegg, in her loudest, severest tone of reproof. 'Little gells as cut their own hair should be whipped and fed on bread and water – not come and sit down with their aunts and uncles.'

'Ay, ay,' said uncle Glegg, meaning to give a playful turn to this denunciation, 'she must be sent to jail, I think, and they'll cut the rest of her hair off there, and make it all even.'

'She's more like a gypsy nor ever,' said aunt Pullet in a pitying tone; 'it's very bad luck, sister, as the gell should be so brown – the boy's fair enough. I doubt it'll stand in her way i' life to be so brown.'

'She's a naughty child, as'll break her mother's heart,' said Mrs Tulliver, with the tears in her eyes.

Maggie seemed to be listening to a chorus of reproach and, getting up from her chair, she ran to her father, hid her face on his shoulder, and burst out into loud sobbing.

'Come, come, my wench,' said her father, soothingly, putting his arm round her, 'never mind; you was i' the right to cut it off if it plagued you; give over crying; father'll take your part.'

Delicious words of tenderness! Maggie never forgot any of these moments when her father 'took her part;' she kept them in her heart.

'How your husband does spoil that child, Bessy!' said Mrs Glegg, in a loud 'aside' to Mrs Tulliver. 'It'll be the ruin of her, if you don't take care.'

Mrs Tulliver's domestic sorrows seemed at this moment to have reached the point at which insensibility begins. She took no notice of her sister's remark, but dispensed the pudding, in mute resignation.

With the dessert there came entire deliverance for Maggie, for the children were told they might have their nuts and wine in the summer-house, since the day was so mild.

Mrs Tulliver had her special reason for this permission: now the dinner was despatched, and every one's mind disengaged, it was the right moment to communicate Mr Tulliver's intention concerning Tom, and it would be as well for Tom himself to be absent. Mrs Tulliver had a sighing sense that her husband would do as he liked, whatever sister Glegg said, or sister Pullet either, but at least they would not be able to say, if the thing turned out ill, that Bessy had fallen in with her husband's folly without letting her own friends know a word about it.

'Mr Tulliver,' she said, interrupting her husband in his talk with Mr Deane, 'it's time now to tell the children's aunts and uncles what you're thinking of doing with Tom, isn't it?'

'Very well,' said Mr Tulliver, rather sharply, 'I've no objections to tell anybody what I mean to do with him. I've settled,' he added, looking towards Mr Glegg and Mr Deane, 'to send him to a Mr Stelling, a parson, down at King's Lorton – an uncommon clever fellow, I understand – as'll put him up to most things.'

There was a rustling demonstration of surprise in the company. Mr Pullet was the first to give utterance to his astonishment.

'Why, what can you be going to send him to a parson for?' he said.

'Why, because the parsons are the best schoolmasters, by what I can make out,' said poor Mr Tulliver, who, in the maze of this puzzling world, laid hold of any clue with great readiness and tenacity. 'Jacobs at th' academy's no parson, and he's done very bad by the boy; and I made up my mind, if I sent him to school again, it should be to somebody different to Jacobs. And this Mr Stelling, by what I can make out, is the sort o' man I want. And I mean my boy to go to him at Midsummer,' he concluded, in a tone of decision.

'You'll have to pay a swinging half-yearly bill, then, eh, Tulliver? The clergymen have highish notions, in general,' said Mr Deane, taking snuff vigorously, as he always did when wishing to maintain a neutral position.

'What! do you think the parson'll teach him to know a good sample o' wheat when he sees it, neighbour Tulliver?' said Mr Glegg, who, having retired from business, felt that it was not only allowable but becoming in him to take a playful view of things.

'Why, you see; I've got a plan i' my head about Tom,' said Mr Tulliver, pausing after that statement and lifting up his glass.

'Well, if I may be allowed to speak, and it's seldom as I am,' said Mrs Glegg, with a tone of bitter meaning, 'I should like to know what good is to come to the boy, by bringin' him up above his fortin.'

'Why,' said Mr Tulliver, not looking at Mrs Glegg, but at the male part of his audience, 'you see, I've made up my mind to put him to some business, as he can go into without capital, and I want to give him an eddication as he'll be even wi' the lawyers and folks, and put me up to a notion now an' then.'

Mrs Glegg emitted a long sort of guttural sound with closed lips that smiled in mingled pity and scorn.

'It 'ud be a fine deal better for some people,' she said, after that introductory note, 'if they'd let the lawyers alone.'

'Is he at the head of a grammar school, then, this clergyman – such as that at Market Bewley?' said Mr Deane.

'No – nothing o' that,' said Mr Tulliver. 'He won't take more than two or three pupils – and so he'll have the more time to attend to 'em, you know.'

'But he'll want the more pay, I doubt,' said Mr Glegg.

'Ay, ay, a cool hundred a-year – that's all,' said Mr Tulliver, with some pride at his own spirited course. 'But then, you know, it's an investment; Tom's eddication 'ull be so much capital to him.'

'Ay, there's something in that,' said Mr Glegg.

'Bless me!' said Mr Deane, introducing a new idea, 'why, now I come to think of it, somebody said Wakem was going to send *his* son – the deformed lad – to a clergyman, didn't they, Susan?'

'I can give no account of it, I'm sure,' said Mrs Deane, closing her lips very tightly again.

'Well,' said Mr Tulliver, speaking all the more cheerfully, 'if Wakem thinks o' sending his son to a clergyman, depend on it I shall make no mistake i' sending Tom to one. Wakem's as big a scoundrel as Old Harry ever made, but he knows the length of every man's foot he's got to deal with. Ay, ay, tell me who's Wakem's butcher, and I'll tell you where to get your meat.'

'But lawyer Wakem's son's got a hump-back,' said Mrs Pullet, 'it's more nat'ral to send *him* to a clergyman.'

'Yes,' said Mr Glegg, interpreting Mrs Pullet's observation with erroneous plausibility, 'you must consider that, neighbour Tulliver; Wakem's son isn't likely to follow any business. Wakem 'ull make a gentleman of him, poor fellow.'

'Mr Glegg,' said Mrs G., in a tone which implied that her

indignation would fizz and ooze a little, though she was determined to keep it corked up, 'you'd far better hold your tongue. Mr Tulliver doesn't want to know your opinion nor mine neither. There's folks in the world as know better than everybody else.'

'Why, I should think that's you, if we're to trust your own tale,' said Mr Tulliver, beginning to boil up.

'Oh, *I* say nothing,' said Mrs Glegg, sarcastically. 'My advice has never been asked, and I don't give it.'

'It'll be the first time, then,' said Mr Tulliver. 'It's the only thing you're over-ready at giving.'

'I've been over-ready at lending, then, if I haven't been over-ready at giving,' said Mrs Glegg. 'There's folk I've lent money to as perhaps I shall repent o' lending money to kin.'

'Come, come, come,' said Mr Glegg, soothingly. But Mr Tulliver was not to be hindered of his retort.

'You've got a bond for it, I reckon,' he said; 'and you've had your five per cent, kin or no kin.'

'Sister,' said Mrs Tulliver, pleadingly, 'drink your wine, and let me give you some almonds and raisins.'

'Bessy, I'm sorry for you,' said Mrs Glegg. 'It's poor work, talking o' almonds and raisins.'

'Lors, sister Glegg, don't be so quarrelsome,' said Mrs Pullet, beginning to cry a little, 'it's very bad among sisters.'

'I should think it *is* bad,' said Mrs Glegg. 'Things are come to a fine pass when one sister invites the other to her house o' purpose to quarrel with her and abuse her.'

'Softly, softly, Jane – be reasonable,' said Mr Glegg.

But while he was speaking, Mr Tulliver, who had by no means said enough to satisfy his anger, burst out again.

'Who wants to quarrel with you?' he said. 'It's you as can't let people alone, but must be gnawing at 'em for ever. I should never want to quarrel with any woman if she kept her place.'

'My place, indeed!' said Mrs Glegg, getting rather more shrill. 'There's your betters, Mr Tulliver, as are dead and in their grave, treated me with a different sort o' respect to what you do – *though* I've got a husband as'll sit by and see me abused by them as 'ud never ha' had the chance if there hadn't been them in our family as married worse than they might ha' done.'

'If you talk o' that,' said Mr Tulliver, 'my family's as good as yours – and better, for it hasn't got a damned ill-tempered woman in it.'

'Well!' said Mrs Glegg, rising from her chair, 'I don't know whether you think it's a fine thing to sit by and hear me swore at, Mr Glegg; but I'm not going to stay a minute longer in this house. You can stay behind, and come home with the gig – and I'll walk home.'

'Dear heart, dear heart!' said Mr Glegg in a melancholy tone, as he followed his wife out of the room.

'Mr Tulliver, how could you talk so?' said Mrs Tulliver, with the tears in her eyes.

'Let her go,' said Mr Tulliver, too hot to be damped by any amounts of tears. 'Let her go, and the sooner the better: she won't be trying to domineer over *me* again in a hurry.'

'Sister Pullet,' said Mrs Tulliver, helplessly, 'do you think it 'ud be any use for you to go after her and try to pacify her?'

'Better not,' said Mr Deane. 'You'll make it up another day.'

'Then, sisters, shall we go and look at the children?' said Mrs Tulliver, drying her eyes.

No proposition could have been more seasonable. Mr Tulliver felt very much as if the air had been cleared of obtrusive flies now the women were out of the room. There were few things he liked better than a chat with Mr Deane. And now the women were gone, they could carry on their serious talk without frivolous interruption.

8

Mr Tulliver Shows His Weaker Side

'Suppose sister Glegg should call her money in – it 'ud be very awkward for you to have to raise five hundred pounds now,' said Mrs Tulliver to her husband that evening.

Mrs Tulliver had lived thirteen years with her husband, yet she retained in all the freshness of her early married life a facility of saying things which drove him in the opposite direction to the one she desired, and did so today with undulled alacrity.

This observation of hers tended directly to convince Mr Tulliver that it would not be at all awkward for him. He declared that Mrs Glegg might do as she liked about calling in her money – he should pay it in, whether or not. He was not going to be beholding to his wife's sisters.

Mrs Tulliver cried a little in a quiet way as she put on her night-cap; but presently sank into a comfortable sleep, lulled by the thought that she would talk everything over with her sister Pullet tomorrow, when she was to take the children to Garum Firs to tea.

Her husband lay awake rather longer, for he too was thinking of a visit he would pay on the morrow, and his ideas on the subject were not of so vague and soothing a kind as those of his amiable partner.

Mr Tulliver, when under the influence of a strong feeling, had a promptitude in action that may seem inconsistent with that painful sense of the complicated puzzling nature of human affairs under which his more dispassionate deliberations were conducted. It was owing to this promptitude that Mr Tulliver was on horseback the next day on his way to Basset to see his sister Moss and her husband. For having made up his mind irrevocably that he would pay Mrs Glegg her loan of five hundred pounds, it naturally occurred to him that he had a promissory note for three hundred pounds lent to his brother-in-law Moss.

Mr Tulliver was held to be a much more substantial man than he really was. He had been always used to hear pleasant jokes about his advantages as a man who worked his own mill, and owned a pretty bit of land; and these jokes naturally kept up his sense that he was a man of considerable substance, and if it had not been for the recurrence of half-yearly payments, Mr Tulliver would really have forgotten that there was a mortgage of two thousand pounds on his very desirable freehold.

That was not altogether his own fault, since one of the thousand pounds was his sister's fortune, which he had had to pay on her marriage; and a man who has neighbours that *will* go to law with him, is not likely to pay off his mortgages, especially if he enjoys the good opinion of acquaintances who want to borrow a hundred pounds on security too lofty to be represented by parchment. Our friend Mr Tulliver had a good-natured fibre in him, and did not like to give harsh refusals even to a sister, who had quite thrown herself away in marriage, and had crowned her mistakes by having an eighth baby. On this point Mr Tulliver was conscious of being a little weak; but this morning he was in a mood more becoming a man of business, and in the course of his ride along the Basset lanes he got up a due amount of irritation against Moss as a man without capital, who, the more you tried to help him out of the mud, would sink the farther in. It would do him good rather than harm, now, if he were obliged to raise this three hundred pounds: Mr Tulliver had been too easy with his brother-in-law, and because he had let the interest run on for two years, Moss was likely enough to think that he should never be troubled about the principal. But Mr Tulliver was determined not to encourage such shuffling people any longer; and a ride along the Basset lanes was not likely to enervate a man's resolution by softening his temper. Basset had a poor soil, poor roads, a poor non-resident landlord, a poor non-resident vicar, and rather less than half a curate, also poor. Nothing could be less pacifying to Mr Tulliver than the behaviour of the farmyard gate, which he no sooner attempted to push open with his riding-stick, than it acted as gates without the upper hinge are known to do, to the peril of shins, whether equine or human. He was about to get down and lead his horse through the damp dirt of the hollow farmyard, shadowed drearily by the large half-timbered buildings, up to the long line of tumble-down dwelling-houses standing on a raised causeway; but the timely appearance of a cowboy saved him that frustration of a plan he had determined on – namely, not to get down from his horse during this visit. If a man means to be hard, let him keep in his saddle and speak from that height, above the level of pleading eyes, and with the command of a distant horizon. Mrs Moss heard the sound of the horse's feet, and, when her brother rode up, was already outside the kitchen door, with a half-weary smile on her face, and a black-eyed baby in her arms. Mrs Moss's face bore a faded resemblance to her brother's; baby's little fat hand, pressed against her cheek, seemed to show more strikingly that the cheek was faded.

'Brother, I'm glad to see you,' she said, in an affectionate tone. 'I didn't look for you today. How do you do?'

'Oh, ... pretty well, Mrs Moss ... pretty well,' answered the brother, with cool deliberation. She knew at once that her brother was not in a good humour: he never called her Mrs Moss except when he was angry, and when they were in company.

'Your husband isn't in the house, I suppose?' added Mr Tulliver, after a grave pause, during which four children had run out.

'No,' said Mrs Moss, 'but he's only in the potato-field yonders. Georgy, run to the Far Close in a minute, and tell father your uncle's come. You'll get down, brother, won't you, and take something?'

'No, no; I can't get down. I must be going home again directly,' said Mr Tulliver, looking at the distance.

'And how's Mrs Tulliver and the children?' said Mrs Moss, humbly, not daring to press her invitation.

'Oh ... pretty well. Tom's going to a new school at Midsummer – a deal of expense to me. It's bad work for me, lying out o' my money.'

'I wish you'd be so good as let the children come and see their cousins some day. My little uns want to see their cousin Maggie. And me so fond of her – there's nobody 'ud make a bigger fuss with her, according to what they've got. And I know she likes to come, for she's a loving child, and how quick and clever she is, to be sure!'

If Mrs Moss had been one of the most astute women in the world, instead of being of the simplest, she could have thought of nothing more likely to propitiate her brother than this praise of Maggie. He seldom found anyone volunteering praise of 'the little wench': it was usually left entirely to himself to insist on her merits. But Maggie always appeared in the most amiable light to her aunt Moss. In spite of himself, Mr Tulliver's eyes got milder, and he did not look away from his sister, as he said, 'Ay: she's fonder o' you than o' the other aunts. She takes after our family: not a bit of her mother's in her.'

'Moss says she's just like what I used to be,' said Mrs Moss, 'though I was never so quick and fond o' the books. But I think my Lizzy's like her – *she's* sharp. Come here, Lizzy, my dear, and let your uncle see you: he hardly knows you; you grow so fast.'

Lizzy, a black-eyed child of seven, looked very shy when her mother drew her forward, for the small Mosses were much in awe of their uncle from Dorlcote Mill. She was inferior enough to Maggie in fire and strength of expression, to make the resemblance between the two entirely flattering to Mr Tulliver's fatherly love.

'Ay, they're a bit alike,' he said, looking kindly at the little figure in the soiled pinafore. 'They both take after our mother. You've got enough o' gells, Gritty,' he added, in a tone half compassionate, half reproachful.

'Four of 'em, bless 'em,' said Mrs Moss, with a sigh, stroking Lizzy's hair on each side of her forehead; 'as many as there's boys. They've got a brother a-piece.'

'Ah, but they must turn out and fend for themselves,' said Mr Tulliver, feeling that his severity was relaxing, and trying to brace it by throwing out a wholesome hint. 'They mustn't look to hanging on their brothers.'

'No; but I hope their brothers 'ull love the poor things, and remember they came o' one father and mother: the lads 'ull never be the poorer for that,' said Mrs Moss, flashing out with hurried timidity, like a half-smothered fire.

'And the more there is of 'em, the more they must love one another,' Mrs Moss went on. 'Not but what I hope your boy 'ull allays be good to his sister, though there's but two of 'em, like you and me, brother.'

That arrow went straight to Mr Tulliver's heart. He had not a rapid imagination, but the thought of Maggie was very near to him, and he was not long in seeing his relation to his own sister side by side with Tom's relation to Maggie. Would the little wench ever be poorly off, and Tom rather hard upon her?

'Ay, ay, Gritty,' said the miller, with a new softness in his tone; 'but I've allays done what I could for you,' he added, as if vindicating himself from a reproach.

'I'm not denying that, brother, and I'm noways ungrateful,' said poor Mrs Moss. 'But there's the father. What a while you've been, Moss!'

'While, do you call it?' said Mr Moss, feeling out of breath and injured. 'I've been running all the way. Won't you 'light, Mr Tulliver?'

'Well, I'll just get down, and have a bit o' talk with you in the garden,' said Mr Tulliver, feeling that he should be more likely to show a due spirit of resolve if his sister were not present.

He got down, and passed with Mr Moss into the garden. Mr Tulliver sat down on the bench, and opened the conversation by observing, with something like a snarl in his tone—

'Why, you've got wheat again in that Corner Close, I see; and niver a bit o' dressing on it. You'll do no good with it this year.'

Mr Moss, who, when he married Miss Tulliver, had been regarded as the buck of Basset, now wore a beard nearly a week old, and had the depressed, unexpectant air of a machine-horse. He answered in a patient-grumbling tone, 'Why, poor farmers like me must do as they can: they must leave it to them as have got money to play with, to put half as much into the ground as they mean to get out of it.'

'I don't know who should have money to play with, if it isn't them as can borrow money without paying interest,' said Mr Tulliver, who wished to get into a slight quarrel; it was the most natural and easy introduction to calling in money.

'I know I'm behind with the interest,' said Mr Moss, 'but I was so unlucky wi' the wool last year; and what with the Missis being laid up so, things have gone awk'arder nor usual.'

'Ay,' snarled Mr Tulliver, 'there's folks as things 'ull allays go awk'ard with: empty sacks 'ull never stand upright.'

'Well, I don't know what fault you've got to find wi' me, Mr Tulliver,' said Mr Moss, deprecatingly; 'I know there isn't a day-labourer works harder.'

'What's the use o' that,' said Mr Tulliver, sharply, 'when a man marries, an's got no capital to work his farm but his wife's bit o' fortin? I was against it from the first; but you'd neither of you listen to me. And I can't lie out o' my money any longer, for I've got to pay five hundred o' Mrs Glegg's, and there 'ull be Tom an expense to me, as I should find myself short, even saying I'd got back all as is my own. You must look about and see how you can pay me the three hundred pound.'

'Well, if that's what you mean,' said Mr Moss, looking blankly before him, 'we'd better be sold up, an' ha' done with it; I must part wi' every head o' stock I've got, to pay you and the landlord too.'

Poor relations are undeniably irritating. Mr Tulliver had succeeded in getting quite as much irritated with Mr Moss as he had desired, and he was able to say angrily, rising from his seat—

'Well, you must do as you can. I must look to my own business and my own family. I can't lie out o' my money any longer. You must raise it as quick as you can.'

Mr Tulliver walked abruptly out of the arbour as he uttered the last sentence, and, without looking round at Mr Moss, went on to the kitchen-door, where the eldest boy was holding his horse, and his sister was waiting in a state of wondering alarm. 'Won't you come in, brother?' she said, looking anxiously at her husband, who was walking slowly up, while Mr Tulliver had his foot already in the stirrup.

'No, no; good-bye,' said he, turning his horse's head, and riding away.

No man could feel more resolute till he got outside the yard-gate, and a little way along the deep-rutted lane; but before he reached the next turning, he appeared to be smitten by some sudden thought. He checked his horse, and made it stand still for two or three minutes, during which he turned his head from side to side in a melancholy way, as if he were looking at some painful object on more sides than one. Evidently, after his fit of promptitude, Mr Tulliver was relapsing into the sense that this is a puzzling world. He turned his horse, and rode slowly back, giving vent to the climax of feeling which had determined this movement by saying aloud, as he struck his horse, 'Poor little wench! she'll have nobody but Tom, belike, when I'm gone.'

Mrs Moss was again on the doorstep when her brother rode up. She had been crying, but was rocking baby to sleep in her arms now, and made no ostentatious show of sorrow as her brother looked at her, but merely said—

'The father's gone to the field again, if you want him, brother.'

'No, Gritty, no,' said Mr Tulliver, in a gentle tone. 'Don't you fret – that's all – I'll make a shift without the money a bit – only you must be as clever and contriving as you can.'

Mrs Moss's tears came again at this unexpected kindness, and she could say nothing.

'Come, come! – the little wench shall come and see you. I'll bring her and Tom some day before he goes to school. You mustn't fret … I'll allays be a good brother to you.'

'Thank you for that word, brother,' said Mrs Moss.

And so the respectable miller returned along the Basset lanes rather more puzzled than before as to ways and means, but still with the sense of a danger escaped. It had come across his mind that if he were hard upon his sister, it might somehow tend to make Tom hard upon Maggie at some distant day, when her father was no longer there to take her part; this was his confused way of explaining to himself that his love and anxiety for 'the little wench' had given him a new sensibility towards his sister.

9

To Garum Firs

While the possible troubles of Maggie's future were occupying her father's mind, she herself was tasting only the bitterness of the present. The day had begun ill with Maggie. The pleasure of having Lucy to look at, and the prospect of the afternoon visit to Garum Firs, where she would hear uncle Pullet's musical box, had been marred as early as eleven o'clock by the advent of the hairdresser from St Ogg's, who had spoken in the severest terms of the condition in which he had found her hair.

Already, at twelve o'clock, Mrs Tulliver had on her visiting costume, with a protective apparatus of brown holland, as if she had been a piece of satin furniture in danger of flies; Maggie was frowning and twisting her shoulders, that she might if possible shrink away from the prickliest of tuckers, while her mother was remonstrating, 'Don't, Maggie, my dear – don't make yourself so ugly!' and Tom's cheeks were looking particularly brilliant as a relief to his best blue suit, which he wore with becoming calmness; having effected what was always the one point of interest to him in his toilet – he had transferred all the contents of his everyday pockets to those actually in wear.

As for Lucy, she was just as pretty and neat as she had been yesterday; no accidents ever happened to her clothes, and she was never uncomfortable in them, so that she looked with wondering pity at Maggie pouting and writhing under the exasperating tucker. Maggie confined herself to behaving peevishly about the card-houses which they were allowed to build till dinner, as a suitable amusement for boys and girls in their best clothes. Tom could build perfect pyramids of houses; but Maggie's would never bear the laying-on of the roof: it was always so with the things that Maggie made; and Tom had deduced the conclusion that no girls could ever make anything. But it happened that Lucy proved wonderfully clever at building: she handled the cards so lightly, and moved so gently, that Tom condescended to admire her houses as well as his own, the more readily because she had asked him to teach her. Maggie, too, would have admired Lucy's houses, and would have given up her own unsuccessful building to contemplate them, without ill-temper, if her tucker had not made her peevish, and if Tom had not laughed when her houses fell, and told her she was 'a stupid.'

'Don't laugh at me, Tom!' she burst out, angrily, 'I'm not a stupid. I know a great many things you don't.'

'Oh, I daresay, Miss Spitfire! I'd never be such a cross thing as you – making faces like that. Lucy doesn't do so. I like Lucy better than you: *I* wish Lucy was *my* sister.'

'Then it's very wicked and cruel of you to wish so,' said Maggie, starting up hurriedly from her place on the floor, and upsetting Tom's wonderful pagoda. She really did not mean it, but the circumstantial evidence was against her, and Tom turned white with anger, but said nothing: he would have struck her, only he knew it was cowardly to strike a girl, and Tom Tulliver was quite determined he would never do anything cowardly.

Maggie stood in dismay and terror while Tom got up from the floor and walked away from the scattered ruins of his pagoda, and Lucy looked on mutely, like a kitten pausing from its lapping.

'Oh, Tom,' said Maggie, at last, going half-way towards him, 'I didn't mean to knock it down – indeed I didn't.'

Tom took no notice of her. Thus the morning had been made heavy to Maggie, and Tom's persistent coldness to her all through their walk spoiled the fresh air and sunshine for her. He called Lucy to look at the half-built bird's nest, without caring to show it Maggie, and peeled a willow switch for Lucy and himself, without offering one to Maggie.

Still the sight of the peacock opportunely spreading his tail on the stackyard wall, just as they reached Garum Firs, was enough to divert the mind temporarily from personal grievances. Nothing was quite common at Garum Firs: the house had a receding centre, and two wings with battlemented turrets, and was covered with glittering white stucco.

Aunt Pullet appeared at the doorway, and as soon as her sister was within hearing, said, 'Stop the children, for God's sake, Bessy – don't let 'em come up the doorsteps: Sally's bringing the old mat and the duster, to rub their shoes.'

Mrs Pullet's front-door mats were by no means intended to wipe shoes on; the very scraper had a deputy to do its dirty work. Tom rebelled particularly against this shoe-wiping, which he always considered in the light of an indignity to his sex. He felt it as the beginning of the disagreeables incident to a visit at aunt Pullet's.

The next disagreeable was confined to his feminine companions; it was the mounting of the polished oak stairs, which had very handsome carpets rolled up and laid by in a spare bedroom. Sophy's weakness about these polished stairs was always a subject of bitter remonstrance on Mrs Glegg's part; but Mrs Tulliver ventured on no comment, only thinking to herself it was a mercy when she and her children were safe on the landing.

'Mrs Gray has sent home my new bonnet, Bessy,' said Mrs Pullet.

'Has she, sister?' said Mrs Tulliver with an air of much interest. 'And how do you like it?'

'It's apt to make a mess with clothes, taking 'em out and putting 'em in again,' said Mrs Pullet, drawing a bunch of keys from her pocket and looking at them earnestly, 'but it 'ud be a pity for you to go away without seeing it. There's no knowing what may happen.'

'I'm afraid it'll be troublesome to you getting it out, sister,' said Mrs Tulliver, 'but I *should* like to see what sort of a crown she's made you.'

Mrs Pullet rose with a melancholy air and unlocked one wing of a very bright wardrobe, where you may have hastily supposed she would find the new bonnet. Not at all. In this wardrobe Mrs Pullet was seeking something small enough to be hidden among layers of linen – it was a door-key.

'You must come with me into the best room,' said Mrs Pullet.

'May the children come too, sister?' inquired Mrs Tulliver, who saw that Maggie and Lucy were looking rather eager.

'Well,' said aunt Pullet, reflectively, 'it'll perhaps be safer for 'em to come – they'll be touching something if we leave 'em behind.'

So they went in procession along the bright and slippery corridor. Aunt Pullet paused and unlocked a door which opened on a darkened room, in which the outer light, entering feebly, showed what looked like the corpses of furniture in white shrouds. Everything that was not shrouded stood with its legs upwards. Lucy laid hold of Maggie's frock, and Maggie's heart beat rapidly.

Aunt Pullet half-opened the shutter and then unlocked the wardrobe, with a melancholy deliberateness which was quite in keeping with the funereal solemnity of the scene. The delicious scent of rose-leaves that issued from the wardrobe made the process of taking out sheet after sheet of silver-paper quite pleasant to assist at, though the sight of the bonnet at last was an anticlimax to Maggie, who would have preferred something more strikingly preternatural. But few things could have been more impressive to Mrs Tulliver. She looked all round it in silence for some moments, and then said emphatically, 'Well, sister, I'll never speak against the full crowns again!'

It was a great concession, and Mrs Pullet felt it: she felt something was due to it.

'You'd like to see it on, sister?' she said, sadly. 'I'll open the shutter a bit further.'

'Well, if you don't mind taking off your cap, sister,' said Mrs Tulliver.

Mrs Pullet took off her cap, displaying the brown silk scalp with a jutting promontory of curls which was common to the more mature and judicious women of those times, and, placing the bonnet on her head, turned slowly round, like a draper's lay-figure, that Mrs Tulliver might miss no point of view.

'How much might she charge you for that bonnet, sister?' said Mrs Tulliver, whose mind was actively engaged on the possibility of getting a humble imitation of this *chef-d'oeuvre* made from a piece of silk she had at home.

Mrs Pullet screwed up her mouth and shook her head, and then whispered, 'Pullet pays for it; he said I was to have the best bonnet at Garum Church.' She returned the bonnet to the wardrobe and locked it up.

When they went down, uncle Pullet observed, with some acumen, that he reckoned the missis had been showing her bonnet – that was what had made them so long upstairs. With Tom the interval had seemed still longer, for he had been seated in irksome constraint on the edge of a sofa directly opposite his uncle Pullet, who regarded him with twinkling grey eyes.

'Well, young sir, what do you learn at school?' was a standing question with uncle Pullet; whereupon Tom always looked sheepish, rubbed his hand across his face, and answered, 'I don't know.'

The only alleviating circumstance in a *tête-à-tête* with uncle Pullet was that he kept a variety of lozenges and peppermint drops about his person, and when at a loss for conversation, he filled up the void by proposing a mutual solace of this kind.

'Do you like peppermints, young sir?' required only a tacit answer when it was accompanied by a presentation of the article in question.

The appearance of the little girls suggested to uncle Pullet the further solace of small sweet-cakes, of which he also kept a stock under lock and key for his own private eating on wet days; but the three children had no sooner got the tempting delicacy between their fingers than aunt Pullet desired them to abstain from eating it till the tray and the plates came, since with those crisp cakes they would make the floor 'all over' crumbs. Lucy didn't mind that much, for the cake was so pretty, she thought it was rather a pity to eat it; but Tom, watching his opportunity while the elders were talking, hastily stowed it in his mouth at two bites, and chewed it furtively. As for Maggie, becoming fascinated, as usual, by a print of Ulysses and Nausicaa, which uncle Pullet had bought as a 'pretty Scripture thing,' she presently let fall her cake, and in an unlucky movement crushed it beneath her foot – a source of so much agitation to aunt Pullet and conscious disgrace to Maggie, that she began to despair of hearing the musical snuff-box today, till it occurred to her that Lucy was in high favour enough to venture on asking for a tune. So she whispered to Lucy, and Lucy, who always did what she was desired to do, went up quietly to her uncle's knee, and, blushing all over her neck, said, 'Will you please play us a tune, uncle?'

Lucy thought it was by reason of some exceptional talent in uncle Pullet that the snuff-box played such beautiful tunes, and indeed the thing was viewed in that light by the majority of his neighbours in Garum. Mr Pullet had *bought* the box, to begin with, and he understood winding it up, and knew which tune it was going to play beforehand; altogether, the possession of this unique 'piece of music' was a proof that Mr Pullet's character was not of that entire nullity which might otherwise have been attributed to it. But uncle Pullet, when entreated to exhibit his accomplishment, never depreciated it by a too ready consent. 'We'll see about it,' was the answer he always gave. Uncle Pullet had a programme for all great social occasions, and in this way fenced himself in from much painful confusion and perplexing freedom of will.

Perhaps the suspense did heighten Maggie's enjoyment when the fairy tune began: for the first time she quite forgot that Tom was angry with her; her face wore that bright look of happiness, while she sat immovable with her hands clasped, which sometimes comforted her mother with the sense that Maggie could look pretty now and then, in spite of her brown skin. But when the magic music ceased, she jumped up, and, running towards Tom, put her arm round his neck and said, 'Oh, Tom, isn't it pretty?'

Tom had his glass of cowslip wine in his hand, and she jerked him so as to make him spill half of it. He must have been an extreme milksop not to say angrily, 'Look here, now!', especially when his resentment was sanctioned, as it was, by general disapprobation of Maggie's behaviour.

'Why don't you sit still, Maggie?' her mother said peevishly.

'Little gells mustn't come to see me if they behave in that way,' said aunt Pullet.

'Why, you're too rough, little miss,' said uncle Pullet.

Mrs Tulliver, foreseeing nothing but misbehaviour while the children remained indoors, took an early opportunity of suggesting that, now they were rested after their walk, they might go and play out of doors; and aunt Pullet gave permission, only enjoining them not to go off the paved walks in the garden, and if they wanted to see the poultry fed, to view them from a distance on the horse-block; a restriction which had been imposed ever since Tom had been found guilty of running after the peacock, with an illusory idea that fright would make one of its feathers drop off.

Mrs Tulliver's thoughts had been temporarily diverted from the quarrel with Mrs Glegg by millinery and maternal cares, but now the great theme of the bonnet was thrown into perspective, and the children were out of the way, yesterday's anxieties recurred.

'It weighs on my mind so as never was,' she said, by way of opening the subject, 'sister Glegg's leaving the house in that way. I'm sure I'd no wish t' offend a sister.'

'Ah,' said aunt Pullet, 'there's no accounting for what Jane 'ull do. But your husband *is* awk'ard, you know, Bessy. He's never behaved quite so pretty to our family as he should do, and the children take after him – the boy's very mischievous, and runs away from his aunts and uncles, and the gell's rude and brown. I'm sorry for you, Bessy; for you was allays my favourite sister.'

'I know Tulliver's hasty, and says odd things,' said Mrs Tulliver, wiping away one small tear from the corner of her eye, 'but I'm sure he's never been the man, since he married me, to object to my making the friends o' my side o' the family welcome to the house.'

'I don't want to make the worst of you, Bessy, said Mrs Pullet, compassionately, 'for I doubt you'll have trouble enough without that; and your husband's got that poor sister and her children hanging on him, and so given to lawing, they say. I doubt he'll leave you poorly off when he dies. Not as I'd have it said out o' the family.'

This view of her position was naturally far from cheering to Mrs Tulliver. She could not help thinking that her case was a hard one, since it appeared that other people thought it hard.

'I'm sure, sister, I can't help myself,' she said. 'There's no woman strives more for her children; and I'm sure, at scouring-time this Ladyday, I did as much as the two gells put together;

and there's this last elder-flower wine I've made – beautiful! I allays offer it along with the sherry, though sister Glegg will have it I'm so extravagant; and the linen's so in order, as if I was to die tomorrow I shouldn't be ashamed. A woman can do no more nor she can.'

'But it's all o' no use, you know, Bessy,' said Mrs Pullet, holding her head on one side, and fixing her eyes pathetically on her sister, 'if your husband makes away with his money.'

'But what can I do, sister?' said Mrs Tulliver. 'Mr Tulliver's not a man to be dictated to and I'm sure I don't pretend to know anything about putting out money and all that. I could never see into men's business as sister Glegg does.'

'Well, you're like me in that, Bessy,' said Mrs Pullet; 'and I think it 'ud be a deal more becoming o' Jane if she'd have that pier-glass rubbed oftener – there was ever so many spots on it last week – instead o' dictating to folks what they've to do with their money. But Jane and we were allays contrairy: she *would* have striped things, and I like spots. You like a spot too, Bessy: we allays hung together i' that.'

Mrs Pullet, affected by this last reminiscence, looked at her sister pathetically.

'Yes, Sophy,' said Mrs Tulliver, 'I remember our having a blue ground with a white spot both alike – I've got a bit in a bed quilt now; and if you would but go and see sister Glegg, and persuade her to make it up with Tulliver, I should take it very kind of you. You was allays a good sister to me.'

'But the right thing 'ud be for Tulliver to go and make it up with her himself, and say he was sorry for speaking so rash. If he's borrowed money of her, he shouldn't be above that,' said Mrs Pullet, whose partiality did not blind her to principles.

'It's no use talking o' that,' said poor Mrs Tulliver, almost peevishly. 'If I was to go down on my bare knees on the gravel to Tulliver, he'd never humble himself.'

'Well, you can't expect me to persuade *Jane* to beg pardon,' said Mrs Pullet. 'Her temper's beyond everything.'

'I'm not thinking of her begging pardon,' said Mrs Tulliver.

'But if she'd just take no notice, and not call her money in; as it's not so much for one sister to ask of another; time 'ud mend things, and Tulliver 'ud forget all about it, and they'd be friends again.'

'Well, Bessy,' said Mrs Pullet, mournfully, 'I don't want to help you on to ruin. I won't be behindhand i' doing you a good turn, if it is to be done. And I don't like it said among acquaintance as we've got quarrels in the family. I shall tell Jane that; and I don't mind driving to Jane's tomorrow, if Pullet doesn't mind. What do you say, Mr Pullet?'

'I've no objections,' said Mr Pullet, who was perfectly contented with any course the quarrel might take, so that Mr Tulliver did not apply to *him* for money.

After a little further discussion as to whether it would not be better for Mrs Tulliver to accompany them on a visit to sister Glegg, Mrs Pullet, observing that it was tea-time, turned to reach from a drawer a delicate damask napkin, which she pinned before her in the fashion of an apron. The door did, in fact, soon open, but instead of the tea tray, Sally introduced an object so startling that both Mrs Pullet and Mrs Tulliver gave a scream, causing uncle Pullet to swallow his lozenge – for the fifth time in his life, as he afterwards noted.

10

Maggie Behaves Worse than She Expected

The startling object was no other than little Lucy, with one side of her person, from her small foot to her bonnet-crown, wet and discoloured with mud, holding out two tiny blackened hands, and making a very piteous face. To account for this unprecedented apparition in aunt Pullet's parlour, we must return to the moment when the three children went to play out of doors. All the disagreeable recollections of the morning were thick upon Maggie, when Tom, whose displeasure towards her had been considerably refreshed by her causing him to upset his cowslip wine, said, 'Here, Lucy, you come along with me,' and walked off to the area where the toads were, as if there were no Maggie in existence. Seeing this, Maggie lingered at a distance. Lucy was naturally pleased that cousin Tom was so good to her, and it was very amusing to see him tickling a fat toad with a piece of string when the toad was safe down the area, with an iron grating over him. Still Lucy wished Maggie to enjoy the spectacle also; she ran back to Maggie and said, 'Oh, there is such a big, funny toad, Maggie! Do come and see.'

Maggie said nothing, but turned away from her with a deeper frown. Maggie would have thought a little while ago that she could never be cross with pretty little Lucy, but then Tom had always been quite indifferent to Lucy before, and it had been left to Maggie to pet and make much of her. As it was, she was actually beginning to think that she should like to make Lucy cry, especially as it might vex Tom.

Tickling a fat toad is an amusement that it is possible to exhaust, and Tom by and by began to look round for some other mode of passing the time. But in so prim a garden, where they were not to go off the paved walks, there was not a great choice of sport. The only great pleasure such a restriction allowed was the pleasure of breaking it, and Tom began to meditate an insurrectionary visit to the pond, about a field's length beyond the garden.

'I say, Lucy,' he began, nodding his head up and down with great significance, as he coiled up his string again, 'I mean to go to the pond, and look at the pike. You may go with me if you like.'

'Oh, Tom, *dare* you?' said Lucy. 'Aunt said we mustn't go out of the garden.'

'Oh, I shall go out at the other end of the garden,' said Tom. 'Nobody 'ull see us. Besides, I don't care if they do – I'll run off home.'

'But *I* couldn't run,' said Lucy, who had never before been exposed to such severe temptation.

'Oh, never mind – they won't be cross with *you*,' said Tom. 'You say I took you.'

Tom walked along, and Lucy trotted by his side, timidly enjoying the rare treat of doing something naughty – excited also by the mention of that celebrity, the pike, about which she was quite uncertain whether it was a fish or a fowl. Maggie saw them leaving the garden, and could not resist the impulse to follow. Anger and jealousy can no more bear to lose sight of their objects than love, and that Tom and Lucy should do or see anything of which she was ignorant would have been an intolerable idea to Maggie. So she kept a few yards behind them, unobserved by Tom, who was presently absorbed in watching for the pike, a highly interesting monster; he was said to be so very old, so very large, and to have such a remarkable appetite. The pike did not show but Tom caught sight of something in rapid movement in the water, which attracted him to the brink of the pond.

'Here, Lucy!' he said in a loud whisper, 'come here! take care! keep on the grass – don't step where the cows have been!' he added, pointing to a peninsula of dry grass, with trodden mud on each side of it; for Tom's contemptuous conception of a girl included the attribute of being unfit to walk in dirty places.

Lucy came carefully as she was bidden, and bent down to look at what seemed a golden arrow-head darting through the water. It was a water snake, Tom told her, and Lucy at last could see the serpentine wave of its body. Maggie had drawn nearer and nearer – she *must* see it too, though it was bitter to her like everything else, since Tom did not care about her seeing it. At last, she was close by Lucy, and Tom, who had been aware of her approach, turned round and said—

'Now, get away, Maggie. There's no room for you on the grass here. Nobody asked *you* to come.'

There were passions at war in Maggie at that moment, and with a fierce thrust of her small brown arm, she pushed poor little pink-and-white Lucy into the cow-trodden mud.

Then Tom could not restrain himself, and gave Maggie two smart slaps on the arm as he ran to pick up Lucy, who lay crying helplessly. Maggie retreated to the roots of a tree a few yards off. Usually her repentance came quickly after one rash deed, but now

Tom and Lucy had made her so miserable she was glad to spoil their happiness. Why should she be sorry? Tom was very slow to forgive *her*, however sorry she might have been.

'I shall tell mother, you know, Miss Mag,' said Tom, loudly and emphatically, as soon as Lucy was up and ready to walk away. It was not Tom's practice to 'tell,' but here justice clearly demanded that Maggie should be visited with the utmost punishment. Lucy was too entirely absorbed by the evil that had befallen her to think much of the cause, which was entirely mysterious to her. She could never have guessed what she had done to make Maggie angry with her; but she felt that Maggie was very unkind and disagreeable, and made no magnanimous entreaties to Tom that he would not 'tell,' only running along by his side and crying piteously.

'Sally,' said Tom, when they reached the kitchen door, and Sally looked at them in speechless amaze – 'Sally, tell mother it was Maggie pushed Lucy into the mud.'

'But Lors ha' massy, how did you get near such mud as that?' said Sally, making a wry face.

Tom's imagination had not included this question among the foreseen consequences, but it was no sooner put than he foresaw that Maggie would not be considered the only culprit in the case. He walked quietly away from the kitchen door, leaving Sally to that pleasure of guessing.

Sally, as you are aware, lost no time in presenting Lucy at the parlour door, for to have so dirty an object introduced into the house at Garum Firs was too great a weight to be sustained by a single mind.

'Goodness gracious!' aunt Pullet exclaimed, after preluding by an inarticulate scream: 'Keep her at the door, Sally! Don't bring her off the oilcloth, whatever you do.'

'Why, she's tumbled into some nasty mud,' said Mrs Tulliver, going up to Lucy to examine the amount of damage to clothes for which she felt herself responsible to her sister Deane.

'If you please, 'um, it was Miss Maggie as pushed her in,' said Sally; 'Master Tom's been and said so, and they must ha' been to the pond, for it's only there they could ha' got into such dirt.'

'There it is, Bessy; it's what I've been telling you,' said Mrs Pullet, in a tone of prophetic sadness; 'it's your children – there's no knowing what they'll come to.'

Mrs Tulliver was mute, feeling herself a truly wretched mother. Mrs Pullet began to give elaborate directions to Sally how to guard the premises from serious injury in the course of removing the dirt. Meantime tea was to be brought in by the cook, and the two naughty children were to have theirs in an ignominious manner in the kitchen. Mrs Tulliver went out to speak to these naughty children, supposing them to be close at hand; but it was not until after some search that she found Tom leaning with rather a hardened careless air against the white paling of the poultry-yard, and lowering his piece of string on the other side as a means of exasperating the turkey-cock.

'Tom, you naughty boy, where's your sister?' said Mrs Tulliver in a distressed voice.

'I don't know,' said Tom; his eagerness for justice on Maggie had diminished since he had seen clearly that it could hardly be brought about without the injustice of some blame on his own conduct.

'Why, where did you leave her?' said his mother, looking round.

'Sitting under the tree against the pond,' said Tom, apparently indifferent to everything but the string and the turkey-cock.

'Then go and fetch her in this minute, you naughty boy. And how could you think o' going to the pond, and taking your sister where there was dirt? You know she'll do mischief, if there's mischief to be done.'

It was Mrs Tulliver's way, if she blamed Tom, to refer his misdemeanour, somehow or other, to Maggie.

The idea of Maggie sitting alone by the pond roused an habitual fear in Mrs Tulliver's mind, and she mounted the horse-block to satisfy herself by a sight of that fatal child, while Tom walked – not very quickly – on his way towards her.

'They're such children for the water, mine are,' she said aloud.

'They'll be brought in dead and drownded some day. I wish that river was far enough.'

But when she not only failed to discern Maggie, but presently saw Tom returning from the pool alone, this hovering fear entered and took complete possession of her, and she hurried to meet him.

'Maggie's nowhere about the pond, mother,' said Tom. You may conceive the terrified search for Maggie, and the difficulty of convincing her mother that she was not in the pond. Mrs Pullet observed that the child might come to a worse end if she lived – there was no knowing; and Mr Pullet, confused and overwhelmed by this revolutionary aspect of things, reached down a key to unlock the goose-pen, as a likely place for Maggie to lie concealed in.

Tom, after a while, started the idea that Maggie was gone home and the suggestion was seized as a comfort by his mother.

'Sister, for goodness' sake, let 'em put the horse in the carriage and take me home – we shall perhaps find her on the road. Lucy can't walk in her dirty clothes,' she said, looking at that innocent victim, wrapped up in a shawl, and sitting with naked feet on the sofa.

Aunt Pullet was quite willing to take the shortest means of restoring her premises to order and quiet, and it was not long before Mrs Tulliver was in the chaise, looking anxiously at the most distant point before her. What the father would say if Maggie was lost was a question that predominated over every other.

11

Maggie Tries to Run Away from Her Shadow

Maggie's intentions, as usual, were on a larger scale than Tom had imagined. She would run away and go to the gypsies. That was by no means a new idea to Maggie; she had been so often told she was like a gypsy and 'half wild,' that when she was miserable it seemed to her the only way of being entirely in harmony with circumstances, would be to live in a little brown tent on the commons; the gypsies, she considered, would gladly receive her and pay her much respect on account of her superior knowledge. Today Maggie thought her misery had reached a pitch at which gypsydom was her only refuge, and she rose from her seat on the roots of the tree with the sense that this was a great crisis in her life; she would run straight away till she came to Dunlow Common, where there would certainly be gypsies, and cruel Tom, and the rest of her relations who found fault with her should never see her any more. She thought of her father as she ran along, but she reconciled herself to the idea of parting with him, by determining that she would secretly let him know that she was well and happy, and always loved him very much.

Maggie soon got out of breath with running, but by the time Tom got to the pond again, she was at the distance of three long fields and felt a delightful sense of privacy in creeping along by the hedgerows. She was used to wandering about the fields by herself. Sometimes she had to climb over high gates, but that was a small evil; she was getting out of reach very fast, and she should probably soon come within sight of Dunlow Common, or at least of some other common, for she had heard her father say that you couldn't go very far without coming to a common. She hoped so, for she was getting rather tired and hungry. It was still broad daylight but it seemed to her that she had been walking a very great distance indeed, and it was really surprising that the common did not come within sight. At last, however, the green fields came to an end, and Maggie found herself looking through the bars of a gate into a lane with a wide margin of grass on each side of it. She had never seen such a wide lane before, and, without her knowing why, it gave her the impression that the common could not be far off; perhaps it was because she saw a donkey with a log to his foot feeding on the grassy margin, for she had seen a donkey with that pitiable encumbrance on Dunlow Common when she had been across it in her father's gig. She crept through the bars of the gate and walked on with new spirit.

It was not without a leaping of the heart that she caught sight of a small pair of bare legs sticking up, feet uppermost, by the side of a hillock; she was too much agitated at the first glance to see the ragged clothes and the dark shaggy head attached to them. It was a boy asleep, and Maggie trotted along faster and more lightly, lest she should wake him: it did not occur to her that he was one of her friends the gypsies. But the fact was so, for at the next bend in the lane, Maggie actually saw the little semicircular black tent with the blue smoke rising before it, which was to be her refuge. She even saw a tall female figure by the column of smoke – doubtless the gypsy-mother; it was astonishing to herself that she did not feel more delighted. But it was startling to find the gypsies in a lane, after all, and not on a common. The tall figure, who proved to be a young woman with a baby on her arm, walked slowly to meet her. Maggie looked up rather tremblingly and was reassured by this face, with the bright dark eyes and the long hair; it was really something like what she used to see in the glass before she cut her hair off.

'My little lady, where are you going to?' the gypsy said, in a tone of coaxing deference.

It was delightful, and just what Maggie expected: the gypsies saw at once that she was a little lady, and were prepared to treat her accordingly.

'Not any farther,' said Maggie, feeling as if she were saying what she had rehearsed in a dream. 'I'm come to stay with *you*, please.'

'That's pritty; come, then. Why, what a nice little lady you are, to be sure,' said the gypsy, taking her by the hand.

There was quite a group round the fire when they reached it. An old gypsy-woman was seated on the ground nursing her knees, and occasionally poking a skewer into the round kettle that sent forth an odorous steam: two small shock-headed children were lying prone and resting on their elbows, something like small sphinxes; and a placid donkey was bending his head over a tall girl, who, lying on her back, was scratching his nose. The slanting sunlight fell kindly upon them, and the scene was really very pretty and comfortable, Maggie thought, only she hoped they would soon set out the tea-cups. It was a little confusing, though, that the young woman began to speak to the old one in a language which Maggie did not understand, while the tall girl sat up and stared at her without offering any salutation. At last the old woman said—

'What! my pretty lady, are you come to stay with us? Sit ye down and tell us where you come from.'

It was just like a story; Maggie liked to be called pretty lady and treated in this way. She sat down and said—

'I'm come from home because I'm unhappy, and I mean to be a gypsy. I'll live with you, if you like, and I can teach you a great many things.'

'Such a clever little lady,' said the woman with the baby, sitting down by Maggie, and allowing baby to crawl; 'and such a pritty bonnet and frock,' she added, taking off Maggie's bonnet and looking at it while she made an observation to the old woman, in the unknown language. The tall girl snatched the bonnet and put it on her own head hindforemost, with a grin; but Maggie was determined not to show any weakness on this subject, as if she were susceptible about her bonnet.

'I don't want to wear a bonnet,' she said, 'I'd rather wear a red handkerchief, like yours' (looking at her friend by her side); 'my hair was quite long till yesterday, when I cut it off: but I daresay it will grow again very soon,' she added apologetically, thinking it probable the gypsies had a strong prejudice in favour of long hair.

'Oh, what a nice little lady! – and rich, I'm sure,' said the old woman. 'Didn't you live in a beautiful house at home?'

'Yes, my home is pretty, and I'm very fond of the river, where we go fishing – but I'm often very unhappy. I should have liked to bring my books with me, but I came away in a hurry, you know. But I can tell you almost everything there is in my books, I've read them so many times – and that will amuse you. Did you ever hear about Columbus?'

Maggie's eyes had begun to sparkle and her cheeks to flush – she was really beginning to instruct the gypsies, and gaining great influence over them. The gypsies themselves were not without amazement at this talk, though their attention was divided by the contents of Maggie's pocket, which the friend at her right hand had by this time emptied without attracting her notice.

'Is that where you live, my little lady?' said the old woman, at the mention of Columbus.

'Oh, no!' said Maggie with some pity; 'Columbus was a very wonderful man, who found out half the world, you know, but perhaps it's rather too long to tell before tea ... *I want my tea so.*'

The last words burst from Maggie, in spite of herself, with a sudden drop from patronising instruction to simple peevishness.

'Why, she's hungry, poor little lady,' said the younger woman. 'Give her some o' the cold victual. You've been walking a good way, I'll be bound, my dear. Where's your home?'

'It's Dorlcote Mill,' said Maggie. 'My father is Mr Tulliver, but we mustn't let him know where I am, else he'll fetch me home again.'

'Here's a bit o' nice victual, then,' said the old woman, handing to Maggie a lump of dry bread, which she had taken from a bag of scraps, and a piece of cold bacon.

'Thank you,' said Maggie, looking at the food without taking it; 'but will you give me some bread-and-butter and tea instead? I don't like bacon.'

'We've got no tea nor butter,' said the old woman.

'Oh, a little bread and treacle would do,' said Maggie.

'We ha'n't got no treacle,' said the old woman crossly, whereupon there followed a sharp dialogue between the two women in their unknown tongue, and one of the small sphinxes snatched at the bread-and-bacon, and began to eat it. The old woman, seeming to forget Maggie's hunger, poked the skewer into the pot with new vigour, and the younger crept under the tent, and reached out some platters and spoons. Maggie trembled a little, and was afraid the tears would come into her eyes. Meanwhile the tall girl gave a shrill cry, and presently came running up the boy, whom Maggie had passed as he was sleeping – a rough urchin about the age of Tom. He stared at Maggie, and there ensued much incomprehensible chattering. She felt very lonely, and was quite sure she should begin to cry before long: the gypsies didn't seem to mind her at all, and she felt quite weak among them. But the springing tears were checked by a new terror, when two men came up. The elder of the two carried a bag, which he flung down, addressing the women in a loud and scolding tone, which they answered by a shower of treble sauciness; while a black cur ran barking up to Maggie, and threw her into a tremor that only found a new cause in the curses with which the younger man called the dog off, and gave him a rap with a great stick he held in his hand.

Both the men now seemed to be inquiring about Maggie. At last the younger woman said in her previous deferential coaxing tone—

'This nice little lady's come to live with us: aren't you glad?'

'Ay, very glad,' said the younger man, who was looking at Maggie's silver thimble, and other small matters that had been taken from her pocket. He returned them all except the thimble to the younger woman, with some observation, and she immediately restored them to Maggie's pocket, while the men seated themselves, and began to attack the contents of the kettle – a stew of meat and potatoes – which had been taken off the fire and turned out into a yellow platter.

'We've got nothing nice for a lady to eat,' said the old woman, in her coaxing tone. 'And she's so hungry, sweet little lady.'

'Here, my dear, try if you can eat a bit o' this,' said the younger woman, handing some of the stew on a brown dish with an iron spoon to Maggie, who, remembering that the old woman had seemed angry with her for not liking the bread-and-bacon, dared not refuse the stew, though fear had chased away her appetite.

Maggie's ideas about the gypsies had undergone a rapid modification in the last five minutes. From having considered them very respectful companions, amenable to instruction, she had begun to think that they meant perhaps to kill her as soon as it was dark. It was no use trying to eat the stew, and yet the thing she most dreaded was to offend the gypsies, by betraying her extremely unfavourable opinion of them.

'What! you don't like the smell of it, my dear,' said the young woman, observing that Maggie did not even take a spoonful of the stew. 'Try a bit – come.'

'No, thank you,' said Maggie, summoning all her force for a desperate effort, and trying to smile in a friendly way. 'I haven't time. I think I must go home now, and come again another day, and then I can bring you a basket with some jam-tarts and things.'

Maggie rose from her seat as she threw out this illusory prospect, but her hope sank when the old gypsy-woman said, 'Stop a bit, stop a bit, little lady – we'll take you home, all safe, when we've done supper; you shall ride home, like a lady.'

Maggie sat down again, with little faith in this promise, though she presently saw the tall girl putting a bridle on the donkey, and throwing a couple of bags on his back.

'Now, then, little missis,' said the younger man, rising, and leading the donkey forward, 'what's the name o' the place where you live?'

'Dorlcote Mill is my home,' said Maggie, eagerly.

'What! a big mill a little way this side o' St Ogg's?'

'Yes,' said Maggie. 'Is it far off? I think I should like to walk there, if you please.'

'No, no, it'll be getting dark, we must make haste. And the donkey'll carry you as nice as can be – you'll see.'

He lifted Maggie as he spoke, and set her on the donkey. She felt relieved that it was not the old man who seemed to be going with her, but she had only a trembling hope that she was really going home.

'Here's your pretty bonnet,' said the younger woman, putting that recently-despised but now welcome article of costume on Maggie's head; 'and you'll say we've been very good to you, won't you? and what a nice little lady we said you was.'

'Oh, yes, thank you,' said Maggie. 'I'm very much obliged to you.'

It now appeared that the man also was to be seated on the donkey, holding Maggie before him, and she was as incapable of remonstrating against this arrangement as the donkey himself, though no nightmare had ever seemed to her more horrible. When the woman had patted her on the back, and said 'Good-bye,' the donkey, at a strong hint from the man's stick, set off at a rapid walk along the lane towards the point Maggie had come from an hour ago.

Poor Maggie was terrified in this entirely natural ride on a short-paced donkey, with a gypsy behind her, who considered that he was earning half-a-crown. The red light of the setting sun seemed to have a portentous meaning.

At last – oh, sight of joy! – this lane, the longest in the world, was coming to an end, was opening on a broad high-road, where there was actually a coach passing! And there was a finger-post at the corner: she had surely seen that finger-post before – 'To St Oggs, 2 miles.' The gypsy really meant to take her home, then: he was probably a good man, after all. This idea became stronger as she felt more and more certain that she knew the road quite well and, as they reached a cross-road, Maggie caught sight of some one coming on a white-faced horse.

'Oh, stop, stop!' she cried out. 'There's my father! Oh, father, father!'

The sudden joy was almost painful, and before her father reached her, she was sobbing. Great was Mr Tulliver's wonder, for he had made a round from Basset, and had not yet been home.

'Why, what's the meaning o' this?' he said, checking his horse, while Maggie slipped from the donkey and ran to her father's stirrup.

'The little miss lost herself, I reckon,' said the gypsy. 'She'd come to our tent at the far end o' Dunlow Lane, and I was bringing her where she said her home was. It's a good way to come arter being on the tramp all day.'

'Oh, yes, father, he's been very good to bring me home,' said Maggie. 'A very kind, good man!'

'Here, then, my man,' said Mr Tulliver, taking out five shillings.

'It's the best day's work *you* ever did. I couldn't afford to lose the little wench; here, lift her up before me.'

'Why, Maggie, how's this, how's this!' he said, as they rode along, while she hid her head against her father, and sobbed. 'How came you to be rambling about and lose yourself?'

'Oh, father,' sobbed Maggie, 'I ran away because I was so unhappy – Tom was so angry with me. I couldn't bear it.'

'Pooh, pooh,' said Mr Tulliver, soothingly, 'you mustn't think o' running away. What 'ud father do without his little wench?'

'Oh, no, I never will again, father – never.'

Mr Tulliver spoke his mind very strongly when he reached home and the effect was seen in the remarkable fact that Maggie never heard one reproach from her mother, or one taunt from Tom, about this foolish business of her running away to the gypsies. Maggie was rather awe-stricken by this unusual treatment, and sometimes thought that her conduct had been too wicked to be alluded to.

12

Mr and Mrs Glegg at Home

In order to see Mr and Mrs Glegg at home, we must enter the town of St Ogg's – that venerable town with the red-fluted roofs and the broad warehouse gables, where the black ships unlade themselves of their burthens from the far North, and carry away, in exchange, the precious inland products, the well-crushed cheese and the soft fleeces.

Everywhere the brick houses have a mellow look. In Mrs Glegg's day the shop windows were small and unpretending; for the farmers' wives and daughters who came to do their shopping on market-days were not to be withdrawn from their regular, well-known shops; and the tradesmen had no wares intended for customers who would go on their way and be seen no more.

This was the general aspect of things at St Ogg's when Mrs Glegg had had her quarrel with Mr Tulliver. Mrs Glegg had both a front and a back parlour in her excellent house, so that she had two points of view from which she could observe the weaknesses of her fellow-beings, and reinforce her thankfulness for her own exceptional strength of mind. From her front windows she could look down the Tofton Road, leading out of St Ogg's, and note the growing tendency to 'gadding about' in the wives of men not retired from business; and from her back windows she could look down the pleasant garden and orchard which stretched to the river, and observe the folly of Mr Glegg in spending his time among 'them flowers and vegetables.' For Mr Glegg, having retired from active business as a woolstapler, for the purpose of enjoying himself through the rest of his life, habitually relaxed by doing the work of two ordinary gardeners. The economising of a gardener's wages might perhaps have induced Mrs Glegg to wink at this folly, if it were possible for a healthy female mind even to simulate respect for a husband's hobby.

Mr Glegg on his side, too, had a double source of mental occupation. On the one hand, he surprised himself by his discoveries in natural history, finding that his piece of garden-ground contained wonderful caterpillars, slugs, and insects, which, so far as he had heard, had never before attracted human observation; his second subject of meditation was the 'contrairiness' of the female mind, as typically exhibited in Mrs Glegg. Mr Glegg had chosen the eldest Miss Dodson as a handsome embodiment of female prudence and thrift, and being himself of a money-getting, money-keeping turn, had calculated on much conjugal harmony. But in that curious compound, the feminine character, it may easily happen that the flavour is unpleasant in spite of excellent ingredients; and a fine systematic stinginess may be accompanied with a seasoning that quite spoils its relish. Now good Mr Glegg himself was stingy in the most amiable manner: his neighbours called him 'near,' which always means that the person in question is a lovable skinflint. There was no humbug or hypocrisy about Mr Glegg: his eyes would have watered with true feeling over the sale of a widow's furniture, which a five-pound note from his side-pocket would have prevented. And Mr Glegg was just as fond of saving other people's money as his own; he would have ridden as far round to avoid a turnpike when his expenses were to be paid for him, as when they were to come out of his own pocket. This inalienable habit of saving, as an end in itself, belonged to the industrious men of business of a former generation, who, having once pinched from real necessity, retained even in the midst of their comfortable retirement the habit of regarding life as an ingenious process of nibbling out one's livelihood without leaving any perceptible deficit. Mr Glegg was one of these men and knowing this, you will be the better able to understand why he had not swerved from the conviction that he had made an eligible marriage, in spite of the too pungent seasoning that nature had given to the eldest Miss Dodson's virtues. A man with an affectionate disposition, who finds a wife to concur with his fundamental idea of life, easily comes to persuade himself that no other woman would have suited him so well, and does a little daily snapping and quarrelling without any sense of alienation. Mr Glegg, being of a reflective turn, and no longer occupied with wool, had much wondering meditation on the peculiar constitution of the female mind as unfolded to him in his domestic life; and yet he thought Mrs Glegg's household ways a model for her sex; it struck him as a pitiable irregularity in other women if they did not roll up their table-napkins with the same tightness and emphasis as Mrs Glegg did, if their pastry had a less leathery consistence, and their damson cheese a less venerable hardness than hers.

Mr Glegg's unmistakable kind-heartedness was shown in this, that it pained him more to see his wife at variance with others – even with Dolly, the servant – than to be in a state of cavil with her himself; and the quarrel between her and Mr Tulliver vexed him so much that it quite nullified the pleasure he would otherwise have had in the state of his early cabbages, as he walked in his garden before breakfast the next morning. Still he went in to breakfast with some slight hope that, now Mrs Glegg had 'slept upon it,' her anger might be subdued enough to give way to her usually strong sense of family decorum.

There was one evening-cloud which had always disappeared from Mrs Glegg's brow when she sat at the breakfast-table: it was her fuzzy front of curls; for as she occupied herself in household matters in the morning, it would have been a mere extravagance to put on anything superfluous as a fuzzy curled front. By half-past ten, decorum demanded the front: until then Mrs Glegg could economise it, and society would never be any the wiser. But the absence of that cloud only left it more apparent that the cloud of severity remained; and Mr Glegg, perceiving this, as he sat down to his milk-porridge, which it was his old frugal habit to stem his morning hunger with, prudently resolved to leave the first remark to Mrs Glegg. It was a hard case, that a vigorous mood for quarrelling, so highly capable of using any opportunity, should not meet with a single remark from Mr Glegg on which to exercise itself. But by and by it appeared that his silence would answer the purpose.

'Well, Mr Glegg! it's a poor return I get for making you the wife I've made you all these years. If this is the way I'm to be treated.'

Mr Glegg paused from his porridge and looked up.

'Why, Mrs G., what have I done now?'

'Done now, Mr Glegg? *done now*? ... I'm sorry for you.'

Not seeing his way to any pertinent answer, Mr Glegg reverted to his porridge.

'There's husbands in the world,' continued Mrs Glegg after a pause, 'as 'ud have known how to do something different to siding with everybody else against their own wives. I've allays heard as it's the husband's place to stand by the wife, instead o' rejoicing and triumphing when folks insult her.'

'Now, what call have you to say that?' said Mr Glegg, rather warmly. 'When did I rejoice or triumph over you?'

'There's ways o' doing things worse than speaking out plain, Mr Glegg. I'd sooner you'd tell me to my face as you make light of me, than try to make out as everybody's in the right but me, and come to your breakfast in the morning, as I've hardly slept an hour this night, and sulk at me as if I was the dirt under your feet.'

'Sulk at you?' said Mr Glegg angrily. 'You're like a tipsy man as thinks everybody's had too much but himself.'

'Don't lower yourself with using coarse language to *me*, Mr Glegg!' said Mrs Glegg, in a tone of energetic compassion. 'A man in your place should set an example, and talk more sensible.'

'Yes; but will you listen to sense?' retorted Mr Glegg, sharply. 'The best sense I can talk to you is what I said last night – as you're i' the wrong to think o' calling in your money, when it's safe enough if you'd let it alone, all because of a bit of a tiff, and I was in hopes you'd ha' altered your mind this morning. But if you'd like to call it in, don't do it in a hurry now, and breed more enmity in the family – but wait till there's a pretty mortgage to be had without any trouble. You'd have to set the lawyer to work now to find an investment, and make no end o' expense.'

Mrs Glegg felt there was really something to this, but she tossed her head and emitted a guttural interjection to indicate that her silence was only an armistice, not a peace. And, in fact, hostilities soon broke out again.

'I'll thank you for my cup o' tea, now, Mrs G.,' said Mr Glegg, seeing that she did not proceed to give it him as usual, when he had finished his porridge. She lifted the teapot with a slight toss of the head, and said—

'I'm glad to hear you'll *thank* me, Mr Glegg. It's little thanks *I* get for what I do for folks i' this world. Though there's never a woman o' *your* side i' the family, Mr Glegg, as is fit to stand up with me. Not but what I've allays conducted myself civil to your kin, though my equils they aren't, and nobody shall make me say it.'

'You'd better leave finding fault wi' my kin till you've left off quarrelling with your own, Mrs G.,' said Mr Glegg, with angry sarcasm. 'I'll trouble you for the milk-jug.'

'That's as false a word as ever you spoke, Mr Glegg,' said the lady, pouring out the milk with unusual profuseness. 'And you know it's false, I'm not the woman to quarrel with my own kin.'

'Why, what did you call it yesterday, then, leaving your sister's house in a tantrum?'

'I'd no quarrel wi' my sister, Mr Glegg, and it's false to say it. Mr Tulliver's none o' my blood, and it was him quarrelled with me, and drove me out o' the house. But perhaps you'd have had me stay and be swore at, Mr Glegg.'

'Did ever anybody hear the like i' this parish?' said Mr Glegg, getting hot. 'A woman, with everything provided for her, and allowed to keep her own money the same as if it was settled on her, and with a gig new stuffed and lined at no end o' expense, and provided for when I die beyond anything she could expect … to go on i' this way! It's beyond everything as God A'mighty should ha' made women so.'

'Well, Mr Glegg, if those are your feelings, it's best they should be known,' said Mrs Glegg, taking off her napkin, and folding it in an excited manner. 'But if you talk o' my being provided for beyond what I could expect, I beg leave to tell you as I'd a right to expect a many things as I don't find. It's well if you're not cried shame on by the county for your treatment of me …'

Here Mrs Glegg's voice intimated that she was going to cry, and breaking off from speech, she rang the bell violently.

'Dolly,' she said, rising from her chair, and speaking in rather a choked voice, 'light a fire upstairs, and put the blinds down. Mr Glegg, you'll please to order what you'd like for dinner. I shall have gruel.'

Mrs Glegg walked across the room to the small book-case, and took down Baxter's 'Saints' Everlasting Rest,' which she carried with her upstairs. It was the book she was accustomed to lay open before her on special occasions: on wet Sunday mornings, or when she heard of a death in the family, or when, as in this case, her quarrel with Mr Glegg had been set an octave higher than usual.

But Mrs Glegg carried something else upstairs with her, which, together with the 'Saints' Rest' and the gruel, may have had some influence in gradually calming her feelings, and making it possible for her to endure existence on the ground-floor shortly before tea-time. This was, partly, Mr Glegg's suggestion, that she would do well to let her five hundred lie still until a good investment turned up; and, further, his parenthetic hint at his handsome provision for her in case of his death. Mr Glegg, like all men of his stamp, was extremely reticent about his will; and Mrs Glegg, in her gloomier moments, had forebodings that, like other husbands of whom she had heard, he might cherish the mean project of heightening her grief at his death by leaving her poorly off, in which case she was firmly resolved that she would have scarcely any weeper on her bonnet, and would cry no more than if he had been a second husband. But if he had really shown her any testamentary tenderness, it would be touching to survive Mr Glegg, and talk eulogically of him as a man who had done the right thing by her, notwithstanding his numerous poor relations – finally, to be looked up to by her own family and the neighbour-hood, as a 'widow well left' – all this made a flattering and concili-atory view of the future. So that when good Mr Glegg, restored to good-humour by much hoeing, and moved by the sight of his wife's empty chair, with her knitting rolled up in the corner, went upstairs to her and observed that the bell had been tolling for poor Mr Morton, Mrs Glegg answered magnanimously, quite as if she had been an uninjured woman. 'Ah! then, there'll be a good business for somebody to take to.'

Mr and Mrs Glegg talked quite amicably about the Tullivers that evening. Mr Glegg went the length of admitting that Tulliver was a sad man for getting into hot water, and was like enough to run through his property; and Mrs Glegg, meeting this acknowl-edgement half-way, declared that it was beneath her to take notice of such a man's conduct, and that, for her sister's sake, she would let him keep the five hundred a while longer, for when she put it out on a mortgage she should only get four per cent.

13

Mr Tulliver Further Entangles the Skein of Life

Owing to this new adjustment of Mrs Glegg's thoughts, Mrs Pullet found her task of mediation the next day surprisingly easy. Mrs Glegg, indeed, checked her rather sharply for thinking it would be necessary to tell her elder sister what was the right mode of behaviour in family matters.

'It's not to be expected, I suppose,' observed Mrs Glegg, by way of winding up the subject, 'as I shall go to the mill again before Bessy comes to see me; but I shall bear no malice, and when Mr Tulliver speaks civil to me, I'll speak civil to him. Nobody has any call to tell me what's becoming.'

'Then I may call and tell Bessy everything be as it was before?' Mrs Pullet said, just before parting.

'Yes; you may, Sophy,' said Mrs Glegg; 'you may tell Mr Tulliver, and Bessy too, as I'm not going to behave ill because folks behave ill to me: I know it's my place, as the eldest, to set an example and I do it. Nobody can say different of me, if they'll keep to the truth.'

Mrs Glegg being in this state of satisfaction in her own lofty magnanimity, I leave you to judge what effect was produced on her by the reception of a short letter from Mr Tulliver, that very evening, after Mrs Pullet's departure, informing her that she needn't trouble her mind about her five hundred pounds, for it should be paid back to her in the course of the next month at farthest, together with the interest due thereon until the time of payment. And furthermore, that Mr Tulliver had no wish to behave uncivilly to Mrs Glegg, and she was welcome to his house whenever she liked to come, but he desired no favours from her, either for himself or his children.

It was poor Mrs Tulliver who had hastened this catastrophe. She thought if she told him when he came in to tea that sister Pullet was gone to try and make everything up with sister Glegg, so that he needn't think about paying in the money, it would give a cheerful effect to the meal. Mr Tulliver had never slackened in his resolve to raise the money, but now he at once determined to write a letter to Mrs Glegg, which should cut off all possibility of mistake. Mrs Pullet gone to beg and pray for *him*, indeed! Mr Tulliver did not willingly write a letter, and found the relation between spoken and written language, briefly known as spelling, one of the most puzzling things in this puzzling world. Nevertheless, like all fervid writing, the task was done in less time than usual.

Mrs Glegg did not alter her will in consequence of this letter, and cut off the Tulliver children from their sixth and seventh share in her thousand pounds; for she had her principles. No one must be able to say of her when she was dead that she had not divided her money with perfect fairness among her own kin; not to do so was a prospective disgrace that would have embittered her life.

But though the letter could not shake Mrs Glegg's principles, it made the family breach much more difficult to mend; and as to the effect it produced on Mrs Glegg's opinion of Mr Tulliver – she begged to be understood from that time forth that she had nothing whatever to say about him: his state of mind, apparently, was too corrupt for her to contemplate it for a moment. It was not until the evening before Tom went to school, at the beginning of August, that Mrs Glegg paid a visit to her sister Tulliver, sitting in her gig all the while, and showing her displeasure by markedly abstaining from all advice and criticism, for, as she observed to her sister Deane, 'Bessy must bear the consequences o' having such a husband, though I'm sorry for her,' and Mrs Deane agreed that Bessy was pitiable.

Mr Tulliver's prompt procedure entailed on him further promptitude in finding the convenient person who was desirous of lending five hundred pounds on bond. 'It must be no client of Wakem's,' he said to himself; and yet at the end of a fortnight it turned out to the contrary; because Wakem's client was the only convenient person to be found.

BOOK SECOND

School-time

1

Tom's 'First Half'

Tom Tulliver's sufferings during the first quarter he was at King's Lorton, under the distinguished care of the Rev Walter Stelling, were rather severe. He had not been there a fortnight before it was evident to him that life, complicated not only with the Latin grammar but with a new standard of English pronunciation, was a very difficult business, made all the more obscure by a thick mist of bashfulness. Tom was never an exception among boys for ease of address; but the difficulty of enunciating a monosyllable in reply to Mr or Mrs Stelling was so great, that he even dreaded to be asked at table whether he would have more pudding. Yet it was impossible for Tom to despise Mr Stelling. If there were anything that was not thoroughly genuine about him, it lay beyond Tom's power to detect it.

Mr Stelling was a well-sized, broad-chested man, not yet thirty, with flaxen hair standing erect, and large lightish-grey eyes, which were always very wide open; he had a sonorous bass voice, and an air of defiant self-confidence inclining to brazenness. He had entered on his career with great vigour, and intended to make a considerable impression on his fellow-men. He had a true British determination to push his way in the world. As a schoolmaster, in the first place; for there were capital masterships of grammar-schools to be had, and Mr Stelling meant to have one of them. But as a preacher also. The style of preaching he had chosen was the extemporaneous, which was held little short of the miraculous in rural parishes like King's Lorton. Some passages of Massillon and Bourdaloue, which he knew by heart, were really very effective when rolled out in Mr Stelling's deepest tones; but as comparatively feeble appeals of his own were delivered in the same loud and impressive manner, they were often thought quite as striking by his hearers. In short, Mr Stelling was a man who meant to rise in his profession, and to rise by merit. A clergyman who has such vigorous intentions naturally gets a little into debt at starting; it is not to be expected that he will live in the meagre style of a man who means to be a poor curate all his life, and if the few hundreds Mr Timpson advanced towards his daughter's fortune did not suffice for the purchase of handsome furniture, together with a stock of wine, a grand piano, and the laying out of a superior flower-garden, it followed in the most rigorous manner, either that these things must be procured by some other means, or else that the Rev Mr Stelling must go without them – which last alternative would be an absurd procrastination of the fruits of success, where success was certain. Mr Stelling felt equal to anything; he would become celebrated by shaking the consciences of his hearers, and he would by-and-by edit a Greek play, and invent several new readings. He had not yet selected the play, for having been married little more than two years, his leisure time had been much occupied with attentions to Mrs Stelling.

But the immediate step to future success was to bring on Tom Tulliver during this first half-year; for, by a singular coincidence, there had been some negotiation concerning another pupil from the same neighbourhood, and it might further a decision in Mr Stelling's favour, if it were understood that young Tulliver, who, Mr Stelling observed in conjugal privacy, was rather a tough cub, had made prodigious progress in a short time. It was on this ground that he was severe with Tom about his lessons: he was clearly a boy whose powers would never be developed through the medium of the Latin grammar, without the application of some sternness. Not that Mr Stelling was a harsh-tempered or unkind man – quite the contrary: he was jocose with Tom at table, and corrected his provincialisms and his deportment in the most playful manner; but poor Tom was only the more cowed and confused by this double novelty, for he had never been used to jokes at all like Mr Stelling's; and for the first time in his life he had a painful sense that he was all wrong somehow. There are two expensive forms of education, either of which a parent may procure for his son by sending him as solitary pupil to a clergyman: one is, the enjoyment of the reverend gentleman's undivided neglect; the other is, the endurance of the reverend gentleman's undivided attention. It was the latter privilege for which Mr Tulliver paid a high price in Tom's initiatory months at King's Lorton.

That respectable miller and maltster had left Tom behind, and driven homeward in a state of great mental satisfaction. Mr Tulliver thought the Rev Mr Stelling was the shrewdest fellow he had ever met with and was not by any means an exception in mistaking brazenness for shrewdness: most laymen thought Stelling shrewd, and a man of remarkable powers generally: it was chiefly by his clerical brethren that he was considered rather a dull fellow. But the miller had no doubt this first-rate man was acquainted with every branch of information, and knew exactly what Tom must learn in order to become a match for the lawyers.

As for Mrs Tulliver – finding that Mrs Stelling's views as to the airing of linen and the frequent recurrence of hunger in a growing boy entirely coincided with her own – she expressed great contentment to her husband, when they drove away, at leaving Tom with a woman who, in spite of her youth, seemed quite sensible and motherly, and asked advice as prettily as could be.

'They must be very well off, though,' said Mrs Tulliver, 'for everything's as nice as can be all over the house, and that watered-silk she had on cost a pretty penny. Sister Pullet has got one like it.'

'Ah,' said Mr Tulliver, 'he's got some income besides the curacy, I reckon. Perhaps her father allows 'em something. There's Tom 'ull be another hundred to him, and not much trouble either, by his own account: he says teaching comes natural to him. That's wonderful now,' added Mr Tulliver, turning his head on one side, and giving his horse a meditative tickling on the flank.

Perhaps it was because teaching came naturally to Mr Stelling that he set about it with that uniformity of method and independence of circumstances. With unerring instinct he set to work at his natural method of instilling the Eton Grammar and Euclid into the mind of Tom Tulliver. Mr Stelling was very far from being led astray by enthusiasm, either religious or intellectual: he had no doubt that he was doing the very best thing for Mr Tulliver's boy. Mr Stelling's duty was to teach the lad in the only right way – indeed, he knew no other.

He very soon set down poor Tom as a thoroughly stupid lad; for though by hard labour he could get particular declensions into his brain, anything so abstract as the relation between cases and terminations could by no means get such a lodgement there as to enable him to recognise a chance genitive or dative. This struck Mr Stelling as something more than natural stupidity: he suspected obstinacy, or, at any rate, indifference. 'You feel no interest in what you're doing, sir,' Mr Stelling would say, and the reproach was painfully true. Tom had never found any difficulty in discerning a pointer from a setter when once he had been told the distinction, and his perceptive powers were not at all deficient. Tom could predict with accuracy what number of horses were cantering behind him, he could throw a stone right into the centre of a given ripple, he could guess to a fraction how many lengths of his stick it would take to reach across the playground, and could draw almost perfect squares on his slate without any measurement. But Mr Stelling took no note of these things: he only observed that Tom's faculties failed him before the abstractions hideously symbolised to him in the pages of the Eton Grammar, and that he was in a state bordering on idiocy with regard to the demonstration that two given triangles must be equal – though he could discern with great promptitude and certainty the fact that they *were* equal.

Tom had a large share of pride, which had hitherto found itself very comfortable in the world, but now this same pride met with nothing but bruises and crushings. He was too clear-sighted not to be aware that Mr Stelling's standard of things was quite different, was certainly something higher in the eyes of the world, than that of the people he had been living amongst, and that, brought in contact with it, he, Tom Tulliver, appeared uncouth and stupid; he was by no means indifferent to this, and his pride got into an uneasy condition which quite nullified his boyish self-satisfaction.

Tom's spirit was further depressed by a new means of mental development, which had been thought of for him out of school hours. Mrs Stelling had lately had her second baby, and as nothing could be more salutary for a boy than to feel himself useful, Mrs Stelling considered she was doing Tom a service by setting him to watch the little cherub Laura while the nurse was occupied with the sickly baby. It was quite a pretty employment for Tom to take little Laura out in the sunniest hour of the autumn day – it would help to make him feel that Lorton Parsonage was a home for him, and that he was one of the family. The little cherub Laura, not being an accomplished walker at present, had a ribbon fastened round her waist, by which Tom held her as if she had been a little dog during the minutes in which she chose to walk; but as these were rare, he was for the most part carrying this fine child round and round the garden, within sight of Mrs Stelling's window – according to orders.

If Tom had had a worse disposition, he would certainly have hated the little cherub Laura, but he was too kind-hearted a lad for that – there was too much in him of the fibre that turns to true manliness, and to protecting pity for the weak. I am afraid he hated Mrs Stelling but he couldn't help liking to amuse little Laura. She was a sort of playfellow – and oh, how Tom longed for playfellows! In his secret heart he yearned to have Maggie with him, and was almost ready to dote on her exasperating acts of forgetfulness; though, when he was at home, he always represented it as a great favour on his part to let Maggie trot by his side on his pleasure excursions.

And before this dreary half-year was ended, Maggie actually

came. Mrs Stelling had given a general invitation for the little girl to come and stay with her brother: so when Mr Tulliver drove over to King's Lorton late in October, Maggie came too.

'Well, my lad,' he said to Tom, when Mr Stelling had left the room to announce the arrival to his wife, and Maggie had begun to kiss Tom freely, 'you look rarely! School agrees with you.'

Tom wished he had looked rather ill.

'I don't think I *am* well, father,' said Tom; 'I wish you'd ask Mr Stelling not to let me do Euclid – it brings on the toothache, I think.'

(The toothache was the only malady to which Tom had ever been subject.)

'Euclid, my lad – why, what's that?' said Mr Tulliver.

'Oh, I don't know: it's definitions, and axioms, and triangles, and things. It's a book I've got to learn in – there's no sense in it.'

'Go, go!' said Mr Tulliver, reprovingly, 'you must learn what your master tells you. He knows what it's right for you to learn.'

'*I'll* help you now, Tom,' said Maggie, with a little air of patronising consolation.

'*You* help me, you silly little thing!' said Tom; he quite enjoyed the idea of confounding Maggie by showing her a page of Euclid. 'I should like to see you doing one of *my* lessons! Why, I learn Latin too! Girls never learn such things. They're too silly.'

'I know what Latin is very well,' said Maggie, confidently. 'Latin's a language. There are Latin words in the Dictionary. There's bonus, a gift.'

'Now, you're just wrong there, Miss Maggie!' said Tom, secretly astonished. '"Bonus" means "good," as it happens – bonus, bona, bonum.'

'Well, that's no reason why it shouldn't mean "gift,"' said Maggie. 'It may mean several things – almost every word does. There's "lawn" – it means the grassplot, as well as the stuff pockethandkerchiefs are made of.'

'Well done, little 'un,' said Mr Tulliver, laughing, while Tom felt rather disgusted with Maggie's knowingness, though beyond measure cheerful at the thought that she was going to stay with him.

Mrs Stelling, in her pressing invitation, did not mention a longer time than a week for Maggie's stay; but Mr Stelling, who took her between his knees, and asked her where she stole her dark eyes from, insisted that she must stay a fortnight. Maggie thought Mr Stelling was a charming man, and Mr Tulliver was quite proud to leave his little wench where she would have an opportunity of showing her cleverness to appreciating strangers. So it was agreed that she should not be fetched home till the end of the fortnight.

'Now, then, come with me into the study, Maggie,' said Tom, as their father drove away.

'Oh, what books!' Maggie exclaimed, as she saw the book-cases in the study. 'How I should like to have as many books as that!'

'Why, you couldn't read one of 'em,' said Tom, triumphantly. 'They're all Latin.'

'No, they aren't,' said Maggie. 'I can read the back of this ... "History of the Decline and Fall of the Roman Empire."'

'Well, what does that mean? *You* don't know,' said Tom, wagging his head.

'But I could soon find out,' said Maggie, scornfully. 'I should look inside, and see what it was about.'

'You'd better not, Miss Maggie,' said Tom, seeing her hand on the volume. 'Mr Stelling lets nobody touch his books without leave, and *I* shall catch it, if you take it out.'

'Oh, very well! Let me see all *your* books, then,' said Maggie, turning to throw her arms round Tom's neck, and rub his cheek with her small round nose.

Tom, with the gladness of his heart at having dear old Maggie to dispute with and crow over again, drew her towards him. 'Come, it's time for me to learn my lessons. See here! what I've got to do,' said Tom, showing her his theorem, while she pushed her hair behind her ears, and prepared herself to prove her capability of helping him in Euclid. She began to read with full confidence in her own powers, but presently, becoming quite bewildered, her face flushed with irritation. It was unavoidable – she must confess her incompetency, and she was not fond of humiliation.

'It's nonsense!' she said, 'nobody need want to make it out.'

'Ah, there now, Miss Maggie!' said Tom, drawing the book away, and wagging his head at her, 'you see you're not so clever as you thought you were.'

Maggie found the Latin Grammar quite soothing after her mathematical mortification; for she delighted in new words, and quickly found that there was an English Key at the end, which would make her very wise about Latin, at slight expense. She presently made up her mind to skip the rules in the Syntax – the examples became so absorbing. These mysterious sentences, snatched from an unknown context, gave boundless scope to her imagination, and were all the more fascinating because they were in a peculiar tongue of their own, which she could learn to interpret. It was really very interesting – and afforded her a great deal of pleasant conjecture, when Tom called out—

'Now, then, Magsie, give us the Grammar!'

'Oh, Tom, it's such a pretty book!' she said, as she jumped out of the large arm-chair to give it him; 'it's much prettier than the Dictionary. I could learn Latin very soon. I don't think it's at all hard.'

'Oh, I know what you've been doing,' said Tom; 'you've been reading the English at the end. Any donkey can do that.'

Tom seized the book and opened it with a determined and business-like air, as much as to say that he had a lesson to learn which no donkeys would find themselves equal to. Maggie, rather piqued, turned to the book-cases to amuse herself with puzzling out the titles.

They were presently fetched to spend the rest of the evening in the drawing-room, and Maggie became so animated with Mr Stelling, who, she felt sure, admired her cleverness, that Tom was rather amazed and alarmed at her audacity.

It was a very happy fortnight to Maggie, this visit to Tom. She was allowed to be in the study while he had his lessons, and in her various readings got very deep into the examples in the Latin

Grammar. Mr Stelling liked her immensely, and they were on the best terms. She told Tom she should like to go to school to Mr Stelling, as he did, and learn just the same things. She knew she could do Euclid, for she had looked into it again, and she saw what ABC meant: they were the names of the lines.

'I'm sure you couldn't do it, now,' said Tom; 'and I'll just ask Mr Stelling if you could.'

'I don't mind,' said the little conceited minx. 'I'll ask him myself.'

'Mr Stelling,' she said, that same evening when they were in the drawing-room, 'couldn't I do Euclid, and all Tom's lessons, if you were to teach me instead of him?'

'No; you couldn't,' said Tom, indignantly. 'Girls can't do Euclid: can they, sir?'

'They can pick up a little of everything, I daresay,' said Mr Stelling. 'They've a great deal of superficial cleverness; but they couldn't go far into anything. They're quick and shallow.'

Tom was delighted with this verdict.

'Ha, ha! Miss Maggie!' he said, when they were alone; 'you see it's not such a fine thing to be quick. You'll never go far into anything, you know.'

But when this small apparatus of shallow quickness was fetched away in the gig by Luke, and the study was once more quite lonely for Tom, he missed her grievously. He had really been brighter, and had got through his lessons better, since she had been there; and she had asked Mr Stelling so many questions about the Roman Empire, and whether there really ever was a man who said, in Latin, 'I would not buy it for a farthing or a rotten nut,' or whether that had only been turned into Latin, that Tom had actually come to a dim understanding of the fact that there had once been people upon the earth who were so fortunate as to know Latin without learning it through the medium of the Eton Grammar. This luminous idea was a great addition to his historical acquirements during this half-year, which were otherwise confined to an epitomised history of the Jews.

But the dreary half-year *did* come to an end. How glad Tom

was to see the bright light in the parlour at home, as the gig passed noiselessly over the snow-covered bridge.

2

The Christmas Holidays

This Christmas day, in spite of Tom's fresh delight in home, was not, he thought, somehow or other, quite so happy as it had always been before. Christmas was cheery, but not so Mr Tulliver. He was irate and defiant, and Tom, though he espoused his father's quarrels and shared his father's sense of injury, was not without some of the feeling that oppressed Maggie when Mr Tulliver got louder and more angry in narration and assertion with the increased leisure of dessert. The attention that Tom might have concentrated on his nuts and wine was distracted by a sense that there were rascally enemies in the world, and that the business of grown-up life could hardly be conducted without a good deal of quarrelling. His father's irritable talk made him uncomfortable, though he never accounted to himself for the feeling, or conceived the notion that his father was faulty in this respect.

The particular embodiment of the evil principle now exciting Mr Tulliver's determined resistance was Mr Pivart, who, having lands higher up the Ripple, was taking measures for their irriga-tion, which either were, or would be, or were bound to be (on the principle that water was water), an infringement on Mr Tulliver's legitimate share of water-power. He had no male audience today except Mr Moss, who knew nothing, as he said, of the 'natur' o' mills,' and could only assent to Mr Tulliver's arguments on the *a priori* ground of family relationship and monetary obligation. Mrs Moss, more alive to the subject, and interested in everything that affected her brother, listened and put in a word as often as maternal preoccupations allowed.

'Why, Pivart's a new name hereabout, brother, isn't it?' she said.

'New name? Yes – it is a new name,' said Mr Tulliver, with

angry emphasis. 'This fellow came and bought Bincome's farm out of hand, before anybody else could so much as say "snap." But I'll *Pivart* him!' added Mr Tulliver, lifting his glass with a sense that he had defined his resolution in an unmistakable manner.

'You won't be forced to go to law with him, I hope, brother?' said Mrs Moss, with some anxiety.

'I don't know what I shall be forced to; but I know well enough who's at the bottom of it; he's got Wakem to egg him on. I know Wakem tells him the law can't touch him for it; but there's folks can handle the law besides Wakem. It takes a big raskill to beat him; but there's bigger to be found.'

Mr Tulliver was a strictly honest man, but he considered that in law the ends of justice could only be achieved by employing a stronger knave to frustrate a weaker.

'Gore's no fool – you needn't tell me that,' he observed presently, in a pugnacious tone, as if poor Gritty had been urging that lawyer's capabilities; 'but, you see, he isn't up to the law as Wakem is. And water's a very particular thing. It's plain enough what's the rights and the wrongs of water, if you look at it straightforward; for a river's a river, and if you've got a mill, you must have water to turn it; and it's no use telling me, Pivart's erigation and nonsense won't stop my wheel: I know what belongs to water better than that. Talk to me o' what th' engineers say! I say it's common sense, as Pivart's dykes must do me an injury. But if that's their engineering, I'll put Tom to it by and by, and he shall see if he can't find a bit more sense in th' engineering business than what *that* comes to.'

Tom, looking round with some anxiety at this announcement of his prospects, unthinkingly withdrew a small rattle he was amusing Baby Moss with, whereupon she instantaneously expressed her sentiments in a piercing yell, and was not to be appeased even by the restoration of the rattle, feeling apparently that the original wrong of having it taken from her remained in all its force. Mrs Moss hurried away with her into another room, and Mrs Tulliver accompanied her. The thoroughly justifiable yell being quieted, Mrs Moss looked at her sister-in-law and said—

'I'm sorry to see brother so put out about this water work.'

'It's your brother's way, Mrs Moss; I'd never anything o' that sort before I was married,' said Mrs Tulliver, with a half-implied reproach. She always spoke of her husband as 'your brother' to Mrs Moss, in any case when his line of conduct was not matter of pure admiration. Being always on the defensive towards her own sisters, it was natural that Mrs Tulliver should be keenly conscious of her superiority, even as the weakest Dodson, over a husband's sister, who, besides being poorly off, and inclined to 'hang on' her brother, had the good-natured submissiveness of a large, easy-tempered, untidy, prolific woman, with affection enough in her not only for her own husband and abundant children, but for any number of collateral relations.

'I pray he won't go to law,' said Mrs Moss, 'for there's never any knowing where that'll end. And the right doesn't allays win.'

'As to that,' said Mrs Tulliver, stroking her dress down, 'I think sometimes I shall be drove off my head with the talk about this law and erigation; and my sisters lay all the fault to me, for they don't know what it is to marry a man like your brother – how should they? Sister Pullet has her own way from morning till night.'

'Well,' said Mrs Moss, 'I don't think I should like my husband if he hadn't got any wits of his own. It's a deal easier to do what pleases one's husband, than to be puzzling what else one should do.'

'If people come to talk o' doing what pleases their husband,' said Mrs Tulliver, with a faint imitation of her sister Glegg, 'I'm sure your brother might have waited a long while before he'd have found a wife that 'ud have let him have his say in everything, as I do. It's nothing but law and erigation now, from when we first get up in the morning till we go to bed at night; and I niver contradict; I only say – "Well, Mr Tulliver, do as you like; but whativer you do, don't go to law."'

Mrs Tulliver, as we have seen, was not without influence over her husband. On the composite impulses that were threatening to hurry Mr Tulliver into 'law,' Mrs Tulliver's monotonous pleading had doubtless its share of force; whenever she departed from entire assent to her husband, he saw in her the representative of the Dodson family; and it was a guiding principle with Mr Tulliver, to let the Dodsons know that they were not to domineer over *him*, or – more specifically – that a male Tulliver was far more than equal to four female Dodsons, even though one of them was Mrs Glegg.

But not even a direct argument from that typical Dodson female herself against his going to law, could have heightened his disposition towards it so much as the mere thought of Wakem, continually freshened by the sight of the too able attorney on market-days. Wakem, to his certain knowledge, was (metaphorically speaking) at the bottom of Pivart's irrigation: all lawyers were more or less rascals, but Wakem's rascality was of that peculiarly aggravated kind which placed itself in opposition to that form of right embodied in Mr Tulliver's interests and opinions. And as an extra touch of bitterness, the injured miller had recently, in borrowing the five hundred pounds, been obliged to carry a little business to Wakem's office on his own account. A hook-nosed glib fellow! as cool as a cucumber – always looking so sure of his game! And it was vexatious that Lawyer Gore was not more like him; and confident as Mr Tulliver was in his principle that water was water, and in the direct inference that Pivart had not a leg to stand on in this affair of irrigation, he had an uncomfortable suspicion that Wakem had more law to show against this (rationally) irrefragable inference, than Gore could show for it.

'Father,' said Tom, one evening near the end of the holidays, 'uncle Glegg says Lawyer Wakem *is* going to send his son to Mr Stelling. You won't like me to go to school with Wakem's son, shall you?'

'It's no matter for that, my boy,' said Mr Tulliver; 'don't you learn anything bad of him, that's all. The lad's a poor deformed creatur, and takes after his mother in the face: I think there isn't much of his father in him. It's a sign Wakem thinks high o' Mr Stelling, as he sends his son to him.'

Mr Tulliver in his heart was rather proud of the fact that his son was to have the same advantages as Wakem's.

3

The New Schoolfellow

It was a cold, wet January day on which Tom went back to school.

'Well, Tulliver, we're glad to see you again,' said Mr Stelling, heartily. 'Take off your wrappings and come into the study till dinner. You'll find a bright fire there, and a new companion.'

Tom felt in an uncomfortable flutter as he took off his woollen comforter and other wrappings. He had seen Philip Wakem at St Ogg's, but had always turned his eyes away from him as quickly as possible. He would have disliked having a deformed boy for his companion, even if Philip had not been the son of a bad man. Tom did not see how a bad man's son could be very good. His own father was a good man, and he would readily have fought any one who said the contrary. He was in a state of mingled embarrassment and defiance as he followed Mr Stelling to the study.

'Here is a new companion for you to shake hands with, Tulliver,' said that gentleman on entering the study – 'Master Philip Wakem. I shall leave you to make acquaintance by yourselves. You already know something of each other, I imagine.'

Tom looked confused and awkward, while Philip rose and glanced at him timidly.

Mr Stelling wisely turned away, and closed the door behind him: boys' shyness only wears off in the absence of their elders.

Philip was at once too proud and too timid to walk towards Tom. He thought, or rather felt, that Tom had an aversion to looking at him: every one, almost, disliked looking at him; and his deformity was more conspicuous when he walked. So they remained without shaking hands or even speaking, while Tom went to the fire and warmed himself, every now and then casting furtive glances at Philip, who seemed to be drawing absently first one object and then another on a piece of paper he had before him. As he drew, he was thinking what he could say to Tom, and trying to overcome his own repugnance to making the first advances.

Tom began to look oftener and longer at Philip's face, for he could see it without noticing the hump, and it was really not a disagreeable face. The deformity of Philip's spine was the result of an accident in infancy; but to Tom, Philip was simply a humpback, probably a spiteful fellow, who, not being able to fight you, had cunning ways of doing you a mischief by the sly. This Wakem was a pale, puny fellow, and it was quite clear he would not be able to play at anything worth speaking of; but he handled his pencil in an enviable manner. What was he drawing? Tom was quite warm now, and suddenly walked across the hearth, and looked over Philip's paper.

'Why, that's a donkey with panniers – and a spaniel, and part-ridges in the corn!' he exclaimed, his tongue being completely loosed by surprise and admiration. 'O my buttons! I wish I could draw like that. I'm to learn drawing this half – I wonder if I shall learn to make dogs and donkeys!'

'Oh, you can do them without learning,' said Philip; 'I never learned drawing.'

'Never learned?' said Tom in amazement. 'Why, when I make dogs and horses, and those things, the heads and the legs won't come right; though I can see how they ought to be very well. I can make houses, and all sorts of chimneys and all that. But I daresay I could do dogs and horses if I was to try more,' he added, reflecting that Philip might falsely suppose that he was going to 'knock under,' if he were too frank about the imperfection of his accomplishments.

'Oh yes,' said Philip, 'it's very easy. You've only to look well at things, and draw them over and over again. What you do wrong once, you can alter the next time.'

'But haven't you been taught anything?' said Tom, beginning to have a suspicion that Philip's crooked back might be the source of remarkable faculties. 'I thought you'd been to school a long while.'

'Yes,' said Philip, smiling, 'I've been taught Latin, and Greek, and mathematics – and writing, and such things.'

'Oh, but I say, you don't like Latin, though, do you?' said Tom, lowering his voice confidentially.

'Pretty well; I don't care much about it,' said Philip.

'Ah, but perhaps you haven't got into the *Propria quae maribus*,' said Tom.

Philip felt some bitter complacency in the promising stupidity of this well-made active-looking boy; but made polite by his own extreme sensitiveness, as well as by his desire to conciliate, he checked his inclination to laugh, and said quietly—

'I've done with the grammar; I don't learn that any more.'

'Then you won't have the same lessons as I shall?' said Tom, with a sense of disappointment.

'No; but I shall be very glad to help you if I can.'

Tom did not say 'Thank you,' for he was quite absorbed in the thought that Wakem's son did not seem so spiteful a fellow as might have been expected.

'I say,' he said presently, 'do you love your father?'

'Yes,' said Philip, colouring deeply; 'don't you love yours?'

'Oh, yes ... I only wanted to know,' said Tom, rather ashamed of himself, now he saw Philip colouring and looking uncomfortable. He found much difficulty in adjusting his attitude of mind towards the son of Lawyer Wakem, and it had occurred to him that if Philip disliked his father, that fact might go some way towards clearing up his perplexity.

'Shall you learn drawing now?' he said, changing the subject.

'No,' said Philip. 'My father wishes me to give all my time to other things now. And there are some lessons I'm very fond of. I'm very fond of Greek history, and everything about the Greeks. I should like to have been a Greek and fought the Persians, and then have come home and have written tragedies.'

'Why, were the Greeks great fighters?' said Tom, who saw a vista in this direction. 'Is there anything like David, and Goliath, and Samson, in the Greek history?'

'Oh, there are very fine stories of that sort about the Greeks – about the heroes of early times who killed the wild beasts, as

Samson did. And in the "Odyssey" – that's a beautiful poem – there's a more wonderful giant than Goliath – Polypheme, who had only one eye in the middle of his forehead; and Ulysses, a little fellow, but very wise and cunning, got a red-hot pine-tree and stuck it into his eye, and made him roar like a thousand bulls.'

'Oh, what fun!' said Tom. 'I say, can you tell me all about those stories? Because I shan't learn Greek, you know ...'

'But you may read those stories without knowing Greek. I've got them in English.'

'Oh, but I don't like reading; I'd sooner have you tell them me. But only the fighting ones. Can you tell a good many fighting stories?'

'Oh, yes,' said Philip; 'lots of them, besides the Greek stories. I know no end.'

'You're older than I am, aren't you?' said Tom.

'Why, how old are *you*? I'm fifteen.'

'I'm only going in fourteen,' said Tom. 'And I wish Mr Stelling would let us go fishing. *I* could show you how to fish. You *could* fish, couldn't you? It's only standing, and sitting still.'

Tom, in his turn, wished to make the balance dip in his favour. This hunchback must not suppose that his acquaintance with fighting stories put him on a par with an actual fighting hero like Tom Tulliver. Philip winced under this allusion to his unfitness for active sports, and he answered almost peevishly—

'I can't bear fishing. I think people look like fools sitting watching a line hour after hour and catching nothing.'

'Ah, but you wouldn't say they looked like fools when they landed a big pike, I can tell you,' said Tom, who had never caught anything that was 'big' in his life, but whose imagination was on the stretch with indignant zeal for the honour of sport. Happily for the harmony of this first interview, they were now called to dinner, and Philip was not allowed to develop further his unsound views on the subject of fishing. But Tom said to himself, that was just what he should have expected from a hunchback.

4

'*The Young Idea*'

The alternations of feeling in that first dialogue between Tom and Philip continued to mark their intercourse even after many weeks of schoolboy intimacy. Tom never quite lost the feeling that Philip, being the son of a 'rascal,' was his natural enemy, never thoroughly overcame his repulsion to Philip's deformity. But then, it was impossible not to like Philip's company when he was in a good humour; he could help one so well in one's Latin exercises, which Tom regarded as a kind of puzzle that could only be found out by a lucky chance; and he could tell such wonderful fighting stories. But Philip was not always in a good humour or happy mood. The slight spurt of peevish susceptibility which had escaped him in their first interview was a symptom of a perpetually-recurring mental ailment – half of it nervous irritability, half of it the heart-bitterness produced by the sense of his deformity. In these fits of susceptibility every glance seemed to him to be charged either with offensive pity or with ill-repressed disgust – at the very least it was an indifferent glance, and Philip felt indifference as a child of the south feels the chill air of a northern spring. Poor Tom's blundering patronage when they were out of doors together would sometimes make him turn upon the well-meaning lad quite savagely; and his eyes, usually sad and quiet, would flash with anything but playful lightning. But Philip's self-taught skill in drawing was another link between them; for Tom found, to his disgust, that his new drawing-master gave him no dogs and donkeys to draw, but brooks and rustic bridges and ruins. Mr Tulliver, having a vague intention that Tom should be put to some business which included the drawing out of plans and maps, had complained to Mr Riley, when he saw him at Mudport, that Tom seemed to be learning nothing of that sort; whereupon that obliging adviser had suggested that Tom should have drawing-lessons. Mr Tulliver must not mind paying extra for drawing: let Tom be made a good draughtsman, and he would be able to turn his pencil to any purpose. So it was ordered that Tom should have drawing-lessons; and whom should Mr Stelling have selected as a master if not Mr Goodrich, who was considered quite at the head of his profession within a circuit of twelve miles round King's Lorton? By which means Tom learned to make an extremely fine point to his pencil, and to represent landscape with a 'broad generality,' which, doubtless from a narrow tendency in his mind to details, he thought extremely dull.

Mr Stelling had a fixed opinion that all boys with any capacity could learn; if they were slow, the exercises must be insisted on with increased severity, and a page of Virgil be awarded as a penalty, to encourage and stimulate a too languid inclination to Latin verse.

This was relaxed a little during this second half-year for Tom. Philip was so advanced in his studies, and so apt, that Mr Stelling could obtain credit by his facility, which required little help, much more easily than by the troublesome process of overcoming Tom's dullness. Tom was gradually allowed to shuffle through his lessons with less rigour, and having Philip to help him, he was able to make some show of having applied his mind in a confused and blundering way, without being cross-examined into a betrayal that his mind had been entirely neutral in the matter. He thought school much more bearable under this modification of circumstances; and he went on contentedly enough, picking up a promiscuous education chiefly from things that were not intended as education at all. Nevertheless, there was a visible improvement in Tom under this training.

There was a great improvement in his bearing, for example, and some credit on this score was due to Mr Poulter, the village schoolmaster, who, being an old Peninsular soldier, was employed to drill Tom – a course of high mutual pleasure. Mr Poulter had rather a shrunken appearance, and was tremulous in the mornings, not from age, but from the extreme perversity of the King's Lorton boys, which nothing but gin could enable him to sustain with any firmness. Still, he carried himself with martial erectness, had his clothes scrupulously brushed, and his trousers tightly strapped; and on the Wednesday and Saturday afternoons, when he came to Tom, he was always inspired with gin and old memories, which gave him an exceptionally spirited air. The drilling-lessons were always protracted by episodes of warlike narrative. On afternoons when Mr Poulter's memory was more stimulated than usual, he remembered that the Duke of Wellington had (in strict privacy, lest jealousies should be awakened) expressed his esteem for that fine fellow Poulter. But Tom did not escape irritating his drilling-master occasionally, by his curiosity concerning other military matters than Mr Poulter's personal experience.

'And General Wolfe, Mr Poulter? wasn't he a wonderful fighter?' said Tom, who held the notion that all the martial heroes commemorated on the public-house signs were engaged in the war with Bony.

'Not at all!' said Mr Poulter, contemptuously. 'Nothing o' the sort! One of my sword-cuts 'ud ha' killed a fellow like General Wolfe.'

'Mr Poulter,' Tom would say, at any allusion to the sword, 'I wish you'd bring your sword and do the sword-exercise!'

For a long while Mr Poulter only shook his head in a significant manner at this request, and smiled patronisingly. But one afternoon, when a sudden shower of heavy rain had detained Mr Poulter twenty minutes longer than usual at the Black Swan, the sword was brought – just for Tom to look at.

'And this is the real sword you fought with in all the battles, Mr Poulter?' said Tom, handling the hilt. 'Has it ever cut a Frenchman's head off?'

'Head off? Ah! and would, if he'd had three heads. Ah, but the sword's the thing when you come to close fighting,' said Mr Poulter, drawing the sword so suddenly that Tom leaped back with much agility.

'Oh, but Mr Poulter, if you're going to do the exercise,' said Tom, a little conscious that he had not stood his ground as became an Englishman, 'let me go and call Philip. He'll like to see you.'

'What! the humpbacked lad?' said Mr Poulter, contemptuously. 'What's the use of *his* looking on?'

'Oh, but he knows a great deal about fighting,' said Tom; 'and how they used to fight with bows and arrows, and battle-axes.'

'Let him come then. I'll show him something different from his bows and arrows,' said Mr Poulter, coughing, and drawing himself up, while he gave a little preliminary play to his wrist.

Tom ran in to Philip, who was enjoying his afternoon's holiday at the piano in the drawing-room, picking out tunes for himself and singing them.

'Come, Philip,' said Tom, bursting in; 'come and see old Poulter do his sword-exercise in the carriage-house!'

The jar of this interruption – the discord of Tom's tones coming across the notes to which Philip was vibrating in soul and body, would have been enough to unhinge his temper, even if there had been no question of Poulter the drilling-master; and Tom, in the hurry of seizing something to say to prevent Mr Poulter from thinking he was afraid of the sword when he sprang away from it, had alighted on this proposition to fetch Philip – though he knew well enough that Philip hated to hear him mention his drilling-lessons. Tom would never have done so inconsiderate a thing except under the severe stress of his personal pride.

Philip shuddered visibly as he paused from his music. Then turning red, he said, with violent passion—

'Get away, you lumbering idiot! Don't come bellowing at me – you're not fit to speak to anything but a cart-horse!'

It was not the first time Philip had been made angry by him, but Tom had never before been assailed with verbal missiles that he understood so well.

'I'm fit to speak to something better than you – you poor-spirited imp!' said Tom, lighting up immediately at Philip's fire. 'You know I won't hit you, because you're no better than a girl. But I'm an honest man's son, and *your* father's a rogue – everybody says so!'

Tom, who had for the first time sent a poisoned arrow into Philip's heart, flung out of the room and returned to the carriage-house, where he found Mr Poulter, with a fixed and earnest eye, wasting the perfections of his sword-exercise on probably observant but inappreciative rats. Tom, not without a slight feeling of alarm at Mr Poulter's fixed eye and hungry-looking sword, which seemed impatient for something else to cut besides the air, admired the performance from as great a distance as possible. It was not until Mr Poulter paused and wiped the perspiration from his forehead, that Tom felt the full charm of the sword-exercise, and wished it to be repeated.

'Mr Poulter,' said Tom, when the sword was being sheathed, 'I wish you'd lend me your sword a little while to keep.'

'No, no, young gentleman,' said Mr Poulter, shaking his head decidedly, 'you might do yourself some mischief with it.'

'Oh, I say, do, Mr Poulter! I'd give you my five-shilling piece if you'd let me keep the sword a week. Look here!' said Tom, reaching out the attractively large round of silver. The young dog calculated the effect as well as if he had been a philosopher.

'Well,' said Mr Poulter, with still deeper gravity, 'you must keep it out of sight, you know.'

'Oh, yes, I'll keep it under the bed,' said Tom, eagerly.

'And let me see, now, whether you can draw it out of the sheath without hurting yourself.'

That process having been gone through more than once, Mr Poulter felt that he had acted with scrupulous conscientiousness and said, 'Well, now, Master Tulliver, if I take the crown-piece, it is to make sure as you'll do no mischief with the sword.'

'Oh, no, indeed, Mr Poulter,' said Tom, delightedly handing him the crown-piece, and grasping the sword, which, he thought, might have been lighter with advantage.

'But if Mr Stelling catches you carrying it in?' said Mr Poulter, pocketing the crown-piece while he raised this new doubt.

'Oh, he always keeps in his upstairs study on Saturday afternoons,' said Tom, who disliked anything sneaking, but was not disinclined to a little stratagem in a worthy cause. So he carried off the sword in triumph, mixed with dread – dread that he might encounter Mr or Mrs Stelling – to his bedroom, where, after some consideration, he hid it in the closet behind some hanging clothes. That night he fell asleep in the thought that he would astonish Maggie with it when she came next week to see him, before she went to a boarding-school with Lucy.

5

Maggie's Second Visit

This last breach between the two lads was not readily mended, and for some time they spoke to each other no more than was necessary. Their natural antipathy of temperament made resentment an easy passage to hatred, and in Philip the transition seemed to have begun. Tom had blundered on Philip's tenderest point, and had caused him as much acute pain as if he had studied the means with the nicest precision and the most envenomed spite. Tom saw no reason why they should not make up this quarrel as they had done many others, by behaving as if nothing had happened; for though he had never before said to Philip that his father was a rogue, this idea had so habitually made part of his feeling as to the relation between himself and his dubious schoolfellow that the mere utterance did not make such an epoch to him as it did to Philip. And he had a right to say so, when Philip hectored over *him*, and called him names. But perceiving that his first advances towards amity were not met, he resolved never to appeal to him either about drawing or exercises again. They were only so far civil to each other as was necessary to prevent their state of feud from being observed by Mr Stelling, who would have 'put down' such nonsense with great vigour.

When Maggie came, however, she could not help looking with growing interest at the new schoolfellow, although he was the son of that wicked Lawyer Wakem, who made her father so angry. She had arrived in the middle of school-hours, and had sat by while Philip went through his lessons with Mr Stelling, and was convinced that he must be very clever: she hoped he would think *her* rather clever too, when she came to talk to him. Maggie, moreover, had rather a tenderness for deformed things; she preferred the wry-necked lambs, because it seemed to her that the lambs which were quite strong and well made wouldn't mind so much about being petted; and she was especially fond of petting objects that would think it very delightful to be petted by her. She loved Tom very dearly, but she often wished that he *cared* more about her loving him.

'I think Philip Wakem seems a nice boy, Tom,' she said, when they went out of the study together into the garden, to pass the interval before dinner. 'He couldn't choose his father, you know; and I've read of very bad men who had good sons, as well as good parents who had bad children. You like him, don't you?'

'Oh, he's a queer fellow,' said Tom, curtly, 'and he's as sulky as can be with me, because I told him his father was a rogue. And I'd a right to tell him so, for it was true – and *he* began it, with calling me names. But you stop here by yourself a bit, Magsie, will you? I've got something I want to do upstairs.'

'Can't I go too?' said Maggie, who, in this first day of meeting again, loved Tom's shadow.

'No, it's something I'll tell you about by and by – not yet,' said Tom, skipping away.

In the afternoon the boys were at their books in the study, preparing the morrow's lessons, that they might have a holiday in the evening in honour of Maggie's arrival. Tom was hanging over his Latin Grammar, and Philip, at the other end of the room, was busy with two volumes, with a look of contented diligence that excited Maggie's curiosity; he did not look at all as if he were learning a lesson. She sat on a low stool at nearly a right angle with the two boys, watching first one and then the other; and Philip, looking off his book once towards the fireplace, caught the pair of questioning dark eyes fixed upon him. He thought this sister of Tulliver's seemed a nice little thing, quite unlike her brother; he wished *he* had a little sister.

'I say, Magsie,' said Tom at last, shutting his books and putting them away, 'I've done my lessons now. Come upstairs with me.'

'What is it?' said Maggie, when they were outside the door,

a slight suspicion crossing her mind as she remembered Tom's preliminary visit upstairs. 'It isn't a trick you're going to play me, now?'

'No, no, Maggie,' said Tom, in his most coaxing tone; 'it's something you'll like *ever so*.'

He put his arm round her neck, and she put hers round his waist, and, twined together in this way, they went upstairs.

'I say, Magsie, you must not tell anybody, you know,' said Tom, 'else I shall get fifty lines. Now you go into that corner and hide your face, while I reach it out,' he added. 'I'll tell you when to turn round. You mustn't squeal out, you know.'

'Oh, but if you frighten me, I shall,' said Maggie, beginning to look rather serious.

'You won't be frightened, you silly thing,' said Tom. 'Go and hide your face, and mind you don't peep.'

'Of course I shan't peep,' said Maggie, disdainfully.

But Tom looked round warily as he walked to the closet; then he stepped into the narrow space, and almost closed the door. Maggie kept her face buried without the aid of principle, for in that dream-suggestive attitude she had soon forgotten where she was, and her thoughts were busy with the poor deformed boy, who was so clever, when Tom called out, 'Now then, Magsie!'

Nothing but long meditation and preconcerted arrangement of effects could have enabled Tom to present so striking a figure as he did to Maggie when she looked up. He had had recourse to that unfailing source of the terrible, burnt cork, and had made himself a pair of black eyebrows that met in a satisfactory manner over his nose, and were matched by a less carefully adjusted blackness about the chin. He had wound a red handkerchief round his cloth cap to give it the air of a turban, and his red comforter across his breast as a scarf – an amount of red which, with the tremendous frown on his brow, and the decision with which he grasped the sword, as he held it with its point resting on the ground, would suffice to convey an approximative idea of his fierce and blood-thirsty disposition.

Maggie looked bewildered for a moment, and Tom enjoyed

that moment keenly; but in the next she laughed, clapped her hands together, and said, 'Oh, Tom, you've made yourself like Bluebeard at the show.'

It was clear she had not been struck with the presence of the sword – it was not unsheathed. Her frivolous mind required a more direct appeal to its sense of the terrible, and Tom prepared for his masterstroke. Frowning with a double amount of intention, if not of corrugation, he (carefully) drew the sword from its sheath and pointed it at Maggie.

'Oh, Tom, please don't,' exclaimed Maggie, in a tone of suppressed dread, shrinking away from him into the opposite corner. 'I *shall* scream – I'm sure I shall! Oh, I wish I'd never come upstairs!'

Slowly Tom let down the scabbard on the floor, and then said sternly—

'I'm the Duke of Wellington! March!' stamping forward with the right leg a little bent, and the sword still pointing towards Maggie, who, trembling, and with tear-filled eyes, got upon the bed as the only means of widening the space between them.

Tom proceeded, with the utmost exertion of his force, to such an exhibition of the cut and thrust as would be expected of the Duke of Wellington.

'Tom, I *will not* bear it – I *will* scream,' said Maggie, at the first movement of the sword. 'You'll hurt yourself!'

'One – two,' said Tom resolutely, though at 'two' his wrist trembled a little. 'Three' came more slowly, and with it the sword swung downward, and Maggie gave a loud shriek. The sword had fallen, with its edge on Tom's foot, and in a moment after he had fallen too. Maggie leaped from the bed, still shrieking, and immediately there was a rush of footsteps towards the room. Mr Stelling, from his upstairs study, was the first to enter. He found both the children on the floor. Tom had fainted, and Maggie thought he was dead. In another minute she was sobbing with joy because Tom had opened his eyes: she couldn't sorrow yet that he had hurt his foot – it seemed as if all happiness lay in his being alive.

6

A Love Scene

Poor Tom bore his severe pain heroically, and was resolute in not 'telling' of Mr Poulter more than was unavoidable: the five-shilling piece remained a secret even to Maggie. But there was a terrible dread weighing on his mind – so terrible that he dare ask the surgeon or Mr Stelling, 'Shall I be lame, sir?' He mastered himself so as not to cry out at the pain, but when his foot had been dressed, and he was left alone with Maggie seated by his bedside, the children sobbed together with their heads laid on the same pillow. Tom was thinking of himself walking about on crutches; and Maggie, who did not guess what was in his mind, sobbed for company. Philip watched the surgeon out of the house, and waylaid Mr Stelling to ask the very question that Tom had not dared to ask for himself.

'I beg your pardon, sir – but does Mr Askern say Tulliver will be lame?'

'Oh no, oh no,' said Mr Stelling, 'only for a little while.'

'Did he tell Tulliver so, sir, do you think?'

'No; nothing was said to him on the subject.'

'Then may I go and tell him, sir?'

'Yes, to be sure: now you mention it, I daresay he may be troubling about that. Go to his bedroom, but be very quiet at present.'

It had been Philip's first thought when he heard of the accident – 'Will Tulliver be lame? It will be very hard for him if he is' – and Tom's hitherto unforgiven offences were washed out by that pity. Philip felt that they were no longer in a state of repulsion, but were being drawn into a common current of suffering and sad privation. His imagination did not dwell on the outward calamity and its future effect on Tom's life, but it made vividly present to him the probable state of Tom's feelings.

'Mr Askern says you'll soon be all right again, Tulliver, did you know?' he said, rather timidly, as he stepped gently up to Tom's bed. 'Mr Stelling says you'll walk as well as ever again, by and by.'

Tom looked up with a sudden joy; then he gave a long sigh, and turned his blue-grey eyes straight on Philip's face, as he had not done for a fortnight or more. As for Maggie, this intimation of a possibility she had not thought of before, affected her as a new trouble and she clung to him and cried afresh.

'Don't be a little silly, Magsie,' said Tom, tenderly, feeling very brave now. 'I shall soon get well.'

'Good-bye, Tulliver,' said Philip, putting out his small delicate hand, which Tom clasped immediately with his more substantial fingers.

'I say,' said Tom, 'ask Mr Stelling to let you come and sit with me sometimes, till I get up again, Wakem – and tell me about Robert Bruce, you know.'

After that, Philip spent all his time out of school-hours with Tom and Maggie.

One day, Philip and Maggie were in the study alone together while Tom's foot was being dressed. Philip was at his books, and Maggie leaned on the table near Philip to see what he was doing, for they were quite old friends now, and perfectly at home with each other.

'Maggie,' said Philip, after a minute or two, still leaning on his elbow and looking at her, 'if you had had a brother like me, do you think you should have loved him as well as Tom?'

'Oh, yes, better,' she answered immediately. 'No, not better; because I don't think I *could* love you better than Tom. But I should be so sorry – *so sorry* for you.'

Philip coloured: he had meant to imply, would she love him as well in spite of his deformity, and yet when she alluded to it so plainly, he winced under her pity. Maggie, young as she was, felt her mistake. Hitherto she had instinctively behaved as if she were quite unconscious of Philip's deformity: her own keen sensitiveness and experience under family criticism sufficed to teach her this as well as if she had been directed by the most finished breeding.

'But you are so very clever, Philip, and you can play and sing,' she added quickly. 'I wish you *were* my brother. I'm very fond of you. And you would stay at home with me when Tom went out, and you would teach me everything – wouldn't you?'

'But you'll go away soon, and go to school, Maggie,' said Philip, 'and then you'll forget all about me, and then I shall see you when you're grown up, and you'll hardly take any notice of me.'

'Oh, no, I shan't forget you, I'm sure,' said Maggie.

'I shall never forget *you*, Maggie,' said Philip, 'and when I'm very unhappy, I shall always think of you, and wish I had a sister with dark eyes, just like yours.'

'Why do you like my eyes?' said Maggie, well pleased.

'I don't know,' said Philip. 'They're not like any other eyes. They seem trying to speak – trying to speak kindly. I don't like other people to look at me much, but I like you to look at me, Maggie.'

'Why, I think you're fonder of me than Tom is,' said Maggie, rather sorrowfully. Then, wondering how she could convince Philip that she could like him just as well, although he was crooked, she said—

'Should you like me to kiss you, as I do Tom? I will, if you like.'

'Yes, very much: nobody kisses me.'

Maggie put her arm round his neck and kissed him quite earnestly.

'There now,' she said, 'I shall always remember you, and kiss you when I see you again, if it's ever so long. But I'll go now, because I think Mr Askern's done with Tom's foot.'

When their father came the second time, Maggie said to him, 'Oh, father, Philip Wakem is so very good to Tom – he is such a clever boy, and I *do* love him. And you love him too, Tom, don't you? *Say* you love him,' she added entreatingly.

Tom coloured a little as he looked at his father and said, 'I shan't be friends with him when I leave school, father; but we've made it up now, since my foot has been bad, and he's taught me to play at draughts, and I can beat him.'

'Well, well,' said Mr Tulliver, 'if he's good to you, try and make him amends, and be good to *him*. But don't you be getting too thick with him – he's got his father's blood in him.'

The jarring natures of the two boys effected what Mr Tulliver's admonition alone might have failed to effect: in spite of Philip's new kindness, and Tom's answering regard in this time of his trouble, they never became close friends. When Maggie was gone, and when Tom by and by began to walk about as usual, the friendly warmth that had been kindled by pity and gratitude died out by degrees, and left them in their old relation to each other. Philip was often peevish and contemptuous; and Tom's more specific and kindly impressions gradually melted into the old background of suspicion and dislike towards him as a queer fellow, a humpback, and the son of a rogue.

7

The Golden Gates Are Passed

So Tom went on till he was turned sixteen at King's Lorton, while Maggie was growing, with a rapidity which her aunts considered highly reprehensible, at Miss Firniss's boarding-school in the ancient town of Laceham on the Floss, with cousin Lucy for her companion. She hardly ever saw Philip during the remainder of their school-life; in the Midsummer holidays he was always away at the seaside, and at Christmas she could only meet him at long intervals in the streets of St Oggs's. When they did meet, she remembered her promise to kiss him, but, as a young lady who had been at a boarding-school, she knew now that such a greeting was out of the question, and Philip would not expect it.

But when their father was actually engaged in the long-threatened lawsuit, and Wakem, as the agent at once of Pivart and Old Harry, was acting against him, even Maggie felt, with some sadness, that they were not likely ever to have any intimacy with Philip again: the very name of Wakem made her father angry, and she had once heard him say, that if that crook-backed son lived to inherit his father's ill-gotten gains, there would be a curse upon him. 'Have as little to do with him at school as you can, my lad,' he said to Tom; and the command was obeyed the more easily because Mr Stelling by this time had two additional pupils.

By the time Tom had reached his last quarter at King's Lorton, the years had made striking changes in him. He was a tall youth now, carrying himself without the least awkwardness, and speaking without more shyness than was a becoming symptom of blended diffidence and pride: he wore his tail-coat and his stand-up collars, and watched the down on his lip with eager impatience, looking every day at his virgin razor, with which he had provided himself in the last holidays. Philip had already left – at the autumn quarter – that he might go to the South for the winter, for the sake of his health.

Tom had not heard anything from home for some weeks – a fact which did not surprise him, for his father and mother were not apt to manifest their affection in unnecessary letters – when, to his great surprise, on the morning of a dark cold day near the end of November, he was told, soon after entering the study at nine o'clock, that his sister was in the drawing-room.

Maggie, with braided and coiled hair, was almost as tall as Tom, though she was only thirteen; and she really looked older than he did at that moment. She had thrown off her bonnet and her young face had a strangely worn look, as her eyes turned anxiously towards the door. When Tom entered she did not speak, but only went up to him, put her arms round his neck, and kissed him earnestly. He was used to various moods of hers, and felt no alarm at the unusual seriousness of her greeting.

'Why, how is it you're come so early this cold morning, Maggie? Did you come in the gig?' said Tom, as she backed towards the sofa, and drew him to her side.

'No, I came by the coach. I've walked from the turnpike.'

'But how is it you're not at school? The holidays have not begun yet?'

'Father wanted me at home,' said Maggie, with a slight trembling of the lip. 'I came home three or four days ago.'

'Isn't my father well?' said Tom, rather anxiously.

'Not quite,' said Maggie. 'He's very unhappy, Tom. The lawsuit is ended, and – oh, Tom, he will lose the mill and the land, and everything; he will have nothing left.'

Tom's eyes flashed out one look of surprise at her, before he turned pale and trembled visibly.

Anxiety about the future had never entered Tom's mind. He had never dreamed that his father would 'fail'; *that* was a form of misfortune which he had always heard spoken of as a deep disgrace, and disgrace was an idea that he could not associate with any of his relations, least of all with his father. Tom was awakened now with a violent shock.

Maggie was frightened at Tom's pale, trembling silence. She threw her arms around him at last, and said, with a half sob—

'Oh, Tom – dear, dear Tom, don't fret too much – try and bear it well.'

The action seemed to rouse him, for he shook himself and said, 'I shall go home with you, Maggie. Didn't my father say I was to go?'

'No, Tom, father didn't wish it,' said Maggie, her anxiety about *his* feeling helping her to master her agitation. 'But poor mother wants you to come – she cries so! Oh, Tom, it's very dreadful at home.'

Maggie's lips grew whiter, and she began to tremble almost as Tom had done. The two poor things clung closer to each other – both trembling. When Maggie spoke, it was hardly above a whisper.

'And ... and ... poor father ... He fell off his horse ... He has known nobody but me ever since ... He seems to have lost his senses ... Oh, father, father ...'

With these last words, Maggie's sobs burst forth with the more violence for the previous struggle against them. Tom felt the crushing weight of what seemed unmitigated misfortune. He tightened his arm almost convulsively round Maggie as she sobbed, but his face looked rigid and tearless – his eyes blank – as if a black curtain of cloud had suddenly fallen on his path.

But Maggie soon checked herself abruptly: a single thought had acted on her like a startling sound.

'We must set out, Tom – we must not stay – father will miss me – we must be at the turnpike at ten to meet the coach.' She said this with hasty decision, rubbing her eyes, and rising to seize her bonnet.

Tom at once felt the same impulse, and rose too. 'Wait a minute, Maggie,' he said. 'I must speak to Mr Stelling, and then we'll go.'

He thought he must go to the study, but on his way he met Mr Stelling, who had heard from his wife that Maggie appeared to be in trouble when she asked for her brother; and, now that he thought the brother and sister had been alone enough, was coming to inquire and offer his sympathy.

'Please, sir, I must go home,' Tom said, abruptly, as he met Mr Stelling in the passage. 'I must go back with my sister directly. My father's lost his lawsuit – he's lost all his property – and he's very ill.'

Mr Stelling felt like a kind-hearted man; he foresaw a probable money loss for himself, but this had no appreciable share in his feeling, while he looked with grave pity at the brother and sister for whom youth and sorrow had begun together. When he knew how Maggie had come, and how eager she was to get home again, he hurried their departure, only whispering something to Mrs Stelling, who had followed them.

Tom and Maggie were standing on the door-step, ready to set out, when Mrs Stelling came with a little basket, which she hung on Maggie's arm, saying, 'Do remember to eat something on the way, dear.' Maggie's heart went out towards this woman whom she had never liked, and she kissed her silently.

Mr Stelling put his hand on Tom's shoulder and said, 'God bless you, my boy: let me know how you get on.' Then he pressed Maggie's hand; but there were no audible good-byes.

The two slight youthful figures soon grew indistinct on the distant road. They had entered the thorny wilderness, and the golden gates of their childhood had for ever closed behind them.

BOOK THIRD

The Downfall

1

What Had Happened at Home

When Mr Tulliver first knew the fact that the lawsuit was decided against him, and that Pivart and Wakem were triumphant, every one who happened to observe him at the time thought that he bore the blow remarkably well. He thought so himself: he thought he was going to show that if Wakem or anybody else considered him crushed, they would find themselves mistaken. He could not refuse to see that the costs of this protracted suit would take more than he possessed to pay them; but he appeared to himself to be full of expedients and plans by which he would meet his difficulties, and remain Mr Tulliver of Dorlcote Mill. There was such a rush of projects in his brain, that it was no wonder his face was flushed when he mounted his horse to ride home from Lindum. There was Furley, who held the mortgage on the land – a reasonable fellow, who, Mr Tulliver was convinced, would be glad not only to purchase the whole estate, including the mill and homestead, but would accept Mr Tulliver as tenant, and be willing to advance money to be repaid with high interest out of the profits of the business, which would be made over to him, Mr Tulliver only taking enough barely to maintain himself and his family. The really vexatious business was the fact that some months ago the creditor who had lent him the five hundred pounds to repay Mrs Glegg, had become uneasy about his money (set on by Wakem, of course), and Mr Tulliver, still confident that he should gain his suit, and finding it eminently inconvenient to raise the said sum until that desirable issue had taken place, had rashly acceded to the demand that he should give a bill of sale on his household furniture, and some other effects, as security in lieu of the bond. But now the consequences of this bill of sale occurred to him in a new light, and he remembered that the time was close at hand, when it would be enforced unless the money were repaid.

Mr Tulliver approached St Ogg's, through which he had to pass on his way homeward. But what is it that suggested to him, as he saw the Laceham coach entering the town, to follow it to the coach-office, and get the clerk there to write a letter, requiring Maggie to come home the very next day? Mr Tulliver's own hand shook too much under his excitement for him to write himself, and he wanted the letter to be given to the coachman to deliver to Miss Firniss's school in the morning. There was a craving which he would not account for to himself, to have Maggie near him; she must come back by the coach tomorrow.

To Mrs Tulliver, when he got home, he would admit no difficulties, and scolded down her burst of grief on hearing that the lawsuit was lost, by angry assertions that there was nothing to grieve about. He said nothing to her that night about the bill of sale, for he had kept her in ignorance of the nature of that transaction, and had explained the necessity for taking an inventory of the goods as a matter connected with his will.

The next day Mr Tulliver was again on horseback in the afternoon, on his way to Mr Gore's office at St Ogg's. Gore was to have seen Furley in the morning, and to have sounded him in relation to Mr Tulliver's affairs. But he had not gone half-way when he met a clerk from Mr Gore's office, who was bringing a letter to Mr Tulliver. Mr Gore had been prevented by a sudden call of business from waiting at his office to see Mr Tulliver, but would be at his office at eleven tomorrow morning, and meanwhile had sent some important information by letter.

'Oh!' said Mr Tulliver, taking the letter, but not opening it.

'Then tell Gore I'll see him tomorrow at eleven;' and he turned his horse.

The reading of a letter was not the affair of an instant to Mr Tulliver; so he had put it in his pocket. But by and by it occurred to him that there might be something in the letter Mrs Tulliver must not know about, and if so, it would be better to keep it out of her sight altogether. He stopped his horse, took out the letter, and read it. It was only a short letter; the substance was, that Mr Gore had ascertained, on secret but sure authority, that Furley had been lately much straitened for money, and had parted with his securities – among the rest, the mortgage on Mr Tulliver's property, which he had transferred to – Wakem.

In half an hour after this, Mr Tulliver's own waggoner found him lying by the roadside insensible, with an open letter near him, and his grey horse snuffing uneasily about him.

When Maggie reached home that evening, in obedience to her father's call, he was no longer insensible. About an hour before, he had become conscious, and after vague, vacant looks around him, had muttered something about 'a letter,' which he presently repeated impatiently. At the instance of Mr Turnbull, the medical man, Gore's letter was brought and laid on the bed, and the previous impatience seemed to be allayed. The stricken man lay for some time with his eyes fixed on the letter. But presently he turned his eyes from the letter to the door, and after looking uneasily he said, 'The little wench.'

He repeated the words impatiently from time to time, appearing entirely unconscious of everything except this one importunate want, and giving no sign of knowing his wife or any one else; and poor Mrs Tulliver, her feeble faculties almost paralysed by this sudden accumulation of troubles, went backwards and forwards to the gate to see if the Laceham coach were coming, though it was not yet time.

But it came at last, and set down the poor anxious girl, no longer the 'little wench,' except to her father's fond memory.

'Oh, mother, what is the matter?' Maggie said, with pale lips, as her mother came towards her, crying. She didn't think her father was ill, because the letter had come at his dictation from the office at St Ogg's.

But Mr Turnbull came now to meet her and Maggie ran towards the kind old friend, with a trembling, questioning look.

'Don't alarm yourself too much, my dear,' he said, taking her hand. 'Your father has had a sudden attack, and has not quite recovered his memory. But he has been asking for you, and it will do him good to see you. Keep as quiet as you can; take off your things and come upstairs with me.'

Maggie obeyed. The very quietness with which Mr Turnbull spoke had frightened her susceptible imagination. Her father's eyes were still turned uneasily towards the door when she entered and met the strange, yearning, helpless look that had been seeking her in vain. With a sudden flash and movement, he raised himself in the bed – she rushed towards him, and clasped him with agonised kisses.

But that flash of recognition had been too great a strain on the father's bruised, enfeebled powers. He sank back again in renewed insensibility and rigidity, which lasted for many hours, and was only broken by a flickering return of consciousness, in which he took passively everything that was given to him, and seemed to have a sort of infantine satisfaction in Maggie's near presence.

Mrs Tulliver sent for her sisters, and there was much wailing and lifting up of hands below stairs: both uncles and aunts saw that the ruin of Bessy was complete, and there was a general family sense that a judgement had fallen on Mr Tulliver, which it would be an impiety to counteract by too much kindness. But Maggie heard little of this, scarcely ever leaving her father's bedside, where she sat opposite him with her hand on his. Mrs Tulliver wanted to have Tom fetched home and, at the end of the second day, when Maggie had become more accustomed to her father's fits of insensibility, and to the expectation that he would revive from them, the thought of Tom had become urgent with *her* too; and when her mother sat crying at night Maggie said, 'Let me go for him, and tell him, mother. It would be so hard

for Tom to come home and not know anything about it beforehand.'

And the next morning Maggie went, as we have seen.

2

Mrs Tulliver's Teraphim, or Household Gods

When the coach set down Tom and Maggie, it was five hours
since she had started from home, and she was thinking with some
trembling that her father had perhaps missed her.

She hurried along the gravel-walk and entered the house before
Tom; but in the entrance she was startled by a strong smell of
tobacco. The parlour door was ajar – that was where the smell
came from. It was very strange: could any visitor be smoking at
a time like this? Maggie, after this pause of surprise, was only in
the act of opening the door when Tom came up, and they both
looked into the parlour together. There was a coarse, dingy man,
of whose face Tom had some vague recollection, sitting in his
father's chair, smoking, with a jug and glass beside him.

The truth flashed on Tom's mind in an instant. To 'have the
bailiff in the house' seemed only natural since his father had lost
all his property. But the immediate presence of this disgrace was
so much keener an experience to Tom than the worst form of
apprehension, that he felt at this moment as if his real trouble
had only just begun.

'How do you do, sir?' said the man, taking the pipe out of his
mouth, with rough, embarrassed civility. The two young startled
faces made him a little uncomfortable.

But Tom turned away hastily without speaking: the sight was
too hateful. Maggie had not understood the appearance of this
stranger, as Tom had. She followed him, whispering, 'Who can it
be, Tom? – what is the matter?' Then, with a sudden undefined
dread lest this stranger might have something to do with a change
in her father, she rushed upstairs, checking herself at the bedroom
door to throw off her bonnet, and entered on tiptoe. All was silent

there; her father was lying, heedless of everything around him, with his eyes closed as when she had left him. A servant was there, but not her mother.

'Where's my mother?' she whispered. The servant did not know.

Maggie hastened out, and said to Tom, 'Father is lying quiet; let us go and look for my mother. I wonder where she is.'

Mrs Tulliver was not downstairs – not in any of the bedrooms. There was but one room below the attic which Maggie had left unsearched: it was the store-room, where her mother kept all her linen and all the precious 'best things' that were only unwrapped and brought out on special occasions. Tom, preceding Maggie as they returned along the passage, opened the door of this room, and immediately said, 'Mother!'

Mrs Tulliver was seated there, with all her laid-up treasures. One of the linen-chests was open: the silver teapot was unwrapped from its many folds of paper, and the best china was laid out on the top of the closed linen-chest; and the poor woman was shaking her head and weeping, with a bitter tension of the mouth, over the mark, 'Elizabeth Dodson,' on the corner of some table-cloths she held in her lap.

She dropped them, and started up as Tom spoke.

'Oh, my boy, my boy!' she said, clasping him round the neck. 'To think as I should live to see this day! We're ruined ... everything's going to be sold up ... to think as your father should ha' married me to bring me to this! We've got nothing ... we shall be beggars ... we must go to the workhouse.'

Tom's face flushed as he said—

'But will my aunts let them be sold, mother? Do they know about it? Haven't you sent to them?'

'Yes, I sent Luke directly they'd put the bailies in, and your aunt Pullet's been – and, oh dear, oh dear, she cries so, and says your father's disgraced my family and made it the talk o' the country; and she'll buy the spotted cloths for herself, because she's never had so many as she wanted o' that pattern but she's got more checks a'ready nor she can do with.' (Here Mrs Tulliver began to lay back the table-cloths in the chest, folding and stroking them automatically.) 'And your uncle Glegg's been too, and he says things must be bought in for us to lie down on, but he must talk to your aunt; and they're all coming to consult ...'

Mrs Tulliver burst out crying afresh.

'And I *did* say to him times and times, "Whativer you do, don't go to law" – and what more could I do? I've had to sit by while my own fortin's been spent, and what should ha' been my children's, too. You'll have niver a penny, my boy ... but it isn't your poor mother's fault.'

She put out one arm towards Tom, looking up at him piteously with her helpless, childish blue eyes. The poor lad went to her and kissed her, and she clung to him. For the first time Tom thought of his father with some reproach. His natural inclination to blame, hitherto kept entirely in abeyance towards his father by the predisposition to think him always right, simply on the ground that he was Tom Tulliver's father, was turned into this new channel by his mother's plaints, and with his indignation against Wakem there began to mingle some indignation of another sort. Perhaps his father might have helped bringing them all down in the world, and making people talk of them with contempt; but no one should talk long of Tom Tulliver with contempt. The natural strength and firmness of his nature was beginning to assert itself, urged by the double stimulus of resentment against his aunts, and the sense that he must behave like a man and take care of his mother.

'Don't fret, mother,' he said tenderly. 'I shall soon be able to get money: I'll get a situation of some sort.'

'Bless you, my boy!' said Mrs Tulliver, a little soothed.

Maggie had witnessed this scene with gathering anger. The implied reproaches against her father – her father, who was lying there in a sort of living death – neutralised all her pity for griefs about tablecloths and china; and her anger on her father's account was heightened by some egoistic resentment at Tom's silent concurrence with her mother in shutting her out from the common calamity. She had become almost indifferent to her mother's habitual depreciation of her, but she was keenly alive to any sanction of it, however passive, that she might suspect in Tom. Poor Maggie was by no means made up of unalloyed devotedness, but put forth large claims for herself where she loved strongly. She burst out at last in an agitated, almost violent tone, 'Mother, how can you talk so? as if you cared only for things with *your* name on, and not for what has my father's name too – and to care about anything but dear father himself! – when he's lying there, and may never speak to us again. Tom, you ought to say so too – you ought not to let any one find fault with my father.'

Maggie, almost choked with mingled grief and anger, left the room, and took her old place on her father's bed. Her heart went out to him with a stronger movement than ever, at the thought that people would blame him. Maggie hated blame: she had been blamed all her life, and nothing had come of it but evil tempers. Her father had always defended and excused her, and her loving remembrance of his tenderness was a force within her that would enable her to do or bear anything for his sake.

Tom was a little shocked at Maggie's outburst – telling *him* as well as his mother what it was right to do! But he presently went into his father's room, and the sight there touched him in a way that effaced the slighter impressions of the previous hour. When Maggie saw how he was moved, she went to him and put her arm round his neck as he sat by the bed, and the two children forgot everything else in the sense that they had one father and one sorrow.

3

The Family Council

It was at eleven o'clock the next morning that the aunts and uncles came to hold their consultation. Mr Deane was not coming – he was away on business; but Mrs Deane, appearing punctually in that handsome new gig and the livery-servant driving it, was the first to arrive; and when she had taken her seat in the large parlour, Mrs Tulliver came down to her with her comely face a little distorted, nearly as it would have been if she had been crying.

'Oh, sister, what a world this is!' she exclaimed as she entered: 'what trouble, oh dear!'

'Yes, sister,' Mrs Deane said deliberately, 'this is a changing world, and we don't know today what may happen tomorrow. But it's right to be prepared for all things, and if trouble's sent, to remember as it isn't sent without a cause. I'm very sorry for you as a sister, and if the doctor orders jelly for Mr Tulliver, I hope you'll let me know: I'll send it willingly. For it is but right he should have proper attendance while he's ill.'

'Thank you, Susan,' said Mrs Tulliver, rather faintly, withdrawing her fat hand from her sister's thin one. 'But there's been no talk o' jelly yet.'

The sound of wheels diverted her thoughts. Mr and Mrs Glegg were come, and were almost immediately followed by Mr and Mrs Pullet.

Mrs Pullet entered crying. Mrs Glegg had on her fuzziest front, and garments which appeared to have had a recent resurrection from rather a creasy form of burial; a costume selected with the high moral purpose of instilling perfect humility into Bessy and her children.

'Mrs G., won't you come nearer the fire?' said her husband, unwilling to take the more comfortable seat without offering it to her.

'You see I've seated myself here, Mr Glegg,' returned this superior woman; '*you* can roast yourself, if you like.'

'Well,' said Mr Glegg, seating himself good-humouredly, 'and how's the poor man upstairs?'

'Dr Turnbull thought him a deal better this morning,' said Mrs Tulliver; 'he took more notice, and spoke to me; but he's never known Tom yet – looks at the poor lad as if he was a stranger, though he said something once about Tom and the pony. The doctor says his memory's gone a long way back, and he doesn't know Tom because he's thinking of him when he was little. Eh dear, eh dear!'

'I doubt if he ever gets up again; and if he does, he'll most like be childish, as Mr Carr was, poor man!'

'Sister Pullet,' said Mrs Glegg, severely, 'if I understand right, we've come together this morning to advise and consult about what's to be done in this disgrace as has fallen upon the family, and not to talk o' people as don't belong to us. If we aren't come together for one to hear what the other 'ull do to save a sister and her children from the parish, *I* shall go back. *One* can't act without the other, I suppose, it isn't to be expected as *I* should do everything.'

'Well, Jane,' said Mrs Pullet, 'I don't see as you've been so very forward at doing. I was here yesterday, and looked at all Bessy's linen and things, and I told her I'd buy in the spotted table-cloths. I couldn't speak fairer.'

'I wish it could be managed so as my teapot and chany and the best castors needn't be put up for sale,' said poor Mrs Tulliver, beseechingly, 'and the sugar-tongs, the first things ever I bought.'

'Well, I've no objection to buy some of the best things,' said Mrs Deane, rather loftily; 'we can do with extra things in our house.'

'Best things!' exclaimed Mrs Glegg with severity, which had gathered intensity from her long silence. 'It drives me past patience to hear you all talking o' best things, and buying in this, that, and the other, such as silver and chany. You must bring your mind to your circumstances, Bessy, and not be thinking o' silver and chany; but whether you shall get so much as a flock-bed to lie on, and a blanket to cover you, and a stool to sit on. You must remember, if you get 'em, it'll be because your friends have bought 'em for you, for you're dependent upon *them* for everything; for your husband lies there helpless, and hasn't got a penny i' the world to call his own. And it's for your own good I say this, for it's right you should feel what your state is, and what disgrace your husband's brought on your own family, as you've got to look to for everything – and be humble in your mind.'

Mrs Glegg paused, for speaking with much energy for the good of others is naturally exhausting. Mrs Tulliver, always borne down by the family predominance of sister Jane, said pleadingly—

'I'm sure, sister, I've never asked anybody to do anything, only buy things as it 'ud be a pleasure to 'em to have, so as they mightn't go and be spoiled i' strange houses.'

'Come, come,' said Mr Glegg, kindly, 'don't let us make things too dark. What's done can't be undone. We shall make a shift among us to buy what's sufficient for you; though, as Mrs G. says, they must be useful, plain things. We mustn't be thinking o' what's unnecessary.'

'Mr Glegg,' said Mrs G., 'if you'll be kind enough to let me speak, i'stead o' taking the words out o' my mouth – I was going to say, Bessy, as it's fine talking for you to say as you've never asked us to buy anything for you; let me tell you, you *ought* to have asked us. Pray, how are you to be purvided for, if your own family don't help you? You must go to the parish, if they didn't.'

'I've been thinking,' said Mrs Deane, 'how is it Mr and Mrs Moss aren't here to meet us? It is but right they should do their share.'

'Oh dear!' said Mrs Tulliver, 'I never sent 'em word about Mr Tulliver. I never gave 'em a thought. I wonder Maggie didn't, though, for she was allays so fond of her aunt Moss.'

'Why don't your children come in, Bessy?' said Mrs Pullet, at the mention of Maggie. 'They should hear what their aunts and uncles have got to say: and Maggie – when it's me as have paid for half her schooling, she ought to think more of her aunt Pullet than of aunt Moss.'

'If I'd had *my* way,' said Mrs Glegg, 'the children 'ud ha' been in the room from the first. It's time they knew who they've to look to, and it's right as *somebody* should talk to 'em, and let 'em know their condition i' life, and what they're come down to, and make 'em feel as they've got to suffer for their father's faults.'

'Well, I'll go and fetch 'em, sister,' said Mrs Tulliver, resignedly. She went upstairs to fetch Tom and Maggie, who were both in their father's room, and was on her way down again, when the sight of the store-room door suggested a new thought to her. She went towards it, and left the children to go down by themselves.

The aunts and uncles appeared to have been in warm discussion when the brother and sister entered – both with shrinking reluctance; for though Tom, with a practical sagacity which had been roused into activity by the strong stimulus of the new emotions he had undergone since yesterday, had been turning over in his mind a plan which he meant to propose to one of his aunts or uncles, he felt by no means amicably towards them, and dreaded meeting them all at once. As for Maggie, she was peculiarly depressed this morning: she had been called up, after brief rest, at three o'clock, and had that strange dreamy weariness which comes from watching in a sick-room through the chill hours of early twilight and breaking day. Their entrance interrupted the conversation. The shaking of hands was a melancholy and silent ceremony, till uncle Pullet observed, as Tom approached him—

'Well, young sir, we've been talking as we should want your pen and ink; you can write rarely now, after all your schooling, I should think.'

'Ay, ay,' said uncle Glegg, with admonition which he meant to be kind, 'we must look to see the good of all this schooling. Let us see whether you can do better than I can, as have made my fortin without it. But I doubt high living and high learning 'ull make it harder for you, young man, nor it was for me.'

'But he must do it,' interposed aunt Glegg, energetically, 'whether it's hard or no. He hasn't got to consider what's hard; he must be humble and grateful to his aunts and uncles for what they're doing for his mother and father, as must be turned out into the streets and go to the workhouse, if they didn't help 'em. And his sister, too,' continued Mrs Glegg, looking severely at Maggie, who had sat down on the sofa by her aunt Deane, drawn to her by the sense that she was Lucy's mother, 'she must make up her mind to be humble and work; for there'll be no servants to wait on her any more – she must do the work o' the house, and she must respect and love her aunts as have done so much for her, and saved their money to leave to their nepheys and nieces.'

Tom was still standing before the table in the centre of the group. There was a heightened colour in his face, and he was very far from looking humbled, but he was preparing to say, in a respectful tone, something he had previously meditated, when the door opened and his mother re-entered.

Poor Mrs Tulliver had in her hands a small tray, on which she had placed her silver teapot, a specimen teacup and saucer, the castors, and sugar-tongs.

'See here, sister,' she said, looking at Mrs Deane, as she set the tray on the table, 'I thought, perhaps, if you looked at the teapot again – it's a good while since you saw it – you might use it for every day, or else lay it by for Lucy when she goes to housekeeping. I should be so loath for 'em to buy it at the Golden Lion,' said the poor woman, her tears coming.

'Ah, dear, dear!' said aunt Pullet, shaking her head with deep sadness, 'it's very bad – to think o' the family initials going about everywhere – it niver was so before: you're a very unlucky sister, Bessy.'

'As to disgrace o' the family,' said Mrs Glegg, 'that can't be helped wi' buying teapots. The disgrace is, for one o' the family to ha' married a man as has brought her to beggary. The disgrace is, as they're to be sold up. We can't hinder the country from knowing that.'

Maggie had started up from the sofa at the allusion to her father, but Tom saw her action and flushed face in time to prevent her from speaking. 'Be quiet, Maggie,' he said, authoritatively, pushing her aside. It was a remarkable manifestation of self-command and practical judgement in a lad of sixteen, that when his aunt Glegg ceased, he began to speak in a quiet and respectful manner, though with a good deal of trembling in his voice; for his mother's words had cut him to the quick.

'Then, aunt,' he said, looking straight at Mrs Glegg, 'if you think it's a disgrace to the family that we should be sold up, wouldn't it be better to prevent it altogether? And if you and my aunt Pullet,' he continued, looking at the latter, 'think of leaving any money to me and Maggie, wouldn't it be better to give it now, and pay the debt we're going to be sold up for, and save my mother from parting with her furniture?'

There was silence for a few moments, for every one, including Maggie, was astonished at Tom's sudden manliness of tone. Uncle Glegg was the first to speak.

'Ay, ay, young man – come now! You show some notion o' things. But there's the interest, you must remember; your aunts get five per cent on their money, and they'd lose that if they advanced it – you haven't thought o' that.'

'I could work and pay that every year,' said Tom, promptly. 'I'd do anything to save my mother from parting with her things.'

'Well done!' said uncle Glegg, admiringly. He had been drawing Tom out, rather than reflecting on the practicability of his proposal. But he had produced the unfortunate result of irritating his wife.

'Yes, Mr Glegg!' said that lady, with angry sarcasm. 'It's pleasant work for you to be giving my money away, to go and be sunk in other folk's furniture, and encourage 'em in luxury and extravagance as they've no means of supporting; and I'm to alter my will, or have a codicil made, and leave two or three hundred less behind me when I die – me as have allays done right and been careful, and the eldest o' the family; and my money's to go and be squandered on them as have had the same chance as me, only they've been wicked and wasteful. Sister Pullet, *you* may do as you like, but that isn't *my* sperrit.'

'La, Jane, how fiery you are!' said Mrs Pullet. 'I'm sure you'll have the blood in your head, and have to be cupped. I'm sorry for Bessy and her children – but it's no use for me to think o' doing anything, if you won't meet me half-way.'

Tom's countenance had fallen during this conversation, and his lip quivered; but he was determined to behave like a man. Maggie, on the contrary, after her momentary delight in Tom's speech, had relapsed into her state of trembling indignation. Her mother had been standing close by Tom's side, and had been clinging to his arm ever since he had last spoken: Maggie suddenly started up and stood in front of them, her eyes flashing like the eyes of a young lioness.

'Why do you come, then,' she burst out, 'talking and interfering with us and scolding us, if you don't mean to do anything to help my poor mother – your own sister – if you've no feeling for her when she's in trouble, and won't part with anything, though you would never miss it, to save her from pain? Keep away from us then, and don't come to find fault with my father – he was better than any of you – he was kind – he would have helped *you* if you had been in trouble. Tom and I don't ever want to have any of your money, if you won't help my mother. We'd rather not have it! We'll do without you.'

Maggie, having hurled her defiance at aunts and uncles in this way, stood still, with her large dark eyes glaring at them, as if she were ready to await all consequences.

Mrs Tulliver was frightened; there was something portentous in this mad outbreak; she did not see how life could go on after it. Tom was vexed; it was no *use* to talk so. The aunts were silent with surprise for some moments. At length, in a case of aberration such as this, comment presented itself as more expedient than any answer.

'You haven't seen the end o' your trouble wi' that child, Bessy,' said Mrs Pullet; 'she's beyond everything for boldness and unthankfulness. It's dreadful. I might ha' let alone paying for her schooling, for she's worse nor ever.'

'It's no more than what I've allays said,' followed Mrs Glegg. 'Other folks may be surprised, but I'm not. I've said over and over again – years ago I've said, "Mark my words; that child 'ull come to no good: there isn't a bit of our family in her." And as for her having so much schooling, I never thought well o' that. I'd my reasons when I said *I* wouldn't pay anything towards it.'

'Come, come,' said Mr Glegg, 'let's waste no more time in talking – let's go to business. Tom now, get the pen and ink—'

While Mr Glegg was speaking, a tall dark figure was seen hurrying past the window.

'Why, there's Mrs Moss,' said Mrs Tulliver. 'The bad news must ha' reached her, then;' and she went out to open the door, Maggie eagerly following her.

'That's fortunate,' said Mrs Glegg. 'She can agree to the list o' things to be bought in. It's but right she should do her share when it's her own brother.'

Mrs Moss was in too much agitation to resist Mrs Tulliver as she drew her into the parlour, automatically, without reflecting that it was hardly kind to take her among so many persons in the first painful moment of arrival. The tall, worn, dark-haired woman was a strong contrast to the Dodson sisters as she entered in her shabby dress, with her shawl and bonnet looking as if they had been hastily huddled on, and with that entire absence of self-consciousness which belongs to keenly-felt trouble. Maggie was clinging to her arm; and Mrs Moss seemed to notice no one else except Tom, whom she went straight up to and took by the hand.

'Oh, my dear children,' she burst out, 'you've no call to think well o' me; I'm a poor aunt to you, for I'm one o' them as take all and give nothing. How's my poor brother?'

'Mr Turnbull thinks he'll get better,' said Maggie. 'Sit down, aunt Gritty. Don't fret.'

'Oh, my sweet child, I feel torn i' two,' said Mrs Moss, allowing Maggie to lead her to the sofa, but still not seeming to notice the presence of the rest. 'We've three hundred pounds o' my brother's money, and now he wants it, and you all want it, poor things! – and yet we must be sold up to pay it, and there's my poor children – eight of 'em, and I feel as if I was a robber. But I'm sure I'd no thought as my brother ...'

The poor woman was interrupted by a rising sob.

'Three hundred pounds! Oh, dear, dear,' said Mrs Tulliver, who felt a wife's irritation at having been kept in the dark.

'What madness, to be sure!' said Mrs Glegg. 'A man with a family! He'd no right to lend his money i' that way; and without security, I'll be bound, if the truth was known.'

Mrs Glegg's voice had arrested Mrs Moss's attention, and, looking up, she said—

'Yes, there *was* security: my husband gave a note for it. We're not that sort of people, neither of us, as 'ud rob my brother's children; and we looked to paying back the money, when the times got a bit better.'

'Well, but now,' said Mr Glegg, gently, 'hasn't your husband no way o' raising this money? Because it 'ud be a little fortin, like, for these folks, if we can do without Tulliver's being made a bankrupt. Your husband's got stock: it is but right he should raise the money, as it seems to me – not but what I'm sorry for you, Mrs Moss.'

'Oh, sir, you don't know what bad luck my husband's had with his stock. The farm's suffering so as never was for want o' stock; and we've sold all the wheat, and we're behind with our rent ... not but what we'd like to do what's right, and I'd sit up and work half the night, if it 'ud be any good ... but there's them poor children ... four of 'em such little uns ...'

'Don't cry so, aunt – don't fret,' whispered Maggie, who had kept hold of Mrs Moss's hand.

'Yes, Mrs Moss,' said Mrs Glegg, with decision. 'Yours is a very unlucky family; the more's the pity for *my* sister.'

'Why, there's this to be thought on, Mrs Moss,' said Mr Glegg, 'and it's right to warn you – if Tulliver's made a bankrupt, and he's got a note-of-hand of your husband's for three hundred pounds, you'll be obliged to pay it: th' assignees 'ull come on you for it.'

'Oh dear, oh dear!' said Mrs Tulliver, thinking of the bankruptcy, and not of Mrs Moss's concern in it. Poor Mrs Moss herself listened in trembling submission, while Maggie looked with bewildered distress at Tom to see if *he* showed any signs of understanding this trouble. Tom was only looking thoughtful, with his eyes on the table-cloth.

'Uncle,' said Tom, looking up suddenly from his meditative view of the table-cloth, 'I don't think it would be right for my aunt Moss to pay the money, if it would be against my father's will for her to pay it; would it?'

Mr Glegg looked surprised for a moment or two before he said, 'Why, no, perhaps not, Tom; but then he'd ha' destroyed the note, you know. What makes you think it 'ud be against his will?'

'Why,' said Tom, colouring, but trying to speak firmly, in spite of a boyish tremor, 'I remember quite well, before I went to school to Mr Stelling, my father said to me one night, when we were sitting by the fire together, and no one else was in the room ...'

Tom hesitated a little, and then went on.

'He said something to me about Maggie, and then he said, "I've always been good to my sister, though she married against my will – and I've lent Moss money; but I shall never think of distressing him to pay it: I'd rather lose it. My children must not mind being the poorer for that." And now my father's ill, and not able to speak for himself, I shouldn't like anything to be done contrary to what he said to me.'

'Well, but then, my boy,' said uncle Glegg, whose good feeling led him to enter into Tom's wish, 'we should have to make away wi' the note, you know, if we're to guard against what may happen, supposing your father's made bankrupt ...'

'Then I hope you'll help me to do it, uncle,' said Tom, earnestly. 'If my father shouldn't get well, I should be very unhappy to think anything had been done against his will, that I could hinder. And I'm sure he meant me to remember what he said that evening. I ought to obey my father's wish about his property.'

Even Mrs Glegg could not withhold her approval from Tom's words: she felt that the Dodson blood was certainly speaking in him. Maggie would hardly have restrained herself from leaping on Tom's neck, if her aunt Moss had not prevented her by herself rising and taking Tom's hand, while she said, with rather a choked voice—

'You'll never be the poorer for this, my dear boy, if there's a God above; and if the money's wanted for your father, Moss and me 'ull pay it, the same as if there was ever such security. We'll do as we'd be done by; for if my children have got no other luck, they've got an honest father and mother.'

'Well,' said Mr Glegg, who had been meditating after Tom's words, 'we shouldn't be doing any wrong by the creditors, supposing your father *was* bankrupt. If he meant to give your aunt the money before ever he got into this sad work o' lawing, it's the same as if he made away with the note himself; for he'd made up his mind to be that much poorer. But there's a deal o' things to be considered, young man,' Mr Glegg added, looking admonishingly at Tom, 'when you come to money business, and you may be taking one man's dinner away to make another man's breakfast. You don't understand that, I doubt?'

'Yes, I do,' said Tom, decidedly. 'I know if I owe money to one man, I've no right to give to another. But if my father had made up his mind to give my aunt the money before he was in debt, he had a right to do it.'

'Well done, young man! I didn't think you'd been so sharp,' said uncle Glegg, with much candour. 'But perhaps your father *did* make away with the note. Let us go and see if we can find it in the chest.'

'It's in my father's room. Let us go too, aunt Gritty,' whispered Maggie.

4

A Vanishing Gleam

Mr Tulliver was usually in so apathetic a condition that the exits and entrances into his room were not felt to be of great importance.

They entered very quietly, and Mrs Moss took her seat near the head of the bed, while Maggie sat in her old place on the bed, and put her hand on her father's, without causing any change in his face.

Mr Glegg and Tom had also entered, treading softly, and were busy selecting the key of the old oak chest from the bunch which Tom had brought from his father's bureau. They succeeded in opening the chest – which stood opposite the foot of Mr Tulliver's bed – and propping the lid with the iron holder, without much noise.

'There's a tin box,' whispered Mr Glegg; 'he'd most like put a small thing like a note in there. Lift it out, Tom; but I'll just lift up

these deeds – they're the deeds o' the house and mill, I suppose –
and see what there is under 'em.'

Mr Glegg had lifted out the parchments, and had fortunately
drawn back a little when the iron holder gave way, and the heavy
lid fell with a loud bang, that resounded over the house.

Perhaps there was something in that sound that produced
the instantaneous effect on the frame of the prostrate man. The
chest had belonged to his father and his father's father, and it
had always been rather a solemn business to visit it. In the same
moment when all the eyes in the room were turned upon him, he
started up and looked at the chest, the parchments in Mr Glegg's
hand, and Tom holding the tin box, with a glance of perfect
consciousness and recognition.

'What are you going to do with those deeds?' he said, in his
ordinary tone of sharp questioning whenever he was irritated.
'Come here, Tom. What do you do, going to my chest?'

Tom obeyed, with some trembling: it was the first time his
father had recognised him. But instead of saying anything more
to him, his father continued to look with a growing distinctness
of suspicion at Mr Glegg and the deeds.

'What's been happening, then?' he said sharply. 'What are
you meddling with my deeds for? Is Wakem laying hold of
everything? Why don't you tell me what you've been a-doing?'
he added impatiently.

'No, no, friend Tulliver,' said Mr Glegg, in a soothing tone.
'Nobody's getting hold of anything as yet. We only came to look
and see what was in the chest. You've been ill, you know, and
we've had to look after things a bit. But let's hope you'll soon be
well enough to attend to everything yourself.'

Mr Tulliver looked round him meditatively – at Tom, at Mr
Glegg, and at Maggie; then suddenly appearing aware that some
one was seated by his side at the head of the bed, he turned sharply
round and saw his sister.

'Eh, Gritty!' he said, in the half-sad, affectionate tone in which
he had been wont to speak to her. 'What! you're there, are you?
How could you manage to leave the children?'

'Oh, brother!' said good Mrs Moss, too impulsive to be prudent, 'I'm thankful I'm come now to see you yourself again – I thought you'd never know us any more.'

'What! have I had a stroke?' said Mr Tulliver, anxiously.

'A fall from your horse – shook you a bit – that's all, I think,' said Mr Glegg.

Mr Tulliver fixed his eyes on the bed-clothes, and remained silent for two or three minutes. A new shadow came over his face. He looked up at Maggie first, and said in a lower tone, 'You got the letter, then, my wench?'

'Yes, father,' she said, kissing him with a full heart. She felt as if her father were coming back to her from the dead, and her yearning to show him how she had always loved him could be fulfilled.

'Where's your mother?' he said, so preoccupied that he received the kiss as passively as some quiet animal might have received it.

'She's downstairs with my aunts, father: shall I fetch her?'

'Ay, ay: poor Bessy!' and his eyes turned towards Tom as Maggie left the room.

'You'll have to take care of 'em both if I die, you know, Tom. You'll be badly off, I doubt. But you must see and pay everybody. And mind – there's fifty pound o' Luke's as I put into the business – he gave it me a bit at a time, and he's got nothing to show for it. You must pay him first thing.'

Uncle Glegg involuntarily shook his head, and looked more concerned than ever, but Tom said firmly—

'Yes, father. And haven't you a note from my uncle Moss for three hundred pounds? We came to look for that. What do you wish to be done about it, father?'

'Ah! I'm glad you thought o' that, my lad,' said Mr Tulliver. 'I allays meant to be easy about that money, because o' your aunt. You mustn't mind losing that money, if they can't pay it – and it's like enough they can't. The note's in that box, mind! I allays meant to be good to you, Gritty,' said Mr Tulliver, turning to his sister; 'but, you know, you aggravated me when you would have Moss.'

At this moment Maggie re-entered with her mother, who came in much agitated by the news that her husband was quite himself again.

'Well, Bessy,' he said, as she kissed him, 'you must forgive me if you're worse off than you ever expected to be. But it's the fault o' the law – it's none o' mine,' he added angrily. 'It's the fault o' raskills! Tom – you mind this: if ever you've got the chance, you make Wakem smart. If you don't, you're a good-for-nothing son.'

Mr Tulliver was getting excited, and an alarming flush was on his face, and with the last words the poor man fell again, rigid and insensible. Though this was only a recurrence of what had happened before, it struck all present as if it had been death, not only from its contrast with the completeness of the revival, but because his words had all had reference to the possibility that his death was near.

Mr Turnbull was sent for; but when he heard what had passed, he said this complete restoration, though only temporary, was a hopeful sign, proving that there was no permanent lesion to prevent ultimate recovery.

Tom was clear upon two points – that his uncle Moss's note must be destroyed, and that Luke's money must be paid, if in no other way, out of his own and Maggie's money now in the savings bank. There were subjects, you perceive, on which Tom was much quicker than on the niceties of classical construction, or the relations of a mathematical demonstration.

5

Tom Applies His Knife to the Oyster

The next day, at ten o'clock, Tom was on his way to St Ogg's, to see his uncle Deane, who was to come home last night, his aunt had said; and Tom had made up his mind that his uncle Deane was the right person to ask for advice about getting some employment.

It was a dark, chill, misty morning. And Tom was very unhappy: he felt the humiliation as well as the prospective hardships of his lot with all the keenness of a proud nature; and with all his resolute dutifulness towards his father there mingled an irrepressible indignation against him which gave misfortune the less endurable aspect of a wrong. Since these were the consequences of going to law, his father was really blamable, as his aunts and uncles had always said he was; and it was a significant indication of Tom's character, that though he thought his aunts ought to do something more for his mother, he felt nothing like Maggie's violent resentment against them for showing no eager tenderness and generosity. Why should people give away their money plentifully to those who had not taken care of their own money? Tom saw some justice in severity; and all the more, because he had confidence in himself that he should never deserve that just severity. It was very hard upon him that he should be put at this disadvantage in life by his father's want of prudence; but he was not going to complain and to find fault with people because they did not make everything easy for him. He would ask no one to help him, more than to give him work and pay him for it. He would be like his uncle Deane – get a situation in some great house of business and rise fast. It was intolerable to think of being poor and looked down upon all one's life. He would provide for his mother and sister, and make every one say that he was a man of high character.

Walking along the street with a firm, rapid step, Tom made haste to reach the warehouse offices of Guest & Co., where he expected to find his uncle Deane. But this was Mr Deane's morning at the bank, a clerk told him, with some contempt for his ignorance.

At the bank Tom was admitted into the private room where his uncle was, immediately after sending in his name. Mr Deane was auditing accounts; but he looked up as Tom entered, and, putting out his hand, said, 'Well, Tom, nothing fresh the matter at home, I hope? How's your father?'

'Much the same, thank you, uncle,' said Tom, feeling nervous.

'But I want to speak to you, please, when you're at liberty.'

'Sit down, sit down,' said Mr Deane, relapsing into his accounts, in which he and the managing-clerk remained so absorbed for the next half-hour that Tom began to wonder whether he should have to sit in this way till the bank closed, but at last there was a change: his uncle took a pen and wrote something with a flourish at the end.

'Well, Tom,' said Mr Deane, when they were alone, turning his substantial person a little in his chair, and taking out his snuff-box, 'what's the business, my boy?' Mr Deane, who had heard from his wife what had passed the day before, thought Tom was come to appeal to him for some means of averting the sale.

'I hope you'll excuse me for troubling you, uncle,' said Tom, colouring, but speaking in a tone which, though tremulous, had a certain proud independence in it; 'but I thought you were the best person to advise me what to do.'

'Ah!' said Mr Deane, reserving his pinch of snuff, and looking at Tom with new attention, 'let us hear.'

'I want to get a situation, uncle, so that I may earn some money,' said Tom, who never fell into circumlocution.

'A situation?' said Mr Deane, and then took his pinch of snuff with elaborate justice to each nostril.

'Why, let me see, how old are you?' said Mr Deane, as he threw himself backward again.

'Sixteen – I mean, I am going in seventeen,' said Tom.

'Let me see – your father had some notion of making you an engineer, I think?'

'But I don't think I could get any money at that for a long while, could I?'

'That's true; but people don't get much money at anything, my boy, when they're only sixteen. You've had a good deal of schooling, however: I suppose you're pretty well up in accounts, eh? You understand book-keeping?'

'No,' said Tom, rather falteringly. 'But Mr Stelling says I write a good hand, uncle. That's my writing,' added Tom, laying on the table a copy of the list he had made yesterday.

'Ah! that's good, that's good. But, you see, the best hand in the world'll not get you a better place than a copying-clerk's, if you know nothing of book-keeping – nothing of accounts. And a copying-clerk's a cheap article.'

Tom coloured, and burst out, with new energy—

'I should like to enter into some business where I can get on – a manly business, where I should have to look after things, and get credit for what I did. And I shall want to keep my mother and sister.'

'Ah, young gentleman,' said Mr Deane, 'that's sooner said than done – sooner said than done.'

'But didn't *you* get on in that way, uncle?' said Tom, a little irritated that Mr Deane did not enter more rapidly into his views. 'I mean, didn't you rise from one place to another through your abilities and good conduct?'

'Ay, ay, sir,' said Mr Deane. 'But I'll tell you how I got on. I kept my eyes and ears open, sir, and I made my master's interest my own. Why, with only looking into what went on in the mill, I found out how there was a waste of five hundred a year that might be hindered. Why, sir, I hadn't more schooling to begin with than a charity boy; but I saw pretty soon that I couldn't get on far without mastering accounts, and I learned 'em between working hours, and paid for it out of my own earnings – often out of my own dinner and supper. And I looked into the nature of all the things we had to do with in the business, and picked up knowledge as I went about my work, and turned it over in my head. If I got places, sir, it was because I made myself fit for 'em. If you want to slip into a round hole, you must make a ball of yourself – that's where it is.'

'Well, uncle,' said Tom with a slight complaint in his tone, 'that's what I should like to do. Can't I get on in the same way?'

'In the same way?' said Mr Deane, eyeing Tom with quiet deliberation. 'You'll have to begin at a low round of the ladder, let me tell you, if you mean to get on in life.'

Tom bit his lips hard; he felt as if the tears were rising, and he would rather die than let them.

'You want me to help you to a situation,' Mr Deane went on; 'well, I've no fault to find with that. I'm willing to do something for you. But the best chance for you 'ud be to have a place on a wharf, or in a warehouse, where you'd learn the smell of things – but you wouldn't like that, I'll be bound; you'd have to stand cold and wet, and be shouldered about by rough fellows. You're too fine a gentleman for that.'

Mr Deane paused and looked hard at Tom, who certainly felt some inward struggle before he could reply—

'I would rather do what will be best for me in the end, sir. Is there any place at liberty that you know of now, uncle, that I should do for? I should like to set to work at once,' said Tom.

'Stop a bit, stop a bit; we mustn't be in too great a hurry. You must bear in mind, if I put you in a place you're a bit young for, because you happen to be my nephew, I shall be responsible for you. It remains to be seen whether you're good for anything.'

'I hope I should never do you any discredit, uncle,' said Tom, 'I care about my own credit too much for that.'

'Well done, Tom, well done! That's the right spirit, and I never refuse to help anybody if they've a mind to do themselves justice.'

'I'd better set about learning book-keeping, hadn't I, uncle?' said Tom, anxious to prove his readiness to exert himself.

'Yes, yes, you can't do amiss there. But ... ah, Spence, you're back again. Well, Tom, there's nothing more to be said just now, I think, and I must go to business again. Good-bye. Remember me to your mother.'

Mr Deane put out his hand with an air of friendly dismissal, and Tom had not courage to ask another question, especially in the presence of Mr Spence. So he went out again into the cold damp air. He had to call at his uncle Glegg's about the money in the savings bank, and by the time he set out again, the mist had thickened, and he could not see very far before him; but going along River Street again, he was startled, when he was within two yards of the projecting side of a shop-window, by the words 'Dorlcote Mill' in large letters on a hand-bill, placed as if on purpose to stare at him! It was the catalogue of the sale to take place the next week – it was a reason for hurrying faster out of the town.

Poor Tom formed no vision of the distant future as he made his way homeward; he only felt that the present was very hard. Apparently he, Tom Tulliver, was likely to be held of small account in the world, and for the first time he felt a sinking of heart under the sense that he really was very ignorant, and could do very little. Tom had been used to being so entirely satisfied with himself but now he suddenly felt at a disadvantage.

'What did my uncle Deane say, Tom?' said Maggie, putting her arm through Tom's as he was warming himself rather drearily by the kitchen fire. 'Did he say he would give you a situation?'

'No, he didn't say that. He didn't quite promise me anything; he seemed to think I couldn't have a very good situation. I'm too young.'

'But didn't he speak kindly, Tom?'

'Kindly? Pooh! what's the use of talking about that? I wouldn't care about his speaking kindly, if I could get a situation. But it's such a nuisance and bother – I've been at school all this while learning Latin and things – not a bit of good to me – and now my uncle says, I must set about learning book-keeping and calculation, and those things. He seems to make out I'm good for nothing.'

Tom's mouth twitched with a bitter expression as he looked at the fire.

'Oh, what a pity I wasn't taught book-keeping by double entry and after the Italian system, as Lucy Bertram was, then I could teach you, Tom.'

'*You* teach! Yes, I daresay. That's always the tone you take,' said Tom.

'Dear Tom, I was only joking,' said Maggie, putting her cheek against his coat-sleeve.

'But it's always the same, Maggie,' said Tom, with the little frown he put on when he was about to be justifiably severe. 'You're always setting yourself up above me and every one else, and I've wanted to tell you about it several times. You think you know better than any one, but you're almost always wrong. I can judge much better than you can.'

Poor Tom! He had just come from being lectured and made to feel his inferiority: the reaction of his strong, self-asserting nature must take place somehow; and here was a case in which he could justly show himself dominant. Maggie's cheek flushed and her lip quivered with conflicting resentment and affection, and a certain awe as well as admiration of Tom's firmer and more effective character. She did not answer immediately; very angry words rose to her lips, but they were driven back again, and she said at last—

'You often think I'm conceited, Tom, when I don't mean what I say at all in that way. I don't mean to put myself above you. But you are always so harsh to me, Tom.'

With the last words the resentment was rising again.

'No, I'm not harsh,' said Tom, with severe decision. 'I'm always kind to you; and so I shall be: I shall always take care of you. But you must mind what I say.'

Their mother came in now, and Maggie rushed away, that her burst of tears, which she felt must come, might not happen until she was safe upstairs.

6

Tending to Refute the Popular Prejudice against the Present of a Pocket-knife

In that dark time of December, the sale of the household furniture lasted beyond the middle of the second day. Mr Tulliver, who had begun, in his intervals of consciousness, to manifest an irritability which often appeared to have as a direct effect the recurrence of spasmodic rigidity and insensibility, had lain in this living death throughout the critical hours when the noise of the sale came nearest to his chamber. The wife and children had sat imprisoned in the silent chamber, watching the large prostrate figure on the bed, and trembling lest the blank face should suddenly show some response to the sounds which fell on their own ears with such obstinate, painful repetition.

But it was over at last. Mrs Tulliver's blond face seemed aged ten years by the last thirty hours: the poor woman's mind had been busy divining when her favourite things were being knocked down by the terrible hammer. Such things bring lines in well-rounded faces, and broaden the streaks of white among the hairs that once looked as if they had been dipped in pure sunshine. Already, at three o'clock, Kezia, the good-hearted, bad-tempered housemaid, who regarded all people that came to the sale as her personal enemies, had begun to scrub and swill with an energy much assisted by a continual low muttering against 'folks as came to buy up other folks's things.'

It was between five and six o'clock, near the usual tea-time, when Kezia came upstairs and said that Master Tom was wanted. The person who wanted him was in the kitchen, and in the first moments, by the imperfect fire and candle-light, Tom had not even an indefinite sense of any acquaintance with the rather broad-set but active figure, perhaps two years older than himself, that looked at him with a pair of blue eyes set in a disc of freckles, and pulled some curly red locks with a strong intention of respect. A low-crowned, oilskin-covered hat, and a certain shiny deposit of dirt on the rest of the costume, suggested a calling that had to do with boats; and this did not help Tom's memory.

'Sarvant, Mister Tom,' said he of the red locks, with a smile which seemed to break through a self-imposed air of melancholy. 'You don't know me again, I doubt,' he went on, as Tom continued to look at him inquiringly; 'but I'd like to talk to you by yourself a bit, please.'

'There's a fire i' the parlour, Master Tom,' said Kezia.

'Come this way, then,' said Tom, wondering if this young fellow belonged to Guest & Co.'s Wharf, for his imagination ran continally towards that particular spot, and uncle Deane might any time be sending for him to say that there was a situation at liberty.

The bright fire in the parlour was the only light that showed
the few chairs, the bureau, the carpetless floor, and the one table
– no, not the *one* table: there was a second table, in a corner,
with a large Bible and a few other books upon it. It was this new
strange bareness that Tom felt first, before he thought of looking
again at the face which was also lit up by the fire, and which stole
a half-shy, questioning glance at him as the entirely strange voice
said—

'Why! you don't remember Bob, then, as you gen the pocket-
knife to, Mr Tom?'

The rough-handled pocket-knife was taken out in the same
moment, and the largest blade opened by way of irresistible
demonstration.

'What! Bob Jakin?' said Tom – not with any cordial delight,
for he felt a little ashamed of that early intimacy symbolised by
the pocket-knife, and was not at all sure that Bob's motives for
recalling it were entirely admirable.

'Ay, ay, Bob Jakin – if Jakin it must be, 'cause there's so many
Bobs as you went arter the squerrils with. An' there was niver
nobody else gen me nothin' but what I got by my own sharpness,
only you, Mr Tom.'

'Well, Bob,' said Tom, with a slight air of patronage, the foregoing reminiscences having disposed him to be as friendly as was
becoming, though there was no part of his acquaintance with Bob
that he remembered better than the cause of their parting quarrel;
'is there anything I can do for you?'

'Why, no, Mr Tom,' answered Bob, shutting up his knife with a
click and returning it to his pocket, where he seemed to be feeling
for something else. 'I shouln't ha' come back upon you now ye're
i' trouble, an' folks say as the master'll niver lift up his yead no
more. I shall niver grow down'ards again, Mr Tom, an' you war
the little chap as I liked the best when I war a little chap, for all
you leathered me, and wouldn't look at me again. I'n seen chaps
as 'ud stand starin' at a bough till their eyes shot out, afore they'd
see as a bird's tail warn't a leaf. It's poor work goin' wi' such raff
– but you war allays a rare un at shying, Mr Tom, an' I could

trusten to you for droppin' down wi' your stick in the nick o' time at a runnin' rat, or a stoat, or that, when I war a-beatin' the bushes.'

Bob had drawn out a dirty canvas bag, and would perhaps not have paused just then if Maggie had not entered the room and darted a look of surprise and curiosity at him, whereupon he pulled his red locks again with due respect. But the next moment the sense of the altered room came upon Maggie with a force that overpowered the thought of Bob's presence. Her eyes had immediately glanced from him to the place where the book-case had hung and below it the small table with the Bible and the few other books.

'Oh, Tom,' she burst out, clasping her hands, 'where are the books? Are those all they've left us?'

'I suppose so,' said Tom, with a sort of desperate indifference.

'Oh, but, Tom,' said Maggie, her eyes filling with tears, as she rushed up to the table to see what books had been rescued. 'Our dear old "Pilgrim's Progress" that you coloured with your little paints; and that picture of Pilgrim with a mantle on, looking just like a turtle – oh dear!' Maggie went on, half sobbing as she turned over the few books. 'I thought we should never part with that while we lived!'

Maggie turned away from the table and threw herself in a chair, with the big tears ready to roll down her cheeks – quite blinded to the presence of Bob, who was looking at her with with perceptions more perfect than his comprehension.

'Well, Bob,' said Tom, feeling that the subject of the books was unseasonable, 'I suppose you just came to see me because we're in trouble? That was very good-natured of you.'

'I'll tell you how it is, Master Tom,' said Bob, beginning to untwist his canvas bag. 'You see, I'n been with a barge this two 'ear – if it wasn't when I was tentin' the furnace, between whiles, at Torry's Mill. But a fortni't ago I'd a rare bit o' luck – a fire i' Torry's Mill, an' I doused it, else it 'ud ha' set th' oil alight, an' the genelman gen me ten suvreigns. Here they are – all but one! I'n changed one o' the suvreigns to buy my mother a goose for dinner, an' I'n bought a blue plush wescoat, an' a sealskin cap. So I'll thank you to take the nine suvreigns, Mr Tom, and set yoursen up with 'em somehow – if it's true as the master's broke. They mayn't go fur enough – but they'll help.'

Tom was touched keenly enough to forget his pride and suspicion.

'You're a very kind fellow, Bob,' he said, colouring, with that little diffident tremor in his voice, which gave a certain charm even to Tom's pride and severity, 'and I shan't forget you again, though I didn't know you this evening. But I can't take the nine sovereigns: I should be taking your little fortune from you, and they wouldn't do me much good either.'

'Wouldn't they, Mr Tom?' said Bob, regretfully. 'Now don't say so 'cause you think I want 'em. I aren't a poor chap! An' I'm such a lucky chap: an' I doubt you aren't quite so lucky, Mr Tom – th' old master isn't, anyhow – an' so you might take a slice o' my luck, an' no harm done. Come, think better on it, Mr Tom, for old 'quintance sake – else I shall think you bear me a grudge.'

Bob pushed the sovereigns forward, but before Tom could speak, Maggie – clasping her hands, and looking at Bob, said—

'Why, I think you're the kindest person in the world!'

Bob smiled with pleasure at this handsome eulogy – especially from a young lass who, as he informed his mother that evening, had 'such uncommon eyes, they looked somehow as they made him feel nohow.'

'No, indeed, Bob, I can't take them,' said Tom; 'but don't think I feel your kindness less because I say no. I don't want to take anything from anybody, but to work my own way. And those sovereigns wouldn't help me much – they wouldn't, really – if I were to take them. Let me shake hands with you instead.'

Tom put out his pink palm, and Bob was not slow to place his hard, grimy hand within it.

'Let me put the sovereigns in the bag again,' said Maggie; 'and if ever Tom or my father wants help that you can give, we'll let you know – won't we, Tom? That's what you would like – to have us always depend on you as a friend that we can go to – isn't it, Bob?'

'Yes, Miss, and thank you,' said Bob, reluctantly taking the money; 'that's what I'd like – anything as you like. An' I wish you good-bye, Miss, and good-luck, Mr Tom, and thank you for shaking hands wi' me, *though* you wouldn't take the money.'

7

How a Hen Takes to Stratagem

The days passed, and while Mr Tulliver was slowly becoming himself again, his lot was hastening towards its moment of most palpable change. By the beginning of the second week in January the bills were out advertising the sale, under a decree of Chancery, of Mr Tulliver's farming and other stock, to be followed by a sale of the mill and land, held in the proper after-dinner hour at the Golden Lion. The miller himself, unaware of the lapse of time, fancied himself still in that first state of his misfortunes when expedients might be thought of; and often in his conscious hours talked in a feeble, disjointed manner, of plans he would carry out when he 'got well.' The wife and children were not without hope of an issue that would at least save Mr Tulliver from leaving the old spot, and seeking an entirely strange life. For uncle Deane had been induced to interest himself in this stage of the business. It would not, he acknowledged, be a bad speculation for Guest & Co. to buy Dorlcote Mill, and carry on the business, which was a good one, and might be increased by the addition of steam-power; in which case Tulliver might be retained as manager. Still Mr Deane would say nothing decided about the matter: the fact that Wakem held the mortgage on the land might put it into his head to bid for the whole estate, and further, to outbid the cautious firm of Guest & Co., who did not carry on business on sentimental grounds. Mr Deane was obliged to tell Mrs Tulliver something to that effect, when he rode over to the mill to inspect the books.

Still, it was clear that Mr Deane was kindly disposed towards the Tullivers. One day he had brought Lucy, who was come home for the Christmas holidays, and the little blond angel-head had pressed itself against Maggie's darker cheek with many kisses and some tears. Perhaps Lucy's anxious pitying questions about her poor cousins helped to make uncle Deane more prompt in finding Tom a place in the warehouse, and in putting him in the way of getting evening lessons in book-keeping and calculation.

That might have cheered the lad and fed his hopes a little, if there had not come at the same time the much-dreaded blow of finding that his father must be a bankrupt, after all; the deficiency at the bank, as well as the other debts, which would make the assets shrink into unequivocal disproportion. He was sadly in want of something to keep up his spirits a little in the unpleasant newness of his position – suddenly transported from the easy carpeted *ennui* of study-hours at Mr Spelling's, to the companionship of sacks and hides, and bawling men thundering down heavy weights at his elbow. The first step towards getting on in the world was a chill, dusty, noisy affair, and implied going without one's tea in order to stay in St Ogg's and have an evening lesson from a one-armed elderly clerk, in a room smelling strongly of bad tobacco. Tom's young pink-and-white face had its colours very much deadened by the time he took off his hat at home, and sat down with keen hunger to his supper. No wonder he was a little cross if his mother or Maggie spoke to him.

But all this while Mrs Tulliver was brooding over a scheme by which she, and no one else, would avert the result most to be dreaded, and prevent Wakem from entertaining the purpose of bidding for the mill. Mrs Tulliver had begun to think that she had been too passive in life; and that, if she had applied her mind to business, and taken a strong resolution now and then, it would have been all the better for her and her family. Nobody, it appeared, had thought of going to speak to Wakem on this business of the mill; and yet, Mrs Tulliver reflected, it would have been quite the shortest method of securing the right end. And now that Mrs Tulliver had come to the conclusion that her husband was very much in the wrong to bring her into this trouble, she was inclined to think that his opinion of Wakem was wrong too. The attorney might be a very reasonable man – why not? He had married a Miss Clint, and at the time Mrs Tulliver had heard of that marriage, she knew no harm of Wakem. And certainly towards herself – whom he knew to have been a Miss Dodson – it was out of all possibility that he could entertain anything but goodwill, when it was once brought home to his observation that she, for her part, had never wanted to go to law, and indeed was at present disposed to take Mr Wakem's view of all subjects rather than her husband's. In fact, if that attorney saw a respectable matron like herself disposed 'to give him good words,' why shouldn't he listen to her representations? For she would put the matter clearly before him, which had never been done yet.

This unusual concentration of thought naturally gave Mrs Tulliver an unusual power of device and determination; and a day or two before the sale, to be held at the Golden Lion, when there was no longer any time to be lost, she carried out her plan by a stratagem. There were pickles in question – a large stock of pickles and ketchup which Mrs Tulliver possessed, and which Mr Hyndmarsh the grocer would certainly purchase if she could transact the business in a personal interview, so she would walk with Tom to St Ogg's that morning: and when Tom urged that she might let the pickles be, at present – he didn't like her to go about just yet – she appeared so hurt at this conduct in her son that he gave way, and they walked together until she turned towards Danish Street, where Mr Hyndmarsh retailed his grocery, not far from the offices of Mr Wakem.

That gentleman was not yet come to his office: would Mrs Tulliver sit down by the fire in his private room and wait for him? She had not long to wait before the punctual attorney entered, knitting his brow with an examining glance at the stout blond woman who rose, curtsying deferentially.

'Mrs Tulliver, I think?' said Mr Wakem, a tallish man, with an aquiline nose and abundant iron-grey hair.

'Yes, sir. Miss Elizabeth Dodson as was.'

'Pray be seated. You have some business with me?'

'Well, sir, yes,' said Mrs Tulliver, beginning to feel alarmed at her own courage, now she was really in presence of the formidable man, and reflecting that she had not settled with herself how she should begin. Mr Wakem felt in his waistcoat-pockets and looked at her in silence.

'I hope, sir,' she began at last, 'I hope, sir, you're not a-thinking as I bear you any ill-will because of my husband's losing his lawsuit, and the bailies being put in, and the linen being sold – oh dear ... for I wasn't brought up in that way. I'm sure you remember my father, sir, for he was close friends with Squire Darleigh, and we allays went to the dances. And as for going to law, and losing money, and having sales before you're dead, I never saw anything o' that before I was married, nor for a long while after. And as for being drawn t' abuse you as other folks abuse you, sir, *that* I niver was, and nobody can say it of me.'

Mrs Tulliver shook her head a little, and looked at the hem of her pocket-handkerchief.

'I've no doubt of what you say, Mrs Tulliver,' said Mr Wakem, with cold politeness. 'But what do you want to ask me?'

'Why, sir, if you'll be so good,' said Mrs Tulliver, starting a little, and speaking more hurriedly, 'if you'll be so good not to buy the mill an' the land – only my husband 'ull be like mad at your having it.'

Something like a new thought flashed across Mr Wakem's face as he said, 'Who told you I meant to buy it?'

'Why, sir, it was Mr Glegg and Mr Deane; and Mr Deane thinks as Guest & Co. 'ud buy the mill and let Mr Tulliver work it for 'em, if you didn't bid for it and raise the price. And it 'ud be such a thing for my husband to stay where he is, if he could get his living: for it was his father's before him, the mill was, and his grandfather built it.'

'What! Guest & Co. would keep the mill in their own hands, I suppose, and pay your husband wages?'

'Oh dear, sir, it's hard to think of,' said poor Mrs Tulliver, a little tear making its way, 'as my husband should take wage. But it 'ud look more like what used to be, to stay at the mill than to go anywhere else.'

'Well, but if I bought the mill, and allowed your husband to act as my manager in the same way, how then?' said Mr Wakem.

'Oh, sir, I doubt he could niver be got to do it, not if the very mill stood still to beg and pray of him. For your name's like poison to him, it's so as never was; and he looks upon it as you've been the ruin of him all along. I've allays told him he was wrong ...'

'He's a pig-headed, foul-mouthed fool!' burst out Mr Wakem, forgetting himself.

'Oh dear, sir!' said Mrs Tulliver, frightened at a result so different from the one she had fixed her mind on; 'I wouldn't wish to contradict you, but it's like enough he's changed his mind with this illness – he's forgot a many things he used to talk about ...'

Mr Wakem rose, opened the door, and called to one of his clerks.

'You must excuse me for interrupting you, Mrs Tulliver; I have business that must be attended to; and I think there is nothing more necessary to be said.'

Poor Mrs Tulliver could make no answer to the attorney's 'good morning,' but curtsied and walked out in silence.

Although, when Mr Wakem entered his office that morning, he had had no intention of purchasing Dorlcote Mill, Mrs Tulliver had suggested to him several determining motives, and he was one of those men who can be prompt without being rash, because their motives run in fixed tracks, and they have no need to reconcile conflicting aims.

Wakem had not the same sort of inveterate hatred towards Tulliver that Tulliver had towards him. If Mr Tulliver had ever seriously injured or thwarted the attorney, Wakem would not have refused him the distinction of being a special object of his vindictiveness. But when Mr Tulliver called Wakem a rascal at the market dinner-table, the attorney's clients were not a whit inclined to withdraw their business from him; the majority of substantial men then present were perfectly contented with the fact that 'Wakem was Wakem;' that is to say, a man who always knew the stepping stones that would carry him through very muddy bits of practice. A man who had made a large fortune, had a handsome house among the trees at Tofton, and decidedly the finest stock of port-wine in the neighbourhood of St Ogg's, was likely to feel himself on a level with public opinion. Tulliver, then, could be no obstruction to Wakem; on the contrary, he was the poor devil whom the lawyer had defeated several times – a hot-tempered fellow, who would always give you a handle against him. To see people who have been only insignificantly offensive to us, reduced in life and humiliated without any special efforts of ours, is apt to have a soothing, flattering influence: Providence, it appears, has undertaken the task of retribution for us; and really, by an agreeable constitution of things, our enemies somehow *don't* prosper.

Wakem was not without this parenthetic vindictiveness towards the uncomplimentary miller; and now Mrs Tulliver had put the notion into his head, it presented itself to him as a pleasure to do the very thing that would cause Mr Tulliver the most deadly mortification – and a pleasure of a complex kind, not made up of crude malice, but mingling with it the relish of self-approbation. To see an enemy humiliated gives a certain contentment, but this is jejune compared with the highly-blent satisfaction of seeing him humiliated by your benevolent action or concession on his behalf. That is a sort of revenge which falls into the scale of virtue, and Wakem was not without an intention of keeping that scale respectably filled. Here was an opportunity of providing for another by making him his own servant. Tulliver, with his rough tongue filed by a sense of obligation, would make a better servant than any chance-fellow who was cap-in-hand for a situation. Tulliver was known to be a man of proud honesty. But there were good reasons for purchasing Dorlcote Mill, quite apart from any benevolent vengeance on the miller. It was really a capital investment; besides, Guest & Co. were going to bid for it. Mr Guest and Mr Wakem were on friendly dining terms, and the attorney liked to predominate over a ship-owner and mill-owner who was a little too loud in the town affairs as well as in his table-talk. For Wakem was not a mere man of business: he was considered a pleasant fellow in the upper circles of St Ogg's – had certainly been an excellent husband and father: at church, when he went there, he sat under the handsomest of mural monuments erected to the memory of his wife. Most men would have married again under his circumstances, but he was said to be more tender to his deformed son than most men were to their best-shapen offspring. Not that Mr Wakem had not other sons besides Philip; but towards them he held only a chiaroscuro parentage, and provided for them in a grade of life duly beneath his own. In this face, indeed, there lay the clenching motive to the purchase of Dorlcote Mill. While Mrs Tulliver was talking, it had occurred to the rapid-minded lawyer, among all the other circumstances of the case, that his purchase would, in a few years to come, furnish a highly suitable position for a certain favourite lad whom he meant to bring on in the world.

8

Daylight on the Wreck

It was a clear frosty January day on which Mr Tulliver first came downstairs. This resolution to come downstairs was heard with trembling by the wife and children. Mrs Tulliver said Tom must not go to St Ogg's at the usual hour – he must wait and see his father downstairs; and Tom complied, though with an intense inward shrinking from the painful scene. The hearts of all three had been more deeply dejected than ever during the last few days. For both mill and land had been knocked down to Wakem, who had been over the premises, and had laid before Mr Deane and Mr Glegg, in Mrs Tulliver's presence, his willingness to employ Mr Tulliver, in case of his recovery, as a manager of the business. This proposition had occasioned much family debating. Uncles and aunts were almost unanimously of opinion that such an offer ought not to be rejected. Here was an opportunity for Mr Tulliver to provide for his wife and daughter without any assistance from his wife's relations, and without that too evident descent into pauperism which makes it annoying to respectable people to meet the degraded member of the family by the wayside.

'Tom,' Maggie said, when they were out of their father's room together, 'we *must* try to make father understand a little of what has happened before he goes downstairs. But we must get my mother away. She will say something that will do harm. Ask Kezia to fetch her down, and keep her engaged with something in the kitchen.'

Kezia was equal to the task. Having declared her intention of staying till the master could get about again, 'wage or no wage,' she had found a certain recompense in keeping a strong hand over her mistress. On this particular occasion there were drying clothes to be fetched in: she wished to know if one pair of hands could do everything indoors and out, and observed that *she* should have thought it would be good for Mrs Tulliver to put on her bonnet, and get a breath of fresh air by doing that needful piece of work. Poor Mrs Tulliver went submissively downstairs: to be ordered about by a servant was the last remnant of her household dignities – she would soon have no servant to scold her.

Mr Tulliver was resting in his chair a little after the fatigue of dressing, and Maggie and Tom were seated near him, when Luke entered to ask if he should help master downstairs.

'Ay, ay, Luke, stop a bit, sit down,' said Mr Tulliver, pointing his stick towards a chair.

Mr Tulliver leaned forward, resting his elbows on the armchair, and looking on the ground as if in search of something: the idea that much had happened of which he knew nothing had often transiently arrested him before, but it came upon him now with entire novelty.

'Father,' said Tom, 'you needn't trouble your mind about business until you are quite well: everything is settled about that for the present – about the mill and the land and the debts.'

'What's settled, then?' said his father, angrily.

'Don't you take on too much about it, sir,' said Luke. 'You'd ha' paid iverybody if you could – that's what I said to Master Tom – I said you'd ha' paid iverybody if you could.'

Good Luke felt, after the manner of contented hard-working men whose lives have been spent in servitude, that sense of natural fitness in rank which made his master's downfall a tragedy to him. He was urged, in his slow way, to say something that would express his share in the family sorrow, and these words, which he had used over and over again to Tom when he wanted to decline the full payment of his fifty pounds out of the children's money, were the most ready to his tongue. They were just the words to lay the most painful hold on his master's bewildered mind.

'Paid everybody?' he said, with vehement agitation, his face flushing. 'Why ... have they sold me up, then?' he said, more calmly, as if he were possessed simply by the desire to know what had happened.

'Everything is sold, father; but we don't know all about the mill and the land yet,' said Tom, anxious to ward off any question leading to the fact that Wakem was the purchaser.

'You must not be surprised to see the room look very bare downstairs, father,' said Maggie.

'Let us go – help me down, Luke – I'll go and see everything,' said Mr Tulliver, leaning on his stick, and stretching out his other hand towards Luke.

'Ay, sir,' said Luke, as he gave his arm to his master, 'you'll make up your mind to't a bit better when you've seen iverything: you'll get used to't.'

Maggie ran on before to see that all was right in the dreary parlour, where the fire, dulled by the frosty sunshine, seemed part of the general shabbiness. She stood with a beating heart to see him enter and look round for the first time. Tom advanced before him, carrying the leg-rest, and stood beside Maggie on the hearth.

Mr Tulliver paused just inside the door, resting on Luke, and looking round him at all the bare places, which for him were filled with the shadows of departed objects – the daily companions of his life. His faculties seemed to be renewing their strength from getting a footing on this demonstration of the senses.

'Ah!' he said, slowly, moving towards his chair, 'they've sold me up ... they've sold me up.'

Then seating himself, and laying down his stick, while Luke left the room, he looked round again.

'They've left the big Bible,' he said. 'It's got everything in – when I was born and married – bring it me, Tom.'

The quarto Bible was laid open before him at the fly-leaf, and while he was reading with slowly-travelling eyes, Mrs Tulliver entered the room, but stood in mute surprise to find her husband down already, and with the great Bible before him. He seemed to be pausing over the record of his sister's birth and marriage, as if it were suggesting new thoughts to him: then he suddenly looked up at Tom, and said, in a sharp tone of alarm—

'They haven't come upo' Moss for the money as I lent him, have they?'

'No, father,' said Tom; 'the note was burnt.'

Mr Tulliver turned his eyes on the page again, and presently said—

'Ah ... Elizabeth Dodson ... it's eighteen year since I married her.'

'Come next Ladyday,' said Mrs Tulliver, going up to his side and looking at the page.

Her husband fixed his eyes earnestly on her face.

'Poor Bessy,' he said, 'you was a pretty lass then – everybody said so – and I used to think you kept your good looks rarely. But you're sorely aged ... don't you bear me ill-will ... I meant to do well by you ... we promised one another for better or for worse ...'

'But I never thought it 'ud be so for worse as this,' said poor Mrs Tulliver.

'Oh, mother,' said Maggie, 'don't talk in that way.'

'No, I know you won't let your poor mother speak ... that's been the way all my life ... your father never minded what I said ... it 'ud have been o' no use for me to beg and pray ... and it 'ud be no use now, not if I was to go down o' my hands and knees ...'

'Don't say so, Bessy,' said Mr Tulliver, whose pride, in these first moments of humiliation, was in abeyance to the sense of some justice in his wife's reproach. 'If there's anything left as I could do to make you amends, I wouldn't say you nay.'

'Then we might stay here and get a living, and I might keep among my own sisters ... and me been such a good wife to you, and never crossed you from week's end to week's end ... and they all say so ... they say it 'ud be nothing but right ... only you're so turned against Wakem.'

'Mother,' said Tom, severely, 'this is not the time to talk about that.'

'Let her be,' said Mr Tulliver. 'Say what you mean, Bessy.'

'Why, now the mill and the land's all Wakem's, and he's got everything in his hands, what's the use o' setting your face against him? – when he says you may stay here, and says you may manage the business, and have thirty shillings a week, and a horse to ride about to market? And where have we got to put our heads? We must go into one o' the cottages in the village ... and me and my children brought down to that ... and all because you must set your mind against folks till there's no turning you.'

Mr Tulliver had sunk back in his chair, trembling.

'You may do as you like wi' me, Bessy,' he said in a low voice; 'I've been the bringing of you to poverty ... I'm nought but a bankrupt – it's no use standing up for anything now.'

'Father,' said Tom, 'I don't agree with my mother or my uncles, and I don't think you ought to submit to be under Wakem. I get a pound a week now, and you can find something else to do when you get well.'

'Say no more, Tom, say no more: I've had enough for this day. Give me a kiss, Bessy, and let us bear one another no ill-will: we shall never be young again ... this world's been too many for me.'

9

An Item Added to the Family Register

There were times when poor Tulliver thought the fulfilment of his promise to Bessy was something quite too hard for human nature: but there were many feelings arguing on her side, besides the sense that life had been made hard to her by having married him. He saw a possibility, by much pinching, of saving money out of his salary towards paying a second dividend to his creditors, and it would not be easy elsewhere to get a situation such as he could fill.

But the strongest influence of all was the love of the old premises where he had run about when he was a boy, just as Tom had done after him. It was when he got able to walk about and look at all the old objects, that he felt the strain of his clinging affection for the old home as part of his life, part of himself. He couldn't bear to think of himself living on any other spot than this, where he knew the sound of every gate and door, and felt that the shape and colour of every roof and weather-stain and broken hillock was good, because his growing senses had been fed on them.

'Ay, Luke,' he said, one afternoon, as he stood looking over the orchard gate, 'I remember the day they planted those apple-trees. My father was a huge man for planting – and I used to stand i' the cold with him, and follow him about like a dog.'

Then he turned round, and, leaning against the gate-post, looked at the opposite buildings.

'The old mill 'ud miss me, I think, Luke.'

'Ay, sir,' said Luke, with soothing sympathy, 'you'd be a deal better here nor in some new place. I can't abide new places mysen. It's poor work, changing your country-side.'

The walk was finished in silence after this. Mr Tulliver had relapsed from his recollections into a painful meditation on the choice of hardships before him. Maggie noticed that he was unusually absent that evening at tea; and afterwards he sat leaning forward in his chair, looking at the ground, moving his lips, and shaking his head from time to time.

'Why, how is it Tom doesn't come?' said Mr Tulliver, impatiently.

'Dear heart! is it time? I must go and get his supper,' said Mrs Tulliver, laying down her knitting, and leaving the room.

'It's nigh upon half-past eight,' said Mr Tulliver. 'He'll be here soon. Go, go and get the big Bible, and open it at the beginning, where everything's set down. And get the pen and ink.'

Maggie obeyed, wondering: but her father gave no further orders, and only sat listening for Tom's footfall on the gravel. There was a strange light in his eyes that rather frightened Maggie.

'There he is, then,' said Mr Tulliver in an excited way, when the knock came at last. Maggie went to open the door, but her mother came out of the kitchen hurriedly, saying, 'Stop a bit, Maggie; I'll open it.'

Mrs Tulliver had begun to be a little frightened at her boy, but she was jealous of every office others did for him.

'Your supper's ready by the kitchen-fire, my boy,' she said, as he took off his hat and coat. 'You shall have it by yourself, just as you like, and I won't speak to you.'

'I think my father wants Tom, mother,' said Maggie; 'he must come into the parlour first.'

Tom entered with his usual saddened evening face, but his eyes fell immediately on the open Bible and the inkstand, and he glanced with a look of anxious surprise at his father, who was saying—

'Come, come, you're late – I want you.'

'Is there anything the matter, father?' said Tom.

'You sit down – all of you,' said Mr Tulliver peremptorily. 'And, Tom, sit down here; I've got something for you to write i' the Bible.'

They all three sat down, looking at him. He began to speak, slowly, looking first at his wife—

'I've made up my mind, Bessy, and I'll be as good as my word to you. I'll stop in the old place, and I'll serve under Wakem – and I'll serve him like an honest man: there's no Tulliver but what's honest, mind that, Tom' – here his voice rose: 'I'm an honest man, though I shall never hold my head up no more – I'm a tree as is broke—'

He paused and looked on the ground. Then suddenly raising his head, he said, in a louder yet deeper tone—

'But I won't forgive him! I know what they say – he never meant me any harm – but he's a fine gentleman – I know, I know. I shouldn't ha' gone to law, they say. But who made it so as there was no arbitrating and no justice to be got? It signifies nothing to him – I know that; he's one o' them fine gentlemen as get money by doing business for poorer folks, and when he's made beggars of 'em he'll give 'em charity. I won't forgive him! I wish he might be punished with shame till his own son 'ud like to forget him. But he won't – he's too big a raskill to let the law lay hold on him. And you mind this, Tom – you never forgive him neither, if you mean to be my son. There'll maybe come a time when you may make him feel – it'll never come to me – I'n got my head under the yoke. Now write – write it i' the Bible.'

'What am I to write?' said Tom, with gloomy submission.

'Write as your father, Edward Tulliver, took service under John Wakem, the man as had helped to ruin him, because I'd promised my wife to make her what amends I could for her trouble, and because I want to die in th' old place, where I was born and my father was born. Put that i' the right words – you know how – and then write, as I don't forgive Wakem for all that; and for all I'll serve him honest, I wish evil may befall him. Write that.'

There was a dead silence as Tom's pen moved along the paper: Mrs Tulliver looked scared, and Maggie trembled like a leaf.

'Now let me hear what you've wrote,' said Mr Tulliver. Tom read aloud, slowly.

'Now write – write as you'll remember what Wakem's done to your father, and you'll make him and his feel it, if ever the day comes. And sign your name Thomas Tulliver.'

'Oh, no, father, dear father!' said Maggie, almost choked with fear. 'You shouldn't make Tom write that.'

'Be quiet, Maggie!' said Tom. 'I *shall* write it.'

BOOK FOURTH

The Valley of Humiliation

1

The Torn Nest Is Pierced by the Thorns

A time of utmost need was to come to Maggie, with her short span of thirteen years. She was strangely old for her age in everything except in her entire want of that prudence and self-command which were the qualities that made Tom manly in the midst of his intellectual boyishness. And now her lot was beginning to have a still, sad monotony, which threw her more than ever on her inward self. Her father was acting as Wakem's manager on the old spot. Tom went to and fro every morning and evening, and became more and more silent in the short intervals at home. One day was like another, and Tom's interest in life, driven back and crushed on every other side, was concentrating itself into the one channel of ambitious resistance to misfortune. Poor Mrs Tulliver, it seemed, would never recover her old self. It was piteous to see the comely woman getting thinner and more worn under a bodily as well as mental restlessness, which made her often wander about the empty house after her work was done, until Maggie, becoming alarmed about her, would seek her, and bring her down by telling her how it vexed Tom that she was injuring her health by never sitting down and resting herself. Yet amidst this helpless imbecility there was a touching trait of humble self-devoting maternity, which made Maggie feel tenderly towards her poor mother. She would let Maggie do none of the work that was heaviest and most soiling to the hands, and was quite peevish when Maggie attempted to relieve her from her grate-brushing and scouring. She would say: 'it's your mother's place to do that. I can't do the sewing – my eyes fail me.' And she would still brush and carefully tend Maggie's hair, which she had become reconciled to, in spite of its refusal to curl, now it was so long and massy. Maggie was not her pet child; the mother pleased herself with wearing out her own hands to save the hands that had so much more life in them.

The constant presence of her mother's regretful bewilderment was less painful to Maggie than that of her father's sullen incommunicative depression. Mr Tulliver lingered nowhere away from home: he hurried away from market, he refused all invitations to stay and chat, as in old times, in the houses where he called on business. He could not be reconciled with his lot: there was no attitude in which his pride did not feel its bruises; and in all behaviour towards him, whether kind or cold, he detected an allusion to the change in his circumstances. Even the days on which Wakem came to ride round the land and inquire into the business, were not so black to him as those market-days on which he had met several creditors who had accepted a composition from him. To save something towards the repayment of those creditors was the object towards which he was now bending all his thoughts and efforts; and under the influence of this all-compelling demand of his nature, the somewhat profuse man who hated to be stinted or to stint any one else in his own house, was gradually metamorphosed into the keen-eyed grudger of morsels. Mrs Tulliver could not economise enough to satisfy him in their food and firing; and he would eat nothing himself but what was of the coarsest quality. Tom, though depressed and strongly repelled by his father's sullenness, and the dreariness of home, entered thoroughly into his father's feelings about paying the creditors; and the poor lad brought his first quarter's money, with a delicious sense of achievement, and gave it to his father to put into the tin box which held the savings. The little store of sovereigns in the tin box seemed to be the only sight that brought a faint beam of pleasure into the miller's eyes – faint and transient, for it was soon dispelled by the thought that the time would be long – perhaps longer than his life – before the narrow savings could remove the hateful incubus of debt. A deficit of more than five hundred pounds, with the accumulating interest, seemed a deep pit to fill with the savings from thirty shillings a week, even when Tom's probable savings were to be added. On this one point there was entire community of feeling in the four widely differing beings who sat round the dying fire of sticks, which made a cheap warmth for them on the verge of bedtime. To all his requirements of household economy, Mrs Tulliver was submissive: her only rebellion was to smuggle into the kitchen something that would make rather a better supper than usual for Tom.

2

A Voice from the Past

One afternoon, when the chestnuts were coming into flower, Maggie had brought her chair outside the front door, and was seated there with a book on her knees. Her dark eyes had wandered from the book. It had been a more miserable day than usual: her father, after a visit of Wakem's, had had a paroxysm of rage, in which for some trifling fault he had beaten the boy who served in the mill. Once before, since his illness, he had had a similar paroxysm, in which he had beaten his horse, and the scene had left a lasting terror in Maggie's mind lest her father should add to his present misfortune the wretchedness of doing something irretrievably disgraceful. Her eyes had filled with tears.

Suddenly she was roused by the sound of the opening gate and of footsteps on the gravel. It was a man in a sealskin cap and a blue plush waistcoat, carrying a pack on his back, and followed closely by a bull-terrier of brindled coat and defiant aspect.

'Oh, Bob, it's you!' said Maggie, starting up with a smile of pleased recognition; 'I'm so glad to see you.'

'Thank you, Miss,' said Bob, lifting his cap and showing a delighted face, but immediately relieving himself of some accompanying embarrassment by looking down at his dog, and saying in a tone of disgust, 'Get out wi' you, you thunderin' sawney!'

'My brother is not at home yet, Bob,' said Maggie; 'he is always at St Ogg's in the daytime.'

'Well, Miss,' said Bob, 'I should be glad to see Mr Tom – but that isn't just what I'm come for – look here!'

Bob was in the act of depositing his pack on the door-step, and with it a row of small books fastened together with string. Apparently, however, they were not the object to which he wished to call Maggie's attention, but rather something which he had carried under his arm, wrapped in a red handkerchief.

'See here!' he said again, laying the red parcel on the others and unfolding it; 'you won't think I'm a-makin' too free, Miss, I hope, but I lighted on these books, and I thought they might make up to you a bit for them as you've lost; for I heared you speak o' pictures – an' as for pictures, *look* here!'

The opening of the red handkerchief had disclosed a super-annuated 'Keepsake' and six or seven numbers of a 'Portrait Gallery,' in royal octavo; and the emphatic request to look referred to a portrait of George the Fourth in all the majesty of his depressed cranium and voluminous neckcloth.

'There's all sorts o' genelmen here,' Bob went on, turning over the leaves with some excitement. 'An' here,' he said, opening the 'Keepsake,' '*here's* ladies for you. But, lors! I shouldn't know what to say to 'em. They'll be more fittin' company for you, Miss.'

'And you've bought them for me, Bob?' said Maggie, deeply touched by this simple kindness. 'How very, very good of you! But I'm afraid you gave a great deal of money for them.'

'Not me!' said Bob. 'I'd ha' gev three times the money if they'll make up to you a bit for them as was sold away from you, Miss. For I'n niver forgot how you looked when you fretted about the books bein' gone – it's stuck by me as if it was a pictur hingin' before me. An' when I see'd the book open upo' the stall, wi' the lady lookin' out of it wi' eyes a bit like your'n when you was frettin' – you'll excuse my takin' the liberty, Miss – I thought I'd make

free to buy it for you, an' then I bought the books full o' genelmen
to match – an' then' – here Bob took up the small stringed packet
of books – 'I thought you might like a bit more print as well as the
picturs, an' I got these for a say-so – they're cram-full o' print, an'
I thought they'd do no harm comin' along wi' these bettermost
books. An' I hope you won't say me nay, an' tell me as you won't
have 'em, like Mr Tom did wi' the suvreigns.'

'No, indeed, Bob,' said Maggie, 'I'm very thankful to you for
thinking of me. I don't think any one ever did such a kind thing
for me before. I haven't many friends who care for me.'

'Hev a dog, Miss! – they're better friends nor any Christian,'
said Bob, laying down his pack again, which he had taken up with
the intention of hurrying away; for he felt considerable shyness
in talking to a young lass like Maggie. 'I can't give you Mumps,
'cause he'd break his heart to go away from me, but I'd get you a
pup, Miss, an' welcome.'

'No, thank you, Bob. We have a yard dog, and I mayn't keep a
dog of my own. Would Mumps let me pat him?'

'Ay, that would he, and thank you. He knows his company,
Mumps does. Lors, I talk to him by th' hour together, when I'm
walking i' lone places, and if I'n done a bit o' mischief, I allays tell
him. I'n got no secrets but what Mumps knows 'em.' He picked
his pack up. 'I wish you good-evening, Miss.'

'Good-bye, Bob. Thank you very much for bringing me the
books. And come again to see Tom.'

'Yes, Miss,' said Bob; he touched his cap and walked away.

Maggie carried Bob's present of books away to her bedroom,
laying them down there and seating herself on her one stool,
without caring to look at them just yet. She leaned her cheek
against the window-frame, and thought that the light-hearted
Bob had a lot much happier than hers.

Maggie's sense of loneliness, and utter privation of joy, had
deepened with the brightness of advancing spring. Every affection, every delight, the poor child had had, was like an aching
nerve to her. There was no music for her any more – no piano, no
harmonised voices, no delicious stringed instruments, with their

passionate cries of imprisoned spirits sending a strange vibration through her frame. And of all her school-life there was nothing left her now but her little collection of school-books, which she turned over with a sickening sense that she knew them all, and they were all barren of comfort. If she could have had all Scott's novels and all Byron's poems! then, perhaps, she might have found happiness enough to dull her sensibility to her actual daily life. And yet ... they were hardly what she wanted. She wanted some explanation of this hard, real life: the unhappy-looking father, seated at the dull breakfast-table; the childish, bewildered mother; the little sordid tasks that filled the hours, or the more oppressive emptiness of weary, joyless leisure; the need of some tender, demonstrative love; the cruel sense that Tom didn't mind what she thought or felt.

At last Maggie's eyes glanced down on the books that lay on the window-shelf; the 'Christian Year' – that seemed to be a hymn-book, and she laid it down again; but *Thomas à Kempis?* – the name had come across her in her reading, and she felt the satisfaction, which every one knows, of getting some ideas to attach to a name that strays solitary in the memory. She took up the little, old, clumsy book with some curiosity: it had the corners turned down in many places, and some hand, now for ever quiet, had made at certain passages strong pen-and-ink marks, long since browned by time. Maggie turned from leaf to leaf, and read where the quiet hand pointed ...'Know that the love of thyself doth hurt thee more than anything in the world ... it is but little thou sufferest in comparison of them that have suffered so much, were so strongly tempted, so grievously afflicted, so many ways tried and exercised. Thou oughtest therefore to call to mind the more heavy sufferings to others, that thou mayest the easier bear thy little adversities. And if they seem not little unto thee, beware lest dry impatience be the cause thereof ... Blessed are those ears that receive the whispers of the divine voice, and listen not to the whisperings of the world. Blessed are those ears which hearken not unto the voice which soundeth outwardly, but unto the Truth, which teacheth inwardly ...'

A strange thrill of awe passed through Maggie while she read, as if she had been wakened in the night by a strain of solemn music, telling of beings whose souls had been astir while hers was in stupor. She went on from one brown mark to another, where the quiet hand seemed to point, hardly conscious that she was reading – seeming rather to listen while a low voice said—

'Why dost thou here gaze about, since this is not the place of thy rest? In heaven ought to be thy dwelling, and all earthly things are to be looked on as they forward thy journey thither. All things pass away, and thou together with them. Beware thou cleave not unto them, lest thou be entangled and perish ... I have often said unto thee, and now again I say the same, Forsake thyself, resign thyself, and thou shalt enjoy much inward peace ... Then shall all vain imaginations, evil perturbations, and superfluous cares fly away; then shall immoderate fear leave thee, and inordinate love shall die.'

Maggie drew a long breath and pushed her heavy hair back, as if to see a sudden vision more clearly. Here, then, was a secret of life that would enable her to renounce all other secrets – here was a sublime height to be reached without the help of outward things – here was insight, and strength, and conquest, to be won by means entirely within her own soul, where a supreme Teacher was waiting to be heard. It flashed through her like the suddenly apprehended solution of a problem, that all the miseries of her young life had come from fixing her heart on her own pleasure, as if that were the central necessity of the universe; and for the first time she saw the possibility of shifting the position from which she looked at the gratification of her own desires – of taking her stand out of herself, and looking at her own life as an insignificant part of a divinely-guided whole. She read on and on in the old book, devouring eagerly the dialogues with the invisible Teacher, the pattern of sorrow, the source of all strength; returning to it after she had been called away, and reading till the sun went down behind the willows. With all the hurry of an imagination that could never rest in the present, she sat in the deepening twilight forming plans of self-humiliation and entire devotedness; and, in the ardour of first discovery, renunciation seemed to her the entrance into that satisfaction which she had so long been craving in vain.

From what you know of her, you will not be surprised that Maggie threw some exaggeration and wilfulness, some pride and impetuosity even into her self-renunciation: her own life was still a drama for her, in which she demanded of herself that her part should be played with intensity. And so it came to pass that she often lost the spirit of humility by being excessive in the outward act; she often strove after too high a flight and came down with her poor little half-fledged wings dabbled in the mud. For example, she not only determined to work at plain sewing, that she might contribute something towards the fund in the tin box, but she went, in the first instance, in the zeal of self-mortification, to ask for it at a linen-shop in St Ogg's, instead of getting it in a more quiet and indirect way; and could see nothing but what was entirely wrong and unkind, nay, persecuting, in Tom's reproof of her for this unnecessary act. Tom was very hard to her, she used to think, in her long night-watchings – to her who had always loved him so; and then she strove to be contented with that hardness, and to require nothing.

In her first ardour she read so eagerly and constantly three books, the Bible, Thomas à Kempis, and the 'Christian Year' (no longer rejected as a 'hymn-book'), that they filled her mind with a continual stream of rhythmic memories; and she was too ardently learning to see all nature and life in the light of her new faith, to need any other material for her mind to work on, as she sat with her well-plied needle, making shirts and other complicated stitchings.

Hanging diligently over her sewing, Maggie was a sight any one might have been pleased to look at. That new inward life of hers, notwithstanding some volcanic upheavings of imprisoned passions, yet shone out in her face with a tender soft light that mingled itself as added loveliness with the gradually enriched colour and outline of her blossoming youth. Her mother felt the change in her with a sort of puzzled wonder that Maggie should be 'growing up so good;' it was amazing that this once 'contrairy' child was become so submissive, so backward to assert her own will. The mother was getting fond of her tall, brown girl; and Maggie, in spite of her own ascetic wish to have no personal adornment, was obliged to give way to her mother about her hair, and submit to have the abundant black locks plaited into a coronet on the summit of her head.

'Let your mother have that bit o' pleasure, my dear,' said Mrs Tulliver; 'I'd trouble enough with your hair once.'

So Maggie, glad of anything that would soothe her mother, and cheer their long day together, consented to the vain decoration, and showed a queenly head above her old frocks – steadily refusing, however, to look at herself in the glass. Mrs Tulliver liked to call the father's attention to Maggie's hair and other unexpected virtues, but he had a brusque reply to give.

'I knew well enough what she'd be, before now – it's nothing new to me. But it's a pity she isn't made o' commoner stuff – she'll be thrown away: there'll be nobody to marry her as is fit for her.'

BOOK FIFTH

Wheat and Tares

1

In the Red Deeps

The family sitting-room was a long room with a window at each end; one looking towards the croft and along the Ripple to the banks of the Floss, the other into the mill-yard. Maggie was sitting with her work against the latter window when she saw Mr Wakem entering the yard, as usual, on his fine black horse; but not alone, as usual. Some one was with him – a figure in a cloak, on a handsome pony. Maggie had hardly time to feel that it was Philip come back, before they were in front of the window, and he was raising his hat to her; while his father, catching the movement by a side-glance, looked sharply round at them both.

Maggie hurried away from the window and carried her work upstairs; for Mr Wakem sometimes came in and inspected the books, and Maggie felt that the meeting with Philip would be robbed of all pleasure in the presence of the two fathers. Maggie retained her childish gratitude and pity towards Philip, and remembered his cleverness; and in the early weeks of her loneliness she had continually recalled the image of him among the people who had been kind to her in life; often wishing she had him for a brother and a teacher, as they had fancied it might have been, in their talk together. But that sort of wishing had been banished along with other dreams that savoured of seeking her own will; and she thought, besides, that Philip might be altered by his life abroad – he might have become worldly, and really not care about her saying anything to him now. And yet, his face was wonderfully little altered – it was only a larger, more manly copy of the pale small-featured boy's face, with the grey eyes and the boyish waving brown hair; there was the old deformity to awaken the old pity; and after all her meditations, Maggie felt that she really *should* like to say a few words to him. He might still be melancholy, as he always used to be, and like her to look at him kindly. She snatched up her work, trying to repress the rising wishes by forcing her memory to recall snatches of hymns, until she saw Philip and his father returning along the road, and she could go down again.

It was far on in June now, and Maggie was inclined to lengthen the daily walk which was her one indulgence; but this day and the following she was so busy with work which must be finished that she never went beyond the gate, and satisfied her need of the open air by sitting out of doors. One of her frequent walks, when she was not obliged to go to St Ogg's, was to a spot that lay beyond what was called the 'Hill' – an insignificant rise of ground crowned by trees, lying along the side of the road which ran by the gates of Dorlcote Mill with pleasant fields behind it, bounded by the murmuring Ripple. Just where this line of bank sloped down again to the level, a by-road turned off and led to the other side of the rise, where it was broken into very capricious hollows and mounds by the working of an exhausted stone-quarry – so long exhausted that both mounds and hollows were now clothed with brambles and trees, and here and there by a stretch of grass which a few sheep kept close-nibbled. This place, called the Red Deeps, had a charm for Maggie especially in summer, when she could sit on a grassy hollow under the shadow of a branching ash, and listen to the hum of insects or see the sunlight piercing the distant boughs, as if to chase and drive home the truant heavenly blue of the wild hyacinths. In this June time too, the dog-roses were in their glory, and that was an additional reason why Maggie should direct her walk to the Red Deeps, rather than to any other spot, on the first day she was free to wander at her will – a pleasure she loved so well, that sometimes, in her ardours of renunciation, she thought she ought to deny herself the frequent indulgence in it.

You may see her now, as she walks down the favourite turning, and enters the Deeps by a narrow path through a group of Scotch firs; and now she is sure of being unseen, she takes off her bonnet and ties it over her arm. In her seventeenth year, youth and health have withstood well the involuntary and voluntary hardships of her lot, and the nights in which she has lain on the hard floor for a penance have left no obvious trace; the eyes are liquid, the brown cheek is firm and rounded, the full lips are red. With her dark colouring and jet crown surmounting her tall figure, she seems to have a sort of kinship with the grand Scotch firs, at which she is looking up as if she loved them well.

Maggie, while her eyes were still turned upward, became conscious of a moving shadow cast by the evening sun on the grassy path before her, and looked down with a startled gesture to see Philip Wakem, who first raised his hat, and then, blushing deeply, came forward to her and put out his hand. Maggie, too, coloured with surprise, which soon gave way to pleasure. She put out her hand and looked down at the lower deformed figure before her with frank eyes, filled for the moment with nothing but the memory of her child's feelings – a memory that was always strong in her. She was the first to speak.

'You startled me,' she said, smiling faintly; 'I never meet any one here. How came you to be walking here? Did you come to meet *me*?' Maggie felt herself a child again.

'Yes, I did,' said Philip, still embarrassed: 'I wished to see you very much. I watched a long while yesterday on the bank near your house to see if you would come out, but you never came. Then I watched again today, and when I saw the way you took, I kept you in sight and came down the bank, behind there. I hope you will not be displeased with me.'

'No,' said Maggie, with simple seriousness, walking on as if she meant Philip to accompany her, 'I'm very glad you came, for I wished very much to have an opportunity of speaking to you. I've never forgotten how good you were long ago to Tom, and me too; but I was not sure that you would remember us so well.'

'I can't believe that you have thought of me so much as I have thought of you,' said Philip, timidly. 'Do you know, when I was away, I made a picture of you as you looked that morning in the study when you said you would not forget me.'

Philip drew a large miniature-case from his pocket, and opened it. Maggie saw her old self leaning on a table, with her black locks hanging down behind her ears, looking into space with strange, dreamy eyes. It was a water-colour sketch, of real merit as a portrait.

'Oh dear,' said Maggie, smiling, and flushed with pleasure, 'what a queer little girl I was! I really *was* like a gypsy. I daresay I am now,' she added, after a little pause; 'am I like what you expected me to be?'

The words might have been those of a coquette, but the full bright glance Maggie turned on Philip was not that of a coquette. She really did hope he liked her face as it was now, but it was simply the rising again of her innate delight in admiration and love. Philip met her eyes and looked at her in silence for a long moment, before he said quietly, 'No, Maggie.'

The light died out a little from Maggie's face, and there was a slight trembling of the lip. Her eyelids fell lower, but she did not turn away her head, and Philip continued to look at her. Then he said slowly—

'You are very much more beautiful than I thought you would be.'

'Am I?' said Maggie, the pleasure returning in a deeper flush. She turned her face away from him and took some steps, looking straight before her in silence, as if she were adjusting her consciousness to this new idea. Philip seemed to like the silence well. He walked by her side, watching her face, as if that sight left no room for any other wish. They had passed from among the fir-trees, and had now come to a green hollow almost surrounded by an amphitheatre of the pale pink dog-roses. But as the light about them had brightened, Maggie's face had lost its glow. She stood still when they were in the hollows, and, looking at Philip again, she said, in a serious, sad voice—

'I wish we could have been friends – I mean, if it would have been good and right for us. But that is the trial I have to bear in everything: I may not keep anything I used to love when I was little. The old books went; and Tom is different – and my father. It is like death. I must part with everything I cared for when I was a child. And I must part with you: we must never take any notice of each other again. That was what I wanted to speak to you for. I wanted to let you know that Tom and I can't do as we like about such things, and that if I behave as if I had forgotten all about you, it is not out of any bad feeling.'

Maggie spoke with more and more sorrowful gentleness as she went on, and her eyes began to fill with tears. The deepening expression of pain on Philip's face gave him a stronger resemblance to his boyish self, and made the deformity appeal more strongly to her pity.

'I know – I see all that you mean,' he said in a voice that had become feebler from discouragement: 'I know what there is to keep us apart on both sides. But it is not right, Maggie – don't you be angry with me, I am so used to call you Maggie in my thoughts – it is not right to sacrifice everything to other people's unreasonable feelings. I would give up a great deal for *my* father; but I would not give up a friendship or – or an attachment of any sort, in obedience to any wish of his that I didn't recognise as right.'

'I don't know,' said Maggie, musingly. 'Often, when I have been angry and discontented, it has seemed to me that I was not bound to give up anything; and I have gone on thinking till it has seemed to me that I could think away all my duty. But I'm quite sure that whatever I might do, I should wish in the end that I had gone without anything for myself, rather than have made my father's life harder to him.'

'But would it make his life harder if we were to see each other sometimes?' said Philip.

'Oh, I'm sure he wouldn't like it,' said Maggie, in a distressed tone. 'My father feels so strongly about some things. He is not at all happy.'

'No more am I,' said Philip, impetuously: 'I am not happy.'

'Why?' said Maggie, gently. 'At least – I ought not to ask – but I'm very, very sorry.'

Philip turned to walk on, as if he had not patience to stand still any longer, and they went out of the hollow, winding amongst the trees and bushes in silence. After that last word of Philip's Maggie could not bear to insist immediately on their parting.

'I've been a great deal happier,' she said at last, timidly, 'since I have given up thinking about what is easy and pleasant, and being discontented because I couldn't have my own will. Our life is determined for us – and it makes the mind very free when we give up wishing, and only think of bearing what is laid upon us, and doing what is given us to do.'

'But I can't give up wishing,' said Philip, impatiently. 'It seems to me we can never give up longing and wishing while we are thoroughly alive. There are certain things we feel to be beautiful and good, and we *must* hunger after them. I delight in fine pictures – I long to be able to paint such. I strive and strive, and can't produce what I want. That is pain to me, and always *will* be pain, until my faculties lose their keenness, like aged eyes. Then there are many other things I long for' – here Philip hesitated a little, and then said – 'things that other men have, and that will always be denied me. My life will have nothing great or beautiful in it; I would rather not have lived.'

'Oh, Philip,' said Maggie, 'I wish you didn't feel so.' But her heart began to beat with something of Philip's discontent.

'Well then,' said he, turning quickly round and fixing his grey eyes entreatingly on her face, 'I should be contented to live, if you would let me see you sometimes.' Then, checked by a fear which her face suggested, he looked away again, and said more calmly, 'I have no friend to whom I can tell everything – no one who cares enough about me; and if I could only see you now and then, and you would let me talk to you a little, and show me that you cared for me – and that we may always be friends in heart, and help each other – then I might come to be glad of life.'

'But how can I see you, Philip?' said Maggie, falteringly.

'If you would let me see you here sometimes – walk with you here – I would be contented if it were only once or twice in a month. *That* would injure no one's happiness, and it would sweeten my life. Besides,' Philip went on, with all the inventive astuteness of love at one-and-twenty, 'if there is any enmity between those who belong to us, we ought all the more to try and quench it by our friendship – I mean, that by our influence on both sides we might bring about a healing of the wounds that have been made in the past. And I don't believe there is any enmity in my own father's mind: I think he has proved the contrary.'

Maggie shook her head slowly, and was silent, under conflicting thoughts. It seemed to her inclination, that to see Philip now and then, and keep up the bond of friendship with him, was something not only innocent, but good: perhaps she might really help him to find contentment as she had found it. The voice that said this made sweet music to Maggie; but athwart it there came an urgent monotonous warning from another voice which she had been learning to obey: the warning that such interviews implied doing something she would dread to be discovered in – something that, if discovered, must cause anger and pain; and that the admission of anything so near doubleness would act as a spiritual blight. Yet the music would swell out again, like chimes borne onward by a recurrent breeze, persuading her that the wrong lay all in the faults and weaknesses of others, and that there was such a thing as futile sacrifice of one to the injury of another. It was very cruel for Philip that he should be shrunk from, because of an unjustifiable vindictiveness towards his father – poor Philip, whom some people would shrink from only because he was deformed.

'I can't say either yes or no,' she said at last, turning round and walking towards the way she had come; 'I must wait, lest I should decide wrongly. I must seek for guidance.'

'May I come again, then – tomorrow – or next week?'

'I think I had better write,' said Maggie, faltering again. 'I have to go to St Ogg's sometimes, and I can put the letter in the post.'

'Oh, no,' said Philip eagerly; 'that would not be so well. My father might see the letter – and – he has not any enmity, I believe, but he views things differently from me: he thinks a great deal about wealth and position. Pray let me come here once more. *Tell* me when it shall be; or if you can't tell me, I will come as often as I can till I do see you.'

'I think it must be so, then,' said Maggie, 'for I can't be certain of coming here any particular evening.'

Maggie felt a great relief in adjourning the decision. She was free now to enjoy minutes of companionship.

'I can't help thinking,' she said, looking smilingly at him, after a few moments of silence, 'how strange it is that we should have met and talked to each other, just as if it had been only yesterday when we parted at Lorton. And yet we must both be very much altered in those five years. How was it you seemed to have a sort of feeling that I was the same Maggie? I was not quite sure you would care about me now.'

'I have never had any doubt that you would be the same, whenever I might see you,' said Philip. 'I mean, the same in everything that made me like you better than any one else. I don't want to explain that: I don't think any of the strongest effects our natures are susceptible of can ever be explained. We can neither detect the process by which they are arrived at, nor the mode in which they act on us. Certain strains of music affect me so strangely – I can never hear them without their changing my whole attitude of mind for a time, and if the effect would last, I might be capable of heroisms.'

'Ah! I know what you mean about music – *I* feel so,' said Maggie, clasping her hands with her old impetuosity. 'At least,' she added, in a saddened tone, 'I used to feel so when I had any music: I never have any now except the organ at church.'

'And you long for it, Maggie?' said Philip, looking at her with affectionate pity. 'Ah, you can have very little that is beautiful in your life. Have you many books? You were so fond of them when you were a little girl.'

They were come back to the hollow, round which the dog-roses grew, and they both paused under the charm of the evening light, reflected from the pale pink clusters.

'No, I have given up books,' said Maggie, quietly, 'except a very, very few.'

Philip had already taken from his pocket a small volume, and was looking at the back as he said—

'Ah, this is the second volume, I see, else you might have liked to take it home with you. I put it in my pocket because I am studying a scene for a picture.'

Maggie had looked at the back too, and saw the title: it revived an old impression with overmastering force.

'"The Pirate,"' she said, taking the book from Philip's hands. 'Oh, I began that once; I read to where Minna is walking with Cleveland, and I could never get to read the rest. I went on with it in my own head, and I made several endings; but they were all unhappy. I could never make a happy ending out of that beginning. Poor Minna! I wonder what is the real end.'

Maggie spoke rapidly, with glistening eyes.

'Take that volume home with you, Maggie,' said Philip, watching her with delight. 'I don't want it now. I shall make a picture of you instead – you, among the Scotch firs and the slanting shadows.'

Maggie had not heard a word he had said: she was absorbed in a page at which she had opened. But suddenly she closed the book, and gave it back to Philip.

'Do keep it, Maggie,' said Philip, entreatingly; 'it will give you pleasure.'

'No, thank you,' said Maggie, putting it aside with her hand and walking on. 'It would make me in love with this world again, as I used to be – it would make me long to see and know many things – it would make me long for a full life.'

'But you will not always be shut up in your present lot: why should you starve your mind in that way? It is narrow ascetism – I don't like to see you persisting in it, Maggie. Poetry and art and knowledge are sacred and pure.'

'But not for me – not for me,' said Maggie, walking more hurriedly. 'Because I should want too much. I must wait – this life will not last long.'

'Don't hurry away from me without saying "good-bye,"
Maggie,' said Philip, as they reached the group of Scotch firs, and
she continued still to walk along without speaking. 'I must not go
any farther, I think, must I?'

'Oh, no, I forgot; good-bye,' said Maggie, pausing, and putting
out her hand to him. The action brought her feeling back in a
strong current to Philip; and after they had stood looking at each
other in silence for a few moments, with their hands clasped, she
said, withdrawing her hand—

'I'm very grateful to you for thinking of me all those years. It
is very sweet to have people love us. What a wonderful beautiful
thing it seems that God should have made your heart so that you
could care about a queer little girl whom you only knew for a few
weeks! I remember saying to you, that I thought you cared for me
more than Tom did.'

'Ah, Maggie,' said Philip, almost fretfully, 'you would never
love me so well as you love your brother.'

'Perhaps not,' said Maggie, simply, 'but then, you know, the
first thing I ever remember in my life is standing with Tom by the
side of the Floss, while he held my hand: everything before that is
dark to me. But I shall never forget you – though we must keep
apart.'

'Don't say so, Maggie,' said Philip. 'If I kept that little girl in my
mind for five years, didn't I earn some part in her? She ought not
to take herself quite away from me.'

'Not if I were free,' said Maggie; 'but I am not – I must submit.'
She hesitated a moment, and then added, 'And I wanted to say to
you, that you had better not take more notice of my brother than
just bowing to him. He once told me not to speak to you again,
and he doesn't change his mind ... Oh dear, the sun is set. I am
too long away. Good-bye.' She gave him her hand once more.

'I shall come here as often as I can, till I see you again, Maggie.
Have some feeling for *me* as well as for others.'

'Yes, yes, I have,' said Maggie, hurrying away, and quickly
disappearing behind the last fir-tree; though Philip's gaze after
her remained immovable for minutes as if he saw her still.

Maggie went home, with an inward conflict already begun; Philip went home to do nothing but remember and hope. You can hardly help blaming him severely. He was four or five years older than Maggie, and had a full consciousness of his feeling towards her to aid him in foreseeing the character his contemplated interviews with her would bear in the opinion of a third person. But you must not suppose that he was capable of a gross selfishness, or that he could have been satisfied without persuading himself that he was seeking to infuse some happiness into Maggie's life – seeking this even more than any direct ends for himself. He could give her sympathy – he could give her help. There was not the slightest promise of love towards him in her manner; it was nothing more than the sweet girlish tenderness she had shown him when she was twelve: perhaps she would never love him – pehaps no woman ever *could* love him: well, then, he would endure that; he should at least have the happiness of seeing her – of feeling some nearness to her. And he clutched passionately the possibility that she *might* love him: perhaps the feeling would grow, if she could come to associate him with that watchful tenderness which her nature would be so keenly alive to. If any woman could love him, surely Maggie was that woman: there was such wealth of love in her, and there was no one to claim it all. Then – the pity of it, that a mind like hers should be withering in its very youth, like a young forest tree, for want of the light and space it was formed to flourish in! Could he not persuade her out of her system of privation? He would be her guardian angel; he would do anything, bear anything, for her sake – except not seeing her.

2

Aunt Glegg Learns the Breadth of Bob's Thumb

While Maggie's life-struggles had lain almost entirely within her own soul, Tom was engaged in a dustier, noisier warfare, grappling with more substantial obstacles, and gaining more definite conquests. Tom's strong will bound together his integrity, his pride, his family regrets, and his personal ambition, and made them one force, concentrating his efforts and surmounting discouragements. His uncle Deane, who watched him closely, soon began to be rather proud that he had brought into the employment of the firm a nephew who appeared to be made of such good commercial stuff. The real kindness of placing him in the warehouse first was soon evident to Tom, in the hints his uncle began to throw out, that after a time he might perhaps be trusted to travel at certain seasons, and buy in for the firm various vulgar commodities. Already, in the second year, Tom's salary was raised; but all, except the price of his dinner and clothes, went home into the tin box; and he shunned comradeship, lest it should lead him into expenses in spite of himself. Tom had a very strong appetite for pleasure but his practical shrewdness told him that there were certain milestones to be passed, and one of the first was the payment of his father's debts. Having made up his mind on that point, he strode along without swerving, contracting some rather saturnine sternness, as a young man is likely to do who has a premature call upon him for self-reliance. Tom felt intensely that common cause with his father which springs from family pride, and was bent on being irreproachable as a son; but his growing experience caused him to pass much silent criticism on the rashness and imprudence of his father's past conduct: their dispositions were not in sympathy, and Tom's face showed little radiance during his few home hours. Maggie had an awe of him, against which she struggled as something unfair to her consciousness of wider thoughts and deeper motives; but it was of no use to struggle. A character at unity with itself – that performs what it intends, subdues every counteracting impulse, and has no visions beyond the distinctly possible – is strong by its very negations.

You may imagine that Tom's more and more obvious unlikeness to his father was well fitted to conciliate the maternal aunts and uncles; and Mr Deane's favourable reports and predictions to Mr Glegg concerning Tom's qualifications for business, began to be discussed amongst them with various acceptance. He was likely, it appeared, to do the family credit, without causing it any expense and trouble. Mrs Pullet had always thought it strange if Tom's excellent complexion, so entirely that of the Dodsons, did not argue a certainty that he would turn out well, his juvenile disrespect to his aunts only indicating a tinge of Tulliver blood which he had doubtless outgrown. Mr Glegg, who had contracted a cautious liking for Tom ever since his spirited and sensible be-haviour when the execution was in the house, was now warming into a resolution to further his prospects actively – some time, when an opportunity offered of doing so in a prudent manner, without ultimate loss; but Mrs Glegg observed that she was not given to speak without book, as some people were; that those who said least were most likely to find their words made good; and that when the right moment came, it would be seen who could do something better than talk. Uncle Pullet, after silent meditation for a period of several lozenges, came distinctly to the conclusion, that when a young man was likely to do well, it was better not to meddle with him.

Tom, meanwhile, had shown no disposition to rely on any one but himself, though, with a natural sensitiveness towards all indi-cations of favourable opinion, he was glad to see his uncle Glegg look in on him sometimes in a friendly way during business hours, and glad to be invited to dine at his house, though he usually preferred declining on the ground that he was not sure of being punctual. But about a year ago, something had occurred which induced Tom to test his uncle Glegg's friendly disposition.

Bob Jakin, who rarely returned from one of his rounds with-out seeing Tom and Maggie, awaited him on the bridge as he was coming home from St Ogg's one evening, that they might have a little private talk. He took the liberty of asking if Mr Tom had ever thought of making money by trading a bit on his own account. Trading, how? Tom wished to know. Why, by sending out a bit of a cargo to foreign ports; because Bob had a particular friend who had offered to do a little business for him in that way in Laceham goods, and would be glad to serve Mr Tom on the same footing. Tom was interested at once, and begged for full explanation; wondering he had not thought of this plan before. He was so well pleased with the prospect of a speculation that might change the slow process of addition into muliplication, that he at once determined to mention the matter to his father, and get his consent to appropriate some of the savings in the tin box to the purchase of a small cargo. He would rather not have consulted his father, but he had just paid his last quarter's money into the tin box, and there was no other resource. All the savings were there; for Mr Tulliver would not consent to put the money out at interest lest he should lose it. Since he had speculated in the purchase of some corn, and had lost by it, he could not be easy without keeping the money under his eye.

Tom approached the subject carefully, as he was seated on the hearth with his father that evening, and Mr Tulliver listened, leaning forward in his arm-chair and looking up in Tom's face with a sceptical glance. His first impulse was to give a positive refusal, but he was in some awe of Tom's wishes, and since he had had the sense of being an 'unlucky' father, he had lost some of his old peremptoriness and determination to be master. He took the key of the bureau from his pocket, got out the key of the large chest, and fetched down the tin box – slowly, as if he were trying to defer the moment of a painful parting. Then he seated himself against the table, and opened the box with that little padlock-key which he fingered in his waistcoat pocket in all vacant moments. There they were, the dingy bank-notes and the bright sovereigns, and he counted them out on the table – only a hundred and sixteen pounds in two years, after all the pinching.

'How much do you want, then?' he said, speaking as if the words burnt his lips.

'Suppose I begin with the thirty-six pounds, father?' said Tom.

Mr Tulliver separated this sum from the rest, and, keeping his hand over it, said—

'It's as much as I can save out o' my pay in a year.'

'Yes, father: it is such slow work – saving out of the little money we get. And in this way we might double our savings.'

'Ay, my lad,' said the father, keeping his hand on the money, 'but you might lose it – you might lose a year o' my life – and I haven't got many. If you trust to luck, it's sure to be against me. It's Old Harry's got the luck in his hands; and if I lose one year, I shall never pick it up again – death 'ull o'ertake me.'

Mr Tulliver's voice trembled, and Tom was silent for a few minutes before he said—

'I'll give it up, father, since you object to it so strongly.'

But, unwilling to abandon the scheme altogether, he determined to ask his uncle Glegg to venture twenty pounds on condition of receiving five per cent of the profits. That was really a very small thing to ask. So when Bob called the next day at the wharf to know the decision, Tom proposed that they should go together to his uncle Glegg's to open the business; for his diffident pride clung to him, and made him feel that Bob's tongue would relieve him from some embarrassment.

Mr Glegg, at the pleasant hour of four in the afternoon of a hot August day, was naturally counting his wall-fruit to assure himself that the sum total had not varied since yesterday. To him entered Tom, in what appeared to Mr Glegg very questionable companionship: that of a man with a pack on his back – for Bob was equipped for a new journey – and of a huge brindled bull-terrier, who walked with a slow swaying movement from side to side, and glanced from under his eyelids with a surly indifference which might after all be a cover to the most offensive designs.

'Heigh! heigh! keep that dog back, will you?' he shouted, snatching up a stake and holding it before him as a shield when the visitors were within three yards of him.

'Get out wi' you, Mumps,' said Bob, with a kick. 'He's as quiet as a lamb, sir' – an observation which Mumps corroborated by a low growl as he retreated behind his master's legs.

'Why, what ever does this mean, Tom?' said Mr Glegg.

'I came to speak to you about a little matter of business of my own,' said Tom

'Ay – well; but what has this dog got to do with it?' said the old gentleman, getting mild again.

'It's my dog, sir,' said the ready Bob. 'An' it's me as put Mr Tom up to the bit o' business; for Mr Tom's been a friend o' mine iver since I was a little chap: fust thing iver I did was frightenin' the birds for th' old master. An' if a bit o' luck turns up, I'm allays thinkin' if I can let Mr Tom have a pull at it. An' it's a downright roarin' shame, as when he's got the chance o' making a bit o' money wi' sending goods out – ten or twelve per zent clear, when freight an' commission's paid – as he shouldn't lay hold o' the chance for want o' money. An' when there's the Laceham goods – lors! they're made o' purpose for folks as want to send out a little carguy; light, an' take up no room – you may pack twenty pound so as you can't see the passill: an' they're manifacturs as please fools, so I reckon they aren't like to want a market. An' I'd go to Laceham an' buy in the goods for Mr Tom along wi' my own. An' there's the shupercargo o' the bit of a vessel as is goin' to take 'em out. I know him partic'lar; he's a solid man, an' got a family i' the town here. Salt, his name is – an' a briny chap he is too – an' if you don't believe me, I can take you to him.'

Uncle Glegg stood open-mouthed with astonishment at this unembarrassed loquacity, with which his understanding could hardly keep pace. He looked at Bob while Tom, doubtful of his uncle's impression, began to wish he had not brought this singular mouthpiece: Bob's talk appeared less seemly, now some one besides himself was listening to it.

'You seem to be a knowing fellow,' said Mr Glegg at last.

'Ay, sir, you say true,' returned Bob, nodding his head: 'I think my head's all alive inside like an old cheese, for I'm so full o' plans, one knocks another over. If I hadn't Mumps to talk to, I should get top-heavy an' tumble in a fit. I suppose it's because I niver went to school much. I'm gettin' so full o' money, I must hev a wife to spend it for me. But it's botherin' a wife is – and Mumps mightn't like her.'

Uncle Glegg was beginning to find Bob amusing.

'But, come now, let's hear more about this business, Tom,' he said. 'I suppose you want a little sum to make a venture with. But where's all your own money? You don't spend it all – eh?'

'No, sir,' said Tom, colouring; 'but my father is unwilling to risk it, and I don't like to press him. If I could get twenty or thirty pounds to begin with, I could pay five per cent for it, and then I could gradually make a little capital of my own, and do without a loan.'

'Ay ... ay,' said Mr Glegg, in an approving tone; 'that's not a bad notion, and I won't say as I wouldn't be your man. But it 'ull be as well for me to see this Salt, as you talk on. And then ... here's this friend o' yours offers to buy the goods for you. Perhaps you've got somebody to stand surety for you if the money's put into your hands?' added the cautious old gentleman, looking over his spectacles at Bob.

'I don't think that's necessary, uncle,' said Tom. 'At least, I mean it would not be necessary for me, because I know Bob well; but perhaps it would be right for you to have some security.'

'You get your percentage out o' the purchase, I suppose?' said Mr Glegg, looking at Bob.

'No, sir,' said Bob, rather indignantly; 'I didn't offer to get a apple for Mr Tom, o' purpose to hev a bite out of it myself.'

'Well, but it's nothing but right you should have a small percentage,' said Mr Glegg. 'I've no opinion o' transactions where folks do things for nothing. It allays looks bad.'

'Well, then,' said Bob, whose keenness saw at once what was implied, 'I'll tell you what I get by't, an' it's money in my pocket in the end: I make myself look big, wi' makin' a bigger purchase. That's what I'm thinking on. Lors! I'm a 'cute chap – I am.'

'Mr Glegg, Mr Glegg,' said a severe voice from the open parlour window, 'pray are you coming in to tea? – or are you going to stand talking with packmen till you get murdered in the open daylight?'

'Murdered?' said Mr Glegg; 'what's the woman talking of? Here's your nephey Tom come about a bit o' business.'

'If my nephey's come about business, it 'ud be more fitting if you'd bring him into the house, and let his aunt know about it, instead o' whispering in corners.'

'Well, well,' said Mr Glegg, 'we'll come in now.'

'You needn't stay here,' said the lady to Bob, in a loud voice, adapted to the moral not the physical distance between them. 'We don't want anything. I don't deal wi' packmen. Mind you shut the gate after you.'

'Stop a bit; not so fast,' said Mr Glegg: 'I haven't done with this young man yet. Come in, Tom; come in,' he added, stepping in at the French window.

'Mr Glegg,' said Mrs G., in a fatal tone, 'if you're going to let that man and his dog in on my carpet, before my very face, be so good as to let me know. A wife's got a right to ask that, I hope.'

'Don't you be uneasy, mum,' said Bob, touching his cap. 'I'm here upo' Mr Tom's business, an' I'm not the man to take up the time wi' my own.'

'And pray, what *is* this business as is to be kept from me?' said Mrs Glegg.

'A little plan o' nephey Tom's here,' said good-natured Mr Glegg; 'and not altogether a bad un, I think. A little plan for making money: that's the right sort o' plan for young folks as have got their fortin to make – eh, Jane?'

'But I hope it isn't a plan where he expects ivery thing to be done for him by his friends. And pray, what has this packman got to do wi' what goes on in our family? Can't you speak for yourself, Tom, and let your aunt know things, as a nephey should?'

'This is Bob Jakin, aunt,' said Tom, bridling at the irritation that aunt Glegg's voice always produced. 'I've known him ever since we were little boys. He's a very good fellow, and always ready to do me a kindness. And he has had some experience in sending goods out – a small part of a cargo as a private speculation; and he thinks if I could begin to do a little in the same way, I might make some money. A large interest is got in that way.'

'Large int'rest?' said aunt Glegg with eagerness; 'and what do you call large int'rest?'

'Ten or twelve per cent, Bob says, after expenses are paid.'

'Then, why wasn't I let to know o' such things before, Mr Glegg?' said Mrs Glegg, turning to her husband, with a deep grating tone of reproach. 'Haven't you allays told me as there was no getting more nor five per cent?'

'Pooh, pooh, nonsense, my good woman,' said Mr Glegg. 'You couldn't go into trade, could you? You can't get more than five per cent with security.'

'But I can turn a bit o' money for you, an' welcome, mum,' said Bob, 'if you'd like to risk it – not as there's any risk to speak on. But if you'd a mind to lend a bit o' money to Mr Tom, he'd pay you six or seven per zent an' get a trifle for himself as well; an' a good-natur'd lady like you 'ud like the feel o' the money better if your nephey took part on it.'

'What do you say, Mrs G.?' said Mr Glegg. 'I've a notion, when I've made a bit more inquiry, as I shall perhaps start Tom here with a bit of a nest-egg – he'll pay me int'rest, you know – an' if you like to join me wi' twenty pounds, you can – I'll make it fifty. That'll be a pretty good nest-egg – eh, Tom?'

'You're not counting on me, Mr Glegg, I hope,' said his wife. 'You could do fine things wi' my money, I don't doubt.'

'Very well,' said Mr Glegg, rather snappishly, 'then we'll do without you. I shall go with you to see this Salt,' he added, turning to Bob.

'And now, I suppose, you'll go all the other way, Mr Glegg,' said Mrs G., 'and want to shut me out o' my own nephey's business. I never said I wouldn't put money into it – I don't say as it shall be twenty pounds, though you're so ready to say it for me – but he'll see some day as his aunt's in the right not to risk the money she's saved for him till it's proved as it won't be lost.'

'Ay, that's a pleasant sort o' risk, that is,' said Mr Glegg, indiscreetly winking at Tom, who couldn't avoid smiling. But Bob stemmed the injured lady's outburst.

'Ay, mum,' he said admiringly, 'you know what's what – you do. An' it's nothing but fair. *You* see how the first bit of a job answers, an' then you'll come down handsome. Lors, it's a fine thing to hev good kin. I got my bit of a nest-egg, as the master calls it, all by my own sharpness – ten suvreigns it was – wi' dousing the fire at Torry's Mill, an' it's growed an' growed by a bit an' a bit, till I'n got a matter o' thirty pound to lay out, besides makin' my mother comfor'ble. Now then, sir,' continued Bob, shoulder-ing his pack, 'if you please, I'll be glad to go and see about makin' Mr Tom's fortin.'

'Stop a bit, Mr Glegg,' said the lady, as her husband took his hat, 'you never *will* give me the chance o' speaking. You'll go away now, and finish everything about this business, and come back and tell me it's too late for me to speak.'

'Well, Mrs G., say what you mean,' said Mr G., hastily.

'Well, then, I desire as nothing may be done without my know-ing. I don't say as I shan't venture twenty pounds, if you make out as everything's right and safe. And if I do, Tom,' concluded Mrs Glegg, turning impressively to her nephew, 'I hope you'll allays bear it in mind and be grateful for such an aunt. I mean you to pay me interest, you know – I don't approve o' giving; we niver looked for that in *my* family.'

'Thank you, aunt,' said Tom, rather proudly. 'I prefer having the money only lent to me.'

'Very well: that's the Dodson sperrit,' said Mrs Glegg.

Salt – that eminently 'briny chap' – having been discovered in a cloud of tobacco-smoke at the Anchor Tavern, Mr Glegg commenced inquiries which turned out satisfactorily enough to warrant the advance of the 'nest-egg,' to which aunt Glegg con-tributed twenty pounds; and in this modest beginning you see the ground of a fact which might otherwise surprise you – namely, Tom's accumulation of a fund, unknown to his father, that promised in no very long time to meet the more tardy process of saving, and quite cover the deficit. When once his attention had been turned to this source of gain, Tom determined to make the most of it, and lost no opportunity of obtaining information and extending his small enterprises.

At the time of Maggie's first meeting with Philip, Tom had already nearly a hundred and fifty pounds of his own capital; and while they were walking by the evening light in the Red Deeps, he, by the same evening light, was riding into Laceham, proud of being on his first journey on behalf of Guest & Co., and revolving in his mind all the chances that by the end of another year he should have doubled his gains, lifted off the obloquy of debt from his father's name, and perhaps – for he should be twenty-one – have got a new start for himself, on a higher platform of employment. Did he not deserve it? He was quite sure that he did.

3

The Wavering Balance

I said that Maggie went home that evening from the Red Deeps with a mental conflict already begun. You have seen clearly enough, in her interview with Philip, what that conflict was. Suddenly some of the memory-haunting earthly delights were no longer out of her reach. She might have books, converse, affection – she might hear tidings of the world from which her mind had not yet lost its sense of exile; and it would be a kindness to Philip too, who was clearly not happy; and perhaps here was an opportunity indicated for making her mind more worthy of its highest service – perhaps the noblest, completest devoutness could hardly exist without some width of knowledge: *must* she always live in this resigned imprisonment? It was so blameless, so good a thing that there should be friendship between her and Philip; the motives that forbade it were so unreasonable – so unchristian! But the severe monotonous warning came again and again – that she was losing the simplicity and clearness of her life by admitting a ground of concealment, and that, by forsaking the simple rule of renunciation, she was throwing herself under the seductive guidance of illimitable wants. She thought she had won strength to obey the warning before she allowed herself the next week to turn her steps in the evening to the Red Deeps. But while she was resolved to say an affectionate farewell to Philip, how she looked forward to that evening walk in the still, fleckered shade of the hollows, away from all that was harsh and unlovely; to the affectionate admiring looks that would meet her; to the sense of comradeship that childish memories would give to wiser, older talk; to the certainty that Philip would care to hear everything she said, which no one else cared for! It was a half-hour that it would be very hard to turn her back upon, with the sense that there would be no other like it. Yet she said what she meant to say; she looked firm as well as sad.

'Philip, I have made up my mind – it is right that we should give each other up, in everything but memory. I could not see you without concealment – stay, I know what you are going to say – it is other people's wrong feelings that make concealment necessary; but concealment is bad, however it may be caused. I feel that it would be bad for me, for us both. And then, if our secret were discovered, there would be nothing but misery – dreadful anger; and then we must part after all, and it would be harder, when we were used to seeing each other.'

Philip's face had flushed, and there was a momentary eagerness of expression, as if he had been about to resist this decision with all his might. But he controlled himself, and said, with assumed calmness, 'Well, Maggie, if we must part, let us try and forget it for one half-hour: let us talk together a little while – for the last time.'

He took her hand, and Maggie felt no reason to withdraw it: his quietness made her all the more sure she had given him great pain, and she wanted to show him how unwillingly she had given it.

'Let us sit down in the hollow,' said Philip, 'where we stood the last time. See how the dog-roses have strewed the ground, and spread their opal petals over it!'

They sat down at the roots of the slanting ash.

'I've begun my picture of you among the Scotch firs, Maggie,' said Philip, 'so you must let me study your face a little, while you stay, since I am not to see it again. Please, turn your head this way.'

This was said in an entreating voice, and it would have been very hard of Maggie to refuse. The full lustrous face, with the bright black coronet, looked down like that of a divinity well pleased to be worshipped, on the pale-hued, small-featured face that was turned up to it.

'I shall be sitting for my second portrait then,' she said, smiling. 'Will it be larger than the other?'

'Oh, yes, much larger. It is an oil-painting.'

'You seem to think more of painting than of anything now, Philip?'

'Perhaps I do,' said Philip, rather sadly; 'but I think of too many things – sow all sorts of seeds, and get no great harvest from any one of them. I'm cursed with susceptibility in every direction, and effective faculty in none. I care for painting and music; I care for classic literature, and mediaeval literature, and modern literature: I flutter all ways, and fly in none.'

'But surely that is a happiness to have so many tastes – to enjoy so many beautiful things – when they are within your reach,' said Maggie, musingly.

'It might be a happiness to have many tastes if I were like other men,' said Philip, bitterly. 'I might think society at St Ogg's agreeable then. But nothing could make life worth the purchase-money of pain to me, but some faculty that would lift me above the dead level of provincial existence. Yes – there is one thing: a passion answers as well as faculty.'

Maggie did not hear the last words: she was struggling against the consciousness that Philip's words had set her own discontent vibrating again as it used to do.

'I understand what you mean,' she said, 'though I know so much less than you do. I used to think I could never bear life if it kept on being the same every day, and I must always be doing things of no consequence, and never know anything greater. But, dear Philip, is it not right to resign ourselves entirely, whatever may be denied us? I have found great peace in that for the last two or three years – even joy in subduing my own will.'

'Yes, Maggie,' said Philip, vehemently; 'and you are shutting yourself up in a narrow self-delusive fanaticism, which is only a way of escaping pain by starving into dullness all the highest powers of your nature. Joy and peace are not resignation. *You* are not resigned: you are only trying to stupefy yourself.'

Maggie's lips trembled; she felt there was some truth in what Philip said, and yet there was a deeper consciousness that, for any immediate application it had to her conduct, it was no better than falsity. Her double impression corresponded to the double impulse of the speaker. Philip seriously believed what he said, but he said it with vehemence because it made an argument against the resolution that opposed his wishes. But Maggie's face, made more childlike by the gathering tears, touched him with a tenderer, less egoistic feeling. He took her hand and said gently—

'Don't let us think of such things in this short half-hour, Maggie. Let us only care about being together. We shall be friends in spite of separation ... We shall always think of each other. I shall be glad to live as long as you are alive, because I shall think there may always come a time when I can – when you will let me help you in some way.'

'What a dear, good brother you would have been, Philip,' said Maggie, smiling through the haze of tears. 'I think you would have made as much fuss about me, and been as pleased for me to love you, as would have satisfied even me. You would have loved me well enough to bear with me, and forgive me everything. That was what I always longed that Tom should do. I was never satisfied with a *little* of anything. That is why it is better for me to do without earthly happiness altogether. I never felt that I had enough music – I wanted more instruments playing together – I wanted voices to be fuller and deeper. Do you ever sing now, Philip?' she added abruptly.

'Yes,' he said, 'every day, almost. But my voice is only middling – like everything else in me.'

'Oh, sing me something – just one song. I *may* listen to that before I go – something you used to sing at Lorton on a Saturday afternoon, when we had the drawing-room all to ourselves, and I put my apron over my head to listen.'

'*I* know,' said Philip, and Maggie buried her face in her hands, while he sang *sotto voce*, 'Love in her eyes sits playing;' and then said, 'That's it, isn't it?'

'Oh, no, I won't stay,' said Maggie, starting up. 'It will only haunt me. Let us walk, Philip. I must go home.'

She moved away, so that he was obliged to rise and follow her.

'Maggie,' he said, in a tone of remonstrance, 'don't persist in this awful, senseless privation. It makes me wretched to see you benumbing and cramping your nature in this way. You were so full of life when you were a child: I thought you would be a brilliant woman – all wit and bright imagination. And it flashes out in your face still, until you draw that veil of dull quiescence over it.'

'Why do you speak so bitterly to me, Philip?' said Maggie.

'Because I foresee it will not end well: you can never carry on this self-torture. It is mere cowardice to seek safety in negations. No character becomes strong in that way. You will be thrown into the world some day, and then every rational satisfaction of your nature that you deny now, will assault you like a savage appetite.'

Maggie started and paused, looking at Philip with alarm in her face.

'Philip, how dare you shake me in this way? You are a tempter.'

'No, I am not; but love gives insight, Maggie, and insight often gives foreboding. *Listen* to me – *let* me supply you with books; do let me see you sometimes – be your brother and teacher, as you said at Lorton. It is less wrong that you should see me than that you should be committing this long suicide.'

Maggie felt unable to speak. She shook her head and walked on in silence, till they came to the end of the Scotch firs, and she put out her hand in sign of parting.

'Do you banish me from this place for ever, then, Maggie? Surely I may come and walk in it sometimes? If I meet you by chance, there is no concealment in that?'

Maggie felt her heart leap at this subterfuge of Philip's, and there passed over her face that almost imperceptible shock which accompanies any relief. He saw it, and they parted in silence.

4

Another Love-scene

Early in the following April, nearly a year after that dubious parting you have just witnessed, you may, if you like, again see Maggie
entering the Red Deeps through the group of Scotch firs. But it
is early afternoon and not evening, and the edge of sharpness in
the spring air makes her draw her large shawl close about her and
trip along rather quickly; though she looks round, as usual, that
she may take in the sight of her beloved trees. There is a more
eager, inquiring look in her eyes than there was last June, and a
smile is hovering about her lips, as if some playful speech were
awaiting the right hearer. The hearer was not long in appearing.

'Take back your "Corinne,"' said Maggie, drawing a book from
under her shawl. 'You were right in telling me she would do me
no good; but you were wrong in thinking I should wish to be like
her.'

'You agree with me in not liking "Corinne," then?'

'I didn't finish the book,' said Maggie. 'As soon as I came to
the blond-haired young lady reading in the park, I shut it up,
and determined to read no further. I foresaw that that light-
complexioned girl would win away all the love from Corinne
and make her miserable. I'm determined to read no more books
where the blond-haired women carry away all the happiness. I
should begin to have a prejudice against them.'

'Well, perhaps you will avenge the dark women in your own
person, and carry away all the love from your cousin Lucy. She
is sure to have some handsome young man of St Ogg's at her
feet now: and you have only to shine upon him – your fair little
cousin will be quite quenched in your beams.'

'Philip, that is not pretty of you, to apply my nonsense to anything real,' said Maggie, looking hurt. 'As if I, with my old gowns
and want of all accomplishments, could be a rival of dear little
Lucy, who is ten times prettier than I am. Besides, I never go to
aunt Deane's when any one is there: it is only because dear Lucy

is good, and loves me, that she comes to see me, and will have me go to see her sometimes.'

'Maggie,' said Philip, with surprise, 'it is not like you to take playfulness literally.'

'Well,' said Maggie, smiling, 'if you meant that for a joke it was a poor one; but I thought you wanted to remind me that I am vain, and wish every one to admire me most. But it isn't because I'm dark myself. It's because I always care the most about the unhappy people: if the blond girl were forsaken, I should like *her* best. I always take the side of the rejected lover in the stories.'

'Then you would never have the heart to reject one yourself – should you, Maggie?' said Philip, flushing a little.

'I don't know,' said Maggie, hesitatingly. Then with a bright smile – 'I think perhaps I could if he were very conceited; and yet, if he got extremely humiliated afterwards, I should relent.'

'I've often wondered, Maggie,' Philip said, with some effort, 'whether you wouldn't really be more likely to love a man that other women were not likely to love.'

'That would depend on what they didn't like him for,' said Maggie, laughing. 'He might be very disagreeable.'

'But suppose, Maggie – suppose it was a man who had been marked from childhood for a peculiar kind of suffering – and to whom you were the day-star of his life – who loved you, worshipped you, so entirely that he felt it happiness enough for him if you would let him see you at rare moments ...'

Philip paused with a pang of dread lest his confession should cut short this very happiness. A rush of self-consciousness told him that he was besotted to have said all this. Maggie's manner this morning had been as unconstrained and indifferent as ever.

But she was not looking indifferent now. Struck with the unusual emotion in Philip's tone, she had turned quickly to look at him, and as he went on speaking, a great change came over her face. She was quite silent, and, walking on towards the trunk of a fallen tree, she sat down, as if she had no strength. She was trembling.

'Maggie,' said Philip, getting more and more alarmed in every fresh moment of silence, 'I was a fool to say it – forget that I've said it. I shall be contented if things can be as they were.'

The distress with which he spoke urged Maggie to say something. 'I am so surprised, Philip – I had not thought of it.' And the effort to say this brought the tears down too.

'Has it made you hate me, Maggie?' said Philip, impetuously. 'Do you think I am a presumptuous fool?'

'Oh, Philip!' said Maggie, 'how can you think I have such feelings? – as if I were not grateful for *any* love. But I had never thought of your being my lover. It seemed so far off that I should ever have a lover.'

'Then can you bear to think of me as your lover, Maggie?' said Philip, seating himself by her, and taking her hand, in the elation of a sudden hope. '*Do* you love me?'

Maggie turned rather pale: this direct question seemed not easy to answer. But her eyes met Philip's, which were in this moment liquid and beautiful with beseeching love. She spoke with hesitation, yet with sweet, simple, girlish tenderness.

'I think I could hardly love any one better: there is nothing but what I love you for.' She paused a little while, and then added, 'But it will be better for us not to say any more about it – won't it, dear Philip? You know we couldn't even be friends, if our friendship were discovered. I have never felt that I was right in giving way about seeing you – though it has been so precious to me in some ways; and now the fear comes upon me strongly again, that it will lead to evil.'

'But no evil has come, Maggie; and if you had been guided by that fear before, you would only have lived through another dreary benumbing year, instead of reviving into your real self.'

Maggie shook her head. 'It has been very sweet, I know – all the talking together, and the books, and the feeling that I had the walk to look forward to, when I could tell you the thoughts that had come into my head while I was away from you. But it has made me restless: it has made me think a great deal about the world; and I have impatient thoughts again – I get weary of my home – and then it cuts me to the heart afterwards, that I should ever have felt weary of my father and mother. I think what you call being benumbed was better – better for me – for then my selfish desires were benumbed.'

Philip took her hand.

'Don't think of the past now, Maggie; think only of our love. If you can really cling to me with all your heart, every obstacle will be overcome in time: we need only wait. I can live on hope. Look at me, Maggie; tell me again, it is possible for you to love me. Don't look away from me to that cloven tree; it is a bad omen.'

She turned her large dark glance upon him with a sad smile.

'Come, Maggie, say one kind word, or else you were better to me at Lorton. You asked me if I should like you to kiss me – don't you remember? – and you promised to kiss me when you met me again. You never kept the promise.'

The recollection of that childish time came as a sweet relief to Maggie. It made the present moment less strange to her. She kissed him almost as simply and quietly as she had done when she was twelve years old. Philip's eyes flashed with delight, but his next words were words of discontent.

'You don't seem happy enough, Maggie: you are forcing yourself to say you love me, out of pity.'

'No, Philip,' said Maggie. 'I'm telling you the truth. It is all new and strange to me; but I don't think I could love any one better than I love you. I should like always to live with you – to make you happy. I have always been happy when I have been with you. There is only one thing I will not do for your sake; I will never do anything to wound my father. You must never ask that from me.'

'No, Maggie: I will ask nothing – I will bear anything – I'll wait another year only for a kiss, if you will only give me the first place in your heart.'

'No,' said Maggie, smiling. 'I won't make you wait so long as that.' But then, looking serious again, she added, as she rose from her seat—

'But what would your own father say, Philip? Oh, it is quite impossible we can ever be more than friends – brother and sister in secret, as we have been. Let us give up thinking of everything else.'

'No, Maggie, I can't give you up – unless you really only care for me as if I were your brother. Tell me the truth.'

'Philip, what happiness have I ever had so great as being with you? – since I was a little girl – the days Tom was good to me. And your mind is a sort of world to me: you can tell me all I want to know. I think I should never be tired of being with you.'

They were walking hand in hand, looking at each other; Maggie, indeed, was hurrying along, for she felt it time to be gone. But the sense that their parting was near, made her more anxious lest she should have unintentionally left some painful impression on Philip's mind. They stopped to part among the Scotch firs.

'Then my life will be filled with hope, Maggie – and I shall be happier than other men, in spite of all? We *do* belong to each other – for always – whether we are apart or together?'

'Yes, Philip: I should like never to part: I should like to make your life very happy.'

'I am waiting for something else – I wonder whether it will come.'

Maggie smiled, with glistening tears, and then stooped her tall head to kiss the low pale face that was full of pleading, timid love.

5

The Cloven Tree

Secrets are rarely betrayed or discovered according to any programme our fear has sketched out. During a year that Maggie had had the burthen of concealment on her mind, the possibility of discovery had continually presented itself under the form of a sudden meeting with her father or Tom when she was walking with Philip in the Red Deeps. She was aware that this was not one of the most likely events; but it was the scene that most completely symbolised her inward dread.

The day after Maggie's last meeting with Philip, being a Sunday on which Mr Pullet was bound to appear in funeral hat-band and scarf at St Ogg's church, Mrs Pullet made this the occasion of dining with sister Glegg, and taking tea with poor sister Tulliver. Sunday was the one day in the week on which Tom was at home in the afternoon; and today the brighter spirits he had been in of late had flowed over in unusually cheerful open chat with his father, and in the invitation, 'Come, Magsie, you come too!' when he strolled out with his mother in the garden to see the advancing cherry-blossoms. He had been better pleased with Maggie since she had been less odd and ascetic; he was even getting rather proud of her: several persons had remarked in his hearing that his sister was a very fine girl.

'You look very well, my dear,' said aunt Pullet, shaking her head sadly, as they sat round the tea-table. 'I niver thought your girl 'ud be so good-looking, Bessy. But you must wear pink, my dear: that blue thing as your aunt Glegg gave you turns you into a crowflower. Jane never *was* tasty. Why don't you wear that gown o' mine?'

'It is so pretty and so smart, aunt. I think it's too showy for me – at least for my other clothes, that I must wear with it.'

'To be sure, it 'ud be unbecoming if it wasn't well known you've got them belonging to you as can afford to give you such things when they've done with 'em themselves. It stands to reason I must give my own niece clothes now and then – such things as *I* buy every year, and never wear anything out. And as for Lucy, there's no giving to her, for she's got everything o' the choicest. She had got a collar on this blessed day,' continued Mrs Pullet, 'as I don't say I haven't got as good, but I must look out my best to match it.'

'Miss Lucy's called the bell o' St Ogg's, they say: that's a cur'ous word,' observed Mr Pullet.

'Pooh!' said Mr Tulliver, jealous for Maggie, 'she's a small thing, not much of a figure. But fine feathers make fine birds. I see nothing to admire so much in those diminutive women; they look silly by the side o' the men – out o' proportion. When

I chose my wife, I chose her the right size – neither too little nor too big.'

The poor wife, with her withered beauty, smiled complacently.

'But the men aren't *all* big,' said uncle Pullet, not without some self-reference; 'a young fellow may be good-looking and yet not be a six-foot, like Master Tom here.'

'Ah, it's poor talking about littleness and bigness – anybody may think it's a mercy they're straight,' said aunt Pullet. 'There's that mismade son o' Lawyer Wakem's – I saw him at church today. Dear, dear! to think o' the property he's like to have; and they say he's very queer and lonely – doesn't like much company. I shouldn't wonder if he goes out of his mind; for we never come along the road but he's a scrambling out o' the trees and brambles at the Red Deeps.'

This wide statement, by which Mrs Pullet represented the fact that she had twice seen Philip at the spot indicated, produced an effect on Maggie which was all the stronger because Tom sat opposite her, and she was intensely anxious to look indifferent. At Philip's name she had blushed, and the blush deepened every instant from consciousness, until the mention of the Red Deeps made her feel as if the whole secret were betrayed, and she dared not even hold her teaspoon lest she should show how she trembled. She sat with her hands clasped under the table, not daring to look round. Happily, her father was seated on the same side with herself, beyond her uncle Pullet, and could not see her face without stooping forward. Her mother's voice brought first relief – turning the conversation; for Mrs Tulliver was always alarmed when the name of Wakem was mentioned in her husband's presence. Gradually Maggie recovered composure enough to look up; her eyes met Tom's, but he turned away his head immediately; and she went to bed that night wondering if he had gathered any suspicion from her confusion. Perhaps he would think it was only her alarm at her aunt's mention of Wakem before her father: that was the interpretation her mother had put on it.

But Tom was too keen-sighted to rest satisfied with such an

interpretation: he had seen clearly enough that there was something distinct from anxiety about her father in Maggie's excessive confusion. In trying to recall all the details that could give shape to his suspicions, he remembered only lately hearing his mother scold Maggie for walking in the Red Deeps when the ground was wet, and bringing home shoes clogged with red soil: still Tom, retaining all his old repulsion for Philip's deformity, shrank from attributing to his sister the probability of feeling more than a friendly interest in such an unfortunate exception to the common run of men. A love for a deformed man would be odious in any woman – in a sister intolerable. He left home the next morning in a watchful state of mind.

That afternoon, about half-past three o'clock, Tom was standing on the wharf, talking with Bob Jakin about the probability of the good ship *Adelaide* coming in, in a day or two, with results highly important to both of them.

'Eh,' said Bob, parenthetically, as he looked over the fields on the other side of the river, 'there goes that crooked young Wakem. I know him or his shadder as far off as I can see 'em; I'm allays lighting on him o' that side the river.'

A sudden thought seemed to have darted through Tom's mind. 'I must go, Bob,' he said, 'I've something to attend to,' hurrying off to the warehouse, where he left notice for some one to take his place – he was called away home on peremptory business. The swiftest pace and the shortest road took him to the gate, and he was pausing to open it deliberately, that he might walk into the house with an appearance of perfect composure, when Maggie came out at the front door in bonnet and shawl. His conjecture was fulfilled, and he waited for her at the gate. She started violently when she saw him.

'Tom, how is it you are come home? Is there anything the matter?' Maggie spoke in a low tremulous voice.

'I'm come to walk with you to the Red Deeps and meet Philip Wakem,' said Tom, the central fold in his brow, which had become habitual with him, deepening as he spoke.

Maggie stood helpless – pale and cold. By some means, then,

Tom knew everything. At last she said, 'I'm not going,' and turned round.

'Yes, you are; but I want to speak to you first. Where is my father?'

'Out on horseback.'

'And my mother?'

'In the yard, I think, with the poultry.'

'I can go in, then, without her seeing me?'

They walked in together, and Tom, entering the parlour, said to Maggie, 'Come in here.'

She obeyed, and he closed the door behind her.

'Now, Maggie, tell me this instant everything that has passed between you and Philip Wakem.'

'Does my father know anything?' said Maggie, still trembling.

'No,' said Tom, indignantly. 'But he *shall* know, if you attempt to use deceit towards me any further.'

'I don't wish to use deceit,' said Maggie, flushing into resentment at hearing this word applied to her conduct.

'Tell me the truth, then, or my father shall know everything.'

'I tell it for my father's sake, then.'

'Yes, it becomes you to profess affection for your father, when you have despised his strongest feelings.'

'You never do wrong, Tom,' said Maggie tauntingly.

'Not if I know it,' answered Tom, with proud sincerity. 'But I have nothing to say to you beyond this: tell me what has passed between you and Philip Wakem. When did you first meet him in the Red Deeps?'

'A year ago,' said Maggie, quietly. Tom's severity gave her a certain fund of defiance, and kept her sense of error in abeyance. 'You need ask me no more questions. We have been friendly a year. We have met and walked together often. He has lent me books.'

'Is that all?' said Tom, looking straight at her with his frown.

Maggie paused a moment; then, determined to make an end of Tom's right to accuse of her deceit, she said haughtily—

'No, not quite all. On Saturday he told me that he loved me. I didn't think of it before then – I had only thought of him as an old friend.'

'And you *encouraged* him?' said Tom with an expression of disgust.

'I told him that I loved him too.'

Tom was silent a few moments. At last he looked up and said coldly—

'Now, then, Maggie, there are but two courses for you to take; either you vow solemnly to me, with your hand on my father's Bible, that you will never have another meeting or speak another word in private with Philip Wakem, or you refuse, and I tell my father everything; and this month, when by my exertions he might be made happy once more, you will cause him the blow of knowing that you are a disobedient, deceitful daughter, who throws away her own respectability by clandestine meetings with the son of a man that has helped to ruin her father. Choose!' Tom ended with cold decision, going up to the large Bible, drawing it forward.

It was a crushing alternative to Maggie.

'Tom,' she said, urged out of pride into pleading, 'don't ask me that. I will promise you to give up all intercourse with Philip, if you will let me see him once, or even only write to him and explain everything – to give it up as long as it would ever cause any pain to my father ... I feel something for Philip too. *He* is not happy.'

'I don't wish to hear anything of your feelings; I have said exactly what I mean: choose – and quickly, lest my mother should come in.'

'If I give you my word, that will be as strong a bond to me as if I laid my hand on the Bible. I don't require that to bind me.'

'Do what *I* require,' said Tom. 'I can't trust you, Maggie. Put your hand on this Bible, and say, "I renounce all private speech and intercourse with Philip Wakem from this time forth." Else you will bring shame on us all, and grief on my father, and what is the use of my exerting myself and giving up everything else for the sake of paying my father's debts, if you are to bring madness and vexation on him, just when he might be easy and hold up his head once more?'

'Oh, Tom – *will* the debts be paid soon?' said Maggie, clasping her hands, with a sudden flash of joy across her wretchedness.

'If things turn out as I expect,' said Tom. 'But,' he added, his voice trembling with indignation, 'while I have been contriving and working that my father may have some peace of mind before he dies – working for the respectability of our family – you have done all you can to destroy both.'

'Tom,' she said in a low voice, 'it was wrong of me – but I was so lonely – and I was sorry for Philip. And I think enmity and hatred are wicked.'

'Nonsense!' said Tom. 'Your duty was clear enough. Say no more; but promise, in the words I told you.'

'I *must* speak to Philip once more.'

'You will go with me now and speak to him.'

'I give you my word not to meet him or write to him again without your knowledge. That is the only thing I will say. I will put my hand on the Bible if you like.'

'Say it then.'

Maggie laid her hand on the page of manuscript and repeated the promise. Tom closed the book, and said, 'Now, let us go.'

Not a word was spoken as they walked along. Maggie's only hope was that something might, for the first time, have prevented Philip from coming. Her heart beat with double violence when they got under the Scotch firs. Philip always met her soon after she got beyond them. But they passed across the more open green space, and entered the narrow bushy path by the mound. Another turning, and they came so close upon him that both Tom and Philip stopped suddenly within a yard of each other. There was a moment's silence, in which Philip darted a look of inquiry at Maggie's face. He saw an answer there, in the pale parted lips, and the terrified tension of the large eyes.

'Do you call this acting the part of a man and a gentleman, sir?' Tom said, in a voice of harsh scorn, as soon as Philip's eyes were turned on him again.

'What do you mean?' answered Philip, haughtily.

'Mean? Stand farther from me, lest I should lay hands on you, and I'll tell you what I mean. I mean, taking advantage of a young girl's foolishness and ignorance to get her to have secret meetings with you. I mean, daring to trifle with the respectability of a family that has a good and honest name to support.'

'I deny that,' interrupted Philip, impetuously. 'I could never trifle with anything that affected your sister's happiness. She is dearer to me than she is to you; I honour her more than you can ever honour her; I would give up my life to her.'

'Don't talk high-flown nonsense to me, sir! Do you mean to pretend that you didn't know it would be injurious to her to meet you here week after week? Do you pretend you had any right to make professions of love to her, even if you had been a fit husband for her, when neither her father nor your father would ever consent to a marriage between you? And *you* – *you* to try and worm yourself into the affections of a handsome girl who is not eighteen, and has been shut out from the world by her father's misfortunes! That's your crooked notion of honour, is it? I call it base treachery – I call it taking advantage of circumstances to win what's too good for you – what you'd never get by fair means.'

'It is manly of you to talk in this way to *me*,' said Philip, bitterly, his whole frame shaken by violent emotions. 'Giants have an immemorial right to stupidity and insolent abuse. You are incapable even of understanding what I feel for your sister. I feel so much for her that I could even desire to be at friendship with *you*.'

'I should be very sorry to understand your feelings,' said Tom, with scorching contempt. 'What I wish is that you should understand *me* – that I shall take care of *my* sister, and that if you dare to make the least attempt to come near her, or to write to her, or keep the slightest hold on her mind, your puny, miserable body, that ought to have put some modesty into your mind, shall not protect you. I'll thrash you – I'll hold you up to public scorn. Who wouldn't laugh at the idea of *your* turning lover to a fine girl?'

'Tom, I will not bear it – I will listen no longer,' Maggie burst out.

'Stay, Maggie!' said Philip, making a strong effort to speak. Then, looking at Tom, 'You have dragged your sister here, I suppose, that she may stand by while you threaten and insult me. These naturally seemed to you the right means to influence me. But you are mistaken. Let your sister speak. If she says she is bound to give me up, I shall abide by her wishes to the slightest word.'

'It was for my father's sake, Philip,' said Maggie, imploringly. 'Tom threatens to tell my father – and he couldn't bear it: I have promised, I have vowed solemnly, that we will not have any intercourse without my brother's knowledge.'

'It is enough, Maggie. *I* shall not change; but I wish you to hold yourself entirely free. But trust me – remember that I can never seek for anything but good to what belongs to you.'

'Yes,' said Tom, exasperated by this attitude of Philip's, 'you can talk of seeking good for her and what belongs to her now: did you seek her good before?'

'I did – at some risk, perhaps. But I wished her to have a friend for life – who would cherish her, who would do her more justice than a coarse and narrow-minded brother, that she has always lavished her affections on.'

'Yes, my way of befriending her is different from yours; and I'll tell you what is my way. I'll save her from disobeying and disgracing her father: I'll save her from throwing herself away on you – from making herself a laughing-stock – from being flouted by a man like *your* father, because she's not good enough for his son. You know well enough what sort of justice and cherishing you were preparing for her. I'm not to be imposed upon by fine words: I can see what actions mean. Come away, Maggie.'

He seized Maggie's right wrist as he spoke, and she put out her left hand. Philip clasped it an instant, with one eager look, and then hurried away.

Tom and Maggie walked on in silence for some yards. He was still holding her wrist tightly, as if he were compelling a culprit from the scene of action. At last Maggie, with a violent snatch, drew her hand away, and her pent-up long-gathered irritation burst into utterance.

'Don't suppose that I think you are right, Tom, or that I bow to your will. I despise the feelings you have shown in speaking to Philip: I detest your insulting unmanly allusions to his deformity. You have been reproaching other people all your life – you have been always sure you yourself are right: it is because you have not a mind large enough to see that there is anything better than your own conduct and your own petty aims.'

'Certainly,' said Tom, coolly. 'I don't see that your conduct is better, or your aims either. If your conduct, and Philip Wakem's conduct, has been right, why are you ashamed of its being known? Answer me that. I know what I have aimed at in my conduct, and I've succeeded: pray, what good has your conduct brought to you or any one else?'

'I don't want to defend myself,' said Maggie, still with vehemence: 'I know I've been wrong – often, continually. But yet, sometimes when I have done wrong, it has been because I have feelings that you would be the better for, if you had them. If *you* were in fault ever – if you had done anything very wrong, I should be sorry for the pain it brought you; I should not want punishment to be heaped on you. But you have always enjoyed punishing me – you have always been hard and cruel to me: even when I was a little girl, and always loved you better than any one else in the world. You have no pity: you have no sense of your own imperfection and your own sins. It is a sin to be hard; you thank God for nothing but your own virtues – you think they are great enough to win you everything else. You have not even a vision of feelings by the side of which your shining virtues are mere darkness!'

'Well,' said Tom, with cold scorn, 'if your feelings are so much better than mine, let me see you show them in some other way than by conduct that's likely to disgrace us all – than by ridiculous flights first into one extreme and then into another. Pray, how have you shown your love, that you talk of, either to me or my father? By disobeying and deceiving us. I have a different way of showing my affection.'

'Because you are a man, Tom, and have power, and can do something in the world.'

'Then if you can do nothing, submit to those that can.'

'So I *will* submit to what I acknowledge and feel to be right. I will submit even to what is reasonable from my father, but I will not submit to it from you. You boast of your virtues as if they purchased you a right to be cruel and unmanly as you've been today. Don't suppose I would give up Philip Wakem in obedience to you. The deformity you insult would make me cling to him and care for him the more.'

'Very well – that is your view of things,' said Tom, more coldly than ever; 'you need say no more to show me what a wide distance there is between us. Let us remember that in future, and be silent.'

Tom went back to St Ogg's, to fulfil an appointment with his uncle Deane, and receive directions about a journey on which he was to set out the next morning.

Maggie went up to her own room to pour out all that indignant remonstrance, against which Tom's mind was close barred, in bitter tears. Then, when the first burst of unsatisfied anger was gone by, came the recollection of that quiet time before the pleasure which had ended in today's misery had perturbed the clearness and simplicity of her life. She used to think in that time that she had made great conquests and won a lasting stand on serene heights above worldly temptations and conflict. And here she was down again in the thick of a hot strife with her own and others' passions. If she had felt that she was entirely wrong, and that Tom had been entirely right, she could sooner have recovered more inward harmony; but now her penitence and submission were constantly obstructed by resentment that would present itself to her no otherwise than as a just indignation. Her heart bled for Philip: she went on recalling the insults that had been flung at him with so vivid a conception of what he had felt under them, that it was almost like a sharp bodily pain to her.

And yet, how was it that she was now and then conscious of a certain dim background of relief in the forced separation from Philip? Surely it was only because the sense of a deliverance from concealment was welcome at any cost?

6

The Hard-won Triumph

Three weeks later, when Dorlcote Mill was at its prettiest moment in all the year – the great chestnuts in blossom, and the grass all deep and daisied – Tom Tulliver came home to it earlier than usual in the evening, and as he passed over the bridge, he looked with the old deep-rooted affection at the respectable red brick house, which always seemed cheerful and inviting outside, let the rooms be as bare and the hearts as sad as they might, inside. There is a very pleasant light in Tom's blue-grey eyes as he glances at the house-windows: that fold in his brow never disappears, but it is not unbecoming; it seems to imply a strength of will that may possibly be without harshness, when the eyes and mouth have their gentlest expression. His firm step becomes quicker, and the corners of his mouth rebel against the compression which is meant to forbid a smile.

The group in the parlour was sitting in unexpectant silence – Mr Tulliver in his arm-chair, tired with a long ride, and ruminating with a worn look, fixed chiefly on Maggie, who was bending over her sewing while her mother was making the tea.

They all looked up with surprise when they heard the well-known foot.

'Why, what's up now, Tom?' said his father. 'You're a bit earlier than usual.'

'Oh, there was nothing more for me to do, so I came away. Well, mother!'

Tom went up to his mother and kissed her, a sign of unusual good-humour with him. Hardly a word or look had passed between him and Maggie in all the three weeks: but his usual

incommunicativeness at home prevented this from being noticeable to their parents.

'Father,' said Tom, when they had finished tea, 'do you know
exactly how much money there is in the tin box?'

'Only a hundred and ninety-three pound,' said Mr Tulliver.
'You've brought less o' late – but young fellows like to have their
own way with their money. Though I didn't do as I liked before *I*
was of age.' He spoke with rather timid discontent.

'Are you quite sure that's the sum, father?' said Tom: 'I wish
you would take the trouble to fetch the tin box down. I think you
have perhaps made a mistake.'

'How should I make a mistake?' said his father, sharply. 'I've
counted it often enough; but I can fetch it, if you won't believe
me.'

It was always an incident Mr Tulliver liked, in his gloomy life,
to fetch the tin box and count the money.

'Don't go out of the room, mother,' said Tom, as he saw her
moving when his father was gone upstairs.

'And isn't Maggie to go?' said Mrs Tulliver; 'because somebody
must take away the things.'

'Just as she likes,' said Tom indifferently.

That was a cutting word to Maggie. Her heart had leaped with
the sudden conviction that Tom was going to tell their father
the debts could be paid – and Tom would have let her be absent
when that news was told! But she carried away the tray, and came
back immediately. The feeling of injury on her own behalf could
not predominate at that moment.

Tom drew to the corner of the table near his father when the tin
box was set down and opened, and the red evening light falling on
them made conspicuous the worn, sour gloom of the dark-eyed
father and the suppressed joy in the face of the fair-complexioned
son. The mother and Maggie sat at the other end of the table, the
one in blank patience, the other in palpitating expectation.

Mr Tulliver counted out the money, setting it in order on the
table, and then said, glancing sharply at Tom—

'There now! you see I was right enough.'

He paused, looking at the money with bitter despondency.

'There's more nor three hundred wanting – it'll be a fine while before *I* can save that. It's took four years to lay *this* by – it's much if I'm above ground for another four year … I must trusten to you to pay 'em,' he went on, with a trembling voice, 'if you keep i' the same mind now you're coming o' age. But you're like enough to bury me first.'

'No, father,' said Tom, speaking with energetic decision, though there was tremor discernible in his voice too, 'you will live to see the debts all paid. You shall pay them with your own hand.'

His tone implied something more than mere hopefulness or resolution. A slight electric shock seemed to pass through Mr Tulliver, and he kept his eyes fixed on Tom with a look of eager inquiry, while Maggie, unable to restrain herself, rushed to her father's side and knelt down by him. Tom was silent a little while before he went on.

'A good while ago, my uncle Glegg lent me a little money to trade with, and that has answered. I have three hundred and twenty pounds in the bank.'

His mother's arms were round his neck as soon as the last words were uttered, and she said, half-crying—

'Oh, my boy, I knew you'd make iverything right again, when you got a man.'

But his father was silent: the flood of emotion hemmed in all power of speech. Both Tom and Maggie were struck with fear lest the shock of joy might even be fatal. But the blessed relief of tears came. The broad chest heaved, the muscles of the face gave way, and the grey-haired man burst into loud sobs. The fit of weeping gradually subsided, and at last he looked up at his wife and said, in a gentle tone—

'Bessy, you must come and kiss me now – the lad has made you amends. You'll see a bit o' comfort again, belike.'

When she had kissed him, and he had held her hand a minute, his thoughts went back to the money.

'I wish you'd brought me the money to look at, Tom,' he said, fingering the sovereigns on the table; 'I should ha' felt surer.'

'You shall see it tomorrow, father,' said Tom. 'My uncle Deane has appointed the creditors to meet tomorrow at the Golden Lion, and he has ordered a dinner for them at two o'clock. My uncle Glegg and he will both be there. It was advertised in the *Messenger* on Saturday.'

'Then Wakem knows on't!' said Mr Tulliver, his eye kindling with triumphant fire. 'Ah!' he went on with something of his old air of defiance, 'I'll get from under *his* thumb now – though I *must* leave th' old mill. I thought I could ha' held out to die here – but I can't ... We've got a glass o' nothing in the house, have we, Bessy?'

'Yes,' said Mrs Tulliver, drawing out her much-reduced bunch of keys, 'there's some brandy sister Deane brought me when I was ill.'

'Get it me, then, get it me. I feel a bit weak.'

'Tom, my lad,' he said, in a stronger voice, when he had taken some brandy-and-water, 'you shall make a speech to 'em. I'll tell 'em it's you as got the best part o' the money. They'll see I'm honest at last, and ha' got an honest son. Ah! Wakem 'ud be fine and glad to have a son like mine – a fine straight fellow – i'stead o' that poor crooked creatur! You'll prosper i' the world, my lad; you're in the right way for't; and then there's nothing to hinder your getting rich ... And if ever you're rich enough – mind this – try and get th' old mill again.'

Mr Tulliver threw himself back in his chair: his mind, which had so long been the home of nothing but bitter discontent and foreboding, suddenly filled, by the magic of joy, with visions of good fortune.

'Shake hands wi' me, my lad,' he said, suddenly putting out his hand. 'It's a great thing when a man can be proud as he's got a good son. I've had *that* luck.'

Maggie felt no jealousy this evening that, for the first time, she seemed to be thrown into the background in her father's mind.

7

A Day of Reckoning

The next day, when Mr Tulliver was seated at table with his creditors, his eye kindling and his cheek flushed with the consciousness
that he was about to make an honourable figure once more, he
looked more like the proud, confident, warm-hearted and warm-
tempered Tulliver of old times. He made his speech, asserting his
honest principles with his old confident eagerness, alluding to the
rascals and the luck that had been against him, but that he had
triumphed over, to some extent, by hard efforts and the aid of
a good son; and winding up with the story of how Tom had got
the best part of the needful money. But the streak of irritation
and hostile triumph seemed to melt for a little while into purer
fatherly pride and pleasure, when, Tom's health having been
proposed, and uncle Deane having taken occasion to say a few
words of eulogy on his general character and conduct, Tom himself got up and thanked the gentlemen for the honour they had
done him. He was glad that he had been able to help his father in
proving his integrity and regaining his honest name; and, for his
own part, he hoped he should never undo that work and disgrace
that name. But the applause that followed was so great, and Tom
looked so gentlemanly as well as tall and straight, that Mr Tulliver
remarked, in an explanatory manner, to his friends on his right and
left, that he had spent a deal of money on his son's education.

The party broke up in a very sober fashion at five o'clock.
Tom remained in St Ogg's to attend to some business, and Mr
Tulliver mounted his horse to go home. He did not choose any
back street today, but rode slowly, with uplifted head and free
glances, along the principal street all the way to the bridge. Why
did he not happen to meet Wakem? The want of that coincidence
vexed him, and set his mind at work in an irritating way. Perhaps
Wakem was gone out of town today on purpose to avoid seeing
or hearing anything of an honourable action, which might well
cause him some unpleasant twinges.

Simmering in this way, Mr Tulliver approached the yard-gates of Dorlcote Mill, near enough to see a well-known figure coming out of them on a fine black horse. They met about fifty yards from the gates.

'Tulliver,' said Wakem, abruptly, in a haughtier tone than usual, 'what a fool's trick you did – spreading those hard lumps on that Far Close! I told you how it would be; but you men never learn to farm with any method.'

'Oh!' said Tulliver, suddenly boiling up. 'Get somebody else to farm for you, then, as'll ask *you* to teach him.'

'You have been drinking, I suppose,' said Wakem, really believing that this was the meaning of Tulliver's flushed face.

'No,' said Tulliver; 'I want no drinking to help me to make up my mind as I'll serve no longer under a scoundrel.'

'Very well; you may leave my premises tomorrow, then: hold your insolent tongue and let me pass.' (Tulliver was backing his horse across the road to hem Wakem in.)

'No, I *shan't* let you pass,' said Tulliver, getting fiercer. 'I shall tell you what I think of you first.'

'Let me pass, you ignorant brute, or I'll ride over you.'

Mr Tulliver, spurring his horse and raising his whip, made a rush forward, and Wakem's horse, rearing and staggering backward, threw his rider from the saddle and sent him sideways on the ground. But before he could remount, Tulliver was off his horse too. He rushed on Wakem, who was in the act of trying to recover his feet, grasped him by the left arm so as to press Wakem's whole weight on the right arm, which rested on the ground, and flogged him fiercely across the back with his riding-whip. Wakem shouted for help, but no help came, until a woman's scream was heard, and the cry of 'Father, father!'

Suddenly, Wakem felt, something had arrested Mr Tulliver's arm; for the flogging ceased, and the grasp on his own arm was relaxed.

'Get away with you – go!' said Tulliver, angrily. But it was not to Wakem that he spoke. Slowly the lawyer rose, and as he turned his head, saw that Tulliver's arms were being held by a girl –

rather by the fear of hurting the girl that clung to him with all her young might.

'Oh, Luke – mother – come and help Mr Wakem!' Maggie cried, as she heard the longed-for footsteps.

'Help me on to that low horse,' said Wakem to Luke, 'then I shall perhaps manage: though – confound it – I think this arm is sprained.'

With some difficulty, Wakem was heaved on to Tulliver's horse. Then he turned towards the miller and said, with white rage, 'You'll suffer for this, sir. Your daughter is a witness that you've assaulted me.'

'I don't care,' said Mr Tulliver, in a thick, fierce voice; 'go and show your back, and tell 'em I thrashed you. Tell 'em I've made things a bit more even i' the world.'

'Ride my horse home with me,' said Wakem to Luke. 'By the Tofton Ferry – not through the town.'

'Father, come in!' said Maggie, imploringly. Then, seeing that Wakem had ridden off, and that no further violence was possible, she slackened her hold and burst into hysteric sobs, while poor Mrs Tulliver stood by in silence, quivering with fear. But Maggie became conscious that as she was slackening her hold, her father was beginning to grasp her and lean on her. The surprise checked her sobs.

'I feel ill – faintish,' he said. 'Help me in, Bessy – I'm giddy – I've a pain i' the head.'

He walked in slowly, propped by his wife and daughter, and tottered into his arm-chair. The almost purple flush had given way to paleness, and his hand was cold.

'Hadn't we better send for the doctor?' said Mrs Tulliver.

He seemed to be too faint and suffering to hear her; but presently, when she said to Maggie, 'Go and see for somebody to fetch the doctor,' he looked up at her with full comprehension, and said, 'Doctor? no – no doctor. It's my head – that's all. Help me to bed.'

In half an hour after his father had lain down Tom came home. Bob Jakin was with him – come to congratulate 'the old master,' not without some excusable pride that he had had his share in bringing about Mr Tom's good luck; and Tom had thought his father would like nothing better, as a finish to the day, than a talk with Bob. But now Tom could only spend the evening in gloomy expectation of the unpleasant consequences that must follow on this mad outbreak of his father's long-smothered hate. After the painful news had been told, he sat in silence: Tom was dejected by the thought that his exemplary effort must always be baffled by the wrong-doing of others. Maggie was living through, over and over again, the agony of the moment in which she had rushed to throw herself on her father's arm – with a vague, shuddering foreboding of wretched scenes to come.

Tom, tired out by his active day, fell asleep soon, and slept soundly: it seemed to him as if he had only just come to bed, when he waked to see his mother standing by him in the grey light of early morning.

'My boy, you must get up this minute: I've sent for the doctor, and your father wants you and Maggie to come to him.'

'Is he worse, mother?'

'He's been very ill all night with his head, but he doesn't say it's worse – he only said sudden, "Bessy, fetch the boy and girl. Tell 'em to make haste."'

Maggie and Tom reached their father's room almost at the same moment. He was watching for them with an expression of pain on his brow, but with sharpened anxious consciousness in his eyes. Mrs Tulliver stood at the foot of the bed, frightened and trembling, looking worn and aged from disturbed rest. Maggie was at the bedside first, but her father's glance was towards Tom, who came and stood next to her.

'Tom, my lad, it's come upon me as I shan't get up again … This world's been too many for me, my lad, but you've done what you could to make things a bit even. Shake hands wi' me again, my lad, before I go away from you.'

The father and son clasped hands and looked at each other an instant. Then Tom said, trying to speak firmly, 'Have you any wish, father – that I can fulfil, when …'

'Ay, my lad … you'll try and get the old mill back.'

'Yes, father.'

'And there's your mother – you'll try and make her amends, all you can, for my bad luck … and there's the little wench …'

The father turned his eyes on Maggie with a still more eager look, while she, with a bursting heart, sank on her knees, to be closer to the dear, time-worn face which had been present with her through long years, as the sign of her deepest love and hardest trial.

'You must take care of her, Tom … don't you fret, my wench … there'll come somebody as'll love you and take your part … and you must be good to her, my lad. I was good to *my* sister. Kiss me, Maggie … Come, Bessy … You'll manage to pay for a brick grave, Tom, so as your mother and me can lie together.'

He looked away from them all when he had said this, and lay silent for some minutes, while they stood watching him, not daring to move. The morning light was growing clearer for them, and they could see the heaviness gathering in his face, and the dullness in his eyes. His hands moved uneasily, as if he wanted them to remove some obstruction that weighed upon him. For an hour or more the chest heaved, the loud hard breathing continued, getting gradually slower, as the cold dews gathered on the brow.

At last there was total silence, and poor Tulliver's dimly-lighted soul had for ever ceased to be vexed with the painful riddle of this world. Help was come now: Luke and his wife were there, and Mr Turnbull had arrived, too late for everything but to say, 'This is death.'

Tom and Maggie went downstairs together into the room where their father's place was empty. Their eyes turned to the same spot, and Maggie spoke—

'Tom, forgive me – let us always love each other;' and they clung and wept together.

BOOK SIXTH

The Great Temptation

1

A Duet in Paradise

The well-furnished drawing-room, with the open grand piano, and the pleasant outlook down a sloping garden to a boat-house by the side of the Floss, is Mr Deane's. The neat little lady in mourning, whose light-brown ringlets are falling over the coloured embroidery with which her fingers are busy, is of course Lucy Deane; and the fine young man who is leaning down from his chair to snap the scissors in the extremely abbreviated face of the 'King Charles' lying on the young lady's feet, is no other than Mr Stephen Guest, whose air of nonchalant leisure, at twelve o'clock in the day, is the graceful and odoriferous result of the largest oil-mill and the most extensive wharf in St Ogg's.

'My scissors please, if you can renounce the great pleasure of persecuting my poor Minny. Now don't set her growling again. Sit up and behave properly, and then I will tell you some news.'

'What is that?' said Stephen, throwing himself back and hanging his right arm over the corner of his chair. He might have been sitting for his portrait, which would have represented a rather striking young man of five-and-twenty, with a square forehead, short dark-brown hair standing erect, with a slight wave at the end, like a thick crop of corn, and a half-ardent half-sarcastic glance from under his well-marked horizontal eyebrows. 'Is it very important news?'

'Yes – very. It is about something I mentioned to you not very long ago.'

'But you have mentioned many things to me not long ago. Does your feminine tyranny require that when you say the thing you mean is one of several things, I should know it immediately by that mark?'

'Yes, I know you think I am silly.'

'I think you are perfectly charming.'

'But I know you like women to be rather insipid. Philip Wakem betrayed you: he said so one day when you were not here.'

'Oh, I know Phil is fierce on that point. I think he must be love-sick for some unknown lady whom he met abroad.'

'By the by,' said Lucy, pausing in her work, 'it has just occurred to me that I have never found out whether my cousin Maggie will object to see Philip. Tom will not enter a room where Philip is, if he knows it: perhaps Maggie may be the same, and then we shan't be able to sing our glees – shall we?'

'What! is your cousin coming to stay with you?' said Stephen, with a look of slight annoyance.

'Yes; that was my news which you have forgotten. She's going to leave her situation, where she has been nearly two years, poor thing – ever since her father's death; and she will stay with me a month or two – many months, I hope.'

'And am I bound to be pleased at that news?'

'Oh, no, not at all,' said Lucy, with a little air of pique. 'I am pleased, but that, of course, is no reason why *you* should be pleased. There is no girl in the world I love so well as my cousin Maggie.'

'And you will be inseparable, I suppose, when she comes. There will be no possibility of a *tête-à-tête* with you any more, unless you can find an admirer for her. What is the ground of dislike to Philip? He might have been a resource.'

'It is a family quarrel with Philip's father. There were very painful circumstances, I believe. My uncle Tulliver was unfortunate and lost all his property, and I think he considered Mr Wakem was somehow the cause of it. Papa told me there was a dreadful quarrel, the very day before my uncle's death, between him and Mr Wakem, but it was hushed up. That was when you were in London. Papa says my uncle was quite mistaken in many ways: his mind had become embittered. But Tom and Maggie must naturally feel it very painful to be reminded of these things. Maggie was at school with me six years ago, when she was fetched away because of her father's misfortunes, and she has hardly had any pleasure since, I think. She has been in a dreary situation in a school since uncle's death, because she is determined to be independent, and not live with aunt Pullet; and I could hardly wish her to come to me then, because dear mamma was ill, and everything was so sad. That is why I want her to come to me now, and have a long, long holiday.'

'Very sweet and angelic of you,' said Stephen, looking at her with an admiring smile; 'and all the more so if she has the conversational qualities of her mother.'

'Poor aunty! You are cruel to ridicule her. She is very valuable to *me*, I know. She manages the house beautifully and she was a great comfort to me in mamma's illness.'

'Yes, but in point of companionship, one would prefer that she should be represented by her brandy-cherries and cream-cakes. I think with a shudder that her daughter will always be present in person, and have no agreeable proxies of that kind – a fat, blond girl, with round blue eyes, who will stare at us silently.'

'Oh yes!' exclaimed Lucy, laughing wickedly and clapping her hands, 'that is just my cousin Maggie. You must have seen her!'

'No, indeed: I'm only guessing what Mrs Tulliver's daughter must be; and then, if she is to banish Philip, our only apology for a tenor, that will be an additional bore.'

'But I hope that may not be. I think I will ask you to call on Philip and tell him Maggie is coming tomorrow. He is quite aware of Tom's feeling; so he will understand, if you tell him, that I asked you to warn him not to come until I write to ask him.'

'I think you had better write a pretty note for me to take: Phil is so sensitive, you know, the least thing might frighten him off coming at all, and we had hard work to get him. I can never induce him to come to the Park: he doesn't like my sisters, I think. It is only your faëry touch that can lay his ruffled feathers.'

Stephen mastered the little hand that was straying towards the table, and touched it lightly with his lips. Little Lucy felt very proud and happy. She and Stephen were in that stage of courtship which makes the most exquisite moment of youth, the freshest blossom-time of passion – when each is sure of the other's love, but no formal declaration has been made, and all is mutual divination, exalting the most trivial word, the slightest gesture, into thrills delicate and delicious as wafted jasmine scent.

'But it is really odd that you should have hit so exactly on Maggie's appearance and manners,' said the cunning Lucy, moving to reach her desk, 'because she might have been like her brother, you know.'

'Oh, I suppose he is like the father: he seems to be as proud as Lucifer. Not a brilliant companion, though, I should think.'

'I like Tom. He gave me my Minny when I lost Lolo; and papa is very fond of him: he says Tom has excellent principles.'

'Oh, I heard your father and mine talking a little while ago, after dinner. They think of doing something for young Tulliver; he saved them from a considerable loss by riding home in some marvellous way to bring them news about the stoppage of a bank, or something of that sort. I was rather drowsy at the time.'

Stephen rose from his seat, and said—

'Adieu, I must gallop home. I promised to be there at lunch.'

'You will not be able to call on Philip, then? It is of no consequence: I have said everything in my note.'

'You will be engaged with your cousin tomorrow, I suppose?'

'Yes, we are going to have a little family-party. My cousin Tom will dine with us; and poor aunty will have her two children together for the first time. It will be very pretty; I think a great deal about it.'

'But may I come the next day?'

'Oh, yes! Come and be introduced to my cousin Maggie – though you can hardly be said not to have seen her, you have described her so well.'

'Good-bye, then.' And there was that slight pressure of the hands, and momentary meeting of the eyes, which will often leave a little lady with a slight flush and smile on her face. Was not Stephen Guest right in his decided opinion that this slim maiden of eighteen was quite the sort of wife a man would not be likely to repent of marrying? A man likes his wife to be pretty: well, Lucy was pretty, but not to a maddening extent. A man likes his wife to be accomplished, gentle, affectionate, and not stupid; and Lucy had all these qualifications. Stephen was not surprised to find himself in love with her, and was aware that he had sense and independence enough to choose the wife who was likely to make him happy, unbiased by any indirect considerations. He meant to choose Lucy: she was exactly the sort of woman he had always most admired.

2

First Impressions

'He is very clever, Maggie,' said Lucy. She was kneeling on a footstool at Maggie's feet, after placing that dark lady in the large crimson-velvet chair. 'I feel sure you will like him. I hope you will.'

'I shall be very difficult to please,' said Maggie, smiling. 'A gentleman who thinks he is good enough for Lucy must expect to be sharply criticised.'

'Indeed, he's a great deal too good for me. And sometimes, when he is away, I almost think it can't really be that he loves me. But I can never doubt it when he is with me – though I couldn't bear any one but you to know that I feel in that way, Maggie.'

'Oh, then, if I disapprove of him, you can give him up, since you are not engaged,' said Maggie, with playful gravity.

'I would rather not be engaged. When people are engaged, they begin to think of being married soon,' said Lucy, too thoroughly preoccupied to notice Maggie's joke; 'and I should like everything to go on for a long while just as it is. But I have prepared a charming suprise for *him*; I shall have a glorious laugh against him. I shall not tell you what it is, though.'

Lucy rose from her knees and went to a little distance, holding her pretty head on one side, as if she had been arranging Maggie for a portrait, and wished to judge of the general effect.

'I can't think what witchery it is in you, Maggie, that makes you look best in shabby clothes. Now, if I were to put anything shabby on, I should be quite unnoticeable – I should be a mere rag.'

'Oh, quite,' said Maggie, with mock gravity. Lucy, with an air of serious reflection, unfastened her large jet brooch. 'But you must change brooches, Maggie; that little butterfly looks silly on you.'

'But won't that mar the charming effect of my consistent shabbiness?' said Maggie, while Lucy knelt again and unfastened the contemptible butterfly. 'I wish my mother were of your opinion, for she was fretting last night because this is my best frock. I've been saving my money to pay for some lessons: I shall never get a better situation without more accomplishments.'

Maggie gave a little sigh.

'Now, don't put on that sad look again,' said Lucy, pinning the large brooch below Maggie's fine throat. 'You're forgetting that you've left that dreary schoolroom behind you.'

'Yes,' said Maggie. 'One gets a bad habit of being unhappy.'

'But I shall put you under a discipline of pleasure that will make you lose that bad habit,' said Lucy, sticking the black butterfly absently in her own collar.

'You dear, tiny thing,' said Maggie, in one of her bursts of loving admiration, 'you enjoy other people's happiness so much, I believe you would do without any of your own. I wish I were like you.'

'I've never been tried in that way,' said Lucy. 'I've always been so happy. I don't know whether I could bear much trouble; I never had any but poor mamma's death. You *have* been tried, Maggie; and I'm sure you feel for other people quite as much as I do.'

'No, Lucy,' said Maggie, shaking her head slowly, 'I don't enjoy their happiness as you do – else I should be more contented. I often hate myself, because I get angry sometimes at the sight of happy people. I think I get worse as I get older. That seems very dreadful.'

'Now, Maggie!' said Lucy, in a tone of remonstrance, 'I don't believe a word of that. It is all a gloomy fancy – just because you are depressed by a dull, wearisome life.'

'Well, perhaps it is,' said Maggie. 'Perhaps it comes from the school diet. Let us hope it will give way before my mother's custards.'

'Do I look fit to be seen with this little brooch?' said Lucy, going to survey the effect in the chimney-glass.

'Oh, no, Mr Guest will be obliged to go out of the room again if he sees you in it. Pray make haste and put another on.'

Lucy hurried out of the room. Maggie's eyes wandered to the window. The sight of the old scenes had made the rush of memories so painful, that even yesterday she had only been able to rejoice in her mother's restored comfort and Tom's brotherly friendliness as we rejoice in good news of friends at a distance, rather than in the presence of a happiness which we share. Memory and imagination urged upon her a sense of privation too keen to let her taste what was offered in the transient present: her future, she thought, was likely to be worse than her past, for after her years of contented renunciation, she had slipped back into desire and longing: she found joyless days of distasteful occupation harder and harder. The sound of the opening door roused her.

'There is one pleasure, I know, Maggie, that your deepest dismalness will never resist,' said Lucy, beginning to speak as soon as she entered the room. 'That is music, and I mean you to get up your playing again, which used to be so much better than mine.'

'You would have laughed to see me playing the little girls' tunes over and over to them, when I took them to practice,' said Maggie, 'just for the sake of fingering the dear keys again.'

'I know what a wild state of joy you used to be in when the glee-men came round,' said Lucy, taking up her embroidery, 'and we might have all those old glees that you used to love so, if I were certain that you don't feel exactly as Tom does about some things.'

'I should have thought there was nothing you might be more certain of,' said Maggie, smiling.

'I ought rather to have said, one particular thing. Because if you feel just as he does about that, we shall want our third voice. St Ogg's is so miserably provided with musical gentlemen. There are really only Stephen and Philip Wakem who have any knowledge of music, so as to be able to sing a part.'

Lucy had looked up from her work as she uttered the last sentence, and saw that there was a change in Maggie's face.

'Does it hurt you to hear the name mentioned, Maggie? If it does, I will not speak of him again. I know Tom will not see him if he can avoid it.'

'I don't feel at all as Tom does on that subject,' said Maggie, rising and going to the window as if she wanted to see more of the landscape. 'I've always liked Philip Wakem ever since I was a little girl and saw him at Lorton. He was so good when Tom hurt his foot.'

'Oh, I'm so glad!' said Lucy. 'Then you won't mind his coming sometimes, and we can have much more music than we could without him. I'm very fond of poor Philip, only I wish he were not so morbid about his deformity. I suppose it *is* his deformity that makes him so sad – and sometimes bitter.'

'But, Lucy—' said Maggie, trying to arrest the prattling stream.

'Ah, there is the door-bell. That must be Stephen,' Lucy went on. 'One of the things I most admire in Stephen is, that he makes a greater friend of Philip than any one.'

It was too late for Maggie to speak now: the drawing-room door was opening, and Minny was already growling in a small way at the entrance of a tall gentleman, who went up to Lucy and took her hand with a half-polite, half-tender glance and tone of inquiry, which seemed to indicate that he was unconscious of any other presence.

'Let me introduce you to my cousin, Miss Tulliver,' said

Lucy, turning with wicked enjoyment towards Maggie, who now approached from the farther window. 'This is Mr Stephen Guest.'

For one instant Stephen could not conceal his astonishment at the sight of this tall, dark-eyed nymph with her jet-black coronet of hair; the next, Maggie felt herself, for the first time in her life, receiving the tribute of a very deep blush and a very deep bow from a person towards whom she herself was conscious of timidity. This new experience was very agreeable to her – so agreeable, that it almost effaced her previous emotion about Philip. There was a new brightness in her eyes, and a very becoming flush on her cheek, as she seated herself.

'I hope you perceive what a striking likeness you drew the day before yesterday,' said Lucy, with a pretty laugh of triumph.

'This designing cousin of yours quite deceived me, Miss Tulliver,' said Stephen, seating himself by Lucy, and stooping to play with Minny – only looking at Maggie furtively. 'She said you had light hair and blue eyes.'

'Nay, it was you who said so,' remonstrated Lucy. 'I only refrained from destroying your confidence in your own second-sight.'

'I wish I could always err in the same way,' said Stephen, 'and find reality so much more beautiful than my preconceptions.'

'Now you have proved yourself equal to the occasion,' said Maggie, 'and said what it was incumbent on you to say under the circumstances.'

She flashed a slightly defiant look at him: it was clear to her that he had been drawing a satirical portrait of her beforehand. Lucy had said he was inclined to be satirical, and Maggie had mentally supplied the addition – 'and rather conceited.'

'An alarming amount of devil there,' was Stephen's first thought. The second, when she had bent over her work, was, 'I wish she would look at me again.' The next was to answer—

'I suppose all phrases of mere compliment have their turn to be true. A man is occasionally grateful when he says "thank you." It's rather hard upon him that he must use the same words with which all the world declines a disagreeable invitation; don't you think so, Miss Tulliver?'

'No,' said Maggie, looking at him with her direct glance; 'if we use common words on a great occasion, they are the more striking, because they are felt at once to have a particular meaning, like old banners, or everyday clothes, hung up in a sacred place.'

'Then my compliment ought to be eloquent,' said Stephen, really not quite knowing what he said while Maggie looked at him, 'seeing that the words were so far beneath the occasion.'

'No compliment can be eloquent, except as an expression of indifference,' said Maggie, flushing a little.

Lucy was rather alarmed: she thought Stephen and Maggie were not going to like each other. She had always feared lest Maggie should appear too old and clever to please that critical gentleman. 'Why, dear Maggie,' she interposed, 'you have always pretended that you are too fond of being admired, and now, I think, you are angry because some one ventures to admire you.'

'Not at all,' said Maggie; 'I like too well to feel that I am admired, but compliments never make me feel that.'

'I will never pay you a compliment again, Miss Tulliver,' said Stephen.

'Thank you; that will be a proof of respect.'

Poor Maggie! She was so unused to society that she could take nothing as a matter of course, and had never in her life spoken from the lips merely, so that she must necessarily appear absurd to more experienced ladies, from the excessive feeling she was apt to throw into very trivial incidents. But she was even conscious herself of a little absurdity in this instance. It was true she had a theoretic objection to compliments, and had once said impatiently to Philip, that she didn't see why women were to be told with a simper that they were beautiful, any more than old men were to be told that they were venerable: still, to be so irritated by a common practice in the case of a stranger like Mr Stephen Guest, and to care about his having spoken slightingly of her before he had seen her, was certainly unreasonable, and as soon as she was silent she began to be ashamed of herself. It did not occur to her that her irritation was due to the pleasanter emotion which preceded it.

Stephen began to talk of impersonal matters, asking Lucy if she knew when the bazaar was at length to take place, so that there might be some hope of seeing her rain the influence of her eyes on objects more grateful than those worsted flowers that were growing under her fingers.

'Some day next month, I believe,' said Lucy. 'But your sisters are doing more for it than I am: they are to have the largest stall.'

'Ah, yes; but they carry on their manufactures in their own sitting-room, where I don't intrude on them. I see you are not addicted to the fashionable vice of fancy-work, Miss Tulliver,' said Stephen, looking at Maggie's plain hemming.

'No,' said Maggie, 'I can do nothing more difficult or more elegant than shirt-making.'

'And your plain sewing is so beautiful, Maggie,' said Lucy, 'that I think I shall beg a few specimens of you to show as fancy-work. Your exquisite sewing is quite a mystery to me – you used to dislike that sort of work so much in old days.'

'It is a mystery easily explained, dear,' said Maggie, looking up quietly. 'Plain sewing was the only thing I could get money by, so I was obliged to try and do it well.'

Lucy, good and simple as she was, could not help blushing a little: she did not quite like that Stephen should know that – Maggie need not have mentioned it. Perhaps there was some pride in the confession: the pride of poverty that will not be ashamed of itself. But if Maggie had been the queen of coquettes she could hardly have invented a means of giving greater piquancy to her beauty in Stephen's eyes: the quiet admission made Maggie more unlike other women even than she had seemed at first.

Did Lucy intend to be present at the meeting of the Book Club next week? was Stephen's next question.

'No, no,' Lucy answered. 'I want Maggie to have delicious do-nothing days, filled with boating, and chatting, and riding, and driving: that is the holiday she needs.'

'Apropos!' said Stephen, looking at his watch. 'Shall we go out for a row on the river now? The tide will suit for us to go the Tofton way, and we can walk back.'

That was a delightful proposition to Maggie, for it was years since she had been on the river. When she was gone to put on her bonnet, Lucy lingered to give an order to the servant, and took the opportunity of telling Stephen that Maggie had no objection to seeing Philip, so that it was a pity she had sent that note the day before yesterday. But she would write another tomorrow and invite him.

'I'll call on him tomorrow,' said Stephen, 'and bring him with me in the evening, shall I?'

'Oh, yes, pray bring him,' said Lucy. 'And you *will* like Maggie, shan't you?' she added in a beseeching tone. 'Isn't she a dear, noble-looking creature?'

'Too tall,' said Stephen, smiling down upon her, 'and a little too fiery. She is not my type of woman, you know.'

Hardly anything could be more distinctly characteristic of Lucy, than that she both implicitly believed what Stephen said, and was determined that Maggie should not know it. He walked down to the boat-house calculating, by the aid of a vivid imagination, that Maggie must give him her hand at least twice in consequence of this pleasant boating plan, and that a gentleman who wishes ladies to look at him is advantageously situated when he is rowing them in a boat. What then? Had he fallen in love with this surprising daughter of Mrs Tulliver at first sight? Certainly not. Besides, he was in love already, and half-engaged to the dearest little creature in the world; and he was not a man to make a fool of himself in any way. But it was perfectly natural and safe to admire beauty and enjoy looking at it – at least under such circumstances as the present. And there was really something very interesting about this girl, with her poverty and troubles: it was gratifying to see the friendship between the two cousins. Generally, Stephen admitted, he was not fond of women who had any peculiarity of character – but here the peculiarity seemed really of a superior kind; and provided one is not obliged to marry such women, why, they certainly make a variety in social intercourse.

Maggie did not fulfil Stephen's hope by looking at him during the first quarter of an hour: her eyes were too full of the old banks that she knew so well. But presently the rhythmic movement of the oars attracted her, and she thought she should like to learn how to row. This roused her from her reverie, and she asked if she might take an oar. It appeared that she required much teaching, and she became ambitious.

The exercise brought the warm blood into her cheeks, and made her inclined to take her lesson merrily.

'I shall not be satisfied until I can manage both oars, and row you and Lucy,' she said, looking very bright as she stepped out of the boat. Maggie, we know, was apt to forget the thing she was doing, and she had chosen an inopportune moment for her remark: her foot slipped, but happily Mr Stephen Guest held her hand, and kept her up with a firm grasp.

'You have not hurt yourself at all, I hope?' he said, bending to look in her face with anxiety. It was very charming to be taken care of in that kind graceful manner by some one taller and stronger than one's self. Maggie had never felt just in the same way before.

When they reached home again, they found uncle and aunt Pullet seated with Mrs Tulliver in the drawing-room, and Stephen hurried away, asking leave to come again in the evening.

Aunt Pullet, under the certainty that Maggie would be invited to go out with Lucy, probably to Park House, was much shocked at the shabbiness of her clothes, which, when witnessed by the higher society of St Ogg's, would be a discredit to the family, that demanded a strong and prompt remedy; and the consultation as to what would be most suitable to this end from among the superfluities of Mrs Pullet's wardrobe, was one that Lucy as well as Mrs Tulliver entered into with some zeal. Maggie must really have an evening dress as soon as possible, and she was about the same height as aunt Pullet.

'But she's so much broader across the shoulders than I am – it's very ill-convenient,' said Mrs Pullet, 'else she might wear that beautiful black brocade o' mine without any alteration; and her arms are beyond everything,' added Mrs Pullet, sorrowfully, 'she'd never get my sleeves on.'

'Oh, never mind that, aunt: pray send us the dress,' said Lucy. 'I don't mean Maggie to have long sleeves, and I have abundance of black lace for trimming. Her arms will look beautiful.'

3

Confidential Moments

When Maggie went up to her bedroom that night, she set down her candle on the first table that presented itself, and began to walk up and down her room, which was a large one, with a firm, regular, and rather rapid step, which showed that the exercise was the instinctive vent of strong excitement. Her eyes and cheeks had an almost feverish brilliancy; her head was thrown backward, and her hands were clasped with the palms outward, and with that tension of the arms which is apt to accompany mental absorption.

Had anything remarkable happened?

She had been hearing some fine music sung by a fine bass voice. And she was conscious of having been looked at a great deal, in rather a furtive manner, from beneath a pair of well-marked horizontal eyebrows, with a glance that seemed somehow to have caught the vibratory influence of the voice. Such things could have had no perceptible effect on a thoroughly well-educated young lady, with a perfectly balanced mind, who had had all the advantages of fortune, training, and refined society. But in poor Maggie's highly-strung, hungry nature – just come away from a third-rate schoolroom, with all its jarring sounds and petty round of tasks – these apparently trivial causes had the effect of rousing and exalting her imagination in a way that was mysterious to herself. It was not that she thought distinctly of Mr Stephen Guest, or dwelt on the indications that he looked at her with admiration; it was rather that she felt the half-remote presence of a world of love and beauty and delight, made up of vague, mingled images from all the poetry and romance she had ever read, or had ever woven in her dreamy reveries. The music was vibrating in her still – Purcell's music, with its wild passion and fancy. She was in her brighter aerial world again, when a little tap came at the door: of course it was her cousin, who entered in ample white dressing-gown.

'Why, Maggie, haven't you begun to undress?' said Lucy, in astonishment.

'Well, *you* are not very forward,' retorted Maggie, hastily reaching her own pink cotton gown, and looking at Lucy's light-brown hair brushed back in curly disorder.

'Oh, I have not much to do. I shall sit down and talk to you, till I see you are really on the way to bed.'

While Maggie stood and unplaited her long black hair over her pink drapery, Lucy sat down near the toilette-table, watching her with affectionate eyes, and head a little aside, like a pretty spaniel.

'You really *have* enjoyed the music tonight, haven't you, Maggie?'

'Oh, yes, that is what prevents me from feeling sleepy. I think I should have no other mortal wants, if I could always have plenty of music. It seems to infuse strength into my limbs and ideas into my brain. Life seems to go on without effort, when I am filled with music.'

'And Stephen has a splendid voice, hasn't he?'

'Well, perhaps we are neither of us judges of that,' said Maggie, laughing, as she seated herself and tossed her long hair back. 'You are not impartial and *I* think any barrel-organ splendid.'

'But tell me what you think of him, now. Tell me exactly – good and bad too.'

'Oh, I think you should humiliate him a little. A lover should not be so much at ease, and so self-confident. He ought to tremble more.'

'Nonsense, Maggie! As if any one could tremble at me! You think he is conceited – I see that. But you don't dislike him, do you?'

'Dislike him! No. Am I in the habit of seeing such charming

people, that I should be very difficult to please? Besides, how could I dislike any one that promised to make you happy, you dear thing!' Maggie pinched Lucy's dimpled chin.

'We shall have more music tomorrow evening,' said Lucy, looking happy already, 'for Stephen will bring Philip Wakem with him.'

'Oh, Lucy, I can't see him,' said Maggie, turning pale. 'At least, I could not see him without Tom's leave.'

'Is Tom such a tyrant as that?' said Lucy, surprised. 'I'll take the responsibility, then – tell him it was my fault.'

'But, dear,' said Maggie, falteringly, 'I promised Tom very solemnly – before my father's death – I promised him I would not speak to Philip without his knowledge and consent. And I have a great dread of opening the subject with Tom – of getting into a quarrel with him again.'

'But I never heard of anything so strange and unreasonable. What harm can poor Philip have done? May I speak to Tom about it?'

'Oh, no, pray don't, dear,' said Maggie. 'I'll go to him myself tomorrow, and tell him that you wish Philip to come. I've thought before of asking him to absolve me from my promise, but I've not had the courage to determine on it.'

They were both silent for some moments, and then Lucy said—

'Maggie, you have secrets from me, and I have none from you.'

Maggie looked meditatively away from Lucy. Then she turned to her and said, 'I *should* like to tell you about Philip. But, Lucy, you must not betray that you know it to any one – least of all to Philip himself, or to Mr Stephen Guest.'

The narrative lasted long, for Maggie had never before known the relief of such an outpouring. On two points only she was not expansive. She did not betray fully what still rankled in her mind as Tom's great offence – the insults he had heaped on Philip. Angry as the remembrance still made her, she could not bear that any one else should know it all – both for Tom's sake and Philip's. And she could not bear to tell Lucy of the last scene between her father and Wakem, though it was this scene which she had ever since felt to be a new barrier between herself and Philip. She merely said, she saw now that Tom was, on the whole, right in regarding any prospect of love and marriage between her and Philip as put out of the question by the relation of the two families. Of course Philip's father would never consent.

'There, Lucy, you have had my story,' said Maggie, smiling, with the tears in her eyes. 'You see I was adored once.'

Lucy mused a little with her eyes downward, and then added, looking at Maggie, 'It is very beautiful that you should love Philip: I never thought such a happiness would befall him. And in my opinion, you ought not to give him up. There are obstacles now; but they may be done away with in time.'

Maggie tried to smile, but shivered, as if she felt a sudden chill. 'Ah, dear, you are cold,' said Lucy. 'You must go to bed; and so must I. I dare not think what time it is.'

4

Brother and Sister

Maggie was obliged to go to Tom's lodgings in the middle of the day, when he would be coming in to dinner. He was not lodging with entire strangers. Our friend Bob Jakin had, with Mumps's tacit consent, taken not only a wife about eight months ago, but also one of those queer old houses by the water-side, where, as he observed, his wife and mother could keep themselves out of mischief by letting out two 'pleasure-boats,' in which he had invested some of his savings, and by taking in a lodger for the parlour and spare bedroom. Under these circumstances, what could be better for the interests of all parties, than that the lodger should be Mr Tom?

It was Bob's wife who opened the door to Maggie. She was a tiny woman, in comparison with Bob's mother, who filled up the passage in the rear. The tiny woman curtsied and looked up at

Maggie with some awe as soon as she had opened the door; but the words, 'Is my brother at home?' which Maggie uttered smilingly, made her turn round with sudden excitement, and say—

'Eh, mother – tell Bob! – it's Miss Maggie! Come in, Miss, for goodness do,' she went on, opening a side door, and endeavouring to flatten her person against the wall to make the utmost space for the visitor.

Sad recollections crowded on Maggie as she entered the small parlour, which was now all that poor Tom had to call by the name of 'home'. But everything was not strange to her in this new room: the first thing her eyes dwelt on was the large old Bible, and the sight was not likely to disperse the old memories. She stood without speaking.

'If you please to take the privilege o' sitting down, Miss,' said Mrs Jakin, rubbing her apron over a perfectly clean chair.

'Bob is at home, then?' said Maggie, smiling.

'Yes, Miss; I'll go and see,' said Mrs Jakin, disappearing.

But she presently came back, walking with new courage a little way behind her husband, who showed the brilliancy of his blue eyes and regular white teeth in the doorway, bowing respectfully.

'How do you do, Bob?' said Maggie, coming forward and putting out her hand to him; 'I always meant to pay your wife a visit, and I shall come another day on purpose for that, if she will let me. But I was obliged to come today to speak to my brother.'

'He'll be in before long, Miss. He's doin' finely, Mr Tom is: he'll be one o' the first men hereabouts – you'll see that.'

'Well, Bob, I'm sure he'll be indebted to you, whatever he becomes: he said so himself only the other night, when he was talking of you.'

'Eh, Miss, that's his way o' takin' it. But I think the more on't when he says a thing, because his tongue doesn't overshoot him as mine does. But you look rarely, Miss – it does me good to see you. What do you say now, Prissy?' – here Bob turned to his wife. 'Isn't it all come true as I said? Though there isn't many sorts o' goods as I can't over-praise when I set my tongue to't.'

Mrs Bob was able now to smile and curtsy, and say, 'I'd looked forrard like aenything to seein' you, Miss, for my husband's tongue's been runnin' on you, like as if he was light-headed, iver since first he come a-courtin' on me.'

'Well, well,' said Bob, looking rather silly. 'Go an' see after the taters, else Mr Tom 'ull have to wait for 'em.'

'I hope Mumps is friendly with Mrs Jakin, Bob,' said Maggie, smiling. 'I remember you used to say, he wouldn't like your marrying.'

'Eh, Miss,' said Bob, grinning, 'he made up his mind to't when he see'd what a little un she was. He pretends not to see her mostly, or else to think as she isn't full-growed. But about Mr Tom, Miss,' said Bob, looking serious, 'he's as close as a iron biler, he is; but I'm a 'cutish chap, an' it worrets me as Mr Tom 'ull sit by himself so glumpish, a-knittin' his brow, an' a-lookin' at the fire of a night. He should be a bit livelier now – a fine young fellow like him.'

'He thinks so much about business,' said Maggie.

'Ay,' said Bob, speaking lower; 'but do you think it's nothin' else, Miss? He's close, Mr Tom is; but I'm a 'cute chap, I am, an' I thought tow'rt last Christmas as I'd found out a soft place in him. It was about a little black spaniel – a rare bit o' breed – as he made a fuss to get. But since then summat's come over him, as he's set his teeth again' things more nor iver, for all he's had such good luck. An' I wanted to tell *you*, Miss, 'cause I thought you might work it out of him a bit, now you're come. He's a deal too lonely, and doesn't go into company enough.'

'I'm afraid I have very little power over him, Bob,' said Maggie, a good deal moved by Bob's suggestion. It was a totally new idea to her mind, that Tom could have his love troubles. Poor fellow! – and in love with Lucy too! But Bob had already said, 'Here's Mr Tom,' and the outer door was opening.

'There's no time to spare, Tom,' said Maggie, as soon as Bob had left the room. 'I must tell you at once what I came about, else I shall be hindering you from taking your dinner.'

Tom stood with his back against the chimney-piece, and

Maggie was seated opposite the light. He had a presentiment of the subject she was going to speak about, making his voice colder and harder as he said, 'What is it?'

This tone roused a spirit of resistance in Maggie, and she put her request in quite a different form from the one she had predetermined on. She rose from her seat, and, looking straight at Tom, said—

'I want you to absolve me from my promise about Philip Wakem. Or rather, I promised you not to see him without telling you. I am come to tell you that I wish to see him.'

'Very well,' said Tom, still more coldly.

But Maggie had hardly finished speaking in that chill, defiant manner, before she repented, and felt the dread of alienation from her brother.

'Dear Tom. Don't be angry. I shouldn't have asked it, only that Philip, you know, is a friend of Lucy's, and she wishes him to come – has invited him to come this evening; and I told her I couldn't see him without telling you. I shall only see him in the presence of other people. There will never be anything secret between us again.'

Tom looked away from Maggie, knitting his brow more strongly for a little while. Then he turned to her and said, slowly and emphatically—

'You know what is my feeling on that subject, Maggie. While my father was living, I felt bound to use the utmost power over you, to prevent you from disgracing him as well as yourself, and all of us. But now I must leave you to your own choice. You wish to be independent – you told me so after my father's death. My opinion is not changed. If you think of Philip Wakem as a lover again, you must give up me.'

'I don't wish it, dear Tom – at least as things are: I see that it would lead to misery. But I shall soon go away to another situation, and I should like to be friends with him again while I am here. Lucy wishes it.'

The severity of Tom's face relaxed a little.

'I shouldn't mind your seeing him occasionally at my uncle's –

I don't want you to make a fuss on the subject. But I have no confidence in you, Maggie. You would be led away to do anything.'

That was a cruel word. Maggie's lips began to tremble.

'Why will you say that, Tom? It is very hard of you. Have I not done and borne everything as well as I could? And I have kept my word to you – when – when … my life has not been a happy one, any more than yours.'

She was obliged to be childish – the tears would come. When Maggie was not angry, she was as dependent on kind or cold words as a daisy on the sunshine or the cloud: the need of being loved would always subdue her. The brother's goodness came uppermost at this appeal, but it could only show itself in Tom's fashion. He put his hand gently on her arm, and said in the tone of a kind pedagogue—

'Now listen to me, Maggie. I'll tell you what I mean. You're always in extremes – you have no judgement and self-command; and yet you think you know best, and will not submit to be guided. You know I didn't wish you to take a situation. My aunt Pullet was willing to give you a good home, and you might have lived respectably amongst your relations, until I could have provided a home for you with my mother. And that is what I should like to do. I wished my sister to be a lady, and I would always have taken care of you, as my father desired, until you were well married. But your ideas and mine never accord, and you will not give way. Yet you might have sense enough to see that a brother, who goes out into the world and mixes with men, necessarily knows better what is right and respectable for his sister than she can know herself. You think I am not kind; but my kindness can only be directed by what I believe to be good for you.'

'Yes – I know – dear Tom,' said Maggie, trying to control her tears. 'I know you would do a great deal for me; I know how you work, and don't spare yourself. I am grateful to you. But, indeed, you can't quite judge for me. You don't know how differently things affect me from what they do you.'

'Yes, I *do* know: I know it too well. With any one but you, I should think it quite certain that what you witnessed just before my father's death would secure you from ever thinking again of Philip Wakem as a lover. But I don't feel certain of it with you – I never feel certain about anything with *you*. At one time you take pleasure in a sort of perverse self-denial, and at another you have not resolution to resist a thing that you know to be wrong.'

There was a terrible cutting truth in Tom's words. Maggie did not answer directly: her heart was too full, and she sat down, leaning her arm on the table. It was no use trying to make Tom feel that she was near to him. He always repelled her. Her feeling under his words was complicated by the allusion to the last scene between her father and Wakem; and at length that painful, solemn memory surmounted the immediate grievance. No! She did not think of such things with frivolous indifference, and Tom must not accuse her of that. She looked up at him with a grave, earnest gaze, and said—

'I can't make you think better of me, Tom, by anything I can say. But I am not so shut out from all your feelings as you believe me to be. I see as well as you do, that from our position with regard to Philip's father – not on other grounds – it would be wrong for us to entertain the idea of marriage; and I have given up thinking of him as a lover … I am telling you the truth, and you have no right to disbelieve me: I have kept my word to you, and you have never detected me in a falsehood. I should carefully avoid any intercourse with Philip on any other footing than that of quiet friendship. You may think that I am unable to keep my resolutions; but at least you ought not to treat me with hard contempt on the ground of faults that I have not committed yet.'

'Well, Maggie,' said Tom, softening under this appeal, 'I don't want to overstrain matters. I think, all things considered, it will be best for you to see Philip Wakem, if Lucy wishes him to come to the house. I believe what you say – at least you believe it yourself, I know: I can only warn you. I wish to be as good a brother to you as you will let me.'

There was a little tremor in Tom's voice as he uttered the last words, and Maggie's ready affection came back with as sudden a glow as when they were children. She rose and laid her hand on Tom's shoulder.

'Dear Tom, I know you mean to be good. I know you have had a great deal to bear, and have done a great deal. I should like to be a comfort to you – not to vex you. You don't think I'm altogether naughty, now, do you?'

Tom smiled at the eager face: his smiles were very pleasant to see when they did come, for the grey eyes could be tender underneath the frown.

'No, Maggie.'

'And may I come some day and make tea for you, and see this extremely small wife of Bob's again?'

'Yes; but trot away now, for I've no more time to spare,' said Tom, looking at his watch.

'Not to give me a kiss?'

Tom bent to kiss her cheek, and then said—

'There! Be a good girl. I've got a great deal to think of today. I have a long consultation with my uncle Deane this afternoon.'

5

Showing that Tom Had Opened the Oyster

'And now we've settled this Newcastle business, Tom,' said Mr Deane, that same afternoon, as they were seated in the private room at the bank together, 'there's another matter I want to talk to you about.'

Tom knew that the affair his uncle had to speak of was not urgent. Indeed, for the last month or two, there had been hints thrown out to Tom which enabled him to guess that he was going to hear some proposition for his own benefit.

'Let me see – it's going on for seven years now since you applied to me for a situation – eh, Tom?'

'Yes, sir; I'm three-and-twenty now,' said Tom.

'Ah – it's as well not to say that, though; for you'd pass for a good deal older, and age tells well in business. I remember your coming very well: I was naturally a little shy at pushing my nephew, but I'm happy to say you've done me credit, sir; and if I'd had a son o' my own, I shouldn't have been sorry to see him like you.'

'I'm very glad I've given you satisfaction, sir; I've done my best,' said Tom, in his proud, independent way.

'Yes, Tom, you've given me satisfaction. Ours is a fine business – a splendid concern, sir – and there's no reason why it shouldn't go on growing: there's a growing capital, and growing outlets for it; but there's another thing that's wanted for the prosperity of every concern, large or small, and that's men to conduct it – men of the right habits; none o' your flashy fellows, but such as are to be depended on. Now this is what Mr Guest and I see clear enough.'

Tom was getting a little nervous as Mr Deane went on speaking: he was conscious of something he had in his mind to say, which might not be agreeable to his uncle, simply because it was a new suggestion rather than acceptance of the proposition he foresaw.

'It stands to reason,' Mr Deane went on, 'that your being my nephew weighs in your favour; but I don't deny that if you'd been no relation of mine at all, your conduct in that affair of Pelley's bank would have led Mr Guest and myself to make some acknowledgement of the service you've been to us; and, backed by your general conduct and business ability, it has made us determine on giving you a share in the business – a share which we shall be glad to increase as the years go on. I told Mr Guest I would open the subject to you; and when you come back from this northern business, we can go into particulars. This is a great stride for a young fellow, but I'm bound to say you've deserved it.'

'I'm grateful to Mr Guest and you, sir; of course I feel the most indebted to *you*, who first took me into the business, and have taken a good deal of pains with me since.'

Tom spoke with a slight tremor. 'But there's one thing I should like to mention to you, uncle. I've never spoken to you of it before. If you remember, at the time my father's property was sold, there was some thought of your firm buying the mill: I know you thought it would be a very good investment, especially if steam were applied.'

'To be sure, to be sure. But Wakem outbid us.'

'Perhaps it's of no use my mentioning it at present,' Tom went on, 'but I wish you to know it was my father's dying wish that I should try and get it back again whenever I could. I promised my father; and besides that, I'm attached to the place. I shall never like any other so well. And if it should ever suit your views to buy it for the firm, I should have a better chance of fulfilling my father's wish. I shouldn't have liked to mention the thing to you, only you've been kind enough to say my services have been of some value. And I'd give up a much greater chance in life for the sake of having the mill again – I mean, having it in my own hands, and gradually working off the price.'

Mr Deane had listened attentively, and now looked thoughtful.

'I see, I see,' he said, after a while; 'the thing would be possible, if there were any chance of Wakem's parting with the property. He's put that young Jetsome in the place; and he had his reasons when he bought it, I'll be bound.'

'He's a loose fish, that young Jetsome,' said Tom. 'He's taking to drinking, and they say he's letting the business go down. Luke told me about it – our old miller. I was thinking, if things went on in that way, Wakem might be more willing to part with the mill. Luke says he's getting very sour about the way things are going on.'

'Well, I'll turn it over, Tom. I must inquire into the matter, and go into it with Mr Guest. But, you see, it's rather striking out a new branch, and putting you to that, instead of keeping you where you are, which was what we'd wanted.'

'I should be able to manage more than the mill when things were once set properly going, sir. I want to have plenty of work. There's nothing else I care about much.'

There was something rather sad in that speech from a young man of three-and-twenty, even in uncle Deane's business-loving ears.

'Pooh, pooh! you'll be having a wife to care about one of these days, if you get on at this pace in the world. But as to this mill, we mustn't reckon on our chickens too early. However, I promise you to bear it in mind, and when you come back, we'll talk of it again. Come and breakfast with us tomorrow morning, and say good-bye to your mother and sister before you start.'

6

Illustrating the Laws of Attraction

Launched into the higher society of St Ogg's, with a striking person which had the advantage of being quite unfamiliar to the majority of beholders, and with such moderate assistance of costume as you have seen foreshadowed in Lucy's anxious colloquy with aunt Pullet, Maggie was certainly at a new starting-point in life. At Lucy's first evening-party, young Torry fatigued his facial muscles more than usual in order that 'the dark-eyed girl there, in the corner,' might see him in all the additional style conferred by his eye-glass; and several young ladies went home intending to have short sleeves with black lace, and to plait their hair in a broad coronet at the back of their head. The Miss Guests, who associated chiefly on terms of condescension with the families of St Ogg's, took some exception to Maggie's manners. She had a way of not assenting at once to the observations current in good society, and of saying that she didn't know whether those observations were true or not, which gave her an air of *gaucherie*, and impeded the even flow of conversation; but it is a fact that ladies are not the worst disposed towards a new acquaintance of their own sex because she has points of inferiority. And Maggie was so entirely without those pretty airs of coquetry which have the reputation of driving gentlemen to despair, that she won some feminine pity for being so ineffective in spite of her beauty. She had not had many advantages, poor thing! and it must be admitted there was no pretension about her: her abruptness and unevenness of manner were plainly the result of her secluded and lowly circumstances. It was only a wonder that there was no tinge of vulgarity about her, considering what the rest of poor Lucy's relations were: an allusion which always made the Miss Guests shudder a little. It was not agreeable to think of any connection by marriage with such people as the Gleggs and the Pullets; but certainly there was no possible objection to Lucy in herself – no one could help liking her. She would naturally desire that the Miss Guests should behave kindly to this cousin of whom she was so fond, and Stephen would make a great fuss if they were deficient in civility. Under these circumstances the invitations to Park House were not wanting; and elsewhere, also, Miss Deane was too popular and too distinguished a member of society in St Ogg's for any attention towards her to be neglected.

Thus Maggie was introduced for the first time to the young lady's life, and even in the first week she began to be less haunted by her sad memories and anticipations. Life was certainly very pleasant just now: it was becoming very pleasant to dress in the evening, and to feel that she was one of the beautiful things of this spring-time. And there were admiring eyes always awaiting her now; she was no longer an unheeded person, liable to be chid, from whom attention was continually claimed, and on whom no one felt bound to confer any. It was pleasant, too, when Stephen and Lucy were gone out riding, to sit down at the piano alone, and find that the old fitness between her fingers and the keys remained, and revived, like a sympathetic kinship not to be worn out by separation.

Under the charm of her new pleasures, Maggie herself was ceasing to think of her future lot; and her anxiety about her first interview with Philip was losing its predominance: perhaps, unconsciously to herself, she was not sorry that the interview had been deferred.

For Philip had not come the evening he was expected, and Mr Stephen Guest brought word that he was gone to the coast — probably, he thought, on a sketching expedition; but it was not certain when he would return. It was just like Philip – to go off in that way without telling any one. It was not until the twelfth day that he returned, to find both Lucy's notes awaiting him: he had left before he knew of Maggie's arrival.

There were not many hours in those days in which Mr Stephen Guest was not seated by Lucy's side, or standing near her at the piano, or accompanying her on some outdoor excursion: his attentions were clearly becoming more assiduous; and that was what every one had expected. Lucy was very happy: all the happier because Stephen's society seemed to have become much more interesting and amusing since Maggie had been there. Is it an inexplicable thing that a girl should enjoy her lover's society the more for the presence of a third person, and be without the slightest spasm of jealousy that the third person had the conversation habitually directed to her? Not when that girl is as tranquil-hearted as Lucy, thoroughly possessed with a belief that she knows the state of her companions' affections. Besides, it was Lucy by whom Stephen sat, to whom he gave his arm, to whom he appealed as the person sure to agree with him; and every day there was the same tender politeness towards her, the same consciousness of her wants and care to supply them. Was there really the same? It seemed to Lucy that there was more; and it was no wonder that the real significance of the change escaped her. It was a subtle act of conscience in Stephen that even he himself was not aware of. His personal attentions to Maggie were comparatively slight, and there had even sprung up an apparent distance between them, that prevented the renewal of that faint resemblance to gallantry into which he had fallen the first day in the boat. If Stephen came in when Lucy was out of the room – if Lucy left them together – they never spoke to each other; each was oppressively conscious of the other's presence. Yet each looked and longed for the same thing to happen the next day. Neither of them had begun to reflect on the matter. And when Lucy came into the room again, they were once more unconstrained. Maggie could look at Stephen – which, for some reason or other, she always avoided when they were alone – and he could even ask her to play his accompaniment for him, since Lucy's fingers were so busy with that bazaar-work; and lecture her on hurrying the *tempo*, which was certainly Maggie's weak point.

One day – it was the day of Philip's return – Lucy had formed a sudden engagement to spend the evening with Mrs Kenn, whose delicate state of health, threatening to become confirmed illness, obliged her to resign her functions at the coming bazaar into the hands of other ladies, of whom she wished Lucy to be one. The engagement had been formed in Stephen's presence, and he had heard Lucy promise to dine early and call at six o'clock for Miss Torry, who brought Mrs Kenn's request.

'Here is another of the moral results of this idiotic bazaar,' Stephen burst forth, as soon as Miss Torry had left the room, 'taking young ladies from the duties of the domestic hearth into scenes of dissipation among urn-rugs and embroidered reticules! I should like to know what is the proper function of women, if it is not to make reasons for husbands to stay at home, and still stronger reasons for bachelors to go out. If this goes on much longer, the bonds of society will be dissolved.'

'Well, it will not go on much longer,' said Lucy, laughing, 'for the bazaar is to take place on Monday week.'

'Thank Heaven!' said Stephen, and there the subject ended.

Maggie was seated in the drawing-room alone, shortly after dinner, with Minny on her lap, having left her uncle to his wine and his nap, and her mother to the compromise between knitting and nodding, which, when there was no company, she always carried on in the dining-room till tea-time. Maggie was stooping to caress the tiny silken pet, and comforting her for her mistress's absence, when the sound of a footstep on the gravel made her look up, and she saw Mr Stephen Guest walking up the garden, as if he had come straight from the river. Maggie felt her cheeks glowing and her heart beating: it was natural she should be nervous, for she was not accustomed to receive visitors alone. He had seen her look up through the open window, and raised his hat as he walked towards it, to enter that way instead of by the door. He blushed too, and certainly looked as foolish as a young man of some wit and self-possession can be expected to look, as he walked in with a roll of music in his hand, and said with an air of hesitating improvisation—

'You are surprised to see me again, Miss Tulliver – I ought to apologise for coming upon you by surprise, but I wanted to come into the town, and I got our man to row me; so I thought I would bring these things from the "Maid of Artois" for your cousin: I forgot them this morning. Will you give them to her?'

'Yes,' said Maggie, who had risen confusedly with Minny in her arms, and now, not quite knowing what else to do, sat down again.

Stephen laid down his hat, with the music, and sat down in the chair close by her. He had never done so before, and both he and Maggie were quite aware that it was an entirely new position.

'Well, you pampered minion!' said Stephen, leaning to pull the long curly ears that drooped over Maggie's arm. As the speaker did not follow it up by further development, it naturally left the conversation at a standstill. It seemed to Stephen like some action in a dream, that he was obliged to go on stroking Minny's head. Yet it was very pleasant: he only wished he dared look at Maggie, and that she would look at him – let him have one long look into those deep strange eyes of hers, and then he would be satisfied. As for Maggie, she had no distinct thought – only the sense of a presence like that of a closely-hovering broad-winged bird in the darkness, for she was unable to look up, and saw nothing but Minny's black wavy coat.

Stephen at last sat upright sideways in his chair, leaning one hand and arm over the back and looking at Maggie. What should he say?

'We shall have a splendid sunset, I think; shan't you go out and see it?'

'I don't know,' said Maggie. Then, courageously raising her eyes and looking out of the window, 'If I'm not playing cribbage with my uncle.'

A pause: during which Minny is stroked again, but has sufficient insight not to be grateful for it – to growl rather.

'Do you like sitting alone?'

A rather arch look came over Maggie's face, and, just glancing at Stephen, she said, 'Would it be quite civil to say "yes"?'

'It *was* rather a dangerous question for an intruder to ask,' said Stephen, delighted with that glance, and getting determined to stay for another. 'But you will have more than half an hour to yourself after I am gone,' he added, taking out his watch. 'I know Mr Deane never comes in till half-past seven.'

Another pause, during which Maggie looked steadily out of the window, till by a great effort she moved her head to look down at Minny's back again, and said—

'I wish Lucy had not been obliged to go out. We lose our music.'

'We shall have a new voice tomorrow night,' said Stephen. 'Will you tell your cousin that our friend Philip Wakem is come back? I saw him as I went home.'

Maggie gave a little start. But the new images summoned by Philip's name dispersed half the oppressive spell she had been under. She rose from her chair with a sudden resolution, and, laying Minny on her cushion, went to reach Lucy's large work-basket from its corner. Stephen was vexed and disappointed: he thought, perhaps Maggie didn't like the name of Wakem to be mentioned to her in that abrupt way – for he now recalled what Lucy had told him of the family quarrel. It was of no use to stay any longer. Maggie was seating herself at the table with her work, and looking chill and proud; and he – he looked like a simpleton for having come. A gratuitous, entirely superfluous visit of that sort was sure to make a man disagreeable and ridiculous.

At this moment Maggie's ball of knitting-wool rolled along the ground, and she started up to reach it. Stephen rose too, and, picking up the ball, met her with a vexed complaining look that gave his eyes quite a new expression to Maggie, whose own eyes met them as he presented the ball to her.

'Good-bye,' said Stephen, in a tone that had the same beseeching discontent as his eyes. Maggie thought she had perhaps been rude.

'Won't you stay?' she said timidly.

'No, thank you,' said Stephen, looking still into the half-unwilling, half-fascinated eyes, as a thirsty man looks towards the track of the distant brook. 'The boat is waiting for me ... You'll tell your cousin that I brought the music?'

'Yes.'

'And that Philip is come back?'

'Yes.' (Maggie did not notice Philip's name this time.)

'Won't you come out a little way into the garden?' said Stephen, in a still gentler tone; but the next moment he was vexed that she did not say 'No,' for she moved away now towards the open window, and he was obliged to take his hat and walk by her side.

'Do take my arm,' he said, in a low tone, as if it were a secret.

There is something strangely winning to most women in that offer of the firm arm: the help is not wanted physically at that moment, but the presence of strength that is outside them and yet theirs meets a continual want of the imagination. Either on that ground or some other, Maggie took the arm. And they walked together round the grass-plot and under the drooping green of the laburnums, in the same dim dreamy state as they had been in a quarter of an hour before; only that Stephen had had the look he longed for, and Maggie had darting thoughts across the dimness – how came she to be there? – why had she come out?

'Take care of this step,' said Stephen, at last.

'Oh, I will go in now,' said Maggie, feeling that the step had come like a rescue. 'Good evening.'

In an instant she had withdrawn her arm, and was running back to the house. She only threw herself into the low arm-chair, and burst into tears.

'Oh, Philip, Philip, I wish we were together again – so quietly – in the Red Deeps.'

Stephen looked after her a moment, then went on to the boat, and was soon landed at the wharf. He spent the evening in the billiard-room, smoking one cigar after another, and losing 'lives' at pools. But he was determined not to think – not to admit any more distinct remembrance than was urged upon him by the perpetual presence of Maggie. But there came the necessity of walking home in the cool starlight, and with it the necessity of cursing his own folly, and bitterly determining that he would never trust himself alone with Maggie again. It was all madness: he wished he had never seen this Maggie Tulliver, to be thrown into a fever by her in this way: she would make a strange, sweet, troublesome, adorable wife to some man or other, but he would never have chosen her himself.

7

Philip Re-enters

The next morning was very wet: the sort of morning on which male neighbours who have no imperative occupation at home are likely to pay their fair friends an illimitable visit.

'Stephen will come earlier this morning. I know,' said Lucy; 'he always does when it's rainy.'

Maggie made no answer. She was angry with Stephen: she began to think she should dislike him; and if it had not been for the rain, she would have gone to her aunt Glegg's this morning, and so have avoided him altogether. As it was, she must find some reason for remaining out of the room with her mother.

But Stephen did not come earlier, and there was another visitor – a nearer neighbour – who preceded him. When Philip entered the room, he was going merely to bow to Maggie, feeling that their acquaintance was a secret which he was bound not to betray; but when she advanced towards him and put out her hand, he guessed at once that Lucy had been taken into her confidence. It was a moment of some agitation to both, though Philip had spent many hours in preparing for it; but like all persons who have passed through life with little expectation of sympathy, he shrank with the most sensitive pride from any noticeable betrayal of emotion. But Maggie, who had little more power of concealing the impressions made upon her than if she had been constructed of musical strings, felt her eyes getting larger with tears as they took each other's hands in silence. For Philip, who a little while ago was associated continually in Maggie's mind with the sense that Tom might reproach her with some justice, had now, in this short space, become a sort of outward conscience to her, that she might fly to for rescue and strength. Her tranquil, tender affection for Philip, with its root deep down in her childhood – the fact that in him the appeal was more strongly to her pity and womanly devotedness than to her vanity or other egoistic excitability of her nature – seemed now to make a sort of sacred place, a sanctuary where she could find refuge from an alluring influence which the best part of herself must resist, which must bring horrible tumult within, wretchedness without. This new sense of her relation to Philip nullified the anxious scruples she would otherwise have felt, lest she should overstep the limit of intercourse with him that Tom would sanction; and she put her hand to him, and felt the tears in her eyes without any consciousness of an inward check. The scene was just what Lucy expected, and her kind heart delighted in bringing Philip and Maggie together again; though, even with all *her* regard for Philip, she could not resist the impression that her cousin Tom had some excuse for feeling shocked at the physical incongruity between the two. She began to speak as soon as possible to set them at ease.

'This was very good and virtuous of you,' she said, 'to come so soon after your arrival. I think I will pardon you for running away in an inopportune manner, and giving your friends no notice. Come and sit down here,' she went on, placing the chair that would suit him best, 'and you shall find yourself treated mercifully.'

'You will never govern well, Miss Deane,' said Philip, as he seated himself, 'because no one will ever believe in your severity. People will always encourage themselves in misdemeanours by the certainty that you will be indulgent.'

Lucy gave some playful contradictions, but Philip did not hear what it was, for he had naturally turned towards Maggie, and she was looking at him with that open, affectionate scrutiny, which we give to a friend from whom we have been long separated.

What a moment their parting had been! And Philip felt as if he were only in the morrow of it. He felt this so keenly – with such intense, detailed remembrance – with such passionate revival of all that had been said and looked in their last conversation – that with that jealousy and distrust which in diffident natures is almost inevitably linked with a strong feeling, he thought he read in Maggie's glance and manner the evidence of a change. The very fact that he feared and half expected it, would be sure to make this thought rush in, in the absence of positive proof to the contrary.

'I am having a great holiday, am I not?' said Maggie. 'Lucy is like a fairy godmother: she has turned me from a drudge into a princess in no time. I do nothing but indulge myself all day long, and she always finds out what I want before I know it myself.'

'I am sure she is the happier for having you, then,' said Philip. 'And you look well – you are benefiting by the change.'

Artificial conversation of this sort went on a little while, till Lucy exclaimed, with a good imitation of annoyance, that she had forgotten something, and was quickly out of the room.

In a moment Maggie and Philip leaned forward, and the hands were clasped again, with a look of sad contentment like that of friends who meet in the memory of recent sorrow.

'I told my brother I wished to see you, Philip – I asked him to release me from my promise, and he consented.'

'Then we can at least be friends, Maggie? There is nothing to hinder that now?'

'Will not your father object?' said Maggie, withdrawing her hand.

'I should not give you up on any ground but your own wish, Maggie,' said Philip, colouring. 'There are points on which I should always resist my father, as I used to tell you. *That* is one.'

'Then there is nothing to hinder our being friends, Philip – seeing each other and talking to each other while I am here: I shall soon go away again to a new situation.'

'Is that inevitable, Maggie?'

'Yes: I must not stay here long. It would unfit me for the life I must begin again at last. I can't live in dependence – I can't live with my brother – though he is very good to me. He would like to provide for me; but that would be intolerable to me.'

Philip was silent a few moments, and then said, in that high feeble voice which with him indicated the resolute suppression of emotion—

'Is there no other alternative, Maggie? Is that life, away from those who love you, the only one you will allow yourself to look forward to?'

'Yes, Philip,' she said, looking at him pleadingly, as if she entreated him to believe that she was compelled to this course. 'At least, as things are; I don't know what may be in years to come. But I begin to think there can never come much happiness to me from loving: I have always had so much pain mingled with it. I wish I could make myself a world outside it, as men do.'

'Now, you are returning to your old thought in a new form, Maggie – the thought I used to combat,' said Philip, with a slight tinge of bitterness. 'You want to find out a mode of renunciation that will be an escape from pain. I tell you again, there is no such escape possible except by perverting or mutilating one's nature. What would become of me, if I tried to escape from pain? Scorn and cynicism would be my only opium; unless I could fall into some kind of conceited madness, and fancy myself a favourite of Heaven, because I am not a favourite with men.'

The bitterness had taken on some impetuosity as Philip went on speaking: the words were evidently an outlet for some immediate feeling of his own, as well as an answer to Maggie. There was a pain pressing on him at that moment. He shrank with proud delicacy from the faintest allusion to the words of love – of plighted love that had passed between them. It would have seemed to him like reminding Maggie of a promise; it would have had for him something of the baseness of compulsion. He could not dwell on the fact that he himself had not changed; for that too would have had the air of an appeal. His love for Maggie was stamped, even more than the rest of his experience, with the exaggerated sense that he was an exception – that she, that every one, saw him in the light of an exception.

But Maggie was conscience-stricken.

'Yes, Philip,' she said, with her childish contrition when he used to chide her, 'you are right, I know. I do always think too much of my own feelings, and not enough of others' – not enough of yours. I had need have you always to find fault with me and teach me: so many things have come true that you used to tell me.'

Maggie was resting her elbow on the table, leaning her head on her hand and looking at Philip with half-penitent dependent affection as she said this; while he was returning her gaze with an expression that, to her consciousness, gradually became charged with a specific recollection. Had his mind flown back to something that *she* now remembered? – something about a lover of Lucy's? It was a thought that made her shudder: it gave new definiteness to her present position, and to the tendency of what had happened the evening before.

'What is the matter, Maggie? Has something happened?' Philip said, in inexpressible anxiety – his imagination being only too ready to weave everything that was fatal to them both.

'No – nothing,' said Maggie. Philip must not have that odious thought in his mind: she would banish it from her own. 'Nothing,' she repeated, 'except in my own mind. You used to say I should feel the effect of my starved life, as you called it, and I do. I am too eager in my enjoyment of music and all luxuries, now they are come to me.'

She took up her work and occupied herself resolutely, while Philip watched her, really in doubt whether she had anything more than this general allusion in her mind. It was quite in Maggie's character to be agitated by vague self-reproach. But soon there came a violent well-known ring at the door-bell resounding through the house.

'Oh, what a startling announcement!' said Maggie, quite mistress of herself, though not without some inward flutter.

Lucy, after an interval long enough for a few solicitous inquiries, ushered Stephen in.

'Well, old fellow,' he said, going straight up to Philip and shaking him heartily by the hand, bowing to Maggie in passing. 'It's glorious to have you back again; only I wish you'd not go in and out constantly without letting the servants know. This is about the twentieth time I've had to scamper up those countless stairs to that painting-room of yours, all to no purpose, because your people thought you were at home.'

'I've so few visitors – it seems hardly worth while to leave notice of my exit and entrances,' said Philip, feeling rather oppressed just then by Stephen's bright strong presence and strong voice.

'Are you quite well this morning, Miss Tulliver?' said Stephen, turning to Maggie with stiff politeness, and putting out his hand with the air of fulfilling a social duty.

Maggie gave the tips of her fingers, and said, 'Quite well, thank you,' in a tone of proud indifference. Stephen and Maggie had no sooner completed this studied greeting than each felt hurt by the other's coldness. And Stephen, while rattling on in questions to Philip about his recent sketching expedition, was thinking all the more about Maggie because he was not drawing her into the conversation, as he had invariably done before. 'Maggie and Philip are not looking happy,' thought Lucy: 'this first interview has been saddening to them.'

'Let us have some music,' she said to Stephen. 'We ought to take advantage of having Philip and you together. Give us the duet in "Masaniello." Maggie has not heard that, and I know it will suit her.'

'Come, then,' said Stephen, going towards the piano.

'You, please, Philip – you play the accompaniment,' said Lucy, 'and then I can go on with my work. You *will* like to play, shan't you?' she added, with a pretty inquiring look, anxious, as usual, lest she should have proposed what was not pleasant to another; but with yearnings towards her unfinished embroidery.

Philip had brightened at the proposition, for there is no feeling, perhaps, except the extremes of fear and grief, that does not find relief in music – that does not make a man sing or play the better; and Philip had an abundance of pent-up feeling at this moment, as complex as any trio or quartet that was ever meant to express love and jealousy, and resignation and fierce suspicion, all at the same time.

'Oh, yes,' he said, seating himself at the piano, 'it is a way of eking out one's imperfect life and being three people at once – to sing and make the piano sing, and hear them both all the while – or else to sing and paint.'

'Ah, there you are an enviable fellow. I can do nothing with my hands,' said Stephen. 'That has generally been observed in men of greater administrative capacity, I believe. A tendency to predominance of the reflective powers in me! – haven't you observed that, Miss Tulliver?'

Stephen had fallen by mistake into his habit of playful appeal to Maggie, and she could not repress the answering flush and epigram.

'I *have* observed a tendency to predominance,' she said, smiling; and Philip at that moment devoutly hoped that she found the tendency disagreeable.

'Come, come,' said Lucy; 'music, music! We will discuss each other's qualities another time.'

Maggie always tried in vain to go on with her work when music began. She tried harder than ever today; for she knew that it was Stephen's habit always to stand so that he could look at her. But it was of no use: soon all her intentions were lost in the vague state of emotion produced by the inspiring duet – emotion that seemed to make her at once strong for all enjoyment, weak for all resistance. Poor Maggie! She looked very beautiful when her soul was being played on in this way by the inexorable power of sound. Lucy, who at other times had always been at the piano when Maggie was looking in this way, could not resist the impulse to steal up to her and kiss her. Philip, too, caught a glimpse of her now and felt that he had never before seen her under so strong an influence.

'More, more!' said Lucy, when the duet had been encored. 'Oh, play something the while, Philip,' said Lucy, noticing that his fingers were wandering over the keys. 'What is that you are falling into? – something delicious that I don't know.'

'Don't you know that?' said Philip, bringing out the tune more definitely. 'It's from the "Sonnambula" – "*Ah! perchè non posso odiarti.*" I don't know the opera, but it appears the tenor is telling the heroine that he shall always love her though she may forsake him. You've heard me sing it to the English words, "I love thee still."'

It was not quite unintentionally that Philip had wandered into this song, which might be an indirect expression to Maggie of what he could not prevail on himself to say to her directly. Her ears had been open to what he was saying, and when he began to sing, she understood the plaintive passion of the music. That pleading tenor had no very fine qualities as a voice, but it was not quite new to her; it had sung to her by snatches, in a subdued way, among the grassy walks and hollows, and underneath the leaning ash-tree in the Red Deeps. There seemed to be some reproach in the words – did Philip mean that? She wished she had assured him more distinctly in their conversation that she desired not to renew the hope of love between them, *only* because it clashed with her inevitable circumstances. She was touched, not thrilled, by the song: it suggested distinct memories and thoughts, and brought quiet regret in the place of excitement.

'That's the way with you tenors,' said Stephen, who was waiting with music in his hand while Philip finished the song. 'You demoralise the fair sex by warbling your sentimental love and constancy under all sorts of vile treatment. I must administer an antidote, while Miss Deane prepares to tear herself away from her bobbins.'

Stephen rolled out, with saucy energy—

> 'Shall I, wasting in despair.
> Die because a woman's fair?'

and seemed to make all the air in the room alive with a new influence. Lucy, always proud of what Stephen did, went towards the piano with laughing, admiring looks at him; and Maggie, in spite of her resistance to the spirit of the song and to the singer, was borne along by a wave too strong for her.

But angrily resolved not to betray herself, she seized her work, and went on making false stitches and pricking her fingers with much perseverance, not looking up or taking notice of what was going forward, until all the three voices united in 'Let us take the road.'

I am afraid there would have been a subtle, stealing gratification in her mind if she had known how entirely this saucy, defiant Stephen was occupied with her: how he was passing rapidly from a determination to treat her with ostentatious indifference to an irritating desire for some sign of inclination from her – some interchange of subdued word or look with her. It was not long before he found an opportunity, when they had passed to the music of 'The Tempest.' Maggie, feeling the need of a footstool, was walking across the room to get one, when Stephen, who was not singing just then, and was conscious of all her movements, guessed her want, and flew to anticipate her, lifting the footstool with an entreating look at her, which made it impossible not to return a glance of gratitude. And then, to have the footstool placed carefully by a too self-confident personage – not *any* self-confident personage, but one in particular, who suddenly looks humble and anxious, and lingers, bending still, to ask if there is not some draught in that position between the window and the fireplace, and if he may not be allowed to move the work-table for her – these things will summon a little of the too ready, traitorous tenderness into a woman's eyes, compelled as she is in her girlish time to learn her life-lessons in very trivial language. And to Maggie such things had not been everyday incidents, but were a new element in her life, and found her keen appetite for homage quite fresh. That tone of gentle solicitude obliged her to look at the face that was bent towards her, and to say, 'No, thank you;' and nothing could prevent that mutual glance from being delicious to both, as it had been the evening before.

It was but an ordinary act of politeness in Stephen; it had hardly taken two minutes; and Lucy, who was singing, scarcely noticed it. But to Philip's mind, filled already with a vague anxiety, this sudden eagerness in Stephen, and the change in Maggie's face, which was plainly reflecting a beam from his, seemed so strong a contrast with the previous overwrought signs of indifference, as to be charged with painful meaning. He had really seen no communicable ground for suspecting any unusual feeling between Stephen and Maggie: his own reason told him so, and he wanted to go home at once that he might reflect coolly on these false images, till he had convinced himself of their nullity. But then, again, he wanted to stay as long as Stephen stayed – always to be present when Stephen was present with Maggie. It seemed to poor Philip so natural, nay, inevitable, that any man who was near Maggie should fall in love with her! There was no promise of happiness for her if she were beguiled into loving Stephen Guest; and this thought emboldened Philip to view his own love for her in the light of a less unequal offering. He was beginning to play very falsely under this deafening inward tumult, and Lucy was looking at him in astonishment, when Mrs Tulliver's entrance to summon them to lunch came as an excuse for abruptly breaking off the music.

'Ah, Mr Philip!' said Mr Deane, when they entered the dining-room, 'I've not seen you for a long while. Your father's not at home, I think, is he? I went after him to the office the other day, and they said he was out of town.'

'He's been to Mudport on business for several days,' said Philip; 'but he's come back now.'

'As fond of his farming hobby as ever, eh?'

'I believe so,' said Philip, rather wondering at this sudden interest in his father's pursuits.

'Ah!' said Mr Deane, 'he's got some land in his own hands on this side the river as well as the other, I think?'

'Yes, he has.'

'Ah!' continued Mr Deane, as he dispensed the pigeon-pie, 'he must find farming an expensive hobby. And the worst of all hobbies are those that people think they can get money at. They shoot their money down like corn out of a sack then.'

Lucy felt a little nervous under her father's apparently gratuitous criticism of Mr Wakem's expenditure. But Mr Deane became unusually silent and meditative during his luncheon. Lucy, having reasons, which had recently become strong, for an extra interest in what referred to the Wakems, felt an unusual curiosity to know what had prompted her father's question.

With this idea in her head, she resorted to her usual plan when she wanted to tell or ask her father anything particular: she found a reason for her aunt Tulliver to leave the dining-room after dinner, and seated herself on a small stool at her father's knee.

'You don't want to go to sleep yet, papa, *do* you?' she said.

'Not yet. But what do *you* want?' he added fondly.

'I only want to know what made you ask Philip Wakem about his father's farming today, papa? It seemed rather odd, because you never hardly say anything to him about his father; and why should you care about Mr Wakem losing money by his hobby?'

'Something to do with business,' said Mr Deane, waving his hands, as if to repel intrusion into that mystery. 'There's a report that Wakem's mill and farm – Dorlcote Mill, your uncle Tulliver's, you know – isn't answering so well as it did. I wanted to see if your friend Philip would let anything out about his father's being tired of farming.'

'Why? Would you buy the mill, papa, if he would part with it?' said Lucy, eagerly. 'Oh, tell me everything – Maggie says it was one of the last things her father said to Tom, that he must get back the mill.'

'Hush, you little puss,' said Mr Deane. 'You must not say a word about this thing – do you hear? There's very little chance of anybody's getting it out of Wakem's hands. And if he knew that we wanted it with a view to the Tullivers getting it again, he'd be the less likely to part with it.'

'Now, papa,' said Lucy, with a little air of solemnity, 'will you trust me? You must not ask me all my reasons for what I'm going to say – but I have very strong reasons. And I'm very cautious.'

'Well, let us hear.'

'Why, I believe, if you will let me take Philip Wakem into our confidence – let me tell him all about your wish to buy, and why my cousins wish to have it – I believe Philip would help to bring it about, I know he would desire to do it.'

'I don't see how that can be, child,' said Mr Deane, looking puzzled. 'Why should *he* care?' Then, with a sudden penetrating look at his daughter, 'You don't think the poor lad's fond of you, and so you can make him do what you like?'

'No, papa; he cares very little about me – not so much as I care about him. But I have a reason for being quite sure of what I say. Don't you ask me. Only give me leave to do as I think fit about it.'

Lucy rose from her stool to seat herself on her father's knee, and kissed him with that last request.

8

Wakem in a New Light

Before three days had passed Lucy had contrived to have a private interview with Philip during a visit of Maggie's to her aunt Glegg. For a day and a night Philip turned over in his mind with restless agitation all that Lucy had told him in that interview, till he had thoroughly resolved on a course of action. He thought he saw before him now a possibility of altering his position with respect to Maggie, and removing at least one obstacle between them. His plan was as bold as it was thoroughly calculated. Having watched for a moment when his father had nothing more urgent on his hands than the newspaper, he went behind him, laid a hand on his shoulder, and said—

'Father, will you come up into my sanctum, and look at my new sketches? I've arranged them now.'

'I'm getting terribly stiff in the joints, Phil, for climbing those stairs of yours,' said Wakem, looking kindly at his son as he laid down his paper.

'This is a nice place for you, isn't it, Phil?' was, as usual, the first thing he said on entering the painting-room. He liked to remind himself and his son too that his fatherly indulgence had provided the accommodation.

'Come, come,' he said, putting his double eye-glass over his nose, and seating himself to take a general view while he rested, 'you've got a famous show here.'

Philip smiled. He had seated himself on his painting-stool, and had taken a lead-pencil in his hand, with which he was making strong marks to counteract the sense of tremulousness. He watched his father get up, and walk slowly round, till he stopped before a stand on which two pictures were placed – one much larger than the other – the smaller one in a leather case.

'Bless me! what have you here?' said Wakem, startled by a sudden transition from landscape to portrait. 'I thought you'd left off figures. Who are these?'

'They are the same person,' said Philip, with calm promptness, 'at different ages.'

'And what person?' said Wakem sharply, fixing his eyes with a growing look of suspicion on the larger picture.

'Miss Tulliver. The small one is something like what she was when I was at school with her brother at King's Lorton: the larger one is not quite so good a likeness of what she was when I came from abroad.'

Wakem turned round fiercely, with a flushed face, letting his eye-glass fall, and looking at his son with a savage expression for a moment. But he threw himself into the arm-chair again, and thrust his hands into his trouser-pockets, still looking angrily at his son, however. Philip did not return the look, but sat quietly watching the point of his pencil.

'And do you mean to say, then, that you have had any acquaintance with her since you came from abroad?' said Wakem.

'Yes: I saw a great deal of her for a whole year before her father's death. We met often in that thicket – the Red Deeps – near Dorlcote Mill. I love her dearly: I shall never love any other woman.'

'Go on, sir! – and you have corresponded with her all this while?'

'No. I never told her I loved her till just before we parted, and she promised her brother not to see me again or to correspond with me. I am not sure that she loves me. But if she would consent – if she *did* love me well enough – I should marry her.'

'And this is the return you make me for all the indulgences I've heaped on you?' said Wakem, beginning to tremble under an enraged sense of impotence before Philip's calm defiance.

'No, father,' said Philip, looking up at him for the first time; 'I don't regard it as a return. You have been an indulgent father to me; but I have always felt that it was because you had an affectionate wish to give me as much happiness as my unfortunate lot would admit of – not that it was a debt you expected me to pay by sacrificing all my chances of happiness to satisfy feelings of yours, which I can never share.'

'I think most sons would share their father's feelings in this case,' said Wakem, bitterly. 'The girl's father was an ignorant mad brute, who was within an inch of murdering me. The whole town knows it. And the brother is just as insolent, only in a cooler way. He forbade her seeing you, you say; he'll break every bone in your body, for your greater happiness, if you don't care. But you seem to have made up your mind. Of course you are independent of me: you can marry this girl tomorrow, if you like: you are a man of five-and-twenty – you can go your way, and I can go mine. We need have no more to do with each other.'

Wakem rose and walked towards the door, but something held him back. Philip was slow to reply, and when he spoke, his tone had a more incisive quietness and clearness than ever.

'No; I can't marry Miss Tulliver, even if she would have me – if I have only my own resources to maintain her with. I have been brought up to no profession. I can't offer her poverty as well as deformity.'

'Ah, *there* is a reason for your clinging to me, doubtless,' said Wakem, still bitterly. He threw himself into the chair again.

'I expected all this,' said Philip. 'I know these scenes are often happening between father and son. If I were like other men of my age, I might answer your angry words by still angrier – we might part – I should marry the woman I love, and have a chance of being as happy as the rest. But if it will be a satisfaction to you to annihilate the very object of everything you've done for me, you have an advantage over most fathers: you can completely deprive me of the only thing that would make my life worth having.'

Philip paused, but his father was silent.

'You know best what satisfaction you would have, beyond that of gratifying a ridiculous rancour worthy only of wandering savages.'

'Ridiculous rancour!' Wakem burst out. 'What do you mean? Damn it! is a man to be horsewhipped by a boor and love him for it? Besides, there's that cold, proud devil of a son, who said a word to me I shall not forget when we had the settling. He would be as pleasant a mark for a bullet as I know – if he were worth the expense.'

'I don't mean your resentment towards them,' said Philip, who had his reasons for some sympathy with this view of Tom, 'though a feeling of revenge is not worth much, that you should care to keep it. I mean your extending the enmity to a helpless girl, who has too much sense and goodness to share their narrow prejudices. *She* has never entered into the family quarrels.'

'What does that signify? We don't ask what a woman does – we ask whom she belongs to. It's altogether a degrading thing to you – to think of marrying old Tulliver's daughter.'

For the first time in the dialogue, Philip lost some of his self-control, and coloured with anger.

'Miss Tulliver,' he said, with bitter incisiveness, 'is thoroughly refined, and her friends, whatever else they may be, are respected for irreproachable honour and integrity. Find a single person in St Ogg's who will not tell you that a beautiful creature like her would be throwing herself away on a pitiable object like me.'

'Not she!' said Wakem, rising again, and forgetting everything else in a burst of resentful pride, half fatherly, half personal. 'It would be a deuced fine match for her. It's all stuff about an accidental deformity, when a girl's really attached to a man.'

'But girls are not apt to get attached under those circumstances,' said Philip.

'Well, then,' said Wakem, rather brutally, trying to recover his previous position, 'if she doesn't care for you, you might have spared yourself the trouble of talking to me about her – and you might have spared me the trouble of refusing my consent to what was never likely to happen.'

Wakem strode to the door, and, without looking round again, banged it after him.

Philip was not without confidence that his father would be ultimately wrought upon as he had expected, by what had passed; but the scene had jarred upon his nerves. He determined not to meet his father again that day. It was Wakem's habit, when he had no company at home, to go out in the evening – often as early as half-past seven; and as it was far on in the afternoon now, Philip went out for a long ramble, thinking he would not return until his father was out of the house again. He got into a boat, and went down the river to a favourite village, where he dined, and lingered till it was late enough for him to return. If he could once be in the position of Maggie's accepted, acknowledged lover, there would be less room for vague dread. He went up to his painting-room again, and threw himself, with a sense of fatigue, into the arm-chair till he fell into a doze. He was awakened by what seemed a sudden, awful crash.

It was the opening of the door, and he could hardly have dozed more than a few moments, for there was no perceptible change in the evening light. It was his father who entered; and when Philip moved to vacate the chair for him, he said—

'Sit still. I'd rather walk about.'

He stalked up and down the room once or twice, and then standing opposite Philip, with his hands thrust in his side pockets, he said, as if continuing a conversation that had not been broken off—

'But this girl seems to have been fond of you, Phil, else she wouldn't have met you in that way.'

Philip's heart was beating rapidly, and a transient flush passed over his face like a gleam. It was not quite easy to speak at once. 'She liked me at King's Lorton, when she was a little girl, because

I used to sit with her brother a great deal when he had hurt his foot. She had kept that in her memory, and thought of me as a friend of a long while ago. She didn't think of me as a lover, when she met me.'

'Well, but you made love to her at last. What did she say then?' said Wakem, walking about again.

'She said she *did* love me then.'

'Confound it, then, what else do you want? Is she a jilt?'

'She was very young then,' said Philip hesitatingly. 'I'm afraid our long separation, and the idea that events must always divide us, may have made a difference.'

'But she's in the town. I've seen her at church. Haven't you spoken to her since you came back?'

'Yes, at Mr Deane's. But I couldn't renew my proposals to her on several grounds. One obstacle would be removed if you would be willing to think of her as a daughter-in-law.'

Wakem was silent a little while, pausing before Maggie's picture.

'She's not the sort of woman your mother was, though, Phil,' he said at last. 'I saw her at church – she's handsomer than this – deuced fine eyes and fine figure, I saw; but rather dangerous and unmanageable, eh?'

'She's very tender and affectionate; and so simple, without the airs and petty contrivances other women have.'

'Ah?' said Wakem, giving his hand to his son. 'We must keep together, if we can. And now, what am I to do? You must come downstairs and tell me. Am I to go and call on this dark-eyed damsel?'

The barrier once thrown down in this way, Philip could talk freely to his father of their entire relation with the Tullivers – of the desire to get the mill and land back into the family – and of its transfer to Guest & Co. as an intermediate step. He could venture now to be persuasive and urgent, and his father yielded with more readiness than he had calculated on.

'I don't care about the mill,' Wakem said at last, with a sort of angry compliance. 'I've had an infernal deal of bother lately about the mill. But there's one thing you needn't ask me. I shall have no direct transactions with young Tulliver.'

I leave you to imagine the agreeable feelings with which Philip went to Mr Deane the next day, to say that Mr Wakem was ready to open the negotiations, and Lucy's pretty triumph as she appealed to her father whether she had not proved her great business abilities. Mr Deane was rather puzzled, and suspected that there had been something 'going on' among the young people, but it appeared to be entirely propitious.

9

Charity in Full Dress

The culmination of Maggie's career as an admired member of society in St Ogg's was certainly the day of the bazaar, when her simple noble beauty, clad in a white muslin of some soft-floating kind, which I suspect must have come from the stores of aunt Pullet's wardrobe, appeared with marked distinction among the more adorned and conventional women around her. All well-dressed St Ogg's and its neighbourhood were there. Near the great arch over the orchestra was the stone oriel with painted glass, and it was close by this that Lucy had her stall, for the convenience of certain large plain articles which she had taken charge of for Mrs Kenn. Maggie had begged to sit at the open end of the stall, and to have the sale of these articles. But it soon appeared that the gentlemen's dressing-gowns, which were among her commodities, were objects of such general attention and inquiry, as to make her post a very conspicuous one.

As for dear little Lucy herself, her late benevolent triumph about the mill, and all the affectionate projects she was cherishing for Maggie and Philip, helped to give her the highest spirits today, and she felt nothing but pleasure in the evidence of Maggie's attractiveness. It is true, she was looking very charming herself, and Stephen was paying her the utmost attention on this public occasion; jealously buying up the articles he had seen under her making. Stephen purchased absolutely nothing from Maggie, until Lucy said, in rather a vexed undertone—

'See, now; all the things of Maggie's knitting will be gone, and you will not have bought one.'

'Oh, no,' said Stephen, 'see – she has got a customer: there is old Wakem himself just coming up.'

Lucy's eyes turned with anxious interest towards Maggie, to see how she went through this first interview, since a sadly memorable time, with a man towards whom she must have so strange a mixture of feelings; but she was pleased to notice that Wakem had tact enough to enter at once into talk about the bazaar wares, and appear interested in purchasing, smiling now and then kindly at Maggie, and not calling on her to speak much, as if he observed that she was rather pale and tremulous.

'Why, Wakem is making himself particularly amiable to your cousin,' said Stephen, in an undertone to Lucy; 'is it pure magnanimity? you talked of a family quarrel.'

'Oh, that will soon be quite healed, I hope,' said Lucy, becoming a little indiscreet in her satisfaction, and speaking with an air of significance. But Stephen did not appear to notice this and as some lady-purchasers came up, he lounged on towards Maggie's end, handling trifles and standing aloof until Wakem, who had taken out his purse, had finished his transactions.

'My son came with me,' he overheard Wakem saying, 'but he has vanished into some other part of the building, and has left all these charitable gallantries to me. I hope you'll reproach him for his shabby conduct.'

She returned his smile and bow without speaking, and he turned away, only then observing Stephen and nodding to him. Maggie, conscious that Stephen was still there, busied herself with counting money, and avoided looking up. She had been well pleased that he had devoted himself to Lucy today, and had not come near her. They had begun the morning with an indifferent salutation, and both had rejoiced in being aloof from each other.

Stephen moved step by step as if he were being unwillingly dragged, until he had got round the open end of the stall. Maggie went on counting her money till she suddenly heard a deep gentle voice saying, 'Aren't you very tired? Do let me bring you something – some fruit or jelly – mayn't I?'

The unexpected tones shook her like a sudden accidental vibration of a harp close by her.

'Oh, no, thank you,' she said, faintly, and only half looking up for an instant.

'You look so pale,' Stephen insisted, in a more entreating tone. 'I'm sure you're exhausted. I must disobey you, and bring something.'

'No, indeed, I couldn't take it.'

'Are you angry with me? What have I done? *Do* look at me.'

'Pray, go away,' said Maggie, looking at him hopelessly, her eyes glancing immediately from him to the opposite corner of the orchestra, which was half hidden by the folds of the old faded green curtain. Maggie had no sooner uttered this entreaty than she was wretched at the admission it implied; but Stephen turned away at once, and following her upward glance, he saw Philip Wakem seated in the half-hidden corner, so that he could command little more than that angle of the hall in which Maggie sat. An entirely new thought occurred to Stephen, and, linking itself with what he had observed of Wakem's manner, and with Lucy's reply to his observation, it convinced him that there had been some former relation between Philip and Maggie beyond that childish one of which he had heard. More than one impulse made him immediately leave the hall, and go upstairs to the refreshment-room, where, walking up to Philip, he sat down behind him, and put his hand on his shoulder.

'Are you studying for a portrait, Phil?' he said.

'I have been studying expression,' said Philip, curtly.

'What, Miss Tulliver's? It's rather of the savage-moody order today, I think. Her cousin sent me to her with a civil offer to get her some refreshment, but I have been snubbed. There's an antipathy between us, I suppose; I have seldom the honour to please her.'

'What a hypocrite you are!' said Philip, flashing angrily.

'What! because experience must have told me that I'm universally pleasing? I admit the law, but there's some disturbing force here.'

'I am going,' said Philip, rising abruptly.

'So am I – to get a breath of fresh air; this place gets oppressive. I think I have done suit and service long enough.'

The two friends walked downstairs together without speaking. Philip turned through the outer door into the courtyard, but Stephen, saying, 'Oh, by the by, I must call in here,' went on along the passage to one of the rooms at the other end of the building, which were appropriated to the town library. He had the room all to himself, and a man requires nothing less than this, when he wants to dash his cap on the table, throw himself astride a chair, and stare at a high brick wall with a deep frown.

It was at this moment that Dr Kenn, who had quite lately come into the hall, and was now walking down the middle with his hands behind him, taking a general view, fixed his eyes on Maggie for the first time, and was struck with the expression of pain on her beautiful face. He was strongly arrested. Her face had naturally drawn his attention as a new and striking one at church, and he had been introduced to her during a short call on business at Mr Deane's, but he had never spoken more than three words to her. He walked towards her now, and Maggie, perceiving some one approaching, roused herself to look up and be prepared to speak. She felt a childlike, instinctive relief from the sense of uneasiness in this exertion, when she saw it was Dr Kenn's face that was looking at her.

'You find your office rather a fatiguing one, I fear, Miss Tulliver?' said Dr Kenn.

'It is, rather,' said Maggie simply.

'But I can tell Mrs Kenn that you have disposed of her goods very quickly,' he added; 'she will be very much obliged to you.'

'Oh, I have done nothing: the gentlemen came very fast to buy the dressing-gowns and embroidered waistcoats, but I think any of the other ladies would have sold more: I didn't know what to say about them.'

Dr Kenn smiled. 'I hope I'm going to have you as a permanent parishioner now, Miss Tulliver – am I? You have been at a distance from us hitherto.'

'I have been a teacher in a school, and I'm going into another situation of the same kind very soon.'

'Ah? I was hoping you would remain among your friends.'

'Oh, *I must go*,' said Maggie, earnestly, looking at Dr Kenn with an expression of reliance, as if she had told him her history in those three words.

Dr Kenn's ear and eye took in all the signs that this brief confidence of Maggie's was charged with meaning.

'I understand,' he said; 'you feel it right to go. But that will not prevent our meeting again, I hope: it will not prevent my knowing you better, if I can be of any service to you.'

He put out his hand and pressed hers kindly before he turned away. 'She has some trouble or other at heart,' he thought. 'Poor child! There's something wonderfully honest in those beautiful eyes.'

Philip had not spoken to Maggie himself about the removal of obstacles between them on his father's side – he shrank from that; but he had told everything to Lucy, with the hope that Maggie, being informed through her, might give him some encouraging sign that their being brought thus much nearer to each other was a happiness to her. The rush of conflicting feelings was too great for Maggie to say much when Lucy poured forth her triumphant revelation; and Lucy could hardly be surprised that she could do little more than cry with gladness at the thought of her father's wish being fulfilled, and of Tom's getting the mill again in reward for all his hard striving. The details of preparation for the bazaar had then come to usurp Lucy's attention for the next few days, and nothing had been said by the cousins on subjects that were likely to rouse deeper feelings. Philip had been to the house more than once, but Maggie had had no private conversation with him, and thus she had been left to fight her inward battle without interference.

But when the bazaar was fairly ended, and the cousins were

alone again, resting together at home, Lucy said—

'You must give up going to stay with your aunt Moss the day after tomorrow, Maggie: write a note to her, and tell her you have put it off at my request, and I'll send the man with it. She won't be displeased; you'll have plenty of time to go by and by; and I don't want you to go out of the way just now.'

'Yes, indeed I must go, dear; I can't put it off for I'm going away to a new situation on the 25th of June.'

'Maggie!' said Lucy, almost white with astonishment.

'I didn't tell you, dear,' said Maggie, making a great effort to command herself, 'because you've been so busy. But some time ago I wrote to our old governess, Miss Firniss, to ask her to let me know if she met with any situation that I could fill, and the other day I had a letter from her telling me that I could take three orphan pupils of hers to the coast during the holidays, and then make trial of a situation with her as teacher. I wrote yesterday to accept the offer.'

Lucy felt so hurt that for some moments she was unable to speak.

'Maggie,' she said at last, 'how could you be so unkind to me – not to tell me – to take *such* a step – and now!' She hesitated a little, and then added – 'And Philip? I thought everything was going to be so happy. Oh, Maggie – what is the reason? Give it up; let me write. There is nothing now to keep you and Philip apart.'

'Yes,' said Maggie, faintly. 'There is Tom's feeling. He said I must give him up if I married Philip. And I know he will not change – at least not for a long while – unless something happened to soften him.'

'But I will talk to him: he's coming back this week. And this good news about the mill will soften him. And I'll talk to him about Philip. Tom's always very compliant to me: I don't think he's so obstinate.'

'But I must go,' said Maggie, in a distressed voice. 'I must leave some time to pass. Don't press me to stay, dear Lucy.'

Lucy was silent for two or three minutes, looking away and

ruminating. At length she knelt down by her cousin, and, looking up in her face with anxious seriousness, said—

'Maggie, is it that you don't love Philip well enough to marry him? – tell me – trust me.'

Maggie held Lucy's hands tightly in silence a little while. Her own hands were quite cold. But when she spoke, her voice was quite clear and distinct.

'Yes, Lucy, I would choose to marry him. I think it would be the best and highest lot for me – to make his life happy. He loved me first. No one else could be quite what he is to me. But I can't divide myself from my brother for life. I must go away, and wait. Pray, don't speak to me again about it.'

Lucy obeyed in pain and wonder. The next word she said was—

'Well, dear Maggie, at least you will go to the dance at Park House tomorrow, and have some music and brightness, before you go to pay these dull, dutiful visits. Ah! here come aunty and the tea.'

10

The Spell Seems Broken

The suite of rooms opening into each other at Park House looked duly brilliant with lights and flowers, and the personal splendours of sixteen couples, with attendant parents and guardians. The focus of brilliancy was the long drawing-room, where the dancing went foward, under the inspiration of the grand piano; the library, into which it opened at one end, had the more sober illumination of maturity, with caps and cards; and at the other end, the pretty sitting-room, with a conservatory attached, was left as an occasional cool retreat. Lucy, who had laid aside her black for the first time, and had her pretty slimness set off by an abundant dress of white crape, was the acknowledged queen of the occasion; for this was one of the Miss Guests' thoroughly condescending parties, including no member of any aristocracy higher than that of St Ogg's, and stretching to the extreme limits of commercial and professional gentility.

Maggie at first refused to dance, saying that she had forgotten all the figures – it was so many years since she had danced at school; and she was glad to have that excuse, for it is ill dancing with a heavy heart. But at length the music wrought in her young limbs, and the longing came; even though it was the horrible young Torry, who walked up a second time to try and persuade her. She warned him that she could not dance anything but a country dance; but he, of course, was willing to wait for that high felicity, meaning only to be complimentary when he assured her at several intervals that it was a 'great bore' that she couldn't waltz – he would have liked so much to waltz with her. But at last it was the turn of the good old-fashioned dance, which has the least of vanity and the most of merriment in it, and Maggie quite forgot her troublous life in a childlike enjoyment of that half-rustic rhythm which seems to banish pretentious etiquette. She felt quite charitably towards young Torry, as his hand bore her along and held her up in the dance; her eyes and cheeks had that fire of young joy in them which will flame out if it can find the least breath to fan it; and her simple black dress, with its bit of black lace, seemed like the dim setting of a jewel.

Stephen had not yet paid her more than a passing civility. Since yesterday, that inward vision of her which perpetually made part of his consciousness, had been half-screened by the image of Philip Wakem; there was some attachment between her and Philip; at least there was an attachment on his side, which made her feel in some bondage. Here then, Stephen told himself, was another claim of honour which called on him to resist the attraction that was continually threatening to overpower him, which almost made him rush towards Maggie and claim her for himself. Nevertheless he had done what he meant to do this evening: he had kept aloof from her; he had hardly looked at her; and he had been gaily assiduous to Lucy. But now his eyes were devouring Maggie: he felt inclined to kick young Torry out of the dance, and take his place. The possibility that he too should dance with

Maggie and have her hand in his so long, was beginning to possess him like a thirst.

Stephen hardly knew what happened, or in what automatic way he got through the duties of politeness until he was free and saw Maggie seated alone again. He made his way towards her round the couples that were forming for the waltz, and when Maggie became conscious that she was the person he sought, she felt, in spite of all the thoughts that had gone before, a glowing gladness at heart. Her eyes and cheeks were still brightened with her childlike enthusiasm in the dance; her whole frame was set to joy and tenderness; even the coming pain could not seem bitter – she was ready to welcome it as a part of life, for life at this moment seemed a keen vibrating consciousness poised above pleasure or pain. This one, this last night, she might expand unrestrainedly in the warmth of the present, without those chill eating thoughts of the past and the future.

'They're going to waltz again,' said Stephen, bending to speak to her, with that glance and tone of subdued tenderness. 'It is rather dizzy work to look on, and the room is very warm. Shall we walk about a little?'

He took her hand and placed it within his arm; they walked on into the sitting-room and passed on into the conservatory.

'How strange and unreal the trees and flowers look with the lights among them,' said Maggie, in a low voice. 'They look as if they belonged to an enchanted land, and would never fade away – I could fancy they all were made of jewels.'

She was looking at the tier of geraniums as she spoke, and Stephen made no answer: but he was looking at her. Something strangely powerful there was in the light of Stephen's long gaze, for it made Maggie's face turn towards it and look upwards at it – slowly, like a flower at the ascending brightness. And they walked unsteadily on, without feeling that they were walking – without feeling anything but that long grave mutual gaze which has the solemnity belonging to all deep human passion. The hovering thought that they must and would renounce each other made this moment of mute confession more intense in its rapture.

But they had reached the end of the conservatory, and were obliged to pause and turn. The change of movement brought a new consciousness to Maggie: she blushed deeply, turned away her head, and drew her arm from Stephen's, going up to some flowers to smell them. Stephen stood motionless, and still pale.

'Oh, may I get this rose?' said Maggie, making a great effort to say something, and dissipate the burning sense of irretrievable confession. 'I think I am quite wicked with roses – I like to gather them and smell them till they have no scent left.'

Stephen was mute: he was incapable of putting a sentence together, and Maggie bent her arm a little upward towards the large half-opened rose that had attracted her.

A mad impulse seized on Stephen; he darted towards the arm, and showered kisses on it, clasping the wrist.

But the next moment Maggie snatched it from him, and glared at him, quivering with rage and humiliation.

'How dare you?' – she spoke in a deeply shaken, half-smothered voice. 'What right have I given you to insult me?'

She darted from him into the adjoining room, and threw herself on the sofa, panting and trembling.

A horrible punishment was come upon her for her sin of allowing a moment's happiness that was treachery to Lucy, to Philip – to her own better soul. That momentary happiness had been smitten with a blight: Stephen thought more lightly of *her* than he did of Lucy.

As for Stephen, he leaned back against the framework of the conservatory, dizzy with the conflict of passions – love, rage, and confused despair: despair at his want of self-mastery, and despair that he had offended Maggie.

The last feeling surmounted every other, to be by her side again and entreat forgiveness; and she had not been seated more than a few minutes when he came and stood humbly before her. But Maggie's bitter rage was unspent.

'Leave me to myself, if you please,' she said, with impetuous haughtiness, 'and for the future avoid me.'

Stephen turned away, and walked backwards and forwards at

the other end of the room. There was the dire necessity of going back into the dancing-room again, and he was beginning to be conscious of that. They had been absent so short a time, that when he went in again the waltz was not ended.

Maggie, too, was not long before she re-entered. All the pride of her nature was stung into activity: the hateful weakness which had dragged her within reach of this wound to her self-respect, had at least wrought its own cure. The thoughts and temptations of the last month should all be flung away into an unvisited chamber of memory: there was nothing to allure her now; duty would be easy, and all the old calm purposes would reign peacefully once more. She re-entered the drawing-room still with some excited brightness in her face, but with a sense of proud self-command that defied anything to agitate her. She refused to dance again, but she talked quite readily and calmly with every one who addressed her. And when they got home that night, she kissed Lucy with a free heart, almost exulting in this scorching moment, which had delivered her from the possibility of another word or look that would have the stamp of treachery towards that gentle, unsuspicious sister.

The next morning Maggie did not set off to Basset quite so soon as she had expected. Her mother was to accompany her in the carriage, and household business could not be despatched hastily by Mrs Tulliver. So Maggie had to sit waiting, equipped for the drive, in the garden. Lucy was busy in the house wrapping up some bazaar presents for the younger ones at Basset, and when there was a loud ring at the door-bell, Maggie felt some alarm lest Lucy should bring out Stephen to her: it was sure to be Stephen.

But presently the visitor came out into the garden alone, and seated himself by her on the garden-chair. It was not Stephen.

'We can just catch the tips of the Scotch firs, Maggie, from this seat,' said Philip.

They had taken each other's hands in silence, but Maggie had looked at him with a more complete revival of the old childlike affectionate smile than he had seen before, and he felt encouraged.

'Yes,' she said, 'I often look at them, and wish I could see the low sunlight on the stems again.'

'I have been there – I go there – continually,' said Philip. 'I have nothing but the past to live upon.'

A keen remembrance and keen pity impelled Maggie to put her hand in Philip's. They had so often walked hand-in-hand!

'You will go there again soon – won't you, Maggie?' said Philip, getting timid. 'The mill will soon be your brother's home again.'

'Yes; but I shall not be there,' said Maggie. 'I shall only hear of that happiness. I am going away again – Lucy has not told you, perhaps?'

'Then the future will never join on to the past again, Maggie? That book is quite closed?'

The grey eyes that had so often looked up at her with entreating worship, looked up at her now, with a last struggling ray of hope in them, and Maggie met them with her large sincere gaze.

'That book never will be closed, Philip,' she said, with grave sadness; 'I desire no future that will break the ties of the past. But the tie to my brother is one of the strongest. I can do nothing willingly that will divide me always from him.'

'Is that the only reason that would keep us apart for ever, Maggie?' said Philip.

'The only reason,' said Maggie, with calm decision. And she believed it. She looked at the future with a sense of calm choice.

They sat hand-in-hand without looking at each other or speaking for a few minutes. Philip felt that he ought to have been thoroughly happy in that answer of hers: she was as open and transparent as a rock-pool. Why was he not thoroughly happy?

11

In the Lane

Maggie had been four days at her aunt Moss's. She was standing on the causeway with her aunt and a group of cousins feeding the chickens, at that quiet moment in the life of the farmyard before the afternoon milking-time. Maggie, with her bonnet over her arm, was smiling down at the hatch of small fluffy chickens, when her aunt exclaimed—

'Goodness me! who is that gentleman coming in at the gate?'

It was a gentleman on a tall bay horse; and the flanks and neck of the horse were streaked black with fast riding.

'Who is it, my dear?' said Mrs Moss, seeing in Maggie's face the evidence that she knew.

'It is Mr Stephen Guest,' said Maggie, rather faintly. 'My cousin Lucy's – a gentleman who is very intimate at my cousin's.'

Stephen was already close to them, had jumped off his horse, and now raised his hat as he advanced.

'Hold the horse, Willy,' said Mrs Moss to the twelve-year-old boy.

'No, thank you,' said Stephen, pulling at the horse's impatiently tossing head. 'I must be going again immediately. I have a message to deliver to you, Miss Tulliver – on private business. May I take the liberty of asking you to walk a few yards with me?'

He had a half-jaded, half-irritated look. He spoke almost abruptly, as if his errand were too pressing for him to trouble himself about what would be thought by Mrs Moss of his visit and request. Good Mrs Moss, rather nervous in the presence of this apparently haughty gentleman, was inwardly wondering whether she would be doing right or wrong to invite him again to leave his horse and walk in, when Maggie, feeling all the embarrassment of the situation, and unable to say anything, put on her bonnet, and turned to walk towards the gate.

Stephen turned too, and walked by her side, leading his horse.

Not a word was spoken till they were out in the lane, and had walked four or five yards, when Maggie, who had been looking straight before her all the while, turned again to walk back, saying, with haughty resentment—

'There is no need for me to go any farther. I don't know whether you consider it gentlemanly and delicate conduct to place me in a position that forced me to come out with you – or whether you wished to insult me still further by thrusting an interview upon me in this way.'

'Of course you are angry with me for coming,' said Stephen, bitterly. 'Of course it is of no consequence what a man has to suffer – it is only your woman's dignity that you care about.'

Maggie gave a slight start, such as might have come from the slightest possible electric shock.

'As if it were not enough that I'm entangled in this way – that I'm mad with love for you – that I resist the strongest passion a man can feel, because I try to be true to other claims – but you must treat me as if I were a coarse brute, who would willingly offend you. And when, if I had my own choice, I should ask you to take my hand, and my fortune, and my whole life, and do what you like with them! I know I forgot myself. I took an unwarrantable liberty. I hate myself for having done it. But I repented immediately – I've been repenting ever since. You ought not to think it unpardonable: a man who loves with his whole soul, as I do you, is liable to be mastered by his feelings for a moment; but you know – you must believe – that the worst pain I could have is to have pained you – that I would give the world to recall the error.'

Maggie dared not speak – dared not turn her head. The strength that had come from resentment was all gone, and her lips were quivering visibly. She could not trust herself to utter the full forgiveness that rose in answer to that confession.

They were come nearly in front of the gate again, and she paused, trembling.

'You must not say these things – I must not hear them,' she said, looking down in misery, as Stephen came in front of her, to prevent her from going farther towards the gate. 'I'm very sorry for any pain you have to go through; but it is of no use to speak.'

'Yes, it *is* of use,' said Stephen, impetuously. 'It would be of use if you would treat me with some sort of pity and consideration, instead of doing me vile injustice in your mind. I could bear everything more quietly if I knew you didn't hate me for an insolent coxcomb. Look at me – see what a hunted devil I am: I've been riding thirty miles every day to get away from the thought of you.'

Maggie did not – dared not look. But she said gently—

'I don't think any evil of you.'

'Then, dearest, look at me.' said Stephen, in deepest, tenderest tones of entreaty. 'Don't go away from me yet. Give me a moment's happiness – make me feel you've forgiven me.'

A great tear fell from under Maggie's lowered eyelids.

'Yes, I do forgive you,' she said, shaken by those tones, and all the more frightened at herself. 'But pray let me go in again. Pray go away.'

Maggie turned. But Tancred, the bay horse, began to make such spirited remonstrances against this frequent change of direction, that Stephen, catching sight of Willy Moss peeping through the gate, called out, 'Here! just come and hold my horse for five minutes.'

'Oh, no,' said Maggie, hurriedly. 'My aunt will think it so strange.'

'Never mind,' Stephen answered, impatiently; 'they don't know the people at St Ogg's. Lead him up and down just here, for five minutes,' he added to Willy, who was now close to them; and then he turned to Maggie's side, and they walked on. It was clear that she *must* go on now.

'Take my arm,' said Stephen, entreatingly; and she took it, feeling all the while as if she were sliding downwards in a nightmare.

'There is no end to this misery,' she began, struggling to repel the influence by speech. 'It is wicked – base – think of Lucy. And I have other ties,' Maggie went on, at last with a desperate effort, 'even if Lucy did not exist.'

'You are engaged to Philip Wakem?' said Stephen, hastily. 'Is it so?'

'I consider myself engaged to him – I don't mean to marry any one else.'

Stephen was silent again until they had turned out of the

sun into a side lane, all grassy and sheltered. Then he burst out impetuously—

'It is unnatural – it is horrible. Maggie, if you loved me as I love you, we should throw everything else to the winds for the sake of belonging to each other. We should break all these mistaken ties that were made in blindness, and determine to marry each other.'

'I would rather die than fall into that temptation,' said Maggie, with deep, slow distinctness. She drew her arm from his as she spoke.

'Tell me, then, that you don't care for me,' he said, almost violently. 'Tell me that you love some one else better.'

It darted through Maggie's mind that here was a mode of releasing herself from outward struggle – to tell Stephen that her whole heart was Philip's. But her lips would not utter that, and she was silent.

'If you do love me, dearest,' said Stephen, gently, taking up her hand again and laying it within his arm, 'it is better – it is right that we should marry each other. We can't help the pain it will give. It is come upon us without our seeking: it is natural – it has taken hold of me in spite of every effort I have made to resist it. God knows, I've been trying to be faithful to tacit engagements, and I've only made things worse – I'd better have given way at first.'

Maggie was silent. If it were *not* wrong – if she were once convinced of that, and need no longer beat and struggle against this current, soft and yet strong as the summer stream!

'Say "yes," dearest,' said Stephen, leaning to look entreatingly in her face. 'What could we care about in the whole world beside, if we belong to each other?'

Her breath was on his face – his lips were very near hers – but there was a great dread dwelling in his love for her.

Her lips and eyelids quivered; she opened her eyes full on his for an instant, like a lovely wild animal timid and struggling under caresses, and then turned sharp round towards home again.

'And after all,' he went on, in an impatient tone, trying to defeat his own scruples as well as hers, 'I am breaking no positive engagement: if Lucy's affections had been withdrawn from me and given to some one else, I should have felt no right to assert a claim on her. If you are not absolutely pledged to Philip, we are neither of us bound.'

'You don't believe that,' said Maggie, earnestly. 'You feel, as I do, that the real tie lies in the feelings and expectations we have raised in other minds. Else all pledges might be broken, when there was no outward penalty. There would be no such thing as faithfulness.'

'The pledge *can't* be fulfilled,' he said, with impetuous insistence. 'It is unnatural: we can only pretend to give ourselves to any one else. There is wrong in that too – there may be misery in it for *them* as well as for us. Maggie, you must see that – you do see that.'

He was looking eagerly at her face for the least sign of compliance; his large, firm, gentle grasp was on her hand. She was silent for a few moments, with her eyes fixed on the ground; then she drew a deep breath, and said, looking up at him with solemn sadness—

'Oh, it is difficult – life is very difficult! It seems right to me sometimes that we should follow our strongest feeling; but then, such feelings continually come across the ties that all our former life has made for us – the ties that have made others dependent on us – and would cut them in two. Many things are difficult and dark to me; but I see one thing quite clearly – that I must not, cannot seek my own happiness by sacrificing others. I should be haunted by the suffering I had caused. Our love would be poisoned. Don't urge me; help me – help me, *because* I love you.'

'Dearest,' he said, in scarcely more than a whisper, while his arm stole round her, 'I'll do, I'll bear anything you wish. But – one kiss – one – the last – before we part.'

One kiss – and then a long look – until Maggie said, tremulously, 'Let me go – let us make haste back.'

She hurried along, and not another word was spoken. Stephen stood still and beckoned when they came within sight of Willy and the horse, and Maggie went on through the gate. Mrs Moss was standing alone at the door of the old porch: she had sent all the cousins in, with kind thoughtfulness.

'Sit down here a bit, my dear.' She drew Maggie into the porch, and sat down on the bench by her: there was no privacy in the house.

'Oh, aunt Gritty, I'm very wretched. I wish I could have died when I was fifteen. It seemed so easy to give things up then – it is so hard now.'

The poor child threw her arms round her aunt's neck, and fell into long, deep sobs.

12

A Family Party

Maggie left her good aunt Gritty at the end of the week, and went to Garum Firs to pay her visit to aunt Pullet according to agreement. In the meantime, very unexpected things had happened, and there was to be a family party at Garum to discuss and celebrate a change in the fortunes of the Tullivers.

Lucy came so early as to have the start even of aunt Glegg; for she longed to have some undisturbed talk with Maggie about the wonderful news. It seemed – did it not? said Lucy, as if everything, even other people's misfortunes (poor creatures!), were conspiring now to make poor dear aunt Tulliver, and cousin Tom, and naughty Maggie too, if she were not obstinately bent on the contrary, as happy as they deserved to be after all their troubles. To think that the very day – the *very day* – after Tom had come back from Newcastle, that unfortunate young Jetsome, whom Mr Wakem had placed at the mill, had been pitched off his horse in a drunken fit, and was lying at St Ogg's in a dangerous state, so that Wakem had signified his wish that the new purchasers should enter on the premises at once! Aunt Tulliver must certainly go to the mill now, and keep house for Tom: that was rather a loss to Lucy in the matter of household comfort; but then, to think of poor aunty being in her old place again, and gradually getting comforts about her there!

On this last point Lucy had her cunning projects, and when she and Maggie had made their dangerous way down the bright stairs into the handsome parlour, where the very sunbeams seemed cleaner than elsewhere, she directed her manoeuvres, as any other great tactician would have done, against the weaker side of the enemy.

'Aunt Pullet,' she said, seating herself on the sofa, and caressingly adjusting that lady's floating cap-string, 'I want you to make up your mind what linen and things you will give Tom towards housekeeping; because you're always so generous – you give such nice things, you know; and if you set the example, aunt Glegg will follow.'

'That she never can, my dear,' said Mrs Pullet, with unusual vigour, 'for she hasn't got the linen to follow suit wi' mine, I can tell you. She'd niver the taste, not if she'd spend the money. But it's poor work, dividing one's linen before one dies – I niver thought to ha' done that,' Mrs Pullet continued.

'Oh, but, aunt Pullet,' said Lucy, 'you've so much beautiful linen. And suppose you had had daughters! Then you must have divided it, when they were married.'

'Well, I don't say as I won't do it,' said Mrs Pullet, 'for now Tom's so lucky, it's nothing but right his friends should look on him and help him. There's the table-cloths I bought at your sale, Bessy. But I'm not going to give Maggie any more o' my Indy muslin and things, if she's to go into service again, when she might stay and keep me company, and do my sewing for me, if she wasn't wanted at her brother's.'

'Going into service' was the expression by which the Dodson mind represented to itself the position of teacher or governess, and Maggie's return to that menial condition, now circumstances offered her more eligible prospects, was likely to be a sore point with all her relatives, besides Lucy. The subject was revived in aunt and uncle Glegg's presence, over the tea and muffins.

'Hegh, hegh!' said Mr Glegg, good-naturedly patting Maggie

on the back, 'nonsense, nonsense! Don't let us hear of you taking a place again, Maggie. Why, you must ha' picked up half-a-dozen sweethearts at the bazaar: isn't there one of 'em the right sort of article?'

'Mr Glegg,' said his wife, with that shade of increased politeness in her severity which she always put on with her crisper fronts, 'it's respect and duty to her aunts, and the rest of her kin as are so good to her, should have kept my niece from fixing about going away, not sweethearts, if I'm to use such a word, though it was never heared in *my* family.'

'Why, what did they call us, when we went to see 'em, then, eh, neighbour Pullet? They thought us sweet enough then,' said Mr Glegg, winking pleasantly.

'Mr Glegg,' said Mrs G., 'if you're going to be undelicate, let me know.'

'La, Jane, your husband's only joking,' said Mrs Pullet; 'let him joke while he's got health and strength.'

'I'll trouble you for the muffineer, then, Mr Glegg,' said Mrs G., 'if I may be so bold to interrupt your joking. Though it's other people must see the joke in a niece's putting a slight on her mother's eldest sister, as is the head o' the family; and only coming in and out on short visits, all the time she's been in the town, and then settling to go away without my knowledge – as I'd laid caps out on purpose for her to make 'em up for me – and me as have divided my money so equal ...'

'Sister,' Mrs Tulliver broke in anxiously, 'I'm sure Maggie never thought o' going away without staying at your house as well as the others. Not as it's my wish she should go away at all – but quite contrairy. But there's ten days or a fortnight Maggie'll have before she's fixed to go: she can stay at your house just as well, and I'll step in when I can, and so will Lucy.'

'Bessy,' said Mrs Glegg, 'if you'd exercise a little more thought, you might know I should hardly think it was worth while to unpin a bed, and go to all that trouble now, just at the end o' the time, when our house isn't above a quarter of an hour's walk from Mr Deane's. She can come the first thing in the morning, and go back the last at night, and be thankful she's got a good aunt so close to her to come and sit with. I know *I* should, when I was her age.'

'Oh, there is Tom!' exclaimed Lucy, clapping her hands.

Maggie jumped up to kiss Tom as he entered, with strong feeling, at this first meeting since the prospect of returning to the mill had been opened to him; and she kept his hand, leading him to the chair by her side. To have no cloud between herself and Tom was still a perpetual yearning in her. He smiled at her very kindly this evening, and said, 'Well, Magsie, how's aunt Moss?'

'Come, come, sir,' said Mr Glegg, putting out his hand. 'Why, you're such a big man, you carry all before you, it seems. You're come into your luck a good deal earlier than us old folks did – but I wish you joy, I wish you joy.'

'But I hope he'll bear in mind as it's his mother's family as he owes it to,' said Mrs Glegg.

'Tom had the Dodson skin,' said aunt Pullet, 'I said that from the first. And I don't know what *you* mean to do, sister Glegg, but I mean to give him a table-cloth of all my three biggest sizes but one, besides sheets. I don't say what more I shall do; but *that* I shall do.'

'I shall look out what's serviceable, to make a present of to my nephey,' said Mrs Glegg.

When it was time to go home, Tom was to drive home his mother and Lucy. 'You must sit by yourself, aunty,' said that contriving young lady, 'because I must sit by Tom; I've a great deal to say to him.'

In the eagerness of her affectionate anxiety for Maggie, Lucy could not persuade herself to defer a conversation about her with Tom, who, she thought, with this rapid fulfilment of his wish about the mill, must become pliant and flexible. Her nature supplied her with no key to Tom's; and she was puzzled as well as pained to notice the unpleasant change on his countenance when she gave him the history of the way in which Philip had used his influence with his father. She had counted on this revelation as a great stroke of policy, which was to turn Tom's heart towards Philip at once, and, besides that, prove that the elder Wakem was ready to receive Maggie with all the honours of a daughter-in-law.

But Tom's inward criticism of his father's faults did not prevent him from adopting his father's prejudice. Other feelings added their force to produce Tom's bitter repugnance to Philip, and to Maggie's union with him; and notwithstanding Lucy's power over her strong-willed cousin, she got nothing but a cold refusal ever to sanction such a marriage: but of course Maggie could do as she liked – she had declared her determination to be independent. For Tom's part, he held himself bound by his duty to his father's memory, and by every manly feeling, never to consent to any relation with the Wakems.

13

Borne Along by the Tide

In less than a week Maggie was at St Ogg's again – outwardly in much the same position as when her visit there had just begun. It was easy for her to fill her mornings apart from Lucy without any obvious effort; for she had her promised visits to pay to her aunt Glegg, and it was natural that she should give her mother more than usual of her companionship in these last weeks, especially as there were preparations to be thought of for Tom's housekeeping. But Lucy would hear of no pretext for her remaining away in the evenings: she must always come from aunt Glegg's before dinner – 'Else what shall I have of you?' said Lucy, with a tearful pout that could not be resisted.

Maggie, all this time, moved about with a quiescence and even torpor of manner, so contrasted with her usual fitful brightness and ardour, that Lucy would have had to seek some other cause for such a change, if she had not been convinced that the position in which Maggie stood between Philip and her brother, and the prospect of her self-imposed wearisome banishment, were quite enough to account for a large amount of depression. But under this torpor there was a fierce battle of emotions, such as Maggie in all her life of struggle had never known or foreboded. There were moments in which a cruel selfishness seemed to be getting possession of her: why should not Lucy – why should not Philip suffer? *She* had had to suffer through many years of her life; and who had renounced anything for her? And when something like that fullness of existence – love, wealth, ease, refinement, all that her nature craved – was brought within her reach, why was she to forgo it, that another might have it – another, who perhaps needed it less? But amidst all this new passionate tumult there were the old voices making themselves heard with rising power, till, from time to time, the tumult seemed quelled. *Was* that existence which tempted her the full existence she dreamed? Where, then, would be all the memories of early striving, all the deep pity for another's pain, which had been nurtured in her through years of affection and hardship, all the divine presentiment of something higher than mere personal enjoyment which had made the sacredness of life? How had she sunk into this struggle with a temptation that she would once have thought herself as secure from, as from deliberate crime? And yet, since this strange, sweet, subduing influence did not, should not conquer her – since it was to remain simply her own suffering … her mind was meeting Stephen's in that thought of his, that they might still snatch moments of mute confession before the parting came. For was not he suffering too? She saw it daily – saw it in the sickened look of fatigue with which, as soon as he was not compelled to exert himself, he relapsed into indifference towards everything but the possibility of watching her. Could she refuse sometimes to answer that beseeching look which she felt to be following her like a low murmur of love and pain? She refused it less and less, till at last the evening for them both was sometimes made of a moment's mutual gaze: they thought of it till it came, and when it had come, they thought of nothing else. One other thing Stephen seemed now and then to care for, and that was to sing: it was a way of speaking to Maggie. Perhaps he was not distinctly conscious that he was impelled to it by a secret longing – running counter to all his self-confessed resolves – to deepen the hold he had on her.

Philip Wakem was a less frequent visitor, but he came occasionally in the evening, and it happened that he was there when Lucy said, as they sat out on the lawn, near sunset—

'Now Maggie's visits to aunt Glegg are completed, I mean that we shall go out boating every day until she goes. She has not had half enough boating, because of these tiresome visits, and she likes it better than anything. Don't you, Maggie?'

'Better than any sort of locomotion, I hope you mean,' said Philip, smiling at Maggie.

'Should you like to be her boatman?' said Lucy. She looked playful reproach at Stephen, who was sauntering up and down. He took no notice, but still kept aloof: he had done so frequently during Philip's recent visits.

'You don't seem inclined for boating,' said Lucy, when he came to sit down by her on the bench. 'Doesn't rowing suit you now?'

'Oh, I hate a large party in a boat,' he said, almost irritably. 'I'll come when you have no one else.'

Lucy coloured, fearing that Philip would be hurt: it was quite a new thing for Stephen to speak in that way; but he had certainly not been well of late. Philip coloured too, but less from a feeling of personal offence than from a vague suspicion that Stephen's moodiness had some relation to Maggie.

'As Miss Deane didn't know she was excluding others by inviting me,' said Philip, 'I am bound to resign.'

'No, indeed, you shall not,' said Lucy, much vexed. 'I particularly wish for your company tomorrow. The tide will suit at half-past ten: it will be a delicious time for a couple of hours to row to Luckreth and walk back, before the sun gets too hot. And how can you object to four people in a boat?' she added, looking at Stephen.

'I don't object to the people, but the number,' said Stephen, who had recovered himself, and was rather ashamed of his rudeness. 'If I voted for a fourth at all, of course it would be you, Phil. But we won't divide the pleasure of escorting the ladies; we'll take it alternately. I'll go the next day.'

This incident had the effect of drawing Philip's attention with freshened solicitude towards Stephen and Maggie; but when they re-entered the house, music was proposed, and Mrs Tulliver and Mr Deane being occupied with cribbage, Maggie sat apart near the table where the books and work were placed – doing nothing, however, but listening abstractedly to the music. Stephen presently turned to a duet which he insisted that Lucy and Philip should sing: but this evening Philip thought he divined some double intention in every word and look of Stephen's, and watched him keenly – angry with himself all the while for this clinging suspicion. For had not Maggie virtually denied any ground for his doubts on her side? Stephen might be strongly fascinated by her but Philip felt himself rather base for intruding on what must be his friend's painful secret. Still, he watched. Stephen, moving away from the piano, sauntered slowly towards the table near which Maggie sat, and seated himself with his back to the piano looking at Maggie, who had not taken the slightest notice of his approach. She had always additional strength of resistance when Philip was present. But at last she heard the word 'dearest' uttered in the softest tone of pained entreaty. She had never heard that word since the moments in the lane at Basset. Philip could hear no word, but he had moved to the opposite side of the piano, and could see Maggie start and blush, raise her eyes an instant towards Stephen's face, but immediately look apprehensively towards himself. It was not evident to her that Philip had observed her; but a pang of shame, under the sense of this concealment, made her move from her chair and walk to her mother's side to watch the game at cribbage.

Philip went home soon after in a state of hideous doubt mingled with wretched certainty. It was impossible for him now to resist the conviction that there was some mutual consciousness between Stephen and Maggie; and for half the night his irritable, susceptible nerves were pressed upon almost to frenzy by that one wretched fact: he could attempt no explanation that would reconcile it with her words and actions. Maggie was struggling, she was banishing herself. His imagination wrought out the whole story: Stephen was madly in love with her; he must have told her so; she had rejected him, and was hurrying away. But would he give her up, knowing – Philip felt the fact with heart-crushing despair – that she was made half helpless by her feeling towards him?

When the morning came, Philip was too ill to think of keeping his engagement to go in the boat. He wrote a brief note to Stephen, and sent it early by the servant, saying that he was not well enough to fulfil his engagement to Miss Deane. Would Stephen take his excuse, and fill his place?

Lucy had arranged a charming plan, which had made her quite content with Stephen's refusal to go in the boat. She discovered that her father was to drive to Lindum this morning at ten: Lindum was the very place she wanted to go to, to make purchases which must by no means be put off to another opportunity; and aunt Tulliver must go too, because she was concerned in some of the purchases.

'You will have your row in the boat just the same, you know,' she said to Maggie when they went out of the breakfast-room and upstairs together; 'Philip will be here at half-past ten, and it is a delicious morning. Now, don't say a word against it, you dear dolorous thing. What is the use of my being a fairy godmother, if you set your face against all the wonders I work for you?'

Maggie was almost glad of the plan; for perhaps it would bring her some strength and calmness to be alone with Philip again.

The ring of the door-bell was punctual, and she was thinking with half-sad, affectionate pleasure of the surprise Philip would have in finding that he was to be with her alone, when the door opened, and Stephen Guest entered.

In the first moment they were both too much agitated to speak; for Stephen had learned from the servant that the others were gone out. Maggie had started up and sat down again, with her heart beating violently; and Stephen, throwing down his cap and gloves, came and sat by her in silence. She thought Philip would be coming soon; and with great effort – for she trembled visibly – she rose to go to a distant chair.

'He is not coming,' said Stephen, in a low tone. 'He is not well; he asked me to come instead.'

'Lucy is gone to Lindum,' said Maggie, taking off her bonnet, with hurried, trembling fingers. 'We must not go.'

'Very well,' said Stephen, dreamily, looking at her, as he rested his arm on the back of his chair. 'Then we'll stay here.'

'The man is waiting – he has taken the cushions,' she said. 'Will you go and tell him?'

'What shall I tell him?' said Stephen, almost in a whisper.

Maggie made no answer.

'Let us go,' Stephen murmured, entreatingly, rising, and taking her hand to raise her too. 'We shall not be long together.'

And they went. Maggie felt that she was being led down the garden among the roses, being helped with firm tender care into the boat, having the cushion and cloak arranged for her feet, and her parasol opened for her – all by this stronger presence that seemed to bear her along without any act of her own will.

They glided rapidly along. The breath of the young, unwearied day, the delicious rhythmic dip of the oars, the fragmentary song of a passing bird heard now and then, the sweet solitude of a twofold consciousness that was mingled into one by that grave untiring gaze which need not be averted – what else could there be in their minds for the first hour? Some low, subdued, languid exclamation of love came from Stephen from time to time, as he went on rowing idly, half automatically: otherwise, they spoke no word; for what could words have been but an inlet to thought? and thought did not belong to that enchanted haze in which they were. Maggie was only dimly conscious of the banks, as they passed them, and dwelt with no recognition on the villages: she knew there were several to be passed before they reached Luckreth.

But at last Stephen, who had been rowing more and more idly, ceased to row, laid down the oars, folded his arms, and looked down on the water as if watching the pace at which the boat glided without his help. This sudden change roused Maggie. She looked at the far-stretching fields – at the banks close by – and felt that they were entirely strange to her. A terrible alarm took possession of her.

'Oh, have we passed Luckreth – where we were to stop?' she exclaimed.

He went on watching the water, and said, in a strange, dreamy, absent tone, 'Yes – a long way.'

'Oh, what shall I do?' cried Maggie, in an agony. 'We shall not get home for hours – and Lucy – O God, help me!'

She clasped her hands and broke into a sob, like a frightened child.

Stephen moved and sat beside her, and gently drew down the clasped hands.

'Maggie,' he said, in a deep tone of slow decision, 'let us never go home again – till no one can part us – till we are married.'

The unusual tone, the startling words, arrested Maggie's sob, and she sat quite still: as if Stephen might have seen some possibilities that would alter everything, and annul the wretched facts.

'See, Maggie, how everything has come without our seeking – in spite of all our efforts. We never thought of being alone together again: it has all been done by others. See how the tide is carrying us out – away from all those unnatural bonds that we have been trying to make faster round us – and trying in vain. It will carry us on to Torby, and we can land there, and get some carriage, and hurry on to York, and then to Scotland – and never pause a moment till we are bound to each other, so that only death can part us. It is the only right thing, dearest: it is the only way of escaping from this wretched entanglement. Everything has concurred to point it out to us. We have contrived nothing, we have thought of nothing ourselves.'

Stephen spoke with deep, earnest pleading. Maggie listened – passing from her startled wonderment to the yearning after that belief, that the tide was doing it all – that she might glide along with the swift, silent stream, and not struggle any more. But across that stealing influence came the terrible shadow of past thoughts; and the sudden horror lest now, at last, the moment of fatal intoxication was close upon her, called up feelings of angry resistance towards Stephen.

'Let me go!' she said, flashing an indignant look at him, and trying to get her hand free. 'You have wanted to deprive me of any choice. You knew we were come too far – you have dared to take advantage of my thoughtlessness. It is unmanly to bring me into such a position.'

Stung at this reproach, he released her hands, moved back to his former place, and folded his arms, in a sort of desperation at the difficulty Maggie's words had made present to him. If she would not consent to go on, he must curse himself for the embarrassment he had led her into. But the reproach was the unendurable thing: the one thing worse than parting with her was, that she should feel he had acted unworthily towards her. At last he said, in a tone of suppressed rage—

'I didn't notice that we had passed Luckreth till we had got to the next village; and then it came into my mind that we would go on. I can't justify it: I ought to have told you. It is enough to make you hate me – since you don't love me well enough to make everything else indifferent to you – as I do you. Shall I stop the boat, and try to get you out here? I'll tell Lucy that I was mad – and that you hate me – and you shall be clear of me for ever. No one can blame you, because I have behaved unpardonably to you.'

Maggie was paralysed: it was easier to resist Stephen's pleading, than this picture he had called up of himself suffering, while she was vindicated – easier even to turn away from his look of tenderness than from this look of angry misery, that seemed to place her in selfish isolation from him. The indignant fire in her eyes was quenched. She had reproached him for being hurried into irrevocable trespass – she, who had been so weak herself.

'As if I shouldn't feel what happened to you – just the same,' she said, with reproach of another kind – the reproach of love, asking for more trust.

He felt all the relenting in her look and tone – it was heaven opening again. He moved to her side, and took her hand, leaning his elbow on the back of the boat, and saying nothing. He dreaded to utter another word; he dreaded to make another movement, that might provoke another reproach or denial from her. Life hung on her consent: everything else was hopeless, confused, sickening misery. They glided along in this way, both resting in that silence as in a haven, both dreading lest their feelings should be divided again – till they became aware that the clouds had gathered, and that the slightest perceptible freshening of the breeze was growing and growing, till the whole character of the day was altered.

'You will be chill, Maggie, in this thin dress. Let me raise the cloak over your shoulders. Get up an instant, dearest.'

Maggie obeyed: there was an unspeakable charm in being told what to do, and having everything decided for her. She sat down again, covered with the cloak, and Stephen took to his oars again, making haste; for they must try to get to Torby as fast as they could. Maggie was hardly conscious of having said or done anything decisive. Every influence tended to lull her into acquiescence: that dreamy gliding in the boat, which had lasted for four hours, and had brought some weariness and exhaustion – the recoil of her fatigued sensations from the impracticable difficulty of getting out of the boat at this unknown distance from home, and walking for long miles – all helped to bring her into more complete subjection to that strong mysterious charm which made a last parting from Stephen seem the death of all joy – which made the thought of wounding him like the first touch of the torturing iron before which resolution shrank. And then there was the present happiness of being with him, which was enough to absorb all her languid energy.

Presently Stephen observed a vessel coming after them. Several vessels, among them the steamer to Mudport, had passed them with the early tide, but for the last hour they had seen none. He looked more and more eagerly at this vessel, as if a new thought had come into his mind along with it, and then he looked at Maggie, hesitatingly.

'Maggie, dearest,' he said, at last, 'if this vessel should be going to Mudport, or to any convenient place on the coast northward, it would be our best plan to get them to take us on board. You are fatigued – and it may soon rain – it may be a wretched business, getting to Torby in this boat. It's only a trading-vessel, but I daresay you can be made tolerably comfortable. We'll take the cushions out of the boat. It is really our best plan. They'll be glad enough to take us: I've got plenty of money about me; I can pay them well.'

Maggie's heart began to beat with reawakened alarm at this new proposition; but she was silent – one course seemed as difficult as another.

Stephen hailed the vessel. It was a Dutch vessel going to Mudport, the English mate informed him, and, if this wind held, would be there in less than two days.

'We had got out too far with our boat,' said Stephen. 'I was trying to make for Torby. But I'm afraid of the weather, and this lady – my wife – will be exhausted with fatigue and hunger. Take us on board – will you? – and haul up the boat. I'll pay you well.'

Maggie, now really faint and trembling with fear, was taken on board, making an interesting object of contemplation to admiring Dutchmen. The mate feared the lady would have a poor time of it on board, for they had no accommodation for such entirely unlooked-for passengers. The boat-cushions were spread into a couch for Maggie on the poop with all alacrity. But to pace up and down the deck leaning on Stephen – being upheld by his strength – was the first change that she needed: then came food, and then quiet reclining on the cushions, with the sense that no new resolution *could* be taken that day. Everything must wait till tomorrow. Stephen sat beside her, with her hand in his; they could only speak to each other in low tones; only look at each other now and then, for it would take a long while to dull the curiosity of the five men on board. But Stephen was triumphantly happy. Every other thought or care was thrown into unmarked perspective by the certainty that Maggie must be his. The leap had been taken now: he had been tortured by scruples, he had fought fiercely with overmastering inclination, he had hesitated; but repentance was impossible. He murmured forth in fragmentary sentences his happiness – his adoration – his tenderness – his belief that their life together must be heaven – that her presence with him would give rapture to every common day – that to satisfy her lightest wish was dearer to him than all other bliss – that everything was easy for her sake, except to part with her: and now they never *would* part; he would belong to her for ever, and all that was his was hers – had no value for him except as it was hers. To poor Maggie, Stephen's passionate words made the vision of such a life more fully present than it had ever been before; and the vision for the time excluded all realites – all except the hand that pressed hers, and the voice that spoke to her, and the eyes that looked at her with grave, unspeakable love.

There was to be no rain, after all. Maggie was to sleep all night on the poop and she was covered with the warmest wrappings the ship could furnish. It was still early, when the fatigues of the day brought on a drowsy longing for perfect rest, and she laid down her head. She looked up at Stephen, who was still seated by her, hanging over her as he leaned his arm against the vessel's side. Behind all the delicious visions of these last hours, which had flowed over her like a soft stream and made her entirely passive, there was the dim consciousness that the condition was a transient one, and that the morrow must bring back the old life of struggle.

14

Waking

Maggie awoke to the splash of water against the vessel, and the sound of a footstep on the deck, and the awful starlit sky. There was a moment of utter bewilderment before her mind could get disentangled from the confused web of dreams; but soon the whole terrible truth urged itself upon her. Stephen was not by her now: she was alone with her own memory and her own dread.

The irrevocable wrong that must blot her life had been committed: she had brought sorrow into the lives of others – into the lives that were knit up with hers by trust and love. The feeling of a few short weeks had hurried her into the sins her nature had most recoiled from – breach of faith and cruel selfishness; she had rent the ties that had given meaning to duty, and had made herself an outlawed soul, with no guide but the wayward choice of her own passion. She had said she would rather die than fall into the temptation. She felt it now – now that the consequences of such a fall had come before the outward act was completed. There was at least this fruit from all her years of striving after the highest and best – that her soul, though betrayed, beguiled, ensnared, could never deliberately consent to a choice of the lower. And a choice of what? O God – not a choice of joy, but of conscious cruelty and hardness; for could she ever cease to see before her Lucy and Philip, with their murdered trust and hopes? Her life with Stephen could have no sacredness: she must for ever sink and wander vaguely, driven by uncertain impulse; for she had let go the clue of life – that clue which once in the far-off years her young need had clutched so strongly. She had renounced all delights then, before she knew them, before they had come within her reach. Philip had been right when he told her that she knew nothing of renunciation: she had thought it was quiet ecstasy; she saw it face to face now – that sad patient living strength which holds the clue of life – and saw that the thorns were for ever pressing on its brow. The yesterday, which could never be revoked – if she could change it now for any length of inward silent endurance, she would have bowed beneath that cross with a sense of rest.

The sun was rising now, and roused Stephen; he came to sit beside her. The sharp instinct of anxious love saw something to give him alarm in the very first glance. He had a hovering dread of some resistance in Maggie's nature that he would be unable to overcome. He had the uneasy consciousness that he had robbed her of perfect freedom yesterday: there was too much native honour in him, for him not to feel that if her will should recoil, his conduct would have been odious, and she would have a right to reproach him.

But Maggie did not feel that right: she was too conscious of fatal weakness in herself – too full of the tenderness that comes with the foreseen need for inflicting a wound. She let him take her hand when he came to sit down beside her, and smiled at him – only with rather a sad glance; she could say nothing to pain him till the moment of possible parting was nearer. And so they drank their cup of coffee together, and walked about the deck, and heard the captain's assurance that they should be in Mudport by five o'clock, each with an inward burthen; but in him it was an undefined fear, which he trusted to the coming hours to dissipate; in her it was a definite resolve on which she was trying silently to tighten her hold. Stephen was continually, through the morning, expressing his anxiety at the fatigue and discomfort she was suffering, and alluded to landing and to the change of motion and repose she would have in a carriage, wanting to assure himself more completely by pre-supposing that everything would be as he had arranged it. For a long while Maggie contented herself with assuring him that she had had a good night's rest, and that she didn't mind about being on the vessel. But a suppressed resolve will betray itself in the eyes, and Stephen became more and more uneasy as the day advanced, under the sense that Maggie had entirely lost her passiveness. Each time he looked at her, he gathered a stronger dread at the new quiet sadness with which she met his eyes.

'Here we are in sight of Mudport,' he said, at last. 'Now, dearest,' he added, turning towards her with a look that was half-beseeching, 'the worst part of your fatigue is over. On the land we can command swiftness. In another hour and a half we shall be in a chaise together – and that will seem rest to you after this.'

Maggie felt it was time to speak.

'We shall not be together – we shall have parted.'

The blood rushed to Stephen's face.

'We shall not,' he said. 'I'll die first.'

It was as he had dreaded – there was a struggle coming. But

neither of them dared to say another word, till the boat was let down, and they were taken to the landing-place. Here there was a cluster of passengers awaiting the departure of the steamboat to St Ogg's. Maggie had a dim sense, when she had landed, and Stephen was hurrying her along on his arm, that some one had advanced towards her from that cluster as if he were coming to speak to her. But she was hurried along, and was indifferent to everything but the coming trial.

A porter guided them to the nearest inn and posting-house, and Stephen gave the order for the chaise as they passed through the yard. Maggie took no notice of this, and only said, 'Ask them to show us into a room where we can sit down.'

When they entered, Maggie did not sit down, and Stephen, whose face had a desperate determination in it, was about to ring the bell, when she said, in a firm voice—

'I'm not going: we must part here.'

'Maggie,' he said, turning round towards her, and speaking in the tones of a man who feels a process of torture beginning, 'do you mean to kill me? What is the use of it now? The whole thing is done.'

'No, it is not done,' said Maggie. 'Too much is done – more than we can ever remove the trace of. But I will go no farther. Don't try to prevail with me again. I couldn't choose yesterday.'

'Maggie,' he said, at last, and speaking in a tone of imploring wretchedness, 'have some pity – hear me – forgive me for what I did yesterday. I will obey you now – I will do nothing without your full consent. But don't blight our lives for ever by a rash perversity that can answer no good purpose to any one – that can only create new evils. Sit down, dearest; wait – think what you are going to do. Don't treat me as if you couldn't trust me.'

He had chosen the most effective appeal; but Maggie's will was fixed. She had made up her mind to suffer.

'We must not wait,' she said, in a low but distinct voice; 'we must part at once.'

'We *can't* part, Maggie,' said Stephen, more impetuously. 'I can't bear it. What is the use of inflicting that misery on me? The blow – whatever it may have been – has been struck now. Will it help any one else that you should drive me mad?'

'I will not begin any future, even for you,' said Maggie, tremulously, 'with a deliberate consent to what ought not to have been. What I told you at Basset I feel now: I would rather have died than fall into this temptation. It would have been better if we had parted for ever then. But we must part now.'

'We will *not* part,' Stephen burst out, instinctively placing his back against the door – forgetting everything he had said a few moments before; 'I will not endure it. You'll make me desperate – I shan't know what I do.'

Maggie felt her determination growing stronger.

'Remember what you felt weeks ago,' she began, with beseeching earnestness, 'remember what we both felt – that we owed ourselves to others, and must conquer every inclination which could make us false to that debt. We have failed to keep our resolution; but the wrong remains the same.'

'No, it does *not* remain the same,' said Stephen. 'We have proved that it was impossible to keep our resolutions. We have proved that the feeling which draws us towards each other is too strong to be overcome: that natural law surmounts every other; we can't help what it clashes with.'

'It is not so, Stephen – I'm quite sure that is wrong. I have tried to think it again and again; but I see, if we judged in that way, there would be a warrant for all treachery and cruelty – we should justify breaking the most sacred ties that can ever be formed on earth. If the past is not to bind us, where can duty lie?'

'But there are ties that can't be kept by mere resolution,' said Stephen, starting up and walking about again. 'What is outward faithfulness? Would they have thanked us for anything so hollow as constancy without love?'

Maggie did not answer immediately. She was undergoing an inward as well as an outward contest. At last she said, with a passionate assertion of her conviction, as much against herself as against him—

'That seems right – at first; but when I look further, I'm sure it is *not* right. Faithfulness and constancy mean something else besides doing what is easiest and pleasantest to ourselves. They mean renouncing whatever would cause misery to those whom the course of our lives has made dependent on us. I feel no excuse for myself – none. I should never have failed towards Lucy and Philip as I have done, if I had not been weak, selfish, and hard – able to think of their pain without a pain to myself that would have destroyed all temptation. Oh, what is Lucy feeling now? She believed in me – she loved me – she was so good to me. Think of her ...'

Maggie's voice was getting choked as she uttered these last words.

'I *can't* think of her,' said Stephen, stamping as if with pain. 'I can think of nothing but you, Maggie. You demand of a man what is impossible. I felt that once; but I can't go back to it now. And where is the use of *your* thinking of it, except to torture me? You can't save them from pain now; you can only tear yourself from me, and make my life worthless to me. And even if we could go back, and both fulfil our engagements – if that were possible now – it would be hateful – horrible, to think of your ever being Philip's wife – of your ever being the wife of a man you didn't love. We have both been rescued from a mistake.'

A deep flush came over Maggie's face, and she couldn't speak. Stephen sat down again, taking her hand in his, and looking at her with passionate entreaty.

'Maggie! Dearest! If you love me, you are mine. Who can have so great a claim on you as I have? My life is bound up in your love. There is nothing in the past that can annul our right to each other: it is the first time we have either of us loved with our whole heart and soul.'

Maggie was still silent for a little while – looking down. Stephen was in a flutter of new hope: he was going to triumph. But she raised her eyes and met his with a glance that was filled with the anguish of regret – not with yielding.

'No – not with my whole heart and soul, Stephen,' she said, with timid resolution. 'I have never consented to it with my whole mind. I couldn't live in peace if I put the shadow of a wilful sin between myself and God. I have caused sorrow already – I know – I feel it; but I have never deliberately consented to it. It has never been my will to marry you: if you were to win consent from the momentary triumph of my feeling for you, you would not have my whole soul. If I could wake back again into the time before yesterday, I would choose to be true to my calmer affections, and live without the joy of love.'

Stephen loosed her hand, and, rising impatiently, walked up and down the room in suppressed rage.

'Good God!' he burst out, at last, 'what a miserable thing a woman's love is to a man's! I could commit crimes for you – and you can balance and choose in that way. But you *don't* love me: if you had a tithe of the feeling for me that I have for you, it would be impossible to you to think for a moment of sacrificing me. But it weighs nothing with you that you are robbing me of *my* life's happiness.'

Maggie pressed her fingers together almost convulsively as she held them clasped on her lap

'No – I don't sacrifice you – I couldn't sacrifice you,' she said, as soon as she could speak again; 'but I can't believe in a good for you, that I feel – that we both feel is a wrong towards others. We can't choose happiness either for ourselves or for another: we can't tell where that will lie. We can only choose whether we will indulge ourselves in the present moment, or whether we will renounce that, for the sake of obeying the divine voice within us – for the sake of being true to all the motives that sanctify our lives. I know this belief is hard: it has slipped away from me again and again; but I have felt that if I let it go for ever, I should have no light through the darkness of this life.'

'But, Maggie,' said Stephen, seating himself by her again, 'is it possible you don't see that what happened yesterday has altered the whole position of things? It is too late to say what we might have done or what we ought to have done. Admitting the very worst view of what has been done, it is a fact we must act on now; our position is altered; the right course is no longer what it was before. We must accept our own actions, and start afresh from them. Suppose we had been married yesterday? It is nearly the same thing. The effect on others would not have been different. It would only have made this difference to ourselves,' Stephen added, bitterly, 'that you might have acknowledged then that your tie to me was stronger than to others.'

Again a deep flush came over Maggie's face, and she was silent. Stephen thought again that he was beginning to prevail.

'Dearest,' he said, in his deepest, tenderest tone, leaning towards her and putting his arm round her, 'you *are* mine now – the world believes it– duty must spring out of that now: in a few hours you will be legally mine, and those who had claims on us will submit – they will see that there was a force which declared against their claims.'

Maggie's eyes opened wide in one terrified look at the face that was close to hers, and she started up – pale again.

'Oh, I can't do it,' she said, in a voice almost of agony – 'Stephen – don't ask me – don't urge me. I can't argue any longer – I don't know what is wise; but my heart will not let me do it. I see – I feel their trouble now: it is as if it were branded on my mind. *I* have suffered, and had no one to pity me; and now I have made others suffer. It would never leave me; it would embitter your love to me. I *do* care for Philip – in a different way: I remember all we said to each other; I know how he thought of me as the one promise of his life. He was given to me that I might make his lot less hard; and I have forsaken him. And Lucy – she has been deceived – she who trusted me more than any one. I cannot marry you: I cannot take a good for myself that has been wrung out of their misery. I can't set out on a fresh life, and forget that: I must go back to it, and cling to it, else I shall feel as if there were nothing firm beneath my feet.'

'Good God, Maggie!' said Stephen, rising too and grasping her arm, 'you rave. How can you go back without marrying me? You don't know what will be said, dearest. You see nothing as it really is.'

'Yes, I do. But they will believe me. I will confess everything.

Lucy will believe me – she will forgive you, and – and – oh, *some* good will come by clinging to the right. Dear, dear Stephen, let me go! – don't drag me into deeper remorse. My whole soul has never consented – it does not consent now.'

Stephen let go her arm, and sank back on his chair, half stunned by despairing rage.

'Go, then – leave me – don't torture me any longer – I can't bear it.'

Maggie was not conscious of a decision as she turned away from that gloomy averted face, and walked out of the room. What came after? A sense of stairs descended as if in a dream – of flagstones – of a chaise and horses standing – then a street, and a turning into another street where a stage-coach was standing, taking in passengers – and the darting thought that the coach would take her away, perhaps towards home. But she could ask nothing yet; she only got into the coach.

Home – where her mother and brother were – Philip – Lucy – the scene of her very cares and trials – was the haven towards which her mind tended – where she would be rescued from more falling. The thought of Stephen was like a horrible throbbing pain, which yet, as such pains do, seemed to urge all other thoughts into activity. But among her thoughts, what others would say and think of her conduct was hardly present. Love and deep pity and remorseful anguish left no room for that.

The coach was taking her to York – farther away from home; but she did not learn that until she was set down in the old city at midnight. It was no matter: she could sleep there, and start home the next day. She had her purse in her pocket, with all her money in it – a bank-note and a sovereign: she had kept it in her pocket from forgetfulness, after going out to make purchases the day before yesterday.

In the darkness of that night the love she had renounced came back upon her with a cruel charm; she felt herself opening her arms to receive it once more; and then it seemed to slip away and fade and vanish, leaving only the dying sound of a deep, thrilling voice that said, 'Gone – for ever gone.'

The Final Rescue

1

The Return to the Mill

Between four and five o'clock on the afternoon of the fifth day from that on which Stephen and Maggie had left St Ogg's, Tom Tulliver was standing on the gravel-walk outside the old house at Dorlcote Mill. He was master there now: he had half fulfilled his father's dying wish, and by years of steady self-government and energetic work he had brought himself near to the attainment of more than the old respectability which had been the proud inheritance of the Dodsons and Tullivers.

But Tom's face, as he stood in the hot still sunshine of that summer afternoon, had no gladness, no triumph in it. His mouth wore its bitterest expression, his severe brow its hardest and deepest fold. No news of his sister had been heard since Bob Jakin had come back in the steamer from Mudport, and put an end to all improbable suppositions of an accident on the water by stating that he had seen her land from a vessel with Mr Stephen Guest. Would the next news be that she was married – or what? Probably that she was not married: Tom's mind was set to the expectation of the worst that could happen – not death, but disgrace.

As he was walking with his back towards the entrance gate a tall figure approached the gate, and paused to look at him, with a fast-beating heart. Her brother was the human being of whom she had been most afraid, from her childhood upwards: afraid with that fear which springs in us when we love one who is inexorable, unbending. That deep-rooted fear was shaking Maggie now: but her mind was unswervingly bent on returning to her brother, as the natural refuge that had been given her. In her deep humiliation under the retrospect of her own weakness she almost desired to endure the severity of Tom's reproof, to submit in patient silence to that harsh disapproving judgement against which she had so often rebelled: it seemed no more than just to her now – who was weaker than she was?

Maggie had been kept on her bed at York for a day with that prostrating headache which was likely to follow on the terrible strain of the previous day and night. There was an expression of physical pain still about her brow and eyes, and her whole appearance, with her dress so long unchanged, was worn and distressed. She lifted the latch of the gate and walked in – slowly. Tom did not hear the gate; he was just then close upon the roaring dam; but he presently turned, and, lifting up his eyes, saw the figure whose worn look and loneliness seemed to him a confirmation of his worst conjectures. He paused, trembling and white with disgust and indignation.

'Tom,' she began, faintly, 'I am come back to you – I am come back home – for refuge – to tell you everything.'

'You will find no home with me,' he answered with tremulous rage. 'You have disgraced us all. You have disgraced my father's name. You have been a curse to your best friends. You have been base – deceitful; no motives are strong enough to restrain you. I wash my hands of you for ever. You don't belong to me.'

Their mother had come to the door now. She stood paralysed by the double shock of seeing Maggie and hearing Tom's words.

'Tom,' said Maggie, with more courage, 'I am perhaps not so guilty as you believe me to be. I never meant to give way to my feelings. I struggled against them. I was carried too far in the boat to come back on Tuesday. I came back as soon as I could.'

'I can't believe in you any more,' said Tom. 'You have been carrying on a clandestine relation with Stephen Guest – as you did before with another. He went to see you at my aunt Moss's;

you walked alone with him in the lanes; you must have behaved as no modest girl would have done to her cousin's lover, else that could never have happened. You have been using Philip Wakem as a screen to deceive Lucy – the kindest friend you ever had. Go and see the return you have made her: she's ill – unable to speak – my mother can't go near her, lest she should remind her of *you*.'

Maggie was half stunned – too heavily pressed upon by her anguish even to discern any difference between her actual guilt and her brother's accusations, still less to vindicate herself.

'Tom,' she said, crushing her hands together under her cloak, in the effort to speak again, 'whatever I have done, I repent it bitterly. I want to make amends. I will endure anything. I want to be kept from doing wrong again.'

'What *will* keep you?' said Tom, with cruel bitterness. 'Not religion; not your natural feelings of gratitude and honour. I loathe your character and your conduct. You struggled with your feelings, you say. Yes! *I* have had feelings to struggle with; but I conquered them. I have had a harder life than you have had; but I have found *my* comfort in doing my duty. But I will sanction no such character as yours: the world shall know that *I* feel the difference between right and wrong. If you are in want, I will provide for you – let my mother know. But you shall not come under my roof. It is enough that I have to bear the thought of your disgrace: the sight of you is hateful to me.'

Slowly Maggie was turning away with despair in her heart. But the poor frightened mother's love leaped out now, stronger than all dread.

'My child! I'll go with you. You've got a mother. I'll get ready and come with you.'

When his mother appeared with her bonnet on, Tom put money into her hands.

'My house is yours, mother, always,' he said. 'You will come and let me know everything you want – you will come back to me.'

Poor Mrs Tulliver took the money, too frightened to say anything. The only thing clear to her was the mother's instinct that she would go with her unhappy child.

Maggie was waiting outside the gate; she took her mother's hand, and they walked a little way in silence.

'Mother,' said Maggie, at last, 'we will go to Bob Jakin's: his wife will have room for us, if they have no other lodger.'

So they went on their way to St Ogg's – to the old house by the river-side.

Bob himself was at home, with a heaviness at heart which resisted even the new joy and pride of possessing a two months' old baby. He would perhaps not so thoroughly have understood all the dubiousness of Maggie's appearance with Mr Stephen Guest on the quay at Mudport, if he had not witnessed the effect it produced on Tom when he went to report it; and since then, the circumstances which in any case gave a disastrous character to her elopement, had passed beyond the more polite circles of St Ogg's, and had become matter of common talk. So that when he opened the door and saw Maggie standing before him in her sorrow and weariness, he had no questions to ask, except one, which he dared only ask himself – where was Mr Stephen Guest?

The lodgings were vacant, and both Mrs Jakin the larger and Mrs Jakin the less were commanded to make all things comfortable for 'the old Missis and the young Miss' – alas! that she was still 'Miss.'

After a day or two Mrs Tulliver was gone to the mill again for a few hours to see to Tom's household matters. Maggie had wished this: after the first violent outburst of feeling, which came as soon as she had no longer any active purpose to fulfil, she was less in need of her mother's presence; she even desired to be alone with her grief. But she had been solitary only a little while in the old sitting-room that looked on the river, when there came a tap at the door, and turning round her sad face as she said 'Come in,' she saw Bob enter with the baby in his arms, and Mumps at his heels.

'We'll go back, if it disturbs you, Miss,' said Bob.

'No,' said Maggie, in a low voice, wishing she could smile.

Bob, closing the door behind him, came and stood before her.

'You see, we've got a little un, Miss, and I wanted you to look at it, and take it in your arms, if you'd be so good. For we made free to name it after you.'

Maggie could not speak, but she put out her arms to receive the tiny baby, while Mumps snuffed at it anxiously, to ascertain that this transference was all right. Maggie's heart had swelled at this action: she knew well enough that it was a way Bob had chosen to show his sympathy and respect.

'Sit down, Bob,' she said presently, and he sat down in silence, finding his tongue refusing to say what he wanted it to say.

'Bob,' she said, after a few moments, looking down at the baby, 'I have a favour to ask of you.'

'Don't you speak so, Miss,' said Bob, grasping the skin of Mumps's neck; 'if there's anything I can do for you, I should look upon it as a day's earnings.'

'I want you to go to Dr Kenn's, and tell him that I am here, and should be very grateful if he would come to me while my mother is away. She will not come back till evening.'

'Eh, Miss – I'd do it in a minute but Dr Kenn's wife lies dead – she's to be buried tomorrow. I hardly like to go a-nigh him yet.'

'Oh, no, Bob,' said Maggie, 'we must let it be – till after a few days, perhaps – when you hear that he is going about again.'

Bob was silent again for a little while, ruminating much on the possible forms in which he might put a question. At last he said, in a more timid voice than usual—

'Will you give me leave to ask you only one thing, Miss?'

Maggie was rather startled, but she answered, 'Yes, Bob, if it is about myself – not about any one else.'

'Well, Miss, it's this: *Do* you owe anybody a grudge?'

'No, not any one,' said Maggie, looking up at him inquiringly. 'Why?'

'Oh, lors, Miss,' said Bob, pinching Mumps's neck harder than ever, 'I wish you did – an' 'ud tell me – I'd leather him till I couldn't see – I would – an' the Justice might do what he liked to me arter.'

'Oh, Bob,' said Maggie, smiling faintly, 'you're a very good friend to me. But I shouldn't like to punish any one, even if they'd done me wrong; I've done wrong myself too often.'

2

St Ogg's Passes Judgement

It was soon known throughout St Ogg's that Miss Tulliver was come back: she had not, then, eloped in order to be married to Mr Stephen Guest – at all events, Mr Stephen Guest had not married her – which came to the same thing, so far as her culpability was concerned. Public opinion, in these cases, is always of the feminine gender – not the world, but the world's wife: Maggie had returned without a husband – in that degraded and outcast condition to which error is well known to lead; and the world's wife, with that fine instinct which is given her for the preservation of Society, saw at once that Miss Tulliver's conduct had been of the most aggravated kind. Could anything be more detestable? A girl so much indebted to her friends – whose mother as well as herself had received so much kindness from the Deanes – to lay the design of winning a young man's affections away from her own cousin, who had behaved like a sister to her! As for poor Mr Stephen Guest, he was rather pitiable than otherwise: a young man of five-and-twenty is not to be too severely judged in these cases – he is really very much at the mercy of a designing bold girl. And it was clear that he had given way in spite of himself: he had shaken her off as soon as he could; indeed, their having parted so soon looked very black indeed – *for her*. To be sure, he had written a letter, laying all the blame on himself, and telling the story in a romantic fashion so as to try and make her appear quite innocent: of course he could do that! But the refined instinct of the world's wife was not to be deceived. Why – her own brother had turned her from his door: he had seen enough, you might be sure, before he would do that. A truly respectable young man – Mr Tom Tulliver. His sister's disgrace was naturally a heavy blow to him. It was to be hoped that she would go out of the neighbourhood so as to purify the air of St Ogg's from the taint of her presence.

It required nearly a fortnight for fine instinct to assure itself of these inspirations; indeed, it was a whole week before Stephen's letter came, telling his father the facts, and adding that he was gone across to Holland – had drawn upon the agent at Mudport for money – was incapable of any resolution at present.

Maggie, all this while, was too entirely filled with a more agonising anxiety, to spend any thought on the view that was being taken of her conduct by the world of St Ogg's: anxiety about Stephen – Lucy – Philip – beat on her poor heart in a hard, driving, ceaseless storm of mingled love, remorse, and pity. If she had thought of rejection and injustice at all, it would have seemed to her that they had done their worst – that she could hardly feel any stroke from them intolerable since the words she had heard from her brother's lips.

But she was not without practical intentions: the love of independence was too strong a habit for her not to remember that she must get her bread: and when other projects looked vague, she fell back on that of returning to her plain sewing, and so getting enough to pay for her lodging at Bob's. She meant to persuade her mother to return to the mill by and by, and live with Tom again; and somehow or other she would maintain herself at St Ogg's. Dr Kenn would perhaps help her and advise her. She remembered the momentary feeling of reliance that had sprung in her when he was talking with her, and she waited with yearning expectation for the opportunity of confiding everything to him. Her mother called every day at Mr Deane's to learn how Lucy was: the report was always sad – nothing had yet roused her from the feeble passivity which had come on with the first shock. But of Philip, Mrs Tulliver had learned nothing: naturally, no one whom she met would speak to her about what related to her daughter. But at last she summoned courage to go and see sister Glegg, who of course would know everything, and had even been to see Tom at the mill in Mrs Tulliver's absence, though he had said nothing of what had passed on the occasion.

As soon as her mother was gone, Maggie put on her bonnet. She had resolved on walking to the Rectory and asking to see Dr Kenn. It was the first time she had been beyond the door since her return; she had no sooner passed beyond the narrower streets which she had to thread from Bob's dwelling, than she became aware of unusual glances cast at her; and this consciousness made her hurry along nervously, afraid to look to right or left. Presently, however, she came full on Mrs and Miss Turnbull, old acquaintances of her family; they both looked at her strangely, and turned a little aside without speaking. All hard looks were pain to Maggie, but her self-reproach was too strong for resentment. She was about to pass a group of gentlemen, who were standing at the door of the billiard-rooms, and she could not help seeing young Torry step out a little with his glass at his eye, and bow to her with that air of nonchalance which he might have bestowed on a friendly barmaid. Maggie's pride was too intense for her not to feel that sting, even in the midst of her sorrow; and for the first time the thought took strong hold of her that she would have other obloquy cast on her besides that which was felt to be due to her breach of faith towards Lucy. But she was at the Rectory now; there, perhaps, she would find something else than retribution.

She was shown up at once, after being announced, into Dr Kenn's study, where he sat amongst piled-up books, for which he had little appetite, leaning his cheek against the head of his youngest child, a girl of three. The child was sent away with the servant, and when the door was closed, Dr Kenn said, placing a chair for Maggie—

'I was coming to see you, Miss Tulliver; you have anticipated me; I am glad you did.'

Maggie looked at him with her childlike directness as she had done at the bazaar, and said, 'I want to tell you everything.' But her eyes filled fast with tears as she said it, and all the pent-up excitement of her humiliating walk would have its vent before she could say more.

'Do tell me everything,' Dr Kenn said, with quiet kindness in his grave firm voice. 'Think of me as one to whom a long experience has been granted, which may enable him to help you.'

In rather broken sentences, and with some effort, at first, but soon with the greater ease that came from a sense of relief in the confidence, Maggie told the brief story of a struggle that must be the beginning of a long sorrow. Only the day before Dr Kenn had been made acquainted with the contents of Stephen's letter, and he had believed them at once, without the confirmation of Maggie's statement. That involuntary plaint of hers, '*Oh, I must go,*' had remained with him as the sign that she was undergoing some inward conflict.

When she had ended, Dr Kenn was silent for some minutes: there was a difficulty on his mind. He rose, and walked up and down the hearth with his hands behind him. At last he seated himself again, and said, looking at Maggie—

'Your inexperience of the world, Miss Tulliver, prevents you from anticipating fully the very unjust conceptions that will probably be formed concerning your conduct – conceptions which will have a baneful effect, even in spite of known evidence to disprove them.'

'Oh, I do – I begin to see,' said Maggie, unable to repress this utterance of her recent pain. 'I know I shall be insulted: I shall be thought worse than I am.'

'You perhaps do not yet know,' said Dr Kenn, with a touch of more personal pity, 'that a letter is come which ought to satisfy every one who has known anything of you, that you chose the steep and difficult path of a return to the right, at the moment when that return was most of all difficult.'

'Oh – where is he?' said poor Maggie, with a flush and tremor that no presence could have hindered.

'He is gone abroad: he has written of all that passed to his father. He has vindicated you to the utmost; and I hope the communication of that letter to your cousin will have a beneficial effect on her.'

Dr Kenn waited for her to get calm again before he went on.

'That letter, as I said, ought to suffice to prevent false impressions concerning you. But I am bound to tell you, Miss Tulliver, that not only the experience of my whole life, but my observation within the last three days, makes me fear that there is hardly any evidence which will save you from the painful effect of false imputations. The persons who are the most incapable of a conscientious struggle such as yours, are precisely those who will be likely to shrink from you; because they will not believe in your struggle. I fear your life here will be attended not only with much pain, but with many obstructions. For this reason – and for this only – I ask you to consider whether it will not perhaps be better for you to take a situation at a distance, according to your former intention. I will exert myself at once to obtain one for you.'

'Oh, if I could but stop here!' said Maggie. 'I have no heart to begin a strange life again. If I remained here, I could perhaps atone in some way to Lucy – to others: I could convince them that I'm sorry. And,' she added, with some of the old proud fire flashing out, 'I will not go away because people say false things of me. They shall learn to retract them. If I must go away at last, because – because others wish it, I will not go now.'

'Well,' said Dr Kenn, after some consideration, 'if you determine on that, Miss Tulliver, you may rely on all the influence my position gives me. I am bound to aid and countenance you, by the very duties of my office as a parish priest. I will add, that personally I have a deep interest in your peace of mind and welfare.'

'The only thing I want is some occupation that will enable me to get my bread and be independent,' said Maggie. 'I shall not want much. I can go on lodging where I am.'

'I must think over the subject maturely,' said Dr Kenn, 'and in a few days I shall be better able to ascertain the general feeling. I shall come to see you: I shall bear you constantly in mind.'

When Maggie had left him, Dr Kenn stood ruminating with his hands behind him, and his eyes fixed on the carpet, under a painful sense of doubt and difficulty.

3

Showing that Old Acquaintances Are Capable of Surprising Us

When Maggie was at home again, her mother brought her news of an unexpected line of conduct in aunt Glegg. When, at last, she learned from Tom that Maggie had come home, and gathered from him what was her explanation of her absence, she burst forth in severe reproof of Tom for admitting the worst of his sister until he was compelled. If you were not to stand by your 'kin' as long as there was a shred of honour attributable to them, pray what were you to stand by? Though Mrs Glegg had always augured ill of Maggie's future at a time when other people were perhaps less clear-sighted, yet fair-play was a jewel, and it was not for her own friends to help to rob the girl of her fair fame, and to cast her out from family shelter to the scorn of the outer world, until she had become unequivocally a family disgrace. She quarrelled with Mr Glegg, whose kindness, flowing entirely into compassion for Lucy, made him as hard in his judgement of Maggie as Mr Deane himself was; and, fuming against her sister Tulliver because she did not at once come to her for advice and help, shut herself up in her own room with Baxter's 'Saints' Rest' from morning till night, denying herself to all visitors, till Mr Glegg brought from Mr Deane the news of Stephen's letter. Then Mrs Glegg laid aside Baxter, and was ready to meet all comers.

Again she had a scene of remonstrance with Tom, all the more severe in proportion to the greater strength of her present position. But Tom, like other immovable things, seemed only the more rigidly fixed under that attempt to shake him. Poor Tom! he judged by what he had been able to see; and the judgement was painful enough to himself. He thought he had the demonstration of facts observed through years by his own eyes which gave no warning of their imperfection, that Maggie's nature was utterly untrustworthy, and too strongly marked with evil tendencies to be safely treated with leniency. There had arisen in Tom a repulsion towards Maggie that derived its very intensity from their early childish love in the time when they had clasped tiny fingers together, and their later sense of nearness in a common duty and a common sorrow: the sight of her, as he had told her, was hateful to him. Mrs Glegg allowed that Maggie ought to be punished – she was not a woman to deny that – she knew what conduct was; but punished in proportion to the misdeeds proved against her, not to those which were cast upon her by people outside her own family, who might wish to show that their own kin were better.

'Your aunt Glegg scolded me so as niver was, my dear,' said poor Mrs Tulliver, when she came back to Maggie, 'as I didn't go to her before – she said it wasn't for her to come to me first. But she spoke the kindest word as has ever been spoke by you yet, my child. For she says you shall have a shelter in her house, if you'll go to her dutiful, and she'll uphold you against folks as say harm of you when they've no call. And I told her I thought you couldn't bear to see nobody but me, you was so beat down with trouble; but she said, "*I* won't throw ill words at her but I'll give her good advice; an' she must be humble." It's wonderful o' Jane; for I'm sure she used to throw everything I did wrong at me whativer it was.'

'Oh, mother,' said poor Maggie, shrinking from the thought of all the contact her bruised mind would have to bear, 'tell her I'm very grateful – I'll go to see her as soon as I can; but I can't see any one just yet, except Dr Kenn. I've been to him – he will advise me, and help me to get some occupation. I can't live with any one, or be dependent on them, tell aunt Glegg; I must get my own bread. But did you hear nothing of Philip Wakem?'

'No, my dear; but I've been to Lucy's, and I saw your uncle, and he says they got her to listen to the letter, and she took notice o' Miss Guest, and asked questions, and the doctor thinks she's on the turn to be better. What a world this is – what trouble, oh dear! The law was the first beginning, and it's gone from bad to worse all of a sudden, just when the luck seemed on the turn.' This was the first lamentation that Mrs Tulliver had let slip to Maggie, but old habit had been revived by the interview with sister Glegg.

'My poor, poor mother!' Maggie burst out, cut to the heart with pity and compunction, and throwing her arms round her mother's neck, 'I was always naughty and troublesome to you. And now you might have been happy if it hadn't been for me.'

'Eh, my dear,' said Mrs Tulliver, leaning towards the warm young cheek; 'I must put up wi' my children – I shall never have no more; and if they bring me bad luck, I must be fond on it – there's nothing else much to be fond on, for my furnitur' went long ago. And you'd got to be very good once!'

Still two or three more days passed, and Maggie heard nothing of Philip; anxiety about him was becoming her predominant trouble, and she summoned courage at last to inquire about him of Dr Kenn, on his next visit to her. He did not even know if Philip was at home. But Philip could hardly have been ill, or it would have been known through the calling in of the medical man; it was probable that he was gone out of the town for a little while. Maggie sickened under this suspense, and her imagination began to live more and more persistently in what Philip was enduring. What did he believe about her?

At last Bob brought her a letter, without a postmark, directed in a hand which she knew. Her mother was in the room, and Maggie, in violent agitation, hurried upstairs that she might read the letter in solitude. She read it with a throbbing brow.

'MAGGIE,

   – I believe in you – I know you never meant to deceive me – I know you tried to keep faith in me, and to all. I believed this before I had any other evidence of it than your own nature. The night after I last parted from you I suffered torments. I had seen what convinced me that you were not free; that there was another whose presence had a power over you which mine never possessed; but through all the suggestions – almost murderous suggestions – of rage and jealousy, my mind made its way to belief in your truthfulness. I foresaw that he would not relinquish you, and I believed then, as I believe now, that the strong attraction which drew you together proceeded only from one side of your characters, and belonged to that partial, divided action of our nature which makes half the tragedy of the human lot. I have felt the vibration of chords in your nature that I have continually felt the want of in his. But perhaps I am wrong; perhaps I feel about you as the artist does about the scene over which his soul has brooded with love: he would tremble to see it confided to other hands; he would never believe that it could bear for another all the meaning and the beauty it bears for him.

'I dared not trust myself to see you that morning; I was filled with selfish passion; I was shattered by a night of conscious delirium. I told you long ago that I had never been resigned even to the mediocrity of my powers: how could I be resigned to the loss of the one thing which had ever come to me on earth, with the promise of such deep joy as would give a new and blessed meaning to the foregoing pain – the promise of another self that would lift my aching affection into the divine rapture of an ever-springing, ever-satisfied want?

'But the miseries of that night had prepared me for what came before the next. It was no surprise to me. I was certain that he had prevailed on you to sacrifice everything to him, and I waited with equal certainty to hear of your marriage. I measured your love and his by my own. But I was wrong, Maggie. There is something stronger in you than your love for him.

'I will not tell you what I went through in that interval. But even in its utmost agony – even in those terrible throes that love must suffer before it can be disembodied of selfish desire – my love for you sufficed to withhold me from suicide, without the aid of any other motive. In the midst of my egoism, I yet could not bear to come like a death-shadow across the feast of your joy. I could not bear to forsake the world in which you still lived and might need me; it was part of the faith I had vowed to you – to wait and endure. Maggie,

that is a proof of what I write now to assure you of – that
no anguish I have had to bear on your account has been too
heavy a price to pay for the new life into which I have entered
in loving you.

'Then – dear one – in spite of all, you have been the
blessing of my life. Let no self-reproach weigh on you because
of me. It is I who should rather reproach myself for having
urged my feelings upon you, and hurried you into words that
you have felt as fetters. You meant to be true to those words;
you *have* been true. I can measure your sacrifice by what I
have known in only one half-hour of your presence with me,
when I dreamed that you might love me best. But, Maggie,
I have no just claim on you for more than affectionate
remembrance.

'For some time I have shrunk from writing to you, because
I have shrunk even from the appearance of wishing to thrust
myself before you, and so repeating my original error. But
you will not misconstrue me. I know that we must keep
apart for a long while; cruel tongues would force us apart, if
nothing else did. But I shall not go away. The place where you
are is the one where my mind must live, wherever I might
travel. And remember that I am unchangeably yours: yours
– not with selfish wishes – but with a devotion that excludes
such wishes.

'God comfort you – my loving, large-souled Maggie. If
every one else has misconceived you, remember that you
have never been doubted by him whose heart recognised you
ten years ago.

'Do not believe any one who says I am ill, because I am
not seen out of doors. I have only had nervous headaches –
no worse than I have sometimes had them before. But the
overpowering heat inclines me to be perfectly quiescent in
the daytime. I am strong enough to obey any word which
shall tell me that I can serve you by word or deed. – Yours to
the last,

'PHILIP WAKEM'

As Maggie knelt by the bed sobbing, with that letter pressed under her, her feelings again and again gathered themselves in a whispered cry, always in the same words—

'O God, is there any happiness in love that could make me forget *their* pain?'

4

Maggie and Lucy

By the end of the week Dr Kenn had made up his mind that there was only one way in which he could secure to Maggie a suitable living at St Ogg's. Even with his twenty years' experience as a parish priest, he was aghast at the obstinate continuance of imputations against her in the face of evidence. He himself wanted a daily governess for his younger children; and though he had hesitated in the first instance to offer this position to Maggie, the resolution to protect with the utmost force of his personal and priestly character against her being crushed and driven away by slander, was now decisive. Maggie gratefully accepted an employment that gave her duties as well as a support: her days would be filled now, and solitary evenings would be a welcome rest. She no longer needed the sacrifice her mother made in staying with her, and Mrs Tulliver was persuaded to go back to the mill.

But now it began to be discovered that Dr Kenn, exemplary as he had hitherto appeared, had his crotchets – possibly his weaknesses. Maggie had not taken her daily walks to the Rectory for many weeks, before the dreadful possibility of her some time or other becoming the Rector's wife had been talked of so often in confidence, that ladies were beginning to discuss how they should behave to her in that position. For Dr Kenn, it had been understood, had sat in the schoolroom half an hour one morning, when Miss Tulliver was giving her lessons; nay, he had sat there every morning: he had once walked home with her – he almost *always* walked home with her – and if not, he went to see her in the evening. What an artful creature she was! What a *mother f⁓*

those children! It was enough to make poor Mrs Kenn turn in her grave, that they should be put under the care of this girl only a few weeks after her death. Would he be so lost to propriety as to marry her before the year was out?

The Miss Guests saw an alleviation to the sorrow of witnessing a folly in their Rector: at least their brother would be safe; and their knowledge of Stephen's tenacity was a constant ground of alarm to them, lest he should come back and marry Maggie. They were not among those who disbelieved their brother's letter; but they had no confidence in Maggie's adherence to her renunciation of him; they suspected that she had shrunk rather from the elopement than from the marriage, and that she lingered in St Ogg's, relying on his return to her. They had always thought her disagreeable; they now thought her artful and proud. On the very first hint of gossip concerning Maggie and Dr Kenn, the report was conveyed in Miss Guest's letter to her brother.

Maggie had frequent tidings through her mother, or aunt Glegg, or Dr Kenn, of Lucy's gradual progress towards recovery, and her thoughts tended continually towards her uncle Deane's house: she hungered for an interview with Lucy, if it were only for five minutes – to utter a word of penitence, to be assured by Lucy's own eyes and lips that she did not believe in the willing treachery of those whom she had loved and trusted. But she knew that even if her uncle's indignation had not closed his house against her, the agitation of such an interview would have been forbidden to Lucy. Only to have seen her without speaking, would have been some relief. But Lucy was not yet able to go to church, or any place where Maggie could see her; and even the hope of that departed, when the news was told her by aunt Glegg, that Lucy was really going away in a few days to Scarborough with the Miss Guests, who had been heard to say that they expected their brother to meet them there.

Only those who have known what hardest inward conflict is, can know what Maggie felt as she sat in her loneliness the evening after hearing that news from Mrs Glegg – only those who have known what it is to dread their own selfish desires.

She sat without candle in the twilight, with the window wide open towards the river; the sense of oppressive heat adding itself undistinguishably to the burthen of her lot. Hearing the door open, she thought Mrs Jakin was coming in with her supper, but the next moment, without her having discerned the sound of a footstep, she felt a light hand on her shoulder, and heard a voice close to her saying, 'Maggie!'

The face was there – changed, but all the sweeter: the hazel eyes were there, with their heart-piercing tenderness.

'Maggie!' the soft voice said. 'Lucy!' answered a voice with a sharp ring of anguish in it; and Lucy threw her arms round Maggie's neck, and leaned her pale cheek against the burning brow.

'I stole out,' said Lucy, almost in a whisper, while she sat down close to Maggie and held her hand, 'when papa and the rest were away. Alice is come with me. I asked her to help me. But I must only stay a little while, because it is so late.'

It was easier to say that at first than to say anything else. They sat looking at each other. It seemed as if the interview must end without more speech. Each felt that there would be something scorching in the words that would recall the irretrievable wrong. But soon, as Maggie looked, every distinct thought began to be overflowed by a wave of loving penitence, and words burst forth with a sob.

'God bless you for coming, Lucy.'

The sobs came thick on each other after that.

'Maggie, dear, be comforted,' said Lucy now, putting her cheek against Maggie's again. 'Don't grieve.' And she sat still, hoping to soothe Maggie with that gentle caress.

'I didn't mean to deceive you, Lucy,' said Maggie, as soon as she could speak. 'It always made me wretched that I felt what I didn't like you to know … It was because I thought it would all be conquered, and you might never see anything to wound you.'

'I know, dear,' said Lucy. 'I know you never meant to make me unhappy … It is a trouble that has come on us all: you have more to bear than I have – and you gave him up, when … you did what it must have been very hard to do.'

They were silent again a little while, sitting with clasped hands, and cheeks leaned together.

'Lucy,' Maggie began again, '*he* struggled too. He wanted to be true to you. He will come back to you. Forgive him – he will be happy then …'

These words were wrung forth from Maggie's deepest soul, with an effort like the convulsed clutch of a drowning man. Lucy trembled and was silent.

A gentle knock came at the door. It was Alice, the maid, who entered and said—

'I daren't stay any longer, Miss Deane. They'll find it out and there'll be such anger at your coming out so late.'

Lucy rose and said, 'Very well, Alice – in a minute.'

'I'm to go away on Friday, Maggie,' she added, when Alice had closed the door again. 'When I come back, and am strong, they will let me do as I like. I shall come to you when I please then.'

'Lucy,' said Maggie, with another great effort, 'I pray to God continually that I may never be the cause of sorrow to you any more.'

She pressed the little hand that she held between hers, and looked up into the face that was bent over hers. Lucy never forgot that look.

'Maggie,' she said, in a low voice, that had the solemnity of confession in it, 'you are better than I am. I can't …'

She broke off there, and said no more. But they clasped each other again in a last embrace.

5

The Last Conflict

In the second week of September, Maggie was again sitting in her lonely room. It was past midnight, and the rain was beating heavily against the window, driven with fitful force by the rushing, loud-moaning wind. For, the day after Lucy's visit, there had been a sudden change in the weather: the heat and drought had given way to cold variable winds, and heavy falls of rain at intervals; and she had been forbidden to risk the contemplated journey until the weather should become more settled. In the counties higher up the Floss, the rains had been continuous, and the completion of the harvest had been arrested. And now, for the last two days, the rains on this lower course of the river had been incessant, so that the old men had shaken their heads and talked of sixty years ago, when the same sort of weather, happening about the equinox, brought on the great floods, which swept the bridge away, and reduced the town to great misery. But Bob Jakin, naturally prone to take a hopeful view of his own luck, laughed at his mother when she regretted their having taken a house by the river-side; observing that but for that they would have had no boats, which were the most lucky of possessions in case of a flood that obliged them to go to a distance for food.

But the careless and the fearful were alike sleeping in their beds now, for it was past midnight: all, except some solitary watchers such as Maggie. She was seated in her little parlour towards the river with one candle, that left everything dim in the room, except a letter which lay before her on the table. That letter, which had come to her today, was one of the causes that had kept her up far on into the night.

Two days before Maggie received that letter, she had been to the Rectory for the last time. The heavy rain would have prevented her from going since; but there was another reason. Dr Kenn, at first enlightened only by a few hints as to the new turn which gossip and slander had taken in relation to Maggie, had recently been made more fully aware of it by an earnest remonstrance from one of his male parishioners against the indiscretion of persisting in the attempt to overcome the prevalent feeling in the parish by a course of resistance. Dr Kenn, having a conscience void of offence in the matter, was still averse to give way before a public sentiment that was odious and contemptible; but he was finally wrought upon by the consideration of the peculiar responsibility attached to his office, of avoiding the appearance of evil – an 'appearance' that is always dependent on the average quality of surrounding minds. He made up his mind that he must advise Maggie to go away from St Ogg's for a time; and he performed that difficult task with as much delicacy as he could. He begged her to allow him to write to a clerical friend of his, who might possibly take her into his own family, as governess; and, if not, would probably know of some other available position for a young woman in whose welfare Dr Kenn felt a strong interest.

Poor Maggie listened with a trembling lip: she could say nothing but a faint 'thank you – I shall be grateful;' and she walked back to her lodgings, through the driving rain, with a new sense of desolation. She must be a lonely wanderer; she must begin a new life, in which she would have to rouse herself to receive new impressions – and she was so unspeakably, sickeningly weary! But ought she to complain? Ought she to shrink in this way from the long penance of life, which was all the possibility she had of lightening the load to some other sufferers, and so changing that passionate error into a new force of unselfish human love? All the next day she sat in her lonely room, with a window darkened by the cloud and the driving rain, thinking of that future, and wrestling for patience.

And on the third day – this day of which she just sat out the close – the letter had come which was lying on the table before her.

The letter was from Stephen. He was come back from Holland: he was at Mudport again, unknown to any of his friends; and had written to her from that place, enclosing the letter to a person whom he trusted in St Ogg's. From beginning to end it was a passionate cry of reproach: an appeal against her useless sacrifice of him – of herself: against that perverted notion of right which led her to crush all his hopes, for the sake of a mere idea, and not any substantial good – *his* hopes, whom she loved, and who loved her with that single overpowering passion, that worship, which a man never gives to a woman more than once in his life.

'They have written to me that you are to marry Kenn. As if I should believe that! Perhaps they have told you some such fables about me. Perhaps they tell you I've been "travelling." My body has been dragged about somewhere; but *I* have never travelled from the hideous place where you left me – where I started up from the stupor of helpless rage to find you gone.

'Maggie! whose pain can have been like mine? Whose injury is like mine? Who besides me has met that long look of love that has burnt itself into my soul, so that no other image can come there? Maggie, call me back to you! – call me back to life and goodness! I am banished from both now. I have no motives: I am indifferent to everything. Two months have only deepened the certainty that I can never care for life without you. Write me one word – say "Come!" In two days I should be with you. Maggie – have you forgotten what it was to be together? – to be within reach of a look – to be within hearing of each other's voice?'

When Maggie first read this letter she felt as if her real temptation had only just begun. For hours she felt as if her struggle had been in vain. For hours every other thought that she strove to summon was thrust aside by the image of Stephen waiting for the single word that would bring him to her. She did not *read* the letter: she heard him uttering it, and the voice shook her with its old strange power. All the day before she had been filled with the vision of a lonely future through which she must carry the burthen of regret, upheld only by clinging faith. And here – close within her reach – urging itself upon her even as a claim – was another future, in which hard endurance and effort were to be exchanged for easy delicious leaning on another's loving strength! And yet that promise of joy in the place of sadness did not make the dire force of the temptation to Maggie. It was Stephen's tone of misery, it was the doubt in the justice of her own resolve, that made the balance tremble, and made her once start from her seat to reach the pen and paper, and write 'Come!'

But close upon that decisive act, her mind recoiled: and the sense of contradiction with her past self in her moments of strength and clearness, came upon her like a pang of conscious degradation. No – she must wait – she must pray – the light that had forsaken her would come again: she should feel again what she had felt, when she had fled away, under an inspiration strong enough to conquer agony – to conquer love: she should feel again what she had felt when Lucy stood by her, when Philip's letter had stirred all the fibres that bound her to the calmer past.

She sat quite still, far on into the night: with no impulse to change her attitude, without active force enough even for the mental act of prayer: only waiting for the light that would surely come again. It came with the memories that no passion could long quench: the long past came back to her, and with it the fountains of self-renouncing pity and affection, of faithfulness and resolve. The words that were marked by the quiet hand in the little old book that she had long ago learned by heart, rushed even to her lips, and found a vent for themselves in a low murmur that was quite lost in the loud driving of the rain against the window and the loud moan and roar of the wind: 'I have received the Cross, I have received it from Thy hand; I will bear it, and bear it till death, as Thou hast laid it upon me.'

But soon other words rose that could find no utterance but in a sob: 'Forgive me, Stephen! It will pass away. You will come back to her.'

She took up the letter, held it to the candle, and let it burn slowly on the hearth. Tomorrow she would write to him the last word of parting.

'I will bear it, and bear it till death …' With that cry of despair, Maggie fell on her knees against the table, and buried her sorrow-stricken face.

At that moment Maggie felt a startling sensation of sudden cold about her knees and feet: it was water flowing under her. She started up: the stream was flowing under the door that led into the passage. She was not bewildered for an instant – she knew it was the flood!

The tumult of emotion she had been enduring for the last twelve hours seemed to have left a great calm in her: without screaming, she hurried with the candle upstairs to Bob Jakin's bedroom. The door was ajar; she went in and shook him by the shoulder.

'Bob, the flood is come! it is in the house! let us see if we can make the boats safe.'

She lighted his candle, while the poor wife, snatching up her baby, burst into screams; and then she hurried down again to see if the waters were rising fast. There was a step down into the room at the door leading from the staircase; she saw that the water was already on a level with the step. While she was looking, something came with a tremendous crash against the window, and sent the leaded panes and the old wooden framework inwards in shivers – the water pouring in after it.

'It is the boat!' cried Maggie. 'Bob, come down to get the boats!'

And without a moment's shudder of fear, she plunged through the water, which was rising fast to her knees, and by the glimmering light of the candle she had left on the stairs, she mounted on to the window-sill, and crept into the boat, which was left with the prow lodging and protruding through the window. Bob was not long after her, hurrying without shoes or stockings, but with the lanthorn in his hand.

'Why, they're both there – both the boats,' said Bob, as he got into the one where Maggie was. 'It's wonderful this fastening isn't broke too, as well as the mooring.'

In the excitement of getting into the other boat, unfastening it, and mastering an oar, Bob was not struck with the danger Maggie incurred. The fact that Maggie had been up, had waked him, and had taken the lead in activity, gave Bob a vague impression of her as one who would help to protect, not need to be protected. She too had got possession of an oar, and had pushed off, so as to release the boat from the overhanging window-frame.

'The water's rising so fast,' said Bob, 'I doubt it'll be in at the chambers before long – th' house is so low. I've more mind to get Prissy and the child and the mother into the boat, if I could, and trusten to the water – for th' old house is none so safe. And if I let go the boat … but *you*,' he exclaimed, suddenly lifting the light of his lanthorn on Maggie, as she stood in the rain with the oar in her hand and her black hair streaming.

Maggie had no time to answer, for a new tidal current swept along the line of the houses, and drove both boats out on to the wide water, with a force that carried them far past the meeting current of the river.

In the first moments Maggie felt nothing, thought of nothing.

The whole thing had been so rapid – so dream-like: she sank down on the seat clutching the oar mechanically, and for a long while had no distinct conception of her position. The first thing that waked her to fuller consciousness was the cessation of the rain, and a perception that the darkness was divided by the faintest light, which parted the overhanging gloom from the immeasurable watery level below. She was driven out upon the flood – that awful visitation of God which her father used to talk of – which had made the nightmare of her childish dreams. And with that thought there rushed in the vision of the old home – and Tom – and her mother.

What was happening to them at the mill? The flood had once nearly destroyed it. They might be in danger – in distress: her mother and her brother, alone there, beyond reach of help! Her whole soul was strained now on that thought; and she saw the long-loved faces looking for help into the darkness, and finding none.

She was floating in smooth water now – perhaps far on the over-flooded fields. There was no sense of present danger to check the outgoing of her mind to the old home; and she strained her eyes against the curtain of gloom that she might seize the first sight of her whereabout – that she might catch some faint suggestion of the spot towards which all her anxieties tended.

Yes – she must be out on the fields – those were the tops of hedgerow trees. Which way did the river lie? Looking behind her, she saw the lines of black trees: looking before her there were none: then, the river lay before her. She seized an oar and began to paddle the boat forward with the energy of wakening hope: the dawning seemed to advance more swiftly, now she was in action. Onward she paddled and rowed by turns in the growing twilight: her wet clothes clung round her, and her streaming hair was dashed about by the wind, but she was hardly conscious of any bodily sensations – except a sensation of strength, inspired by mighty emotion.

She must get her boat into the current of the Floss, else she would never be able to pass the Ripple and approach the house: this was the thought that occurred to her, as she imagined with more and more vividness the state of things round the old home. But then she might be carried very far down, and be unable to guide her boat out of the current again. For the first time distinct ideas of danger began to press upon her; but there was no choice of courses, no room for hesitation, and she floated into the current. Swiftly she went now, without effort; more and more clearly in the lessening distance and the growing light she began to discern the objects that she knew must be the well-known trees and roofs; nay, she was not far off a rushing muddy current that must be the strangely altered Ripple.

She had passed the mouth of the Ripple, then: *now*, she must use all her skill and power to manage the boat and get it if possible out of the current. She could see now that the bridge was broken down: she could see the masts of a stranded vessel far out over the watery field. But no boats were to be seen moving on the river – such as had been laid hands on were employed in the flooded streets.

With new resolution Maggie seized her oar, and stood up again to paddle; but the now ebbing tide added to the swiftness of the river, and she was carried along beyond the bridge. She could hear shouts from the windows overlooking the river, as if the people there were calling to her. It was not till she had passed on nearly to Tofton that she could get the boat clear of the current. Then she took to both her oars and rowed with all her might across the watery fields, back towards the mill. Colour was beginning to awake now, and as she approached the Dorlcote fields, she could discern the tints of the trees – could see the old Scotch firs far to the right, and the home chestnuts – but the house stood firm; drowned up to the first storey, but still firm – or was it broken in at the end towards the mill?

With panting joy that she was there at last – joy that overcame all distress – Maggie neared the front of the house. At first she heard no sound: she saw no object moving. Her boat was on a level with the upstairs window. She called out in a loud piercing voice—

'Tom, where are you? Mother, where are you? Here is Maggie!'

Soon, from the window of the attic in the central gable, she heard Tom's voice—

'Who is it? Have you brought a boat?'

'It is I, Tom – Maggie. Where is mother?'

'She is not here: she went to Garum the day before yesterday. I'll come down to the lower window.'

'Alone, Maggie?' said Tom, in a voice of deep astonishment, as he opened the middle window on a level with the boat.

'Yes, Tom: God has taken care of me, to bring me to you. Get in quickly. Is there no one else?'

'No,' said Tom, stepping into the boat, 'I fear the man is drowned: he was carried down the Ripple, I think, when part of the mill fell with the crash of trees and stones against it: I've shouted again and again, and there has been no answer. Give me the oars, Maggie.'

It was not till Tom had pushed off and they were on the wide water – he face to face with Maggie – that the full meaning of what had happened rushed upon his mind. It came with so over-powering a force – it was such a new revelation to his spirit, of the depths in life that had lain beyond his vision, which he had fancied so keen and clear – that he was unable to ask a question. They sat mutely gazing at each other: Maggie with eyes of intense life looking out from a weary, beaten face – Tom pale with a certain awe and humiliation. Thought was busy though the lips were silent: and though he could ask no question, he guessed a story of almost miraculous divinely-protected effort. But at last a mist gathered over the blue-grey eyes, and the lips found a word they could utter: the old childish – 'Magsie!'

Maggie could make no answer but a long deep sob of that mysterious wondrous happiness that is one with pain.

As soon as she could speak, she said, 'We will go to Lucy, Tom: we'll go and see if she is safe, and then we can help the rest.'

Tom rowed with untired vigour, and with a different speed from poor Maggie's. The boat was soon in the current of the river again, and soon they would be at Tofton.

Nothing else was said; a new danger was being carried towards them by the river. Some wooden machinery had just given way on one of the wharves, and huge fragments were being floated along. The sun was rising now, and the wide area of watery desolation was spread out in dreadful clearness around them – in dreadful clearness floated onwards the hurrying, threatening masses. A large company in a boat that was working its way along under the Tofton houses, observed their danger, and shouted, 'Get out of the current!'

But that could not be done at once, and Tom, looking before him, saw death rushing on them. Huge fragments, clinging together in fatal fellowship, made one wide mass across the stream.

'It is coming, Maggie!' Tom said, in a deep hoarse voice, loosing the oars, and clasping her.

The next instant the boat was no longer seen upon the water – and the huge mass was hurrying on in hideous triumph.

The boat reappeared – but brother and sister had gone down in an embrace never to be parted: living through again in one supreme moment, the days when they had clasped their little hands in love, and roamed the daisied fields together.

6

Conclusion

Nature repairs her ravages – repairs them with her sunshine, and with human labour. The desolation wrought by that flood had left little visible trace on the face of the earth, five years after.

And every man and woman mentioned in this history was still living – except those whose end we know.

Nature repairs her ravages – but not all. The uptorn trees are not rooted again; the parted hills are left scarred: if there is a new growth, the trees are not the same as the old, and the hills underneath their green vesture bear the marks of the past rending. To the eyes that have dwelt on the past, there is no thorough repair.

Dorlcote Mill was rebuilt. And Dorlcote churchyard – where the brick grave that held a father whom we know, was found with the stone laid prostrate upon it after the flood – had recovered all its grassy order and decent quiet.

Near that brick grave there was a tomb erected, very soon after the flood, for two bodies that were found in close embrace; and it was visited at different moments by two men who both felt that their keenest joy and keenest sorrow were for ever buried there.

One of them visited the tomb again with a sweet face beside him – but that was years after.

The other was always solitary. His great companionship was among the trees of the Red Deeps, where the buried joy seemed still to hover – like a revisiting spirit.

The tomb bore the names of Tom and Maggie Tulliver, and below the names it was written—

'In their death they were not divided.'

The End

About this Compact Edition

The Mill on the Floss, George Eliot's second full-length novel, was published in April 1860. In this present edition, which uses only the author's language, some lengthy descriptions and passages of dialogue have been reduced in the interests of narrative directness: the author's use of her own voice has been cut but not omitted. The local setting, historical period and atmosphere are all felt and seen as background to the poignant story of Maggie Tulliver, her parents and her brother Tom: the humour is evident early, in the dialogue (often dialect) of the family aunts, but the tragic elements of the story are as ever-present as the tidal river of the title.